D1409556

VENUS
RISING

VENUS RISING

Anonymous

CARROLL & GRAF PUBLISHERS, INC.

NEW YORK

Copyright © 1996 by Carroll & Graf Publishers, Inc.

First Carroll & Graf edition 1996
Second Carroll & Graf edition 1999

First Carroll & Graf edition of *Venus Remembered* 1985
Original title *Pangs of Venus*

First Carroll & Graf edition of *Venus Unbound* 1985
Original titles *Flossie: A Venus at Fifteen* and *Evaline*

First Carroll & Graf edition of *Venus Unmasked* 1988

Carroll & Graf Publishers, Inc.
19 West 21st Street
New York, NY 10010-6805

ISBN: 0-7867-0672-4

Manufactured in the United States of America

Venus
Unbound

FLOSSIE

PREFACE

IN PRESENTING TO A CRITICAL PUBLIC THIS
narrative of a delightful experience, I am conscious of an inability to do justice to the indescribable charm of my subject.

A true daughter of the Paphian goddess, Flossie added to the erotic allurements inherited from
her immortal mother a sense of humour which
is not traceable in any of the proceedings on
Mount Ida or elsewhere. Those of my readers,
who have had the rare good fortune to meet with
the combination, will not gainsay my assertion
that it is an incomparable incentive to deeds of
love.

If some of those deeds, as here set down,
should seem to appertain to a somewhat advanced school of amatory action, I beg objectors

to remember that Flossie belongs to the end of the century, *when such things are done*, to the safety, comfort and delight of vast numbers of fair English girls, and to the unspeakable enjoyment of their adorers.

* *Credo experto.* *

So, in the words of the City toastmaster: —

"Pray silence, gentlemen, for your heroine, Flossie: a Venus of Fifteen."

J. A.

POSTSCRIPT. — Flossie has herself revised this unpretending work, and has added a footnote here and there which she trusts may not be regarded as painful interruptions to a truthful tale.

All thine the new wine of desire
   The fruit of four lips as they clung
Till the hair and the eyelids took fire;
   The fan of a serpentine tongue,
The froth of the serpents of pleasure,
   More salt than the foam of the sea,
Now felt as a flame, now at leisure
            As wine-shed for me!

They were purple of rainment, and golden,
   Filled full of thee, fiery with wine,
Thy lovers, in haunts unbeholden,
   In marvellous chambers of thine.
They are fled and their footprints escape us
   Who appraise thee, adore, and abstain,
O daughter of Death and Priamus!
            Our Lady of Pain.
                              A. C. Swinburne

CHAPTER I

"My love, she's but a lassie yet"

TOWARDS THE END OF A BRIGHT SUNNY AFTER-
noon in June, I was walking in one of the quieter
streets of Piccadilly, when my eye was caught
by two figures coming in my direction. One
was that of a tall, finely-made woman about
27, who would under other circumstances, have
received something more than an approving
glance. But it was her companion that rivetted
my gaze of almost breathless admiration. This
was a young girl of fifteen, of such astounding
beauty of face and figure as I had never seen
or dreamt of. Masses of bright, wavy, brown
hair fell to her waist. Deep violet eyes looked
out from under long curling lashes, and seemed
to laugh in unison with the humorous curves of
the full red lips. These and a thosand other
charms I was to know by heart later on, but
what struck me most at this view, was the extraordinary size and beauty of the girl's bust,
shown to all possible advantage by her dress

15

which, in the true artistic French style, crept in between her breasts, outlining their full and perfect form with loving fidelity. Tall and lithe, she moved like a young goddess, her short skirt shewing the action of a pair of exquisitely moulded legs, to which the tan-coloured open-work silk stockings were plainly designed to invite attention. Unable to take my eyes from this enchanting vision, I was approaching the pair, when to my astonishment, the elder lady suddenly spoke my name.

"You do not remember me, Captain Archer." For a moment I was at a loss, but the voice gave me the clue.

"But I do," I answered, "you are Miss Letchford, who used to teach my sisters."

"Quite right. But I have given up teaching, for which fortunately there is no longer any necessity. I am living in a flat with my dear little friend here. Let me introduce you, — Flossie Eversley — Captain Archer."

The violet eyes laughed up at me; and the red lips parted in a merry smile. A dimple appeared at the corner of the mouth. I was done for! Yes; at thirty-five years of age, with more than my share of experiences in every phase of love, I went down before this lovely girl with her childish face smiling at me above the budding womanhood of her rounded breasts, and confessed myself defeated!

A moment of two later, I had passed from them with the address of the flat in my pocket, and under promise to go down to tea on the next day.

At midday I received the following letter:

Dear Captain Archer,

"I am sorry to be obliged to be out when you come; and yet not altogether sorry, because I should like you to know Flossie very well. She is an orphan, without a relation in the world. She is just back from a Paris school. In years she is of course a child, but in tact and knowledge she is a woman; also in figure, as you can see for yourself! She is of an exceedingly warm and passionate nature, and a look that you gave her yesterday was not lost upon her. In fact, to be quite frank, she has fallen in love with you! You will find her a delightful companion. Use her *very* tenderly, and she will do anything in the world for you. Speak to her about life in the French school; she loves to talk of it. I want her to be happy, and I think you can help. Remember she is only just fifteen.

"Yours sincerely,
"*Eva Letchford.*"

17

Flossie: a Venus of fifteen

I must decline any attempt to describe my feelings on receiving this remarkable communication. My first impulse was to give up the promised call at the flat. But the flower-like face, the soft red lips and the laughing eyes passed before my mind's eye, followed by an instant vision of the marvelous breasts and the delicate shapely legs in their brown silk stockings, and I knew that fate was too strong for me. For it was of course impossible to misunderstand the meaning of Eva Letchford's letter, and indeed, when I reached the flat, she herself opened the door to me, whispering as she passed out, "Flossie is in there, waiting for you. You two can have the place to yourselves. One last word. You have been much in Paris, have you not? So has Flossie. She is *very* young — *and there are ways* — Good-bye."

I passed into the next room. Flossie was curled up in a long chair, reading. Twisting her legs from under her petticoats with a sudden movement that brought into full view her delicately embroidered drawers, she rose and came towards me, a rosy flush upon her cheeks, her eyes shining, her whole bearing instinct with an enchanting mixture of girlish coyness and anticipated pleasure. Her short white skirt swayed as she moved across the room, her

breasts stood out firm and round under the
close-fitting woven silk jersey; what man of
mortal flesh and blood could withstand such
allurements as these! Not I, for one! In a moment, she was folded in my arms. I rained
kisses on her hair, her forehead, her eyes, her
cheeks, and then, grasping her body closer and
always closer to me, I glued my lips upon the
scarlet mouth and revelled in a long and maddeningly delicious kiss — a kiss to be ever remembered — so well remembered now, indeed,
that I must make some attempt to describe it.
My hands were behind Flossie's head, buried in
her long brown hair. Her arms were round my
body, locked and clinging. At the first impact,
her lips were closed, but a moment later they
parted, and slowly, gently, almost as if in the
performance of some solemn duty, the rosy
tongue crept into my mouth, and bringing with
it a flood of the scented juices from her throat,
curled amorously round my own, whilst her
hands dropped to my buttocks, and standing on
tiptoe, she drew me to her with such extraordinary to be already in conjunction. Not a word
was spoken on either side — indeed, under the
circumstances, speech was impossible, for our
tongues had twined together in a caress of unspeakable sweetness, which neither would be the

first to forego. At last, the blood was coursing through my veins at a pace that became unbearable and I was compelled to unglue my mouth from hers. Still silent, but with love and longing in her eyes, she pressed me into a low chair, and seating herself on the arm, passed her hand behind my head, and looking full into my eyes, whispered my name in accents that were like the sound of a running stream. I kissed her open mouth again and again, and then, feeling that the time had come for some little explanation:

"How long will it be before your friend Eva comes back?" I asked.

"She has gone down into the country, and won't be here till late this evening."

"Then I may stay with you, may I?"

"Yes, do, do, *do*, Jack. Do you know, I have got seats for an Ibsen play to-night, I was wondering . . . if . . . you would . . . take me!"

"Take *you* — to an Ibsen play — with your short frocks, and all that hair down your back! Why, I don't believe they'd let us in?"

"Oh, if *that's* all, wait a minute."

She skipped out of the room with a whisk of her petticoats and a free display of brown silk legs. Almost before I had time to wonder what she was up to, she was back again. She had put on a long skirt of Eva's, her hair was coiled on the top of her head, she wore my "billycock" hat and a pair of blue pincenez, and carrying a crutch-handled stick, she advanced upon me with a defiant air, and glaring down over the top of her glasses, she said in a deep masculine voice:

"Now, sir if you're ready for Ibsen, *I* am. Or if your tastes are so *low* that you can't care about a play, I'll give you a skirtdance."

As she said this, she tore off the long dress, threw my hat on to a sofa, let down her hair with a turn of the wrist, and motioning me to the piano, picked up her skirts and began to dance.

Enchanted as I was by the humour of her quick change to the "Ibsen woman," words are vain to describe my feelings as I feebly tinkled a few bars on the piano and watched the dancer.

Every motion was the perfection of grace and yet no Indian Nautch-girl could have more skillfully expressed the idea of sexual allurement. Gazing at her in speechless admiration, I saw the violet eyes glow with passion, the full red lips part, the filmy petticoats were lifted higher and higher; the loose frilled drawers gleamed white. At last breathless and panting, she fell back upon a chair, her eyes closed, her legs parted, her breasts heaving. A mingled perfume came to my nostrils — half *"odor di faemina,"* half the scent of white rose from her hair and clothes.

I flung myself upon her.

"Tell me, Flossie darling, what shall I do first?

The answer came, quick and short.

"Kiss me — *between my legs!*"

In an instant, I was kneeling before her. Her legs fell widely apart. Sinking to a sitting posture, I plunged my head between her thighs. The petticoats incommoded me a little, but I soon managed to arrive at the desired spot. Somewhat to my surprise, instead of finding the lips closed and barricaded as is usual in the case of young girls, they were ripe, red and pouting, and as my mouth closed eagerly upon the delicious orifice and my tongue found and pressed upon the trembling clitoris, I knew that my qualms of conscience had been vain. My utmost powers were now called into play and I sought, by every means I possessed, to let Flossie know that I was no halfbaked lover. Passing my arms behind her, I extended my tongue to its utmost length and with rapid agile movements penetrated the scented recesses. Her hands locked themselves under my head, soft gasps of pleasure came for her lips, and as I delivered at last an effective attack upon the erect clitoris, her fingers clutched my neck, and with a sob of delight, she crossed her legs over my back, and pressing my head towards her, held me with a convulsive grasp, whilst the aromatic essence of her being flowed softly into my enchanted mouth.

As I rose to my feet, she covered her face with her hands and I saw a blue eye twinkle out between the fingers with an indescribable mixture of bashfulness and fun. Then, as if suddenly remembering her self, she sat up, dropped her petticoats over her knees, and looking up at me from under the curling lashes, said in a tone of profound melancholy.

"Jack, am I not a *disgraceful* child! All the same, I wouldn't have missed *that* for a million pounds."

"Nor would I, little sweetheart; and whenever you would like to have it again —"

"No, no, it is your turn now."

"What! Flossie; you don't mean to say —"

"But I *do* mean to say it, and to *do* it too. Lie down on that sofa at once, sir."

"But, Flossie, I really — "

Without another word she leapt at me, threw her arms round my neck and fairly bore me down on to the divan. Falling on the top of me, she twined her silken legs round mine and gently

23

pushing the whole of her tongue between my lips, began to work her body up and down with a wonderful sinuous motion which soon brought me to a state of excitement bordering on frenzy. Then, shaking a warning finger at me to keep still, she slowly slipped to her knees on the floor.

In another moment, I felt the delicate fingers round my straining yard. Carrying it to her mouth she touched it ever so softly with her tongue; then slowly parting her lips she pushed it gradually between them, keeping a grasp of the lower end with her hand which she moved gently up and down. Soon the tongue began to quicken its motion, and the brown head to work rapidly in a perpendicular direction. I buried my hands under the lovely hair, and clutched the white neck towards me, plunging the nut further and further into the delicious mouth until I seemed almost to touch the uvula. Her lips, tongue and hands now worked with redoubled ardour, and my sensations became momentarily more acute, until with a cry I besought her to let me withdraw. Shaking her head with great emphasis, she held my yard in a firmer grasp, and passing her disengaged hand behind me, drew me towards her face, and with an unspeakable clinging action of her mouth, carried out the delightful act of love to its logical conclusion, declining to remove her lips until, some minutes after, the last remaining evidences of the late crisis had completely disappeared.

Then and not till then, she stood up, and bending over me, as I lay, kissed me on the forehead, whispering: —

"There! Jack, now I love you twenty times more than ever." *)

I gazed into the lovely face in speechless adoration.

"Why don't you say something?" she cried, "Is there anything else you want me to do?"

"Yes," I answered, "there is."

"Out with it, then."

"I am simply dying to see your breasts, naked."

"Why, you darling, of course, you shall! Stay there a minute."

Off she whisked again, and almost before I could realise she had gone, I looked up and she was before me. She had taken off everything but her chemise and stockings, the former lowered beneath her breasts.

---

*) "This is a fact, as every girl knows who has ever gamahuched and been gamahuched by the man or boy she loves. As a *link*, it beats fucking out of the field. I've tried both and I *know*."   *Flossie*

Any attempt to describe the beauties thus laid bare to my adoring gaze must necessarily fall absurdly short of the reality. Her neck, throat and arms were full and exquisitely rounded, bearing no trace of juvenile immaturity.

Her breasts, however, were of course the objects of my special and immediate attention.

For size, perfection of form and colour, I had never seen their equals, nor could the mind of man conceive anything so alluring as the coral nipples which stood out firm and erect, craving kisses. A wide space intervened between the two snowy hillocks which heaved a little with the haste of her late exertions, I gazed a moment in breathless delight and admiration, then rushing towards her, I buried my face in the enchanting valley, passed my burning lips over each of the neighbouring slopes and finally seized upon one after the other of the rosy nipples, which I sucked, mouthed and tongued with a frenzy or delight.

The darling little girl lent herself eagerly to my every action, pushing her nipples into my mouth and eyes, pressing her breasts against my face, and clinging to my neck with her lovely naked arms.

Whilst we were thus amourously employed, my little lady had contrived dexterously to slip out of her chemise, and now stood before me naked but for her brown silk stockings and little shoes.

"There, Mr. Jack, now you can see my breasts, and everything else that you like of mine. In future, this will be my full-dress costume for making love to you in. Stop, though; it wants just one touch." And darting out of the room, she came back with a beautiful chain of pearls round her neck, finishing with a pendant of rubies which hung just low enough to nestle in the Valley of Delight, between the wonderful breasts.

"I am, now," she said, "The White Queen of the Gama Huchi Islands. My kingdom is bounded on this side by the piano, and on the other by the furthest edge of the bed in the next room. Any male person found wearing a *stitch* of clothing within those boundaries will be sentenced to lose his p . . . . but soft! who comes here?"

Shading her eyes with her hand she gazed in my direction: —

"Aha! a stranger; and, unless these royal eyes deceive us, a man! He shall see what it is to defy our laws! What ho! within there! Take this person and remove his p . . . ."

"Great Queen!" I said, in a voice of deep

humility, "if you will but grant me two minutes, I will make haste to comply with your laws."

"And we, good fellow, will help you. *(Aside.)*

"Methinks he is somewhat comely*). *(Aloud.)*

"But first let us away with these garments, which are more than aught else a violation of our Gama Huchian Rules, Good! now the shirt. And what, pray, it *this?* We thank you, sir, but we are not requiring any *tent-poles* just now."

"Then if your Majesty will deign to remove your royal fingers I will do my humble best to cause the offending pole to disappear. At present, with your Majesty's hand upon it — !"

"Silence, Sir! Your time is nearly up, and if the last garment be not removed in twenty seconds ... So! you obey. Tis well! You shall see how we reward a faithful subject of our laws." And thrusting my yard between her lips, the Great White Queen of the Gama Huchi Islands sucked in the whole column to the very root, and by dint of working her royal mouth up and down, and applying her royal fingers to the neighbour-

---

*) Don't believe I ever said anything of the sort, but if I did, "methinks" I'd better take this opportunity of withdrawing the statement. *Flossie*

ing appendages, soon drew into her throat a tribute to her greatness, which, from its volume and the time it took in the act of payment, plainly caused her Majesty the most exquisite enjoyment. Of my own pleasure I will only say that it was delirious, whilst in this, as in all other love sports in which we indulged, an added zest was given by the humour and fancy with which this adorable child-woman designed and carried out our amusements. In the present case, the personating of the Great White Queen appeared to afford her especial delight, and going on with the performance, she took a long branch of pampasgrass from its place and waving it over my head, she said: —

"The next ceremony to be performed by a visitor to these realms will, we fear, prove somewhat irksome, but it must be gone through. We shall now place our royal person on this lofty throne. You, sir, will sit upon this footstool before us. We shall then wave our sceptre three times. At the third wave, our knees will part and our guest will see before him the royal spot of love. This he will proceed to salute with a kiss which shall last until we are pleased to signify that we have had enough. Now, most noble guest, open your mouth, *don't* shut your eyes, and prepare! One, two, *three*."

The pampas-grass waved, the legs parted, and nestling between the ivory thighs, I saw the scarlet lips open and show the erected clitoris peeping forth from its nest below the slight brown tuft which adorned the base of the adorable belly. I gazed and gazed in mute rapture, until a sharp strident voice above me said: —

"Now then, there, move on, please; can't have you blocking up the road all day!" Then changing suddenly to her own voice: —

"Jack, if you don't kiss me at once I shall *die!*"

I pressed towards the delicious spot and taking the whole cunt into my mouth passed my tongue upwards along the perfumed lips until it met the clitoris, which thrust itself amourously between my lips, imploring kisses. These I rained upon her with all the ardour I could command, clutching the rounded bottom with feverish fingers and drawing the naked belly closer and ever closer to my burning face, whilst my tongue plunged deep within the scented cunt and revelled in its divine odours and the contraction of its beloved lips.

The Great White Queen seemed to relish this particular form of homage, for it was many minutes before the satin thighs closed, and with the little hands under my chin, she raised my face and looking into my eyes with inexpressible love and sweetness shining from her own, she said simply: —

"Thank you, Jack. You're a darling!" —

By way of answer I covered her with kisses, omitting no single portion of the lovely naked body, the various beauties of which lent themselves with charming zest to my amorous doings. Upon the round and swelling breasts, I lavished renewed devotion, sucking the rosy nipples with a fury of delight, and relishing to the full the quick movements of rapture with which the lithe clinging form was constantly shaken, no less than the divine aroma passing to my nostrils as the soft thighs opened and met again, the rounded arms rose and fell, and with this, the faintly perfumed hair brushing my face and shoulders mingled its odour of tea-rose.

All this was fast exciting my senses to the point of madness, and there were moments when I felt that to postpone much longer the consummation of our amour would be impossible.

I looked at the throbbing breasts, remembered the fragrant lips below that had pouted ripely to meet my kisses, the developed clitoris that told of joys long indulged in. And then . . . And then . . . the sweet girlish face looked up into mine, the violet eyes seemed to take on a pleading expression, and as if reading my thoughts, Flossie pushed me gently into a chair, seated herself on my knee, slipped an arm round my neck, and pressing her cheek to mine, whispered: —

"Poor, *poor* old thing! I know what it wants; and *I* want it too — badly, oh! so badly. But, Jack, you can't guess what a friend Eva has been to me, and I've promised her *not to!* You see I'm only just fifteen, and . . . *the consequences!* There! don't let us talk about it. Tell me all about yourself, and then I'll tell you about me. When you're tired of hearing me talk, you shall stop my mouth with — well, whatever you like. Now sir, begin!"

I gave her a short narrative of my career from boyhood upwards, dry and dull enough in all conscience!

"Yes, yes, that's all very nice and prim and proper," she cried. "But you haven't told me the principal thing of all — when you first began to be — naughty, and with whom?"

I invented some harmless fiction which, I saw, the quickwitted little girl did not believe, and begged her to tell me her own story, which she at once proceeded to do. I shall endeavour to transcribe it, though it is impossible to convey any idea of the humour with which it was delivered, still less of the irrepressible fun which flashed from her eyes at the recollection of her schoolgirl pranks and amourettes. There were, of course, many interruptions*), for most of which I was probably responsible; but, on the whole, in the following chapter will be found a fairly faithful transcript of Flossie's early experiences. Some at least of these I am sanguine, will be thought to have been of a sufficiently appetising character.

---

*) The first of these is a really serious one, but for this the impartial reader will see that the responsibility was divided.

CHAPTER II

"How Flossie Acquired the French tongue."

BEFORE I BEGIN, JACK, I SHOULD LIKE TO hold something nice and solid in my hand, to sort of give me confidence as I go on. Have you got anything about you that would do?"

I presented what seemed to me the most suitable article 'in stock' at the moment.

"Aha!" said Flossie in an affected voice, "the very thing! How *very* fortunate that you should happen to have it ready!"

"Well, madam, you see it is an article we are constantly being asked for by our lady-customers. It is rather an expensive thing — seven pound ten —"

"Yes, it's rather stiff. Still, if you can assure me that it will always keep in its present condition, I shouldn't mind spending a good deal upon it."

"You will find, madam, that anything you may spend upon it will be amply returned to you. Our ladies have always expressed the greatest satisfaction with it."

"Do you mean that you find they come more than once? If so, I'll take it now."

"Perhaps you would allow me to bring it myself —?"

"Thanks, but I think I can hold it quite well in my hand. It won't go off suddenly, will it?"

"Not if it is kept in a cool place, madam."

"And it mustn't be shaken, I suppose, like *that*, for instance?" (shaking it.)

"For goodness gracious sake, take your hand away, Flossie, or there'll be a catastrophe."

"That is a good word, Jack! But do you suppose that if I saw a 'catastrophe' coming I shouldn't know what to do with it?"

"*What* should you do?"

"Why, what *can* you do with a catastrophe of that sort but *swallow it?*"

The effect of this little interlude upon us both was magnetic. Instead of going on with her story, Flossie commanded me to lie upon my back on the divan, and having placed a couple of pillows under my neck, knelt astride of me with her face towards my feet. With one or two caressing movements of her bottom, she arranged herself so that the scarlet vulva rested just above my face. Then gently sinking down, she brought her delicious cunt full upon my mouth from which my tongue instantly darted to penetrate the adorable recess. At the same moment, I felt the brown hair fall upon my thighs, my straining prick plunged between her lips, and was engulphed in her velvet mouth to the very root, whilst her hands played with feverish energy amongst the surrounding parts, and the nipples of her breasts rubbed softly against my belly.

In a very few moments, I had received into my mouth her first tribute of love and was working with might and main to procure a second, whilst she in her turn, wild with pleasure my wandering tongue was causing her, grasped my yard tightly between her lips, passing them rapidly up and down its whole length, curling her tongue round the nut, and maintaining all the time an ineffable sucking action which very soon produced its natural result. As I poured a torrent into her eager mouth, I felt the soft lips which I was kissing contract for a moment upon my tongue and then part again to set free the aromatic flood to which the intensity of her sensations imparted additional volume and sweetness.

The pleasure, we were both experiencing from

this the most entrancing of all the reciprocal acts of love, was too keen to be abandoned after one effort. Stretching my hands upwards to mould and press the swelling breasts and erected nipples, I seized the rosy clitoris anew between my lips, whilst Flossie resumed her charming operations upon my instrument which she gamahuched with ever increasing zest and delight, and even with a skill and variety of action which would have been marvellous in a woman of double her age and experience. Once again the fragrant dew was distilled upon my enchanted tongue, and once again the velvet mouth closed upon my yard to receive the results of its divinely pleasurable ministrations.

Raising herself slowly and almost reluctantly from her position, Flossie laid her naked body at full length upon mine, and after many kisses upon my mouth, eyes and cheeks said, "Now you may go and refresh yourself with a bath while I dress for dinner."

"But where are we going to dine?" I asked.

"You'll see presently. *Go* along, there's a good boy!"

I did as I was ordered and soon came back from the bath-room, much refreshed by my welcome ablutions.

Five minutes later Flossie joined me, looking

lovelier than ever, in a short-sleeved pale blue muslin frock, cut excessively low in front, black openwork silk stockings and little embroidered shoes.

"Dinner is on the table," she said, taking my arm and leading me into an adjoining room where an exquisite little cold meal was laid out, to which full justice was speedily done, followed by coffee made by my hostess, who produced some Benedictine and a box of excellent cigars.

"There, Jack, if you're quite comfy, I'll go on with my story. Shall I stay here, or come and sit on your knee?"

"Well, as far as getting on with the story goes, I think you are better in that chair, Flossie —"

"But I told you I must have something to hold."

"You, you did, and the result was that we didn't get very far with the story, if you remember —"

"Remember! As if I was likely to forget. But look at this," holding up a rounded arm bare to the shoulder. "Am I to understand that you'd rather not have this round your neck?"

Needless to say she was to understand nothing of the sort, and a moment later she was perched upon my knee and having with deft penetrating

39

fingers enough under her magic touch, began her narrative.

"I don't think there will be much to tell you until my school life at Paris begins. My father and mother both died when I was quite small; I had no brothers or sisters, and I don't believe I've got a relation in the world. You mustn't think I want to swagger, Jack, but I am rather rich. One of my two guardians died three years ago and the other is in India and doesn't care a scrap about me. Now and then, he writes and asks how I am getting on, and when he heard I was going to live with Eva (whom he knows quite well) he seemed perfectly satisfied. Two years ago he arranged for me to go to school in Paris.

"Now I must take great care not to shock you, but there's nothing for it but to tell you that about this time I began to have the most wonderful feelings all over me — a sort of desperate longing for something, — I didn't know what — which used to become almost unbearable when I danced or played any game in which a boy or man was near me. At the Paris school was a very pretty girl, named Ylette de Vespertin, who, for some reason I never could understand, took a fancy to me. She was two years older than I, had several brothers and boy cous-

ins at home, and being up to every sort of lark
and mischief, was just the girl I wanted as confidante. Of course she had no difficulty in explaining the whole thing to me, and in the course
of a day or two, I knew everything there was to
know. On the third day of our talks Ylette
slipped a note into my hand as I was going up to
bed. Now, Jack, you must really go and look out
of the window while I tell you what it said:

" '(Chérie,
"Si tu veux te faire sucer la langue, les seins
et le con, viens dans mon lit toute nue ce soir.
C'est moi qui te ferai voir les anges.
" 'Viens de suite à ton
" 'Ylette.' "

"I have rather a good memory, and even if I
hadn't, I don't think I could ever forget the
words of that note, for it was the beginning of a
most delicious time for me.

"I suppose if I had been a well-regulated
young person, I should have taken no notice of
the invitation. As it was, I stripped myself
naked in a brace of shakes, and flew to Ylette's
bedroom which was next door to the one I occupied. I had not realized before what a beautifully made girl she was. Her last garment was

41

just slipping from her as I came in, and I stared in blank admiration at her naked figure which was like a statue in the perfection of its lines. A furious longing to touch it seized me, and springing upon her, I passed my hands feverishly up and down her naked body, until grasping me round the waist, she half dragged, half carried me to the bed, laid me on the edge of it, and kneeling upon the soft rug, plunged her head between my legs, and bringing her lips to bear full upon the *other* lips before her, parted them with a peculiar action of the mouth and inserted her tongue with a sudden stroke which sent perfect waves of delight through my whole body, followed by still greater ecstasy when she went for the particular spot *you* know of, Jack — the one near the top, I mean — and twisting her tongue over it, under it, round it and across it, soon brought about the result she wanted, and in her own expressive phrase 'me faisait voir les anges'.

"Of course I had no experience, but I did my best to repay her for the pleasures he had given me, and as I happen to possess an extremely long and pointed tongue, and Ylette's cunt — oh Jack, *I've said it at last!* Go and look out of the window again; or better still, come and stop my naughty mouth with — I *meant* your tongue, but this will do better still. The wicked monster,

what a size he is! Now put both your hands behind my head, and push him in till he touches
my throat. Imagine he is *somewhere else*,
work like a demon, and for your life, don't stop
until the very end of all things Ah! the dear,
darling, delicious thing! How he throbs with
excitement! I believe he can *see* my mouth
waiting for him. Come, Jack, my darling, my
beloved, let me gamahuche you. I want to feel
this heavenly prick of yours between my lips
and against my tongue, so that I may suck it
and drain every drop that comes from it into my
mouth. Now, Jack *now* . . ."

The red lips closed hungrily upon the object of
their desire, the rosy tongue stretched itself
amorously along the palpitating yard, and twice,
the tide of love poured freely forth to be received with every sign of delight into the velvet
mouth.

Nothing in my experience had ever approached the pleasure which I derived from the
intoxicating contact of this young girl's lips and
tongue upon my most sensitive parts, enhanced
as it was by my love for her, which grew apace,
and by her own intense delight in the adorable
pastime. So keen indeed were the sensations
she procured me that I was almost able to forget the deprivation laid upon me by Flossie's

promise to her friend. Indeed, when I reflected upon her youth, and the unmatched beauty of her girlish shape with its slender waist, smooth satin belly and firm rounded breasts, the whole seemed too perfect a work of nature to be married — at least as yet — by the probable consequences of an act of coition carried to its logical conclusion by a pair of ardent lovers.

So I bent my head once more to its resting place between the snowy thighs, and again drew from my darling little mistress the fragrant treasures of love's sacred store house, lavished upon my clinging lips with gasps and sighs and all possible tokens of enjoyment in the giving.

After this it was time to part, and at Flossie's suggestion I undressed her, brushed out her silky hair and put her into bed. Lying on her white pillow, she looked so fair and like a child that I was for saying goodnight with just a single kiss upon her cheek. But this was not in accordance with her views on the subject. She sat up in bed, flung her arms round my neck, nestled her face against mine and whispered in my ear:

"I'll never give a promise again as long as I live."

It was an awful moment and my resolution all but went down under the strain. But I just managed to resist, and after one prolonged em-

brace, during which Flossie's tongue went twining and twisting round my own with an indescribably lascivious motion, I planted a farewell
kiss full upon the nipple of her left breast,
sucked it for an instant and fled from the room.

On reaching my own quarters I lit a cigar and
sat down to think over the extraordinary good
fortune by which I had chanced upon this
unique liaison. It was plain to me that in Flossie
I had encountered probably the only specimen
of her class. A girl of fifteen, with all the fresh
charm of that beautiful age united to the fascination of a passionate and amorous woman.
Add to these a finely-strung temperament, a
keen sense of humour, and the true artist's striv-
ing after thoroughness in all she did, and it will
be admitted that all these qualities meeting in a
person of quite faultless beauty were enough to
justify the self-congratulations with which I contemplated my present luck, and the rosy visions
of pleasure to come which hung about my
waking and sleeping senses till the morning.

About midday I called at the flat. The door
was opened to me by Eva Letchford.

"I am so glad to see you," she said. "Flossie is
out on her bicycle, and I can say what I want to."

As she moved to the window to draw up the
blind a little, I had a better opportunity of notic-

ing into what a really splendid woman she had developed. Observing my glances of frank admiration, she sat down in a low easy chair opposite to me, crossed her shapely legs, and looking over at me with a bright pleasant smile, said:

"Now, Jack — I may call you Jack, of course, because we are all three going to be great friends — you had my letter the other day. No doubt you thought it a strange document, but when we know one another better, you will easily understand how I came to write it."

"My dear girl, I understand it already. You forget I have had several hours with Flossie. It was her happiness you wanted to secure, and I hope she will tell you our plan was successful"

"Flossie and I have no secrets. She has told me everything that passed between you. She has also told me what did *not* pass between you, and how you did not even try to make her break her promise to me."

"I should have been a brute if I had —"

"Then I am afraid nineteen men out of twenty are brutes — but that's neither here nor there. What I want you to know is that I appreciate your nice feeling, and that some day soon I shall with Flossie's consent take an opportunity of shewing that appreciation in a practical way."

Here she crossed her right foot high over the left knee and very leisurely removed an imaginary speck of dust from the shotsilk stocking.

"Now I must go and change my dress. You'll stay and lunch with us in the coffeeroom, won't you? — that's right. This is my bedroom. I'll leave the door open so that we can talk till Flossie comes. She promised to be in by one o'clock."

We chatted away on indifferent subjects whilst I watched with much satisfaction the operations of the toilette in the next room.

Presently a little cry of dismay reached me:

"Oh dear, oh dear! do come here a minute, Jack. I have pinched one of my breasts with my stays and made a little red mark. Look! *Do* you think it will shew in evening dress?"

I examined the injury with all possible care and deliberation.

"My professional opinion is, madam, that as the mark is only an inch above the nipple we may fairly hope —"

"*Above* the nipple! then I'm afraid it will be a near thing," said Eva with a merry laugh.

"Perhaps a little judicious stroking by an experienced hand might —"

"Naow then there, Naow then!" suddenly came from the door in a hoarse cockney accent.

"You jest let the lydy be, or oi'll give yer somethink to tyke' ome to yer dinner, see if oi don't!"

"Who is this person?" I asked of Eva, placing my hands upon her two breasts as if to shield them from the intruder's eye.

"Person yerself!" said the voice, "Fust thing *you've* a-got ter do is ter leave' old of my donah's breasties and then oi'll *tork* to ver!"

"But the lady has hurt herself, sir, and was consulting me professionally."

There was a moment's pause, during which I had time to examine my opponent when I found to be wearing a red Tam-o'-Shanter cap, a close fitting knitted silk blouse, a short white flannel skirt, and scarlet stockings. This charming figure threw itself upon me open-armed and open-mouthed and kissed me with delightful abandon.

After a hearty laugh over the success of Flossie's latest 'impersonation', Eva pushed us both out of the room, saying. "Take her away, Jack, and see if *she* has got any marks. Those bicycle saddles are rather trying sometimes. We will lunch in a quarter of an hour."

I bore my darling little mistress away to her room, and having helped her to strip off her clothes, I inspected on my knees the region where the saddle might have been expected to gall her, but found nothing but a fair expanse of firm white bottom which I saluted with many lustful kisses upon every spot within reach of my tongue. Then I took her naked to the bathroom, and sponged her from neck to ankles, dried her thoroughly, just plunged my tongue once into her cunt, carried her back to her room, dressed her and presented her to Eva within twenty minutes of our leaving the latter's bedroom.

Below in the coffee-room, a capitally served luncheon awaited us. The table was laid in a sort of little annex to the principal room, and I was glad of the retirement, since we were able to enjoy to the full the constant flow of fun and mimicry with which Flossie brought tears of laughter to our eyes throughout the meal. Eva, too, was gifted with a fine sense of the ridiculous, and as I myself was at least an appreciative audience, the ball was kept rolling with plenty of spirit.

After lunch Eva announced her intention of going to a concert in Piccadilly, and a few minutes later Flossie and I were once more alone.

"Jack," she said, "I feel thoroughly and hopelessly naughty this afternoon. If you like I

49

will go on with my story while you lie on the sofa and smoke a cigar."

This exactly suited my views and I said so.

"Very well, then. First give me a great big kiss with all the tongue you've got about you. Ah! that was good! Now I'm going to sit on this footstool beside you, and I *think* one or two of these buttons might be unfastened, so that I can feel whether the story is producing any effect upon you. Good gracious! why, it's as hard and stiff as a poker already. I really *must* frig it a little —"

"Quite gently and slowly then, *please* Flossie, or —"

"Yes, quite, *quite* gently and slowly, so — Is that nice, Jack?"

"Nice is not the word, darling!"

"Talking of words, Jack, I am afraid I shall hardly be able to finish my adventures without occasionally using a word or two which you don't hear at a Sunday School Class. Do you mind, very much? Of course you can always go and look out of the window, can't you!"

"My dearest little sweetheart, when we are alone together like this, and both feeling extremely naughty, as we do now, any and every word that comes from your dear lips sounds sweet and utterly void of offence to me."

"Very well, then; that makes it ever so much easier to tell my story, and if I *should* become too shocking — well, you know how I love you to stop my mouth, don't you Jack!"

A responsive throb from my imprisoned member gave her all the answer she required.

"Let me see," she began, "where was I? Oh, I remember, in Ylette's bed."

"Yes, she had gamahuched you, and you were just performing the same friendly office for her."

"Of course: I was telling you how the length of my tongue made up for the shortness of my experience, or so Ylette was kind enough to say. I think she meant it too: at any rate she spent several times before I gave up my position between her legs. After this we tried the double gamahuche, which proved a great success because, although she was, as I have told you, two years older than I, we were almost exactly of a height, so that as she knelt over me, her cunt came quite naturally upon my mouth, and her mouth upon my cunt, and in this position we were able to give each other an enormous amount of pleasure."

At this point I was obliged to beg Flossie to remove her right hand from the situation it was occupying.

"What I cannot understand about it," she

went on, "is that there are any number of girls in France, and a good many in England too, who after they have once been gamahuched by another girl don't care about anything else. Perhaps it means that they have never been really in love with a man, because to *me* one touch of your lips in that particular neighbourhood is worth ten thousand kisses from anybody else, male or female and when I have got your dear, darling, delicious prick in my mouth, I want nothing else in the whole wide world, except to give you the greatest possible amount of pleasure and to make you spend down my throat in the quickest possible time —"

"If you really want to beat the record, Flossie, I think there's a good chance now —"

Almost before the words had passed my lips the member in question was between *hers*, where it soon throbbed to the crisis in response to the indescribable sucking action of mouth and tongue of which she possessed the secret.

On my telling her how exquisite were the sensations she procured me by this means she replied:

"Oh, you have to thank Ylette for that! Just before we became friends she had gone for the long holidays to a country house belonging to a young couple who were great friends of hers.

There was a very handsome boy of eighteen or so staying in the house. He fell desperately in love with Ylette and she with him, and he taught her exactly how to gamahuche him so as to produce the utmost amount of pleasure. As she told me afterwards, "Every day, every night, almost ever hour, he would bury his prick in my mouth, frig it against my tongue, and fill my throat with a divine flood. With a charming amiability, he worked incessantly to shew me every kind of gamahuching, all the possible ways of sucking a man's prick. Nothing, said he, should be left to the imagination, which, he explained, can never produce such good results as a few practical lessons given in detail upon a real standing prick, plunged to the very root in the mouth of the girl pupil, to whom one can thus describe on the spot the various suckings, hard, soft, slow or quick, of which it is essential she should know the precise effect in order to obtain the quickest and most copious flow of the perfumed liquor which she desires to draw from her lover."

"I suppose," Ylette went on, "that one invariably likes what one can do well. Anyhow, my greatest pleasure in life is to suck a goodlooking boy's prick. If he likes to slip his tongue into my cunt at the same time, *tant mieux*."

"Unfortunately this delightful boy could only stay a fortnight, but as there were several other young men of the party, and as her lover was wise enough to know that after his recent lessons in the art of love, Ylette could not be expected to be an abstainer, he begged her to enjoy herself in his absence, with the result, as she said that 'au bout d'une semaine il n'y avait pas un vit dans la maison qui ne m'avait tripoté la luette (I), ni une langue qui n'était l'amie intime de mon con.'

"Every one of these instructions Ylette passed on to me, with practical illustrations upon my second finger standing as substitute for the real thing, which, of course, was not to be had in the school at — least not just then.

"She must have been an excellent teacher, for I have never had any other lessons than hers, and yours is the first and only staff of love that I have ever had the honour of gamahuching. However, I mean to make up now for lost time, for I would have you to know, my darling, that I am madly in love with every bit of your body, and that most of all do I adore your angel prick with its coral head that I so love to suck and

---

*) Uvula

plunge into my mouth. Come, Jack, Come! let us have one more double gamahuche. One moment! There! Now I am naked. I am going to kneel over your face with my legs wide apart and my cunt kissing your mouth. Drive the whole of your tongue into it, won't you, Jack, and make it curl round my clitoris. Yes! that's it — just like that. Lovely! Now I can't talk any more, because I am going to fill my mouth with the whole of your darling prick; push; push it down my throat, Jack, and when the time comes, spend your very longest and most. I'm going to frig you a little first and rub you under your balls. Goodness! how the dear thing is standing. In he goes now ... m ... m ... m ... m ... m ... m ... "

A few inarticulate gasps and groans of pleasure were the only sounds audible for some minutes during which each strove to render the sensations of the other as acute as possible. I can answer for it that Flossie's success was complete, and by the convulsive movements of her bottom and the difficulty I experienced in keeping the position of my tongue upon her palpitating clitoris, I gathered that my operations had not altogether failed of their object. In this I was confirmed by the copious and protracted discharge which the beloved cunt delivered into my throat at the same instant as the incomparable mouth received my yard to the very root, and a perfect torrent rewarded her delicious efforts for my enjoyment.

"Ah, Jack! that was just heavenly," she sighed, as she rose from her charming position. *"How you did spend, that time, you darling old boy, and so did I, eh, Jack?"*

"My little angel, I thought you would never have finished," I replied.

"Do you know, Jack, I believe you really did get a little way down my throat, then! At any rate you managed the 'tripotage de luette' that Ylette's friend recommended so strongly!"

"And I don't think I ever got quite so far into your cunt, Flossie."

"That's quite true; I felt your tongue touch a spot it had never reached before. And just wasn't it lovely when you got there! It almost makes me spend again to think of it! But I am not going to be naughty any more. And to show you how truly virtuous I am feeling, I'll continue my story if you like. I want to get on with it, because I know you must be wondering all the time how a person of my age can have come to be so . . . what shall we say, Jack?"

"Larky," I suggested.

"Yes, 'larky' will do. Of course I have always

been 'older than my age' as the saying goes, and my friendship with Ylette and all the lovely things she used to do to me made me 'come on' much faster than most girls. I ought to tell you that I got to be rather a favourite at school, and after it came to be known that Ylette and I were on gamahuching terms, I used to get little notes from almost every girl in the school over twelve, imploring me to sleep with her. One dear little thing even went so far as to give me the measurements of her tongue, which she had taken with a piece of string."

"Oh, I say, Flossie, *come now* — I can swallow a good deal but — "

"You can indeed, Jack, as I have good reason to know! But all the same it's absolutely true. You can't have any conception what French school-girls of fourteen or fifteen are. There is nothing they won't do to get themselves gamahuched, and if a girl is pretty or fascinating or has particularly good legs, or specially large breasts, she may, if she likes, have a fresh admirer's head under her petticoats every day in the week. Of course, it's all very wrong and dreadful, I know, but what else can you expect? In France gamahuching between grown-up men and women is a recognised thing — "

"Not only in France, *nowadays*," I put in.

"So I have heard. But at any rate in France every body does it. Girls at school naturally know this, as they know most things. At that time of life — at *my* time of life, if you like — a girl thinks and dreams of nothing else. She cannot, except by some extraordinary luck, find herself alone with a boy or man. One day her girl chum at school pops her head under her petticoats and gamahuches her deliciously. How can you wonder if from that moment she is ready to go through fire and water to obtain the same pleasure?"

"Go on, Flossie. You are simply delicious to-day!"

"Don't laugh, Jack. I am very serious about it. I don't care how much a girl of (say) my age longs for a boy to be naughty with — it's perfectly right and natural. What I think is bad is that she should *begin* by having a liking for a girl's tongue inculcated into her. I should like to see boys and girls turned loose upon one another once a week or so at authorized gamahuching parties, which should be attended by masters and governesses (who would have to see that the *other* thing was not indulged in, of course). Then the girls would grow up with a good healthy taste for the other sex, and even if they did do a little gamahuching amongst themselves between whiles, it would only be to keep themselves going till the next 'party'. By my plan a boy's prick would be the central object of their desires, as it ought to be. Now *I* think that's a very fine scheme, Jack, and as soon as I am a little older, I shall go to Paris and put it before the Minister of Education!"

"But why wait, Flossie? Why not go now?"

"Well, you see, if the old gentleman (I suppose he is old, isn't he, or he wouldn't be a minister?) — if he saw a girl in short frocks, he would think she had got some private object to serve in regard to the gamahuching parties. Whereas a grown-up person who had plainly left school might be supposed to be doing it unselfishly for the good of the rising generation."

"Yes, I understand that. But when you *do* go, Flossie, please take me or some other respectable person with you, because I don't altogether trust that Minister of Education and whatever the length of your frocks might happen to be at the time, I feel certain that, old or young, the moment you had explained your noble scheme, he would be wanting some practical illustrations on the office arm-chair!"

"How dare you suggest such a thing, Jack! You are to understand, sir, that from henceforth my mouth is reserved for three purposes, to eat with, to talk with, and to kiss you with on whatever part of your person I may happen to fancy at the moment. By the way, you won't mind my making just one exception in favour of Eva, will you? She loves me to make her nipples stand with my tongue; occasionally, too we perform the '*soixant neuf*'."

"When the next performance takes place, may I be there to see?" I ejaculated fervently.

"Oh, Jack, how shocking!"

"Does it shock you, Flossie? Very well, then I withdraw it, and apologise."

"You cannot withdraw it now. You have distinctly stated that you would like to be there when Eva and I have our next gamahuche."

"Well, I suppose I *did* say."

"Silence, sir," said Flossie in a voice of thunder, and shaking her brown head at me with inexpressible ferocity. "You have made a proposal of the most indecent character, and the sentence of the Court is that, at the first possible opportunity, you shall be *held to that proposal!* Meanwhile the Court condemns you to receive 250 kisses on various parts of your body, which it will at once proceed to administer. Now, sir, off with your clothes!"

"Mayn't I keep my . . . "

"No, sir, you may *not!*"

"How Flossie acquired the French tongue"

The sentence of the Court was accordingly carried out to the letter, somewhere about three-fourths of the kisses being applied upon one and the same part of the prisoner to which the Court attached its mouth with extraordinary gusto.

CHAPTER III

Nox Ambrosiana

MY INTERCOURSE WITH THE TENANTS OF THE flat became daily more intimate and more frequent. My love for Flossie grew intensely deep and strong as opportunities increased for observing the rare sweetness and amiability of her character, and the charm which breathed like a spell over everything she said and did. At one moment, so great was her tact and so keen her judgment, I would find myself consulting her on a knotty point with the certainty of getting sound advice; at another the child in her would suddenly break out and she would romp and play about like the veriest kitten. Then there would be yet another reaction, and without a word of warning, she would become amorous and caressing and seizing upon her favourite plaything, would push it into her mouth and suck it in a perfect frenzy of erotic passion. It is hardly necessary to say that these contrasts of mood lent an infinite zest to our liaison and I had almost ceased to long for its more perfect consummation. But one warm June evening, allusion was again made to the subject by Flossie, who repeated her sorrow for the deprivation she declared I must be feeling so greatly.

I assured her that it was not so.

"Well, Jack, if you aren't, *I* am," she cried. "And what is more there is some one else who is 'considerably likewise' as our old gardener used to say."

"What *do* you mean, child?"

She darted into the next room and came back almost directly.

"Sit down there and listen to me. In that room, lying asleep on her bed, is the person whom, after you, I love best in the world. There is nothing I wouldn't do for her, and I'm sure you'll believe this when I tell you that I am going to beg you on my knees, to go in there and do to Eva what my promise to her prevents me from letting you do to me. Now, Jack, I know you love me and you know *dearly* I love you. Nothing can alter *that*. Well, Jack, if you will go into Eva, gamahuche her well and let her gamahuche you (she *adores* it), and then have her thoroughly and in all positions — I shall simply love you a thousand times better than ever."

"But Flossie, my darling, Eva doesn't —"

"Oh, doesn't she! Wait till you get between her legs, and see! Come along: I'll just put you inside the room and then leave you. She is lying outside her bed for coolness — on her side. Lie down quietly *behind* her. She will be almost sure to think it's me, and perhaps you will hear — something interesting. Quick's the word! Come!"

The sight which met my eyes on entering Eva's bedroom was enough to take one's breath away. She lay on her side, with her face towards the door, stark naked, and fast asleep. I crept noiselessly towards her and gazed upon her glorious nudity in speechless delight. Her dark hair fell in a cloud about her white shoulders. Her fine face was slightly flushed, the full red lips a little parted. Below, the gleaming breasts caught the light from the shaded lamp at her bedside, the pink nipples rising and falling to the time of her quiet breathing. One fair round arm was behind her head, the other lay along the exquisitely turned thigh. The good St. Antony might have been pardoned for owning himself defeated by such a picture!

As is usual with a sleeping person who is being looked at, Eva stirred a little, and her lips opened as if to speak. I moved on tiptoe to the other side of the bed, and stripping myself naked, lay down beside her.

Then, without turning round, a sleepy voice said, "Ah, Flossie, are you there? What have you done with Jack? *(a pause)*. When are you going to lend him to me for a night, Flossie? I wish I'd got him here now, between my legs — betwe-e-e-n m-y-y-y le-egs! Oh dear! how randy I do feel to-night. When I *do* have Jack for a night, Flossie, may I take his prick in my mouth before we do the other thing? Flossie — Floss*ee* — why don't you answer? Little darling! I expect she's tired out, and no wonder! Well, I suppose I'd better put something on me and go to sleep too!"

As she raised herself from the pillow, her hand came in contact with my person.

"Angels and Ministers of Grace defend us! What's this? *You*, Jack! *And you've heard what I've been saying?*"

"I'm afraid I have, Eva."

"Well, it doesn't matter: I meant it all, and more besides! Now before I do anything else I simply must run in and kiss that darling Floss for sending you to me. It is just like her, and I can't say anything stronger than *that!*"

"Jack," she said on coming back to the room.

"I warn you that you are going to have a stormy night. In the matter of love, I've gone starving for many months. To-night I'm fairly roused, and when in that state, I believe I am about the most erotic bed-fellow to be found anywhere. Flossie has given me leave to *say* and do anything and everything to you, and I mean to use the permission for all its worth. Flossie tells me that you are an absolutely perfect gamahucher. Now I adore being gamahuched. Will you do that for me, Jack?"

"My dear girl, I should rather think so!"

"Good! But it is not to be all on one side. I shall gamahuche you, too, and you will have to own that I know something of the art. Another thing you may perhaps like to try is what the French call '*fouterie aux seins*'."

"I know all about it, and if I may insert monsieur Jacques between those magnificent breasts of yours, I shall die of the pleasure."

"Good again. Now we come to the legitimate drama, from which you and Floss have so nobly abstained. I desire to be thoroughly and comprehensively fucked to-night — sorry to have to use the word, Jack, but it is the only one that expresses my meaning."

"Don't apologise, dear. Under present circumstances all words are allowable."

"Glad to hear you say that, because it makes conversation so much easier. Now let me take hold of your prick, and frig it a little, so that I may judge what size it attains in full erection. So! he's a fine boy, and I think he will fit my cunt to a turn. I must kiss his pretty head, it looks so tempting. Ah! delicious! See here Jack, I will lie back with my head on the pillow, and you shall just come and kneel over me and have me in the mouth. Push away gaily, just as if you were fucking me, and when you are going to spend, slip one hand under my neck and drive your prick down my throat, and do not *dare* to withdraw it until I have received all you have to give me. Sit upon my chest first for a minute and let me tickle your prick with the nipples of my breasts. Is that nice? Ah! I knew you would like it! *Now* kneel up to my face, and I will suck you."

With eagerly pouting lips and clutching fingers, she seized upon my straining yard, and pressed it into her soft mouth. Arrived there, it was saluted by the velvet tongue which twined itself about the nut in a thousand lascivious motions.

Mindful of Eva's instructions, I began to work the instrument as if it was in another place. At once she laid her hands upon my buttocks and regulated the time of my movements, assisting them by a corresponding action of her head. Once, owing to carelessness on my part, her lips lost their hold altogether; with a little cry, she caught my prick in her fingers and in an instant, it was again between her lips and revelling in the adorable pleasure of their sucking.

A moment later and my hands were under her neck, for the signal, and my very soul seemed to be exhaled from me in response to the clinging of her mouth as she felt my prick throb with the passage of love's torrent.

After a minute's rest, and a word of gratitude for the transcendent pleasure she had given me, I began a tour of kisses over the enchanting regions which lay between her neck and her knees, ending with a protracted sojourn in the most charming spot of all. As I approached this last, she said.

"Please to begin by passing your tongue slowly round the edges of the lips, then thrust it into the lower part at full length and keep it there working it in and out for a little. Then move it gradually up to the top and when there, press your tongue firmly against my clitoris a minute or so. Next take the clitoris between your lips and suck it *furiously*, bite it gently, and slip the point of your tongue underneath it. When I have spent twice, which I am sure to do in the first three minutes, get up and lie between my legs, drive the whole of your tongue into my mouth, and the whole of your prick into my cunt, and fuck me with all your might and main!"

I could not resist a smile at the naiveté of these circumstantial directions. My amusement was not lost upon Eva, who hastened to explain, by reminding me again that it was "ages" since she had been touched by a man. "In gamahuching," she said, "the *details* are everything. In copulation they are not so important, since the principal things that increase one's enjoyment — such as the quickening of the stroke towards the end by the man, and the knowing exactly how and when to apply the *nipping* action of the cunt by the woman — come more or less naturally, especially with practice. But now, Jack, I want to be gamahuched, please."

"And I'm longing to be at you, dear. Come and kneel astride of me, and let me kiss your cunt without any more delay."

Eva was pleased to approve of this position and in another moment, I was slipping my tongue into the delicious cavity which opened wider and wider to receive its caresses, and to enable it to plunge further and further into the perfumed depths. My attentions were next turned to the finely developed clitoris which I found to be extraordinarily sensitive. In fact, Eva's own time limit of three minutes had not been reached, when the second effusion escaped her, and a third was easily obtained by a very few more strokes of the tongue. After this, she laid herself upon her back, drew me towards her and, taking hold of my prick, placed it tenderly between her breasts, and pressing them together with her hands, urged me to enjoy myself in this enchanting position. The length and stiffness imparted to my member by the warmth and softness of her breasts delighted her beyond measure, and she implored me to fuck her without any further delay. I was never more ready or better furnished than at that moment, and after she had once more taken my prick into her mouth for a moment, I slipped down to the desired position between her thighs which she had already parted to their uttermost to receive me. In an instant she had guided the staff of love to the exact spot, and with a heave of her bottom, aided by an answering thrust from me, had buried it to the root within the soft of its natural covering.

Eva's description of herself as an erotic bed-fellow had hardly prepared me for the joys I was to experience in her arms. From the moment the nut of my yard touched her womb, she became as one possessed. Her eyes were turned heavenwards, her tongue twined round my own in rapture, her hands played about my body, now clasping my neck, now working feverishly up and down my back, and ever and again, creeping down to her lower parts where her first and second finger would rest compass-shaped upon the two edges of her cunt, pressing themselves upon my prick as it glided in and out and adding still further to the maddening pleasure I was undergoing. Her breath came in short quick gasps, the calve of her legs sometimes lay upon my own but more often were locked over my loins or buttocks, thus enabling her to time to a nicety the strokes of my body, and to respond with accurately judged thrusts from her own splendid bottom. At last a low musical cry came from her parted lips, she strained me to her naked body with redoubled fury and driving the whole length of her tongue into my mouth, she spent long and deliciously, whilst I flooded her clinging cunt with a torrent of unparalleled volume and duration.

"Jack," she whispered, "I have never enjoyed anything half so much in my life before. I hope you liked it too?"

"I don't think you can expect anyone to say that he "liked" fucking *you*, Eva! One might 'like' kissing your hand, or helping you on with an opera cloak or some minor pleasure of that sort. But to lie between a pair of legs like yours, cushioned on a pair of breasts like yours, with a tongue like yours down one's throat, and one's prick held in the soft grip of a cunt like yours, is to undergo a series of sensations such as don't come twice in a lifetime."

Eva's eyes flashed as she gathered me closer in her naked arms and said.

"*Don't* they, though! In this particular instance I am going to see that they come twice *within half an hour!*"

"Well, I've come twice in less than half an hour and —"

"Oh! I know what you are going to say, but we'll soon put that all right."

A careful examination of the state of affairs was then made by Eva who bent her pretty head for the purpose, kneeling on the bed in a position which enabled me to gaze at my leisure upon all her secret charms.

Her operations meanwhile were causing me

exquisite delight. With an indescribable tenderness of action, soft and caressing as that of a young mother tending her sick child, she slipped the fingers of her left hand under my balls while the other hand wandered luxuriously over the surrounding country and finally came to an anchor upon my prick, which not unnaturally began to show signs of returning vigour. Pleased at the patient's improved state of health, she passed her delicious velvet tongue up and down and round and into a standing position! This sudden and satisfactory result of her ministrations so excited her that, without letting go of her prisoner, she cleverly passed one leg over me as I lay, and behold us in the traditional attitude of the *gamahuche a deux!* I now, for the first time, looked upon Eva's cunt in its full beauty, and I gladly devoted a moment to the inspection before plunging my tongue between the rich red lips which seemed to kiss my mouth as it clung in ecstasy to their luscious folds. I may say here that in point of colour, proportion and beauty of outline, Eva Letchford's cunt was the most perfect I had ever seen or gamahuched, though in after years my darling little Flossie's displayed equal faultlessness, and, as being the cunt of my beloved little sweetheart, whom I adored, it was entitled to and received from me a degree of homage never accorded to any other before or since.

The particular part of my person to which Eva was paying attention soon attained in her mouth a size and hardness which did the highest credit to her skill. With my tongue revelling in its enchanted resting-place, and my prick occupying what a house-agent might truth fully describe as "this most desirable site," I was personally content to remain as we were, whilst Eva, entirely abandoning herself to her charming occupation, had apparently forgotten the object with which she had originally undertaken it. Fearing therefore lest the clinging mouth and delicately twining tongue should bring about the crisis which Eva had designed should take place elsewhere, I reluctantly took my lips from the clitoris they were enclosing at the moment, and called to its owner to stop.

"But Jack, you're just going to spend!" was the plaintive reply.

"Exactly, dear! And how about the 'twice in half an hour'."

"Oh! of course. You were going to fuck me again, weren't you! Well, you'll find Massa Johnson in pretty good trim for the fray," and she laughingly held up my prick, which was really of enormous dimensions, and plunging it downwards let it rebound with a loud report against my belly.

This appeared to delight her, for she repeated it several times. Each time the elasticity seemed to increase and the force of the recoil to become greater.

"The darling!" she cried, as she kissed the coral head. "He is going to his own chosen abiding place. Come! Come! Come! blessed, *blessed* prick. Bury yourself in this loving cunt which longs for you; frig yourself deliciously against the lips which wait to kiss you; plunge into the womb which yearns to receive your life-giving seed; pause as you go by to press the clitoris that loves you. Come, divine, adorable prick! fuck me, fuck me, fuck me! fuck me long and hard: fuck and spare not! — Jack, you are into me, my cunt clings to your prick, do you feel how it nips you? Push, Jack, further; now your balls are kissing my bottom. That's lovely! Crush my breasts with your chest, *cr-r-r-r-ush* them, Jack. Now go slowly a moment, and let your prick gently rub my clitoris. So . . . o . . o . . . Now faster and harder . . . faster still — now your tongue in my mouth, and dig your nails into my bottom. I'm going to spend: fuck, Jack, fuck me, fuck me, fu-u-u-uck me! Heavens! what bliss it is! Ah you're spending too bo ... o ... o ... oth together, both toge ... e e ... ther. Pour it into me, Jack! Flood me, drown me, fill my womb. God! What rapture. Don't stop. Your prick is still hard and long. Drive it into me — touch my navel. Let me get my hand down to frig you as you go in and out. The sweet prick! He's stiffer than ever. How splendid of him! Fuck me again. Jack. Ah! fuck me till to-morrow, fuck me till I die."

I fear that this language in the cold form of print may seem more than a little crude. Yet those who have experience of a beautiful and refined woman, abandoning herself in moments of passion to similar freedom of speech, will own the stimulus thus given to the sexual powers. In the present instance its effect, joined to the lascivious touches and never ceasing efforts to arouse and increase desire of this deliciously lustful girl, was to impart an unprecedented stiffness to my member which throbbed almost to bursting within the enclosing cunt and pursued its triumphant career to such lengths, that even the resources of the insatiable Eva gave out at last, and she lay panting in my arms, where soon afterwards she passed into a quiet sleep. Drawing a silken coverlet over her, I rose with great caution, slipped on my clothes, and in five minutes was on my way home.

CHAPTER IV

*More of Flossie's school-life;
and other matters*

"GOOD MORNING, CAPTAIN ARCHER, I TRUST THAT you have slept well?" said Flossie on my presenting myself at the flat early the next day. "My friend Miss Letchford," she went on, in a prim middleaged tone of voice, "has not yet left her apartment. She complains of having passed a somewhat disturbed night owing to — ahem!"

"Rats in the wainscot?" I suggested.

"No, my friend attributes her sleepless condition to a severe irritation in the — forgive the immodesty of my words — lower part of her person, followed by a prolonged pricking in the same region. She is still feeling the effects, and I found her violently clasping a pillow between her — ahem! — legs, which which she was apparently endeavouring to soothe her feelings."

"Dear me! Miss Eversley, do you think I could

be of any assistance?" *(stepping towards Eva's door.)*

"You are *most* kind, Captain Archer, but I have already done what I could in the way of friction and — other little attentions, which left the poor sufferer somewhat calmer. Now, Jack, you wretch! you haven't kissed me yet . . . That's better! You will not be surprised to hear that Eva has given me a full and detailed description of her sleepless night, in her own language, which I have no doubt you have discovered, is just a bit *graphic* at times."

"Well, my little darling, I did my best, as I knew you would wish me to do. It wasn't difficult with such a bed-fellow as Eva. But charming and amorous as she is, I couldn't help feeling all the time 'if it were only my little Flossie lying under me now!' By the way how utterly lovely you are this morning, Floss."

She was dressed in a short sprigged cotton frock, falling very little below her knees, shot pink and black stockings, and low patent leather shoes with silver buckles. Her long waving brown hair gleamed gold in the morning light, and the deep blue eyes glowed with health and love, and now and again flashed with merriment. I gazed upon her in rapture at her beauty.

"Do you like my frock, Jack? I'm glad. It's the first time I've had it on. It's part of my trousseau."

"Your *what*, Flossie?" I shouted.

"I said my trousseau," she repeated quietly, but with sparks of fun dancing in her sweet eyes. "The fact is, Jack, Eva declared the other day that though I am not married to you, you and I are really on a sort of honeymoon. So, as I have just had a good lot of money from the lawyers, she made me go with her and buy everything new. Look here," *(unfastening her bodice)* "new stays, new chemise, new stockings and oh! Jack, *look!* such *lovely* new drawers — none of your horrid vulgar knickerbockers, trimmings and lovely little tucks all the way up, and quite wide open in front for . . . ventilation I suppose! Feel what soft stuff they are made of! Eva was awfully particular about these drawers. She is always so practical, you know."

"Practical!" I interrupted.

"Yes. What she said was that you would often be wanting to kiss me between my legs when there wasn't time to undress and be naked together, so that I must have drawers made of the finest and most delicate stuff to please you, and with the opening cut extra wide so as not to get in the way of your tongue! Now don't you call that practical?"

"I do indeed! Blessed Eva, that's another good turn I owe her!"

"Well, for instance, there isn't time to undress *now*, Jack, and —"

She threw herself back in her chair and in an instant, I had plunged under the short rose-scented petticoats and had my mouth glued to the beloved cunt once more. In the midst of the delicious operation, I fancied I heard a slight sound from the direction of Eva's door and just then, Flossie locked her hands behind my head and pressed me to her with even more than her usual ardour; a moment later deluging my throat with the perfumed essence of her being.

You darling old boy, how you *did* make me spend that time! I really think your tongue is longer than it was. Perhaps the warmth of Eva's interior has made it grow! Now I must be off to the dressmaker's for an hour or so. By the way, she wants to make my frocks longer. She declares people can see my drawers when I run upstairs."

"Don't you let her do it, Floss."

"*Rather not!* What's the use of buying expensive drawers like mine if you can't show them to a pal! *Good* morning, Captain! Sorry I can't stop. While I'm gone you might just step in and see how my lydy friend's gettin' on. Fust door on the right. *Good* morning!"

For a minute or two, I lay back in my chair and wondered whether I would not take my hat and go. But a moments' further reflection told me that I must do as Flossie directed me. To this decision, I must own, the memory of last night's pleasure and the present demands of a most surprising erection contributed in no small degree. Accordingly, I tapped at Eva's bedroom door.

She had just come from her bath and wore only a peignoir and her stockings. On seeing me, she at once let fall her garment and stood before me in radiant nakedness.

"Look at this", she said, holding out a half-sheet of notepaper. "I found it on my pillow when I woke an hour ago.

" 'If Jack comes this morning I shall send him in to see you while I go to Virginie's. Let him — *anything beginning with "f" or "s" that rhymes with* luck — you.' "A hair of the dog", etc., will do you both good. My time will come. Ha! Ha!"

"Floss."

"Now I ask you, Jack, was there ever such an adorable little darling?"

My answer need not be recorded.

Eva came close to me and thrust her hand inside my clothes.

"Ah! I see you are of the same way of thinking as myself," she said taking hold of my fingers and carrying them on her cunt, which pouted hungrily. "So let us have one good royal fuck and then you can stay here with me while I dress, and I'll tell you anything that Flossie may have left out about her school-life in Paris. Will that meet your views?"

"Exactly," I replied.

"Very well then. As we are going to limit ourselves to *one*, would you mind fucking me *en levrette?*"

"Any way you like, most puissant and fucksome of ladies!"

I stripped off my clothes in a twinkling and Eva placed herself in position, standing on the rug and bending forwards with her elbows on the bed. I reverently saluted the charms thus presented to my lips, omitting none, and then rising from my knees, advanced, weapon in hand, to storm the breach. As I approached, Eva opened her legs to their widest extent, and I drove my straining prick into the mellow cunt, fucking it with unprecedented vigour and delight, as the lips alternately parted and contracted, nipping me with an extraordinary force in response to the pressure of my right forefinger upon the clitoris and of my left upon the nipples of the heaving breasts. Keen as was the enjoyment we were both experiencing the fuck — as in invariably the case with a morning performance — was of very protacted duration, and several minutes had elapsed before I dropped my arms to Eva's thighs and, with my belly glued against her bottom and my face nestling between her shoulder blades, felt the rapturous throbbing of my prick as it discharged an avalanche into the innermost recesses of her womb.

"Don't move, Jack, for Heaven's sake," she cried.

"Don't want to, Eva, I'm quite happy where I am, thank you!"

Moving an inch or two further out from the bed so as to give herself more "play", she

85

started an incredibly provoking motion of her bottom, so skilfully executed that it produced the impression of being almost *spiral*. The action is difficult to describe, but her bottom rose and fell, moved backward and forward, and from side to side in quick alternation, the result being that my member was constantly in contact with, as it were, some fresh portion of the embracing cunt, the soft folds of which seemed by their varied and tender caresses to be pleading to him to emerge from his present state of partial apathy and resume the proud condition he had displayed before.

"Will he come up this way, Jack, or shall I take the dear little man in my mouth and suck him into an erection?"

"I think he'll be all right as he is, dear. Just keep on nipping him with your cunt and push your bottom a little closer to me so that I may feel your naked flesh against mine . . . *that's* it!"

"Ah! the darling prick, he's beginning to swell! he's going to fuck me directly, I know he is! Your finger on my cunt in front, please Jack, and the other hand on my nipples. So! *that's* nice. Oh dear! how I *do* want your tongue in my mouth, but that can't be. Now begin and fuck me slowly at first. Your *second* finger on my clitoris, please, and frig me in time to the motion of your body. Now fuck faster a little, and deeper into me. Push, dear, push like a demon. Pinch my nipple; a little faster on the clitoris. I'm spending! I'm dying of delight! Fuck me, Jack, keep on fucking me. Don't be afraid. Strike against my bottom with all your strength, harder still, harder! Now put your hands down to my thighs and *drag* me on to you. Lovely! grip the flesh of my thighs with your fingers and fuck me to the very womb."

"Eva, look out! I'm going to spend!"

"So am I, Jack. Ah! how your prick throbs against my cunt! Fuck me, Jack, to the last moment, spend your last drop, as I'm doing. One last push up to the hilt — there, keep him in like that and let me have a deluge from you. How exquisite! how adorable to spend together! *One* moment more before you take him out, and let me kiss him with my cunt before I say good-bye."

"What a nip that was, Eva, it felt more like a hand on me than a —"

"Yes", she interrupted, turning round and facing me with her eyes languorous and velvety with lust, "that is my only accomplishment, and I must say I think it's a valuable one! In Paris

I had a friend — but no matter I'm not going to talk about myself, but about Flossie. Sit down in that chair, and have a cigarette while I talk to you. I'm going to stay naked if you don't mind. It's so hot. Now if you're quite comfy, I'll begin."

She seated herself opposite to me, her splendid naked body full in the light from the window near her.

"There is a part of Flossie's school story," began Eva, "which she has rather shrunk from telling you, and so I propose to relate the incident, in which I am sure you will be sufficiently interested. For the first twelve months of her school days in Paris, nothing very special occured to her beyond the cementing of her friendship with Ylette Vespertin. Flossie was a tremendous favourite with the other girls on account of her sweet nature and her extraordinary beauty, and there is no doubt that a great many curly heads were popped under her petticoats at one time and another. All these heads, however, belonged to her own sex, and no great harm was done. But at last there arrived at the convent a certain Camille de Losgrain, who, though by no means averse to the delights of gamahuche, nursed a strong preference for male, as against female charms. Camille speedily struck up an alliance with a handsome boy of seventeen who lived in the house next door. This youth had often seen Flossie and greatly desired her acquaintance. It seems that his bedroom window was on the same level as that of the room occupied by Flossie, Camille and three other girls, all of whom knew him by sight and had severally expressed a desire to have him between their legs. So it was arranged one night that he was to climb on to a buttress below his room, and the girls would manage to haul him into theirs. All this had to be done in darkness, as of course no light could be shewn. The young gentleman duly arrived on the scene in safety — the two eldest girls divested him of his clothes, and then, according to previous agreement, the five damsels sat naked on the edge of the bed in the pitch dark room, and Master Don Juan was to decide, by passing his hands over their bodies, which of the five should be favoured with his attentions. No one was to speak, to touch his person or to make any sign of interest. Twice the youth essayed this novel kind of ordeal by touch, and after a moment's profound silence he said, 'J'ai choisi, c'est la troisieme.' 'La troisieme' was no other than Flossie, the size of whose breasts had at

once attracted him as well as given a clue to
her identity. And now, Jack, I hope the sequel
will not distress you. The other girls accepted
the decision most loyally, having no doubt anticipated it. They laid Flossie tenderly on the bed
and lavished every kind of caress upon her,
gamahuching her with especial tenderness, so
as to open the road as far as possible to the in-
vader. It fortunately turned out to be the case
that the boy's prick was not by any means of
abnormal size, and as the dear little maidenhead had been already subjected to very considerable wear and tear of fingers and
tongues the entrance was, as she told me herself, effected with a minimum of pain and dis-
comfort, hardly felt indeed in the midst of the
frantic kisses upon mouth, eyes, nipples, breasts
and buttocks which the four excited girls rained
upon her throughout the operation. As for the
boy, his enjoyment knew no bounds, and when
his alloted time was up could hardly be persuaded to make the return voyage to his room.
This, however, was at last accomplished, and
the four virgins hastened to hear from their
ravished friend the full true and particular account of her sensations. For several nights
after this, the boy made his appearance in the
room, where he fucked all the other four in

succession, and pined openly for Flossie, who, however, regarded him as belonging to Camille and declined anything beyond the occasional service of his tongue which she greatly relished and which he, of course, as gladly put at her disposal.

"All this happened before my time and was related to me afterwards by Flossie herself. It is only just a year ago that I was engaged to teach English at the convent. Like everyone else who is brought in contact with her, I at once fell in love with Flossie and we quickly became the greatest of friends. Six months ago, came a change of fortune for me, an old bachelor uncle dying suddenly and leaving me a competence. By this time, the attachment between Flossie and myself had become so deep that the child could not bear the thought of parting from me. I too was glad enough of the excuse thus given for writing to Flossie's guardian — who has never taken more than a casual interest in her — to propose her returning to England with me and the establishment of a joint menage. My 'references' being satisfactory, and Flossie having declared herself to be most anxious for the plan, the guardian made no objection and in short — here we are!"

"Well, that's a very interesting story, Eva.

Only — *confound* that French boy and his buttress!"

"Yes, you would naturally feel like that about it, and I don't blame you. Only you must remember that if it hadn't been for the size of Flossie's breasts, and its being done in the dark, and . . ."

"But Eva, you don't mean to tell me the young brute wouldn't have chosen her out of the five if there had been a *light*, do you!"

"No, of course not. What I *do* mean is that it was all a sort of fluke, and that Flossie is really, to all intents and purposes . . . "

"Yes, yes, I know what you would like to say, and I entirely and absolutely agree with you. I *love* Flossie with all my heart and soul and . . . well, that French boy can go to the devil!"

"Miss Eva! Niss Eva!" came a voice outside the door.

"Well, what is it?"

"Oh, if you please, Miss, there's a young man downstairs called for his little account. Says'e's the coals, Miss. I *towld* him you was engaged, Miss?"

"Did you — and what did he say?"

" 'Ow!' 'e sez, 'engyged, *is* she', 'e sez — 'well, you tell'er from me confidential-like, as it's 'igh time she was *married*', 'e sez!"

Our shouts of laughter brought Flossie scampering into the room, evidently in the wildest spirits.

"Horful scandal in 'igh life," she shouted. "A genl'man dish-covered in a lydy's aportments! 'arrowin' details. Speshul! Pyper! Speshul! — Now then, you two, what have you been doing while I've been gone? Suppose you tell me exactly what you've done and I'll tell you exactly what *I've* done!" — then in a tone of cheap melodrama — "Aha! 'ave I surproised yer guilty secret? She winceth! likewise'*e* winceth! in fact they both winceth! Thus h'am I avenged upon the pair!" And kneeling down between us, she pushed a dainty finger softly between the lips of Eva's cunt, and with her other hand took hold of my yard and tenderly frigged it, looking up into our faces all the time with inexpressible love and sweetness shining from her eyes.

"You *dears!*" she said. "It *is* nice to have you two naked together like this!"

A single glance passed between Eva and me, and getting up from our seats we flung ourselves upon the darling and smothered her with kisses. Then Eva, with infinite gentleness and many loving touches, preceded to undress her, handing the dainty garments to me one by one to be laid on the bed near me. As the fair white

breasts came forth from the corset, Eva gave a
little cry of delight, and pushing the lace-edged
chemise below the swelling globes, took one
erect and rosy nipple into her mouth, and putting her hand behind my neck, motioned me to
take the other. Shivers of delight coursed one
another up and down the shapely body over
which our fingers roamed in all directions.
Flossie's remaining garments were soon allowed to fall by a deft touch from Eva, and the
beautiful girl stood before us in all her radiant
nakedness. We paused a moment to gaze upon
the spectacle of loveliness. The fair face
flushed with love and desire; the violet eyes
shone; the full rounded breasts put forth their
coral nipples as if craving to be kissed again;
below the smooth satin belly appeared the silken
tuft that shaded without concealing the red lips
of the adorable cunt; the polished thighs gained
added whiteness by contrast with the dark stockings which clung amorously to the finely
moulded legs.

"Now, Jack, *both together*," said Eva, suddenly.

I divined what she meant and arranging a
couple of large cushions on the wide divan, I
took Flossie in my arms and laid her upon them,
her feet upon the floor. Her legs opened in-

stinctively and thrusting my head between her thighs, I plunged my tongue into the lower part of the cunt, whilst Eva, kneeling over her, upon the divan, attacked the developed clitoris. Our mouths thus met upon the enchanted spot and our tongues filled every corner and crevice of it. My own, I must admit, occasionally wandered downwards to the adjacent regions, and explored the valley of delight in that direction. But wherever we went and whatever we did, the lithe young body beneath continued to quiver from head to foot with excess of pleasure, shedding its treasures now in Eva's mouth, now in mine and sometimes in both at once! But vivid as were the delights she was experiencing, they were of a passive kind only, and Flossie was already artist enough to know that the keenest enjoyment is only obtained when giving and receiving are equally shared. Accordingly I was not surprised to hear her say:

"Jack, could you come up here to me now, please?"

Signing to me kneel astride of her face, she seized my yard, guided it to her lips and then locking her hands over my loins, she alternately tightened and relaxed her grasp, signifying that I was to use the delicious mouth freely as a substitute for the interdicted opening below. The

peculiar sucking action of her lips, of which I
have spoken before, bore a pleasant resemblance to the nipping of an accomplished cunt,
whilst the never-resting tongue, against whose
soft folds M. Jacques frigged himself luxuriously
in his passage between the lips and throat,
added a provocation to the lascivious sport not
to be enjoyed in the ordinary act of coition.
Meanwhile Eva had taken my place between
Flossie's legs and was gamahuching the beloved
cunt with incredible ardour. A sloping mirror
on the wall above enabled me to survey the
charming scene at my leisure, and to observe
the spasms of delight which, from time to time,
shook both the lovely naked forms below me. At
last my own time arrived, and Flossie, alert as
usual for the signs of approaching crisis,
clutched my bottom with convulsive fingers and
held me close pressed against her face, whilst
I flooded her mouth with the stream of love that
she adored. At the same moment the glass told
me that Eva's lips were pushing far into the
vulva to receive the result of their amorous
labours, the passage of which from cunt to
mouth was accompanied by every token of intense enjoyment from both the excited girls.

Rest and refreshment were needed by all
three after the strain of our morning revels, and

so the party broke up for the day after Flossie
had mysteriously announced that she was de-
signing something 'extra special', for the mor-
row.

CHAPTER V

Birthday Festivities

THE NEXT MORNING THERE WAS A NOTE FROM Flossie asking me to come as soon as possible after receiving it.

I hurried to the flat and found Flossie awaiting me, and in one of her most enchanting moods. It was Eva's birthday, as I was now informed for the first time, and to do honour to the occasion, Flossie had put on a costume in which she was to sell flowers at a fancy bazaar a few days later. It consisted of a white Tam-o'-Shanter cap with a straight upstanding feather — a shirt of the thinnest and gauziest white silk falling open at the throat and having a wide sailor collar — a broad lemon-coloured sash, a very short muslin skirt, lemon-coloured silk stockings and high-heeled brown shoes. At the opening of the shirt, a bunch of flame-coloured roses nestled between the glorious breasts, to the outlines of which all possible prominence was given by the softly clinging material. As she stood waiting to hear my verdict, her red lips slightly parted, a rosy flush upon her cheeks, and love and laughter beaming from the radiant eyes, the magic of her youth and beauty seemed to weave a fresh spell around my heart, and a torrent of passionate words burst from my lips as I strained the lithe young form to my breast and rained kisses upon her hair, her eyes, her cheeks and mouth.

She took my hand in her hand and quietly led me to my favourite chair, and then seating herself on my knee, nestled her face against my cheek and said:

"Oh, Jack, Jack, my darling boy, how can you possibly love me like that!" The sweet voice trembled and a tear or two dropped softly from the violet eyes whilst an arm stole round my neck and the red lips were pressed in a long intoxicating kiss upon my mouth.

We sat thus for some time when Flossie jumped from my knee, and said:

"We are forgetting all about Eva. Come in to her room and see what I have done."

We went hand in hand into the bedroom and

found Eva still asleep. On the chairs were laid her dainty garments, to which Flossie silently drew my attention. All along the upper edge of the chemise and corset, round the frills of the drawers and the hem of the petticoat, Flossie had sewn a narrow chain of tiny pink and white rosebuds, as a birthday surprise for her friend. I laughed noiselessly, and kissed her hand in token of my appreciation of the charming fancy.

"Now for Eva's birthday treat," whispered Flossie in my ear. "Go over into that corner and undress yourself as quietly as you can. I will help you."

Flossie's 'help' consisted chiefly in the use of sundry wiles to induce an erection. As these included the slow frigging in which she was such an adept, as well as the application of her rosy mouth and active tongue to every part of my prick, the desired result was rapidly obtained.

"Now, Jack, you are going to have Eva whilst I look on. Some day, my turn will come, and I want to see exactly how to give you the greatest possible amount of pleasure. Come and stand here by me, and we'll wake her up."

We passed round the bed and stood in front of Eva, who still slept on unconscious.

"Ahem!" from Flossie.

The sleeping figure turned lazily. The eyes unclosed and fell upon the picture of Flossie in her flower-girl's dress, standing a little behind me and, with her right hand passed in front of me, vigorously frigging my erected yard, whilst the fingers of the other glided with a softly caressing motion over and under the attendant balls.

Eva jumped up, flung off her nightdress and crying to Flossie *"Don't leave go!"* fell on her knees, seized my prick in her mouth and thrust her hand under Flossie's petticoats. The latter, obeying Eva's cry, continued to frig me deliciously from behind, whilst Eva furiously sucked the nut and upper part, and passing her disengaged hand round my bottom, caused me a new and exquisite enjoyment by inserting a dainty finger into the aperture thus brought within her reach. Flossie now drew close up to me and I could feel the swelling breasts in their thin silken covering pressed again my naked back, whilst her hand quickened its maddeningly provoking motion upon my prick and Eva's tongue pursued its enchanted course with increasing ardour and many luscious convolutions. Feeling I was about to spend, Flossie slipped her hand further down towards the root so as to give room for Eva's mouth to engulph almost the whole yard, a hint which the latter was quick to take, for her lips at once pressed close down to Flossie's fingers and with my hands behind my fair gamahucher's neck, I poured my very soul into her waiting and willing throat.

During the interval which followed, I offered my congratulations to Eva and told her how sorry I was not to have known of her birthday before, so that I might have presented a humble gift of some sort. She hastened to assure me that nothing in the world, that I could have brought, would be more welcome than what I had just given her!

Eva had not yet seen her decorated underclothes and these were now displayed by Flossie with countless merry jokes and quaint remarks. The pretty thought was highly appreciated and nothing would do but our dressing Eva in the flowery garments. When this was done, Flossie suggested a can-can, and the three of us danced a wild *pas-de-trois* until the breath was almost out of our bodies. As we lay panting in various unstudied attitudes of exhaustion, a ring was heard at the door and Flossie, who was the only presentable one of the party went out to answer the summons. She came back in a minute

with an enormous basket of Neapolitan violets.
Upon our exclaiming at this extravagance Flossie gravely delivered herself on the following
statement.

"Though not in a position for the moment to
furnish chapter and verse, I am able to state
with conviction that in periods from which we
are only separated by some twenty centuries or
so, it was customary for ladies and gentlemen
of the time to meet and discuss the business of
pleasure of the hour without the encumbrance
of clothes upon their bodies. The absence of
arrière-pensée shewn by this commendable
practice might lead the superficial to conclude
that these discussions led to no practical results.
Nothing could be further from the truth. The
interviews were invariably held upon a Bank of
Violets (so the old writers tell us), and at a certain point in the proceedings, the lady would fall
back upon this bank with her legs spread open
at the then equivalent to an angle of forty-five.
The gentleman would thereupon take in his right
(or dexter) hand the instrument which our modern brevity of speech has taught us to call his
prick. This, with some trifling assistance on
her part, he would introduce into what the same
latter-day rage for conciseness of expression

leaves us powerless to describe otherwise than as her cunt. On my right we have the modern type of the lady, on my left, that of the gentleman. In the middle, the next best thing to a bank of violets. Ha! you take me at last! Now I'm going to put them all over the bed, and when I'm ready, you, Eva, will kindly oblige by depositing your snowy bottom in the middle, opening your legs and admitting Mr. Jack to the proper position between them."

While delivering this amazing oration, Flossie had gradually stripped herself entirely naked. We both watched her movements in silent admiration as she strewed the bed from end to end with the fragrant blossoms, which filled the room with their delightful perfume. When all was ready, she beckoned to Eva to lay herself on the bed, whispering to her, though not so low but that I could hear.

"Imagine you are Danae. I'll trouble you for the size of Jupiter's prick! Just look at it!" — then much lower, but still audibly — "You're going to be fucked, Eva darling, jolly well fucked! and I'm going to *see* you — *Lovely!*"

The rose-edged chemise and drawers were once more laid aside and the heroine of the day stretched herself voluptuously on the heaped-up flowers, which sent forth fresh streams of fragrance in response to the pressure of the girl's naked body.

"Ah, a happy thought!" cried Flossie. "If you would lie *across* the bed with your legs hanging down, and Jack wouldn't mind standing up to his work, I think I could be of some assistance to you both."

The change was quickly made, a couple of pillows were slipped under Eva's head, and Flossie, kneeling across the other's face, submitted her cunt to be gamahuched by her friend's tongue which at once darted amorously to its place within the vulva. Flossie returned the salutation for a moment and then resting her chin upon the point just above Eva's clitoris, called to me to "come on". I placed myself in position and was about to storm the breach when Flossie found the near proximity of my yard to be too much for her feelings and begged to be allowed to gamahuche me for a minute.

"After that, I'll be quite good," she added to Eva, "and will only *watch*."

Needless to say I made no objection. The result, as was the case with most of Flossie's actions, was increased pleasure to everybody concerned and to Eva as much as anyone inasmuch as the divine sucking of Flossie's rosy lips and lust full tongue produced a sensible hardening and lengthening of my excited member.

After performing this delightful service, she was for moving away, but sounds of dissent were heard from Eva, who flung her arms round Flossie's thighs and drew her cunt down in closer contact with the caressing mouth.

From my exalted position, I could see all that was going on and this added enormously to the sensations I began to experience when Flossie, handling my yard with deft fingers, dropped a final kiss upon the nut, and then guided it to the now impatient goal. With eyes lit up with interest and delight, she watched it disappear within the soft red lips whose movements she was near enough to follow closely. Under these conditions, I found myself fucking Eva with unusual vigour and penetration, whilst she, on her part, returned my strokes with powerful thrusts of her bottom and exquisitely pleasurable contractions of her cunt upon my prick.

Flossie, taking in all this with eager eyes, became madly excited, and at last sprang from her kneeling position on the bed, and taking advantage of an *outward* motion of my body, bent down between us, and pushing the point of her tongue under Eva's clitoris, insisted on my finishing the performance with this charming incentive added. Its effect upon both Eva and myself was electric, and as her clitoris and my prick shared equally in the contact of the tongue, we were not long in bringing the entertainment to an eminently satisfactory conclusion.

The next item in the birthday programme was the exhibition of half a dozen cleverly executed pen and ink sketches — Flossie's gift to Eva — shewing the three of us in attitudes not to be found in the illustrations of the "Young Ladies Journal". A discussion arose as to whether Flossie had not been somewhat flattering to the longitudinal dimensions of the present writer's member. She declared that the proportions were "according to *Cocker*" — obviously, as she wittily said, the highest authority on the question.

"Anyhow, I'm going to take measurements and then you'll see I'm right! In the picture the length of Jack's prick is exactly one-third of the distance from his chin to his navel. Now measuring the real article — Hullo! I *say*, Evie, what *have* you done him!"

In point of fact, the object under discussion

was feeling the effects of his recent exercise and had drooped to a partially recumbent attitude.

Eva, who was watching the proceedings with an air of intense amusement called out.

"Take it between your breasts, Flossie; you will see a difference then!"

The mere prospect of such a lodging imparted a certain amount of vigour to Monsieur Jacques, who was thereupon introduced into the delicious cleft of Flossie's adorable bosom, and in rapture at the touch of the soft flesh on either side of him, at once began to assume more satisfactory proportions.

"But he's not up to his full height yet," said Flossie. "Come and help me, Evie dear; stand behind Jack and frig him whilst I gamahuche him in front. *That's* the way to get him up to concert pitch! When I feel him long and stiff enough in my mouth, I'll get up and take his measure."

The success of Flossie's plan was immediate and complete, and when the measurements were made, the proportions were found to be exactly twenty-one and seven inches respectively, whilst in the drawing they were three inches to one inch. Flossie proceeded to execute a wild war-dance of triumph over this signal vindication of her accuracy, winding up by insisting on my carrying her pick-a-back round the flat. Her enjoyment of this ride was unbounded, as also was mine, for besides the pleasure arising from the close contact of her charming body, she contrived to administer a delicious friction to my member with the calves of her naked legs.

On our return to the bedroom, Eva was sitting on the edge of the low divan.

"Bring her to me here," she cried.

I easily divined what was wanted, and carrying my precious burden across the room, I faced round with my back to Eva. In the sloping glass to the left, I could see her face disappear between the white rounded buttocks, at the same moment that her right moved in front of me and grasped my yard which it frigged with incomparable tenderness and skill. This operation was eagerly watched by Flossie over my shoulder, while she clung to me with arms and legs and rubbed herself against my loins with soft undulating motions like an amorous kitten, the parting lips of her cunt kissing my back and her every action testifying to the delight with which she was receiving the attentions of Eva's tongue upon the neighbouring spot.

My feelings were now rapidly passing beyond my control, and I had to implore Eva to remove her hand, whereupon Flossie, realising the state of affairs, jumped down from her perch, and burying my prick in her sweet mouth, sucked and frigged me in such a frenzy of desire that she had very soon drawn from me the last drop I had to give her.

A short period of calm ensued after this last ebullition, but Flossie was in too mad a mood to-day to remain long quiescent.

"Eva" she suddenly cried, "I believe I am as tall as you nowadays, and I am *quite sure* my breasts are as large as yours. I'm going to measure and see!"

After Eva's height had been found to be only a short inch above Flossie's, the latter proceeded to take the most careful and scientific measurements of the breasts. First came the circumference, then the diameter *over* the nipples, then the diameter omitting the nipples, then the distance from the nipple to the upper and lower edges of the hemispheres, and so on. No dryasdust old savant, staking his reputation upon an absolutely accurate calculation of the earth's surface, could have carried out his task with more ineffable solemnity than did this merry child who, one knew, was all the time secretly bubbling over with the fun of her quaint conceit.

The result was admitted to be what Flossie called it — "a moral victory" for herself, inasmuch as half a square inch, or as Flossie declared, "fifteen thirty-*two-ths*", was all the superiority of area that Eva could boast.

"There's one other measurement I *should* like to have taken," said Eva, "because in spite of my ten years '*de plus*' and the fact that my cunt is not altogether a stranger to the joys of being fucked, I believe that Flossie would win *that* race, and I should like her to have one out of three!"

"*Lovely!*" cried Flossie. "But Jack must be the judge. Here's the tape, Jack: fire away. Now, Evie, come and lie beside me on the edge of the bed, open your legs, and swear to abide by the verdict!"

After a few minutes fumbling with the tape and close inspection of the parts in dispute, I retired to a table and wrote down the following, which I pinned against the window-curtain.

Letchford v. Eversley.

Mesdames,

In compliance with your instructions I have this day surveyed the private premises belonging to the above parties, and have now the honour to submit the following report, plan, and measurements.

As will be seen from the plan, Miss Letchford's cunt is exactly 3 1/16 inches from the underside of clitoris to the base of vulva. Miss Eversley's cunt, adopting the same line of measurement, gives 3 5/8 inches.

I may add that the premises appear to me to be thoroughly desirable in both cases, and to a good, upright and painstaking tenant would afford equally pleasant accommodation in spring, summer, autumn or winter.

A small but well-wooded covert is attached to each, whilst an admirable dairy is in convenient proximity.

With reference to the Eversley property, I am informed that it has not yet been occupied, but in view of its size and beauty, and the undoubted charms of the surrounding country, I confidently anticipated that a permanent and satisfactory tenant (such as I have ventured to describe above), will very shortly be found for it. My opinion of its advantages as a place of residence may, indeed, be gathered from the fact that I am greatly disposed to make an offer in my own person.

Yours faithfully,

J. Archer,

As the two girls stood with their hands behind their backs reading my ultimatum, Flossie laughed uproariously, but I noticed that Eva looked grave and thoughtful.

Had I written anything that annoyed her? I could hardly think so, but while I was meditating on the possibility, half resolved to put it to the test by a simple question, Eva took Flossie and myself by the hand, led us to the sofa and sitting down between us, said:

"Listen to me, you two dears! You, Flossie, are my chosen darling, and most beloved little friend. You Jack, are Flossie's lover, and for her sake as well as for your own, I have the greatest affection for you. You both know all this. Well, I have not the heart to keep you from one another any longer. Flossie, dear, I hereby absolve you from your promise to me. Jack, you have behaved like a brick, as you are. Come here to-morrow at your usual time and I think we shall be able to agree upon '*a tenant for the Eversley property.*'"

This is not a novel of sentiment, and a description of what followed would therefore be out of place. Enough to say that after one wild irrepressible shriek of joy and gratitude from Flossie, the conversation took a sober and serious turn, and soon afterwards we parted for the day.

CHAPTER VI

The tenant in possession

THE NEXT MORNING'S POST BROUGHT ME LET-
ters from both, Eva and Flossie.

"My dear Jack (wrote the former),

"Tomorrow will be a red-letter day for you
two! and I want you both to get the utmost of
delight from it. So let no sort of scruple or com-
punction spoil your pleasure. Flossie is, in
point of physical development, a woman. As
such, she longs to be fucked by the man she
loves. Fuck her therefore with all and more
than all the same skill and determination you
displayed in fucking me. She can think and
talk of nothing else. Come early to-morrow and
bring your admirable prick in its highest state
of efficiency and stiffness!

"Yours
"Eva".

Flossie wrote:

"I cannot sleep a wink for thinking of what is coming to me to-morrow. All the time I keep turning over in my mind how best to make it nice for you. I am practising Eva's 'nip.' I *feel* as if I could do it, but nipping *nothing* is not really practice, is it, Jack? My beloved, I kiss your prick, in imagination. To-morrow I will do it in the flesh, for I warn you that nothing will ever induce me to give up *that*, nor will even the seven inches which I yearn to have in my cunt ever bring me to consent to being depried of the sensation of your dear tongue when it curls between the lips and pays polite attentions to my clitoris! But you shall have me as you like to-morrow, and all days to follow. I am to be in the future.

> "Yours body and soul
> "Flossie."

When I arrived at the flat I found Flossie had put on the costume in which I had seen her the first day of our acquaintance. The lovely little face wore an expression of gravity, as though to shew me she was not forgeting the importance of the occasion. I am not above confessing that, for my part, I was profoundly moved.

We sat beside one another, hardly exchanging a word. Presently Flossie said.

"Whenever you are *ready*, Jack, I'll go to my room and undress."

The characteristic "naiveté of this remark somewhat broke the spell that was upon us, and I kissed her with effusion.

"Shall it be . . . *quite* naked, Jack?"

"Yes, darling, if *you* don't mind."

"All right. When I am ready I'll call to you."

Five minutes later, I heard the welcome summons.

From the moment I found myself in her room, all sense of restraint vanished at a breath. She flew at me in a perfect fury of desire, pushed me by sheer force upon my back on the bed, and lying at full length upon me with her face close to mine, she said.

"Because I was a girl and not a woman, Jack, you have never fucked me. But you are going to fuck me now, and I shall be a woman. But first, I want to be a girl to you still for a few minutes only. I want to have your dear prick in my mouth again; I want you to kiss my cunt in the old delicious way; I want to lock my naked arms round your naked body; and hold you to my face, whilst I wind my tongue round your prick until you spend. Let me do all this,

119

Jack, and then you shall fuck me till the skies fall."

Without giving me time to reply to this frenzied little oration, Flossie had whisked round and was in position for the double gamahuche she desired. Parting her legs to their widest extent on each side of my face, she sank gently down until her cunt came full upon my open mouth. At the same moment I felt my prick seized and plunged deep into her mouth with which she at once commenced the delicious sucking action I knew so well. I responded by driving my tongue to the root into the rosy depths of her perfumed cunt, which I sucked with ever increasing zest and enjoyment, drawing fresh treasures from its inner recesses at every third or fourth stroke of my tongue. Words fail me to describe the unparalleled vigour of her sustained attack upon my erected prick, which she sucked, licked, tongued and frigged with such a furious *abandon* and at the same time with such a subtle skill and knowledge of the sublime art of gamahuching, that the end came with unusual rapidity, and wave after wave of the sea of love broke in ecstasy upon the 'coral strand' of her adorable mouth. For a minute or two more, her lips retained their hold and then, leaving her position, she came and lay down beside me, nestling her naked body against mine, and softly chafing the lower portion of my prick whilst she said:

"Now, Jack darling, I am going to talk to you about the different ways of fucking, because of course you will want to fuck me, and I shall want to be fucked, in every possible position, and in every single part of my body where a respectable young woman may reasonable *ask* to be fucked.

The conversation which followed agreeably filled the intervening time before the delicate touches which Flossie kept constantly applying to my prick caused it to raise its head to a considerable altitude, exhibiting a hardness and rigidity which gave high promise for the success of the coming encounter.

"Good Gracious!" cried Flossie, "do you think I shall ever find room for all that, Jack?"

"For that, and more also, sweetheart," I replied.

"*More!* Why *what* more are you going to put into me?"

"This is the only article I propose to introduce at present, Floss. But I mean that when Monsieur Jacques finds himself for the first time with his head buried between the delicious cushions in *there*" (*touching her belly*) "he

121

will most likely beat his own record in the matter ter of length and stiffness."

"Do you mean, Jack, that he will be bigger with me than he was with Eva?" said Flossie with a merry twinkle.

"Certainly I mean it," was my reply. "To fuck a beautiful girl like Eva must always be immensely enjoyable, but to fuck a young Venus of fifteen, who besides being the perfection of mortal loveliness, is also one's own chosen and adorable little sweetheart — *that* belongs to a different order of pleasure altogether.

"And I suppose, Jack, that when the fifteen-year-old is simply dying to be fucked by her lover, as I am at this moment, the chances are that she may be able to make it rather nice for him, as well as absolutely heavenly for herself. Now I can wait no longer. 'First position' at once, please, Jack. Give me your prick in my hand and I will direct his wandering footsteps."

"He's at the door, Flossie; shall he enter?"

"Yes. Push him in slowly and fuck gently at first, so that I may find out by degrees how much he's going to hurt me. A little further, Jack. Why, he's more than half way in already! Now you keep still and I'll thrust a little with my bottom."

"Why, Floss, you darling, you're nipping me deliciously!"

"Can you feel me Jack? How lovely! Fuck me a little more, Jack, and get in deeper, that's it! Now faster and harder. What glorious pleasure it is!"

"And no pain, darling?"

"Not a scrap. One more good push and he'll be in up to the hilt, won't he? Eva told me to put my legs over your back. Is that right?"

"Quite right, and if you're sure I'm not hurting you, Floss, I'll really begin now and fuck you in earnest."

"That's what I'm here for, Sir," she replied with a touch of her never absent fun even in this supreme moment.

"Here goes, then!" I answered. Having once made up her mind that she had nothing to dread, Flossie abandoned herself with enthusiasm to the pleasures of the moment. Locking her arms round my neck and her legs round my buttocks, she cried to me to fuck her with all my might.

"Drive your prick into me again and again, Jack. Let me feel your belly against mine. Did you feel my cunt nip you then? Ah! how you are fucking me now! — fucking me, fu . . . u . . . ucking me!"

Her lovely eyes turned to heaven, her breath

came in quick short gasps, her fingers wandered feverishly about my body. At last, with a cry, she plunged her tongue into my mouth and, with convulsive undulations of the little body, let loose the floods of her being to join the deluge which, with sensations of exquisite delight, I poured into her burning cunt.

The wild joy of this our first act of coition was followed by a slight reaction and, with a deep sigh of contentment Flossie fell asleep in my arms, leaving my prick still buried in its natural resting-place. Before long, my own eyelids closed and, for an hour or more, we lay thus gaining from blessed sleep fresh strength to enter upon new transports of pleasure.

Flossie was the first to awake, stirred no doubt by the unaccustomed sensations of a swelling prick within her. I awoke to find her dear eyes resting upon my face, her naked arms round my neck and her cunt enfolding my yard with a soft and clinging embrace.

Her bottom heaved gently, and accepting the invitation thus tacitly given, I turned my little sweetheart on her back and, lying luxuriously between her widely parted legs, once more drove my prick deep into her cunt and fucked her with slow lingering strokes, directed upwards so as to bring all possible contact to bear upon the clitoris.

This particular motion afforded her evident delight and the answering thrusts of her bottom were delivered with ever increasing vigour and precision, each of us relishing to the full the efforts of the other to augment the pleasure of the encounter. With sighs and gasps and little cries of rapture, Flossie strained me to her naked breasts, and twisting her legs tightly round my own, cried out that she was spending and implored me to let her feel my emission mix with hers. By dint of clutching her bottom with my hands, driving the whole length of my tongue into her mouth I was just able to manage the simultaneous discharge she coveted, and once more I lay upon her in a speechless ecstasy of consummated passion.

Any one of my readers who has had the supreme good fortune to fuck the girl of his heart will bear me out in saying that the lassitude following upon such a meeting is greater and more lasting than the mere weariness resulting from an ordinary act of copulation 'where love is not'.

Being well aware of this fact, I resolved that my beloved little Flossie's powers should not be taxed any further for the moment, and told her so.

"But Jack," she cried, almost in tears, "we've only done it *one* way, and Eva says there are at least *six!* And oh, I do *love* it so!"

"And so do I, little darling. But also, I love *you*, and I'm not going to begin by giving you and that delicious little caressing cunt of yours more work than is good for you both."

"Oh, dear! I suppose you're right, Jack."

"Of course I'm right, darling. To-morrow I shall come and fuck you again, and the next day, and the next, and many days after that. It will be odd if we don't find ourselves in Eva's six different positions before we've done!"

At this moment Eva herself entered the room.

"Well, Flossie . . . ?" she said.

"Ask Jack!" replied Flossie.

"Well Jack, then . . . ?" said Eva.

"Ask Flossie!" I retorted, and fled from the room.

The adventures I have, with many conscious imperfections, related in the foregoing pages, were full of interest to me, and were, I am disposed to think, not without their moments of attraction for my fellow-actors in the scenes depicted.

It by no means necessarily follows that they will produce a corresponding effect upon the reading public who, in my descriptions of Flossie and her ways, may find only an ineffectual attempt to set forth the charms of what appears to me an absolutely unique temperament. If haply it should prove to be otherwise, I should be glad to have the opportunity of continuing a veritable labour of love by recounting certain further experiences of Eva, Flossie and

Yours faithfully
"Jack."

Eveline

CHAPTER 1

"A temperament like yours, my darling child, requires constant attention. You are no ordinary girl. You have need of change, of variety, of sufficient venereal food to keep you in health. You have developed within you so much vitality, so much necessity for sensual gratification—if I may use the term—that you have urgent need to feed the fire. Like the ancient flame that burned, which still burns, on the altars of the followers of Zoroaster, you must keep it going, replenishing it as may be necessary, never letting it languish. If it does so you will not be well. Eveline will not be herself."

"I feel the force of what you say, dear Papa. I love you devotedly . . . but . . ."

"Yes, my child, I see it, I know it. At my age, with all my various engagements and occupations, I am not likely to be all to you that your nature demands. When you are married . . ."

"Do not speak of that, dear. It will be time enough hereafter. I do not anticipate any pleasure from my married state—not in the sense that my dear Papa can bestow it. I look forward to it with disgust, rather than with satisfaction. And I feel very dejected on the subject."

"Listen to me, Eveline. Your nature requires sexual excitement. You know it as well as I do. It is medicine to you. You must take your medicine or be unhealthy. Take it then, only be careful that you imbibe naught but what is good and wholesome. I would be your doctor if you would follow my advice."

"I am always ready to be guided by your counsel, dear Papa."

"Well then, Eveline, having sufficiently explained my views, which I am sure you understand, I will obtain for you the best medicine."

"And I will take it, for whatever you provide for little Eveline is sure to be nice."

"It shall be something extra nice. Something that will set your pretty mouth watering, your eyes sparkling, your whole being alert with anticipation of enjoyment. Something that will ring sobs of delight from your darling heart, sighs of the most intense rapture from your parted lips, something which shall possess your body and your senses with ecstasy, something irresistible in its noble manhood—solid, stiff, strong!"

"Oh Papa, you excite me too much! I already long for this delicious medicine. When may I commence my course of it? Or is it only in small doses, to be taken sparingly? I am ready for all. Let it be large and solid—stiff and strong!"

"Your capacity for enjoyment is wonderful, my child. You require a male well-furnished with sexual organs in full vigor, robust and extraordinarily well-developed. I will provide you with such. I will enable you to take your fill of pleasure without risk, without danger."

"I think you are right, Papa. In the meantime I want this thing which is always stiff in my hand. See how the head shines! It enters! Oh goodness, dear! How you excite your little girl! Push now! Oh, it comes! It is squirting into me—Oh! Give me all your delicious seed. Dear love! You kill me with pleasure."

"I have in store for you, my darling child, a delicious treat for the senses. To see you enjoy it will be to me also an extreme pleasure. We will roll in ecstasy. Our senses shall float in a world of pleasure. Give me only a few days to arrange it. Your medicine will take a novel form. The medium is deaf and dumb."

"Oh, Papa, how dreadful!"

"By no means, Eveline, we only desire the means, the instrument. So long as that has no surroundings which are positively objectionable or repulsive, it matters little; we shall possess all we require. I promise you that in the present case, it is neither, but on the other hand, attractive in every sense. You will be charmed and even sympathetic when you know more."

"You excite my curiosity, Papa. When may I take the first dose?"

13

"As soon as we are back in town together. They say the implement of love is immense and that its owner is singularly gifted in sexual gratifications."

"Oh, Papa, you are too good to your naughty little Eveline. You offer her a banquet—it will not be medicine. It will be a draught of pleasure. My mouth waters already. I long to taste it."

* * *

Percy had been at Eastbourne three days. We had not altogether lost our time. I determined to run up to town. I went by an early train, alone. I entered the station some 15 minutes before the train started. On the platform was a gentlemanly-looking man in a tweed suit. I thought I had seen his face before. We passed each other. He looked pointedly at me. Certainly I knew his features. I never forget, if I take an interest in a man's appearance. I liked the looks of this tall, well-built fellow in tweed. He appeared to be about 35 or 40 years of age, hale and hearty. I gave him one of my glances as he passed me.

"This way, Miss. First-class. No corridors on this train. You will be all right here. You're all alone at present."

"Thank you, guard. Does the train go without stopping?"

"Stops at Lewes, Miss. That's all—then right up."

I saw my tall friend pass the carriage. Another glance. He stopped, hesitated, then opened the door and got in. He took a seat

14

opposite me. The newspaper appeared to engross his attention until the whistle sounded.

"Would you mind if I were to lower the window? These carriages are stuffy. The morning is so warm."

I made no objection, but smilingly gave my consent.

"How calm and beautiful the sea looks. It seems a pity to leave it."

"Indeed I think so—especially for London."

"You are going to London? How odd! So am I."

I could not be mistaken. I had seen him somewhere before.

"I shall miss the sea very much. We have no sea baths in Manchester. I love my morning dip."

It struck me like a flash. I remembered him now.

"You must have enjoyed it very much, coming from an inland city."

"Well, yes, you see I had a good time. They looked after me well. Always had my machine ready."

"I have no doubt of that."

"Number 33. A new one—capital people— very fine machine."

I suppose I smiled a little. He laughed in reply as he read my thoughts. Then he folded up his paper. I arranged my small reticule. It unfortunately dropped from my hand. He picked it up and presented it to me. His foot touched mine. We conversed. He told me he lived near Manchester. He had been to Eastbourne for a rest. His business had been too much for him, but he was all right now. His gaze was constantly on me. I kept thinking about his appearance all naked on the platform of the bathing machine as old David Jones rowed me past. We stopped at Lewes.

My companion put his head out of the window. He prevented the entry of an old lady by abusing the newspaper boy for his want of activity.

"I think Eastbourne is one of the best bathing places on the coast. You know, where the gentlemen's machines are!"

"I think I know where they keep them."

"Well, I was going to say . . . but . . . well . . . what a funny girl you are! Why are you laughing?"

"Because I was thinking of a funny idea. I was thinking of a friend."

His foot pushed a little closer. Very perceptible was the touch. He never ceased gloating over my person. My gloves evidently had an especial attraction for him. Meanwhile I looked him well over. He was certainly a fine man. He aroused my emotions. I permitted his foot to remain in contact with mine. I even moved it past his so that our ankles touched. His face worked nervously. Poor man, no wonder! He gave me a seaching look. Our glances met. He pressed my leg between his own. His fingers were trembling with that undefined longing for contact with the object of desire I so well understood. I smiled.

"You seem very fond of the ladies."

I said it boldly, with a familiar meaning. He could not fail to understand. I glanced at his leather bag in the rack above.

"I cannot deny the soft impeachment. I am.

Especially when they are young and beautiful."

"Oh, you men. You are dreadfully wicked. What would Mrs. Turner say to that?"

I laughed. He stared with evident alarm. It was a bold stroke. I risked it. Either way I lost nothing.

"How do you know I'm married?"

My shaft had gone home. He had actually missed the first evident fact. He picked it up, however, quickly, before I could reply.

"It appears you know me, you know my name."

"Well, yes, you see I'm not blind."

It was his turn to laugh.

"Ah, you had me there. What a terribly observant woman you are."

He seized my hand before I could regain my attitude. He pressed it with both of his.

"You will not like me any the less, will you?"

"On the contrary, they say married men are the best."

Up to this point my effrontery had led him on. He must have felt that he was on safe ground. My last remark was hardly even equivocal. He evidently took it as it was intended. I was actually excited. The man and the opportunity tempted me. I wanted him. I was delighted with his embarrassment, with his first and fast increasing assurance. He crossed over. He occupied the seat beside me. My gloved hand remained in his.

"I am so glad you think so. You do not know how charming I think you. Married men ought to be good judges, you know."

"I suppose so. I rather prefer them."

He looked into my face and I laughed as I uttered the words. He brought his face very close. He pressed his left hand around my waist. I made no resistance. The carriage gave a sympathetic jerk as it rushed along. Our faces touched. His lips were in contact with mine. It was quite accidental, of course; the line is so badly laid. We kissed.

"Oh, you are nice! How pretty you are!"

He pressed his hot lips again to mine. I thought of the sight I had seen on the bathing machine. My blood boiled. I half-closed my eyes. I let him keep his lips on mine. He pressed me to him. He drew my light form to his stout and well-built body as in a vise. I put my right foot up on the opposite seat. He stared at the pretty, tight little kid boot. He was evidently much agitated.

"Ah, what a lovely boot!"

He touched it with his hand. His fingers ran over the soft cream-colored leather. I wore a pair of Papa's prime favorites. He did not stop there. The trembling hand passed on to my stockings, advancing by stealthy degrees. It was then he tried to push forward the tip of his tongue.

"How beautiful you are and how gentle and kind!"

His arm enfolded me still closer; my bosom pressed his shoulder. His hand advanced further and further up my stocking. I closed my knees resolutely. I gave a hurried glance around.

"Are we quite safe here, do you think?"

"Quite safe and as you see, alone."

Our lips met again. This time I kissed him

boldly. The tip of his active tongue inserted itself between my moist lips.

"Ah how lovely you are! How gloriously pretty!"

"Hush! They might hear us in the next carriage. I am frightened."

"You are deliciously sweet. I long for you dreadfully."

Mr. Turner's hand continued its efforts to reach my knees. I relaxed my pressure a little. He reached my garters above them. In doing so he uncovered my ankles. He feasted his eyes on my calves daintily set off in openwork stockings of a delicate shade.

It was a delicious game of seduction. I enjoyed his lecherous touches. He was constantly becoming more confident in his sudden and uncontrollable passion. He strained me to him. His breath came quick and sweet on my face. I lusted for this man's embrace beyond all power of language to convey. His warm hand reached my plump thigh. I made a pretense to prevent his advance.

"Pray, Oh pray, do not do that! Oh!"

A sudden jerk as we apparently sped over some joints. I relaxed my resistance a little. He took instant advantage of the movement. His finger was on the most sensitive of my private parts. It pressed upon my clitoris. I felt the little thing stiffen, swell and throb under the touch of a man's hand. His excitement increased. He drew me ever closer. He pressed my warm body to his. His kisses, hot and voluptuous, covered my neck and face.

"How divinely sweet you are! The perfume

of your lovely breath is so rapturously nice. Do let me—do—do! I love you."

He held me tight with his left arm. He had withdrawn his right. I was conscious he was undoing his trousers. He had left my skirts in disorder. I saw him pull aside his protruding shirt. I secretly watched his movements out of a corner of my eye while he kept my face close to him. Then appeared all that I had seen in the bathing machine. But standing erect. Red-headed and formidable. A huge limb. He thrust it into full view.

"My darling! My beauty! See this! To what a savage state you have driven me! You will let me, won't you?"

"Oh, for shame, let me go! Pray do not do that! You must not! Your finger hurts. Don't!"

The jolting of the carriage favored his operations. His hand was again between my legs. His second finger pressed my button. His parts were bedewed with the fluid begotten by desire. He was inspecting the premises before taking possession. I only hoped he would not find the accommodation insufficient.

"Oh, pray, don't! Oh, goodness! What a man you are!"

With a sudden movement he slipped around upon his knees, passing one of my legs over his left arm and thus thrust me back on the soft spring seat of the carriage. He threw up my clothes. He was between my thighs. My belly and private parts were exposed to his lascivious operations. I looked over my dress as I attempted to right myself. I saw him kneeling before me in the most indelicate position. His trousers were open. He had loosened his clothing so much that his testicles were out. I saw all in that quick feverish glance. His belly was covered with crisp hair. I saw the dull red head of his big limb drawn downward by the little string as it faced my way, and the slitlike opening from which the men spurt their white sap.

He audaciously took my hand, gloved as it was, and placed it upon his member. It was hard and rigid as wood.

"Feel that—dear girl! Do not be frightened. I will not hurt you. Feel, feel my prick!"

He drew me forward. I felt him as requested. I had ceased all resistance. My willing little hand clasped the immense instrument he called his "prick."

"Now put it there yourself, little girl. It is longing to be into you."

"Oh, my good heavens! It will never go in. You will kill me!"

Nevertheless I assisted him to his enjoyment. I put the nut between the nether lips. He pushed while firmly holding me by both hips. My parts relaxed. My vagina adapted itself as I had been told it could without injury to the most formidable of male organs. The huge thing entered me. He thrust in fierce earnest. He got fairly in.

"Oh, my God! I'm into you now! Oh, how delicious! Hold tight. Let me pull you down to me! Oh, how soft!"

I passed my left arm through the strap. My right clutched him round the neck. He pulled down his hand. He parted the strained lips around his intruding weapon. Then he seized me by the buttocks. He strained me towards him as he pushed. My head fell back—my lips parted. I felt his testicles rubbing close up between my legs. He was into me to the quick.

"Oh, dear, you are too rough. My goodness me! How you are tearing me! Oh! Oh! Ah, it is too much! You darling man. Push—Push—Oh!"

It was too much pleasure. I threw my head back again. I grasped the cushions on either side. I could only gasp and moan now. I moved my head from side to side as he lay down on my belly and enjoyed me. His thing —stiff as a staff—worked up and down in my vagina. I could feel the big plumlike gland pushed forcibly against my womb. I spent over and over again. I was in heaven.

He ground his teeth. He hissed. He lolled his head. He kissed me on the lips, breathing hard and fast. His pleasure was delicious to witness.

"Oh, hold tight, love! I am in an agony of pleasure! I . . . I can't tell you! I never tasted such delicious poking! Oh!"

"Oh dear! Oh dear! You are so large . . . so strong!"

"Don't move! Don't pinch my prick more than you can help, darling girl. Let us go on as long as possible. You are coming again, I can feel you squeezing me. Oh, wait a moment! So! Hold still!"

"Oh, I can feel it at my waist! Oh! Oh You are so stiff"

"I cannot hold much longer, I must spend soon!"

Bang! Bang! Bang!

The train was passing over the joints at Reigate. The alarm was sufficient to retard our climax. It acted as a check to his wild excitement; it was too much pleasure. I threw my head back again. I grasped the cushions on either side. I could not speak. I could not gasp again as before.

"Hold quite still, you sweet little beauty! We do not stop, the seed is quickening up again. Now push! Is that nice? Do you like my big prick? Does it stir you up? You are right, my sweet, I can feel your little womb to the tip."

He assisted me to throw my legs over his shoulders. He seemed to enter me further than ever.

"Oh, you are so large! Oh, good Lord! Go on slowly—don't finish yet. It's so . . . so . . . nice! You're making me come again. Oh!"

"No, dear, I won't finish you before I can help it. You are so nice to poke slowly. Do you like being finished? Do you like to feel a man come?"

"Oh, not so hard! There . . . oh, my! Must I tell you? I . . . I . . . love to feel . . . to feel a man spend . . . all the sweet sperm."

"You'll feel mine very soon. Very soon, you beautiful little angel. Oh! I shall swim in it. There. My prick is in up to the balls! Oh! How you nip it!"

He gave me some exquisite short stabs with his loins. His thing, as hard as wood, was up in my belly as far as it would go. He sank his head on my shoulder.

"Hold still . . . I'm spending! Oh, my God!"

I felt a little gush from him. It flowed in quick jets as he groaned in his ecstasy. I opened my legs and raised my loins to receive it. I clutched right and left at anything and everything. I spent furiously. He gave me a quantity. I was swimming in it. At length he desisted and released me.

A few minutes sufficed in which to arrange ourselves decently. Mr. Turner asked me many questions. I fenced some—I answered others. I led him to believe I was professionally employed in a provincial company. I told him I had been ill and had been resting a short time in Eastbourne. He was delicate enough not to press me for particulars. But he asked for an address. I gave him a country post office. In a few minutes more we stopped on the river bridge to deliver our tickets.

The train rolled into the station. My new friend made his exit. He dexterously slipped two sovereigns into my glove as he squeezed my hand. I was glad. It proved the complete success of my precautions.

I hailed a hansom and drove direct to Swan and Edgars. Outside the station my cab stopped in a crowd. A poor woman thrust a skinny arm and hand towards me with an offer of a box of matches. I took them and substituted one of the sovereigns. As I alighted in Picadilly a ragged little urchin made a dash to turn back the door of my cab. He looked half-starved.

"Have you a mother? How many brothers and sisters?"

"Six of us, lady. Muvver's out of work."

"Take that home as quick as you can!"

He took the other sovereign and dashed off. He had never been taught to say thank you. I discharged the cab. I made sure I was not followed.

* * *

I drove home. I found Mrs. Lockett ready to receive me. It was yet morning. I lunched alone. John was radiant with happiness.

"No more chicken, thank you, John. How is Robin? There are some ginger nuts for him in a bag on the hall table. You see I did not forget him."

"Thank you very much, Miss. It's been dull every since you went away. Mrs. Lockett ain't very lively company. As for Robin, Miss, he's been sulky as possible; the poor thing is quite alone. In the morning he comes up to the bed clothes and stares me in the face, Miss, as much to say 'where've you gone to?' I'm ashamed to look at him."

"Poor dear. Why, John, how shocking! It's quite stiff now."

I had only just tapped it with my fingertips through the red plush breeches. The unruly monster was already stretching itself down his plump thigh as its owner leaned forward to pour me a glass of wine. The door was shut. I let fly a button.

"Oh, John, it's shameful! It's bigger than ever!"

I gave a twist of the wrist. His fat member sprang out into view. I squeezed it as I examined the rubicund top. What a beauty it was! The true perfection of what such things ought to be. I pulled down the skin. I delighted to see the effect of my touches.

"He likes that, John, doesn't he? He seems to enjoy being stroked like a cat."

"Yes, Miss—puts up his back for it. You can almost hear him purr."

"You must not let him get too much excited. We will keep all that for tonight, John. I think we must let him out then. But you cannot be too cautious. Mrs. Lockett sleeps in the wing, doesn't she?"

"Yes, Miss. She always turns the key of the door on the landing when she locks it at night. The maid sleeps on the top floor. There is no one on your floor now, Miss."

I made my arrangements. I finished my lunch, then dressed myself very plainly to go out. John called a cab. I drove straight to my bootmaker in Great Castle Street. Monsieur Dalmaine was not an ordinary bootmaker. He was an artist in boots. He made only for ladies, and his terms would be considered extravagant by the ordinary customer. His shop was small and unpretentious. Personally, he was short and stout, and fair for a Frenchman. He might have been some eight and thirty. His wife kept the accounts and assisted him to collect them. His boots and shoes were not ordinary, either. They were the perfection of his craft. He took real pride in them. The ability of the poor man to turn out boots to my satisfaction, and what seemed of greater importance, to his own, was sufficient. He was in the shop when I entered. Madame

Dalmaine was out collecting accounts as usual on a Monday afternoon.

"Good morning, Mr. Dalmaine. Are my boots *couleur creme*, ready? Have you completed the slight alterations to the pale blue lace boots?"

"Both are at your service, Miss. I will try them on if you will step into the showroom."

There was a small, well-arranged room behind the shop with several large glass cases. In these were deposited boots that had been made for celebrities. They were by no means old or worn, but this most extraordinary man had obtained them from the ladies in question after they had only served a single occasion. Monsieur Dalmaine claimed that they did not please him. He thereupon supplied a second pair. He obtained the first for his *musée*, as he called it.

I sat myself in an easy chair in which he fitted all his lady customers. It was a great event if he made a pair of boots in a fortnight. He had, however, prepared mine considerably within that period. He brought out both pairs. He held them up. He turned them about. His keen little gray eyes sparkled with evident pleasure.

"*Les voila*, Mademoiselle! But they are superb. It is not often that I make for so beautiful a foot. *Mon Dieu!* One would say the foot of Mademoiselle had been sculptured by Canova himself. It is a study."

He knelt before me. He placed my foot, in its openwork silk stocking, upon his knee. He gave one affectionate look at the object. He cast another at his work. He then proceeded to fit the artistic little boot. Several times he inserted my foot. As often he withdrew it to make some trifling adjustment. I tired of his minuteness. I amused myself in worrying the good man by avoiding his grasps. Sometimes I slipped my glossy little silk-covered foot on one side, sometimes on the other. At last it slid from the approaching boot and was jerked between his thighs. There it alighted on the muscular development of Monsieur Dalmaine's most private personal effects. I distinctly felt something pulsate between my toes. The artist of ladies' boots flushed. He was arranging the lace of the new *chaussure*.

"Please give it to me, Monsieur Dalmaine. I have not yet examined it for myself. Is not the toe more pointed than usual? You know I do not wear those hideously impossible toes to my boots."

He handed it up, holding my ankle as he did so. I rubbed my wicked foot a little more gently against his person as I took the boot from his hand. At the same time the man must have seen the half-comical, half-lecherous glance with which I met his eyes. A sudden inspiration almost overwhelmed me. This artist *cordonnier* was a victim of his own creations.

He had fallen in love with his own work like Pygmalion with his statue. The discovery set me on fire at once. What joy to play on this man's weakness. I allowed him to fit on the boot. He smoothed down the yielding kid as it glistened with its soft sheen on my foot. His eyes followed his nervous fingers. His lips moved as though he longed, yet dared not extend his too evident fascination into actual embrace. I then pushed my toe again towards his person. The quick blood of the nervous Frenchman was plainly stirred. There was an unmistakable enlargement in the region of his trouble. My warm foot did not let it subside. I was conscious of a certain throbbing on the sole of my foot.

"How long have you been in business, Monsieur Dalmaine? You evidently have a passion for your work. You are not like the ordinary bootmaker."

"No, Mademoiselle, I am not so. I am a man different. I am one man by myself. No other man understands me. Sometimes a lady comes to see me. I fit them to her. I make the boots for her. She likes my work—she comes again. More work, more boots. But— oh no! she comprehends not. She knows not my heart!"

Monsieur Dalmaine pressed his hand over the part mentioned. He bowed his head with its light curly hair over my legs as he knelt in the pursuit of his calling. His air was impatient, if not content to suffer.

"What is the matter with your heart, then? Is it very susceptible, Monsieur? Or is it really a matter for a physician?"

"Ah, Mademoiselle, can you ask? Can you doubt?"

My active toes were tickling gently all the time between his legs, where something very like a cucumber had gradually developed itself within the folds of his clothing.

"I am afraid your art is too much for you.

You are too much engrossed with fitting the ladies. Why not work for the men?"

"The men! Me! Dalmaine make boots for the beasts? I am not a merchant—*ferrant*—what you call him? *Farrier?* I do not make shoes for the horses! *Mon Dieu!* When I no longer make the *chaussures de dames*, I die! I go dead!"

In the agony of his disgust good Monsieur Dalmaine had seized my foot and ankle in his nervous grasp. He even emphasized his anguish by raising my leg until a portion of my calf was visible. I laughed so heartily that his confusion became even greater. Raising my other foot I almost pushed him backwards in my assumed merriment. Thus he had a chance of a private view, certainly not calculated to calm his excitement. His features proclaimed his delight. A sudden look of sensual pleasure spread over him as he saw my brown-stockinged legs. I let him enjoy the exhibition as long as he liked. My foot was all the time in contact with the cucumber. At last he could stand it no longer. He put down his hand. He himself pressed my little foot upon the most sensitive part.

"Ah, *Mon Dieu,* you are the most beautiful young lady I make for. You do not know what you make me suffer. When I see—when I feel these lovely little boots, I am made! When I make them I have pleasure. When I see them on your beautiful feet I go crack!"

I did not reply in words. I only raised my foot to his face as he knelt. He seized it again. He covered it with kisses. His white apron slipped to one side. The violent erection of his limb was plainly visible in his loose trousers. From the position he occupied I am sure he could see above my garters. I made no scruple in encouraging his passion.

"Poor Monsieur Dalmaine! Are you so very bad?"

"Oh, you most beautiful! I must fuck with you or burst! Oh dear! Oh dear!"

"I should be very sorry to make you suffer. Will it do you good, do you think?"

"I must fuck you! I must fuck! You are the angel of my dreams! I must feel—*il faut que je m'assoucisse avant de mourir!*"

His whole being quivered with excitement as he knelt, his hands convulsively clasping my ankles as I reclined in the easy chair.

"Are we quite sure not to be disturbed? Poor Monsieur Dalmaine, you shall not be disappointed. Only be prudent. Pray, do not hold my legs so high. How dreadfully indecent. Oh, really!"

"But first I must taste of your sweet *parfum*—of your essence divine. I must enjoy. Oh, yes! My beautiful young lady (clasping my foot in both hands) I have wanted you for a long time. Now!"

In another instant he had separated my legs. Plunging forward he had inserted his head between. He forcibly opened a passage. Before I could oppose any resistance to his attack, even had I been so inclined, his face was upon my naked thighs. He pressed forward. In pretending to protect myself, I assisted his design. With a stifled cry of delight he covered my parts with his lips. He drove in his long hot tongue. I felt him sucking my clitoris

31

with all the fury of a satyr. The taste, the perfume appeared to drive him into a frenzy. Finding no further resistance, he clasped me around the loins. He continued his salacious gratification, steeping his mouth in the amorous secretion with which I liberally doused him. I was almost beside myself with the pleasure he was giving me. I spent continuously. Presently his right hand released me. I guessed his object. He raised himself from his recumbent position, but without quitting his vantage ground. His face was red and inflamed with lust. Raging desire had taken possession of the man. I had led him on. It was not in my power to stay him now, I had not long to wait. He tore open the front of his trousers. I saw his limb fiercely erect, red-capped and ready to do its work.

The lewd sight destroyed what little remained of prudence. I raised myself to favor his assault and he threw himself upon my willing body. Neither of us spoke but with a great gasp of acute delight I felt the stiff insertion of the Frenchman's long member into my parts.

Monsieur Dalmaine went to work at once. He was so fiercely charged with unappeased desire that he made all haste to quench his passion on me. In the midst of his desperate thrusts he took care to seize one of my feet in either hand. He thus had me at his mercy.

I felt his powerful movements within my belly where his limb was pushed as far as its great length could carry it. It was very strong and rigid. I enjoyed the act as much as he did. All too soon I knew he was about to discharge. He spent in a burst of semen which overflowed my parts. He sank groaning upon my bosom.

"Oh! Monsieur Dalmaine, is this what you call 'going crack'?"

CHAPTER 2

Our reduced establishment retired early. By 11 o'clock all the inmates had gone to their rooms for the night. Mrs. Lockett was heard to shut her door and turn the key. I thoroughly believe that John had purposely rusted that lock. Sometimes a drop of salt water is as useful as oil, in a different sense. At midnight the mansion was wrapped in slumber—all save John and I. At a quarter past 12 I admitted the footman. I lay with him that night. He entered noiselessly, as he had on felt slippers. I had thought of all. We were absolutely safe and alone. It was delicious to freely gratify one's voluptuous inclinations and indulge without restraint all one's libidinous ideas and conceptions. One great advantage was that under the circumstances John could mount me and moan to his heart's content without fear. My greedy nerves vibrated as I closed the door of my chamber after the impatient good fellow. I motioned him to a seat. He submitted with the prompt obedience of a well-trained menial. Neither of us spoke. He watched me as I undressed.

I intentionally afforded him a delicious prospect. I saw his hands clench, his lips quiver, his nostrils dilate to his intoxications. I let fall my skirts. I stood in my chemise, my corset and my stockings. His greedy eyes followed every movement. I knew I was working the man into a state of almost unendurable longing. It was delightful to me. I grew excited beyond measure. I watched the keen, fierce, lecherous spirit overpowering all reserve—all prudence. I threw myself on the large couch.

"John, you may undress. I want to see you naked."

It had pleased me to act the schoolmistress in my intercourse with this man. It seemed to come natural to me. It served as a silly excuse for my precocious wantonness. It assuaged my amour proper. It gave me unbounded confidence in my character of an innocent led astray by the blandishment of a good-looking, full-grown man. John's natural vanity did the rest. To him I was the condescending young lady of the house seduced by his modest behavior, his rich livery. Above all, his manly proportions and his capacity for affording her sensuous delights.

I therefore looked on while John cast off his coat and divested himself of his striped garment underneath, depositing both within the adjoining room. Then came the turn of his scarlet breeches. I smiled at the semimodest, stupid air with which he let them fall. My mouth watered and my lips parted at the sight of his erect limb. His hairy belly and his shirt were raised.

"Come here, John, I want to feel your Robin."

In another minute my stallion was beside me. My eager hand closed around his huge member. I shook it and caressed it. I lowered my head and sucked it. It was delicious to my overwrought nerves. I took his big testicles in my grasp. I played with them.

"How shall we do it, John?"

"You'll let me do the job for you this time, won't you, Miss? Right into, I mean, Miss? I'll do it beautiful. You'll feel as if you were in heaven when Robin is pushing himself up and down your beautiful belly. It's all very well up against the door, standing up, but lying down with your sweet legs open he gets at it so free. He seems to get up almost to your waist."

As if to give point to his argument the rampant fellow opened my thighs. His face went between, his eager tongue inserted itself in my moist slit. I was in no humor to refuse him anything. I bore down on his thick, sensual lips. The scenes of the day came back to me. They passed as in a panorama before my closed eyes. John luxuriated in his prurient pleasure. I seemed to be exhaling for his delight the concentrated essence of previous luxury. The thought added poignancy to the sensations he caused me. I shivered with ecstasy.

"Oh, John, dear John . . . you are making me come!"

The delighted footman reveled in the solution of bygone pleasure with which I now liberally saturated him. I rose to my feet. Then I beheld his strong member, erect, redheaded, stiff as a bar of metal, threatening an onslaught upon my delicate person. I saw him gloating over my naked slit.

"Hush John. Whisper only. How shall we do it, dear John?"

He clasped me to him. He pressed his big, hairy chest to my tender form. He carried me towards the bed. He sat me upon it.

"Oh, Miss, let me do it so. Let me put it into you. See how stiff I am. It's bursting nearly. It's so full of the cream you are so fond of."

"So, John—on the side of the bed. Now push it into me. Oh! Oh, how big you are, John! Oh! Go slowly. It hurts."

Huge as it was, the big thing went in—up into me, till I felt the two big testicles pressing against my bottom. My stallion was at work upon me. The lewd fellow lolled back his head. He rolled his eyes in his luxury. His hands clutched nervously at my haunches as he pulled me towards him. Then he thrust slowly in and out—up and down in my little belly where he had said he longed to be.

I love to look on a man in this condition, filled with a fiery sense of unappeased desire, struggling in his libidinous embrace, his eyes turned up and burning with lust at the contemplation of the object of his passion extended at his mercy beneath him. The picture is a delicately fond one to my luxurious temperament—it enhances enormously my own enjoyment. It is the sacrifice of modesty upon the altar of lust; it is the reversal of all that is reserved, becoming and dignified. It is this which is its charm. It is the utter abnegation of personal respect, the surrender of virtue to animal passion which is its fascination.

The enjoyment of my poor John came alas to its end as all things must. It grew too poignant to last and finally burst. I was the recipient of his exhausting efforts. He left me bathed in his essence to my intense enjoyment, and to his own loss.

*   *   *

"A telegram for you, Miss. I would not disturb you sooner. Fanny told me you had given orders not to be awakened."

"Oh, thank you, Mrs. Lockett; but I have been awake already a couple of hours. I have even had my tub, you see."

I tore open the telegram. It was from Eastbourne—from Percy.

"Mother has suffered a fresh attack, is extremely unwell. Lord L—— desires you to remain. Await further news."

The further news arrived an hour later. As I had anticipated, it was from the local medical practitioner.

"Lord L—— desires me to inform you that Lady L—— succumbed at three o'clock this morning. He begs you to be calm."

I pass over those particulars. They have no place here. Enough that Lady L—— had paid the inevitable price of her folly, and that poor

Papa was free. Sippett lost a profitable employment. I was told that her luggage was heavy and voluminous when she went away.

* * *

"A gentleman to see you, Miss. He says he has come on business. I told him you could see no one but he insisted. Here is his card."

"Mr. William Dragoon, Bow Street. Quite right, John. I will see this gentleman. Show him into Lord L——'s study. I will come up directly."

The blinds were drawn. The house gave the usual dolorous impression of Society grief. At such times one receives odd visitors, always in business, of course. It was not yet ten o'clock. The situation was already quite accustomed. Everyone went about his duties as usual, only speaking lower and looking solemn instead of simpering.

" I should not have called but that I thought I could do so without fear under the present circumstances. We had the news at six this morning direct from Bow Street."

"I am sure you are very good and you would not have come but for a useful object. I feel bewildered."

"I know—I know. Do not trouble to explain. I only want to caution you. Of course I know your position is a little difficult. Take my advice, will you? That's right. I knew you would —for it is honest. Do not delay your marriage. Listen to me: I told you, little beauty, once, not so long ago, your fortune lies at your feet.

You have only to stoop to win it. It lies so still. But you must act."

"How do you mean? What must I do?"

Dragoon looked cautiously around. He even closed the slide over the keyhole. He waited a moment and listened acutely.

"I know much more than you think. Your groom is not to be trusted. Young men are vain and they boast. He is steady but he is no better than his fellows. You have elected to pick up what lay at your feet. Another trouble arises. Women are plotting. They are devils when they are jealous. Do not delay on account of what has happened. Try to shorten time. Lord Endover is surrounded by interesting women. Women are in his councils also. You are quite safe yet. Strike while the iron is hot; you know what I mean. Do not give him time to let them get at him. They will ruin you if they can."

He looked at me appealingly. His manner was most respectful.

"I really hardly see and yet—I know you are good and honest in what you say. Frankly, I will take your advice. You frighten me. I thought I was so safe—so guarded."

"So you are *as yet*. That is why I have come to reassure you and to caution you. I know all that passes at Endover. Take my advice. And now, good-bye. Look all the facts in the face—*and marry him quick.*"

Dragoon rose. He bowed with an almost mock solemnity which had its significance. In another moment he was gone.

The day passed wearily enough. In the afternoon Lord Endover called. He was all sympathy for me and condolence. His passion was evidently at its zenith. He regarded me as the object of his most cherished desires. The position was difficult. I told him I had not yet seen my Papa. I would consult him. My fiancé was evidently alarmed lest a long delay should be added to his probation. He had my permission to return the day following. I told him he was welcome. I said I desired his companionship and his advice. He left me much pleased and flattered.

I passed the evening with Mrs. Lockett. She brought her needlework to my sitting room. At an early hour I retired to rest. She supplied the place of my maid. I had never known the tender offices of a mother. I was grateful for her sympathy. I cried myself to sleep.

When I rose the next morning I had resolved all my difficulties. I had also carefully laid my plans. I prepared to put them into execution.

For malignity there is no expression to equal the intensity of the simply pronoun, "she," when hissed through the lips in an undertone as another woman speaks of a member of her sex behind her back. It conveys not only the absence of all respect, but the full measure of contempt which can be brought to bear on the absent one.

I felt I was being discussed and probably in quarters where I desired to be at my best. I felt quite equal to the occasion, but there was no time to be lost. I resolved to act at once. Thanks to Dragoon, I was warned and therefore armed.

*   *   *

"Ah, what a pleasure! I never expected to see you, my lovely one, this morning—and so early too. Why, business has been so dull lately that I have closed quite early. The season is a lot too good for us doctors; no colds, no bronchitis. What is London coming to! But you look anxious and not quite so well as usual."

"Well, I am glad to see you, all the same. I am not quite so well, perhaps, as usual. I have had bad news. No, do not ask me about it. You remember our compact; it is because I rely on your word of honor that I am here. I want your advice. I have lost a relative. But that is not the immediate cause of my visit. It has raised complications. I am uncertain what to do for the best."

My tall, fair young disciple of Esculapius consigned the care of his establishment to his lad. He ushered me into his back parlor with a look of radiant delight on his handsome face.

"Now, my beautiful. Tell me how I can be of use. I am entirely at your service. I hope the matter is not very grave. You look weary."

"You remember the conclusions you arrived at regarding the difficulty in the way of . . . of . . . well, I need not be reserved with you, my friend: I mean in the way of conception?"

"Certainly I do and I am still of that opinion. I am absolutely certain that every physician who took the same pains in the examination and who was proficient in his practice would confirm them."

"Then you are still sure I could not bear a child to my husband if I married?"

"Quite sure—and for the matter of that—to no one else."

"But that if I submitted myself to an operation—a slight operation—in that case, I should have the same chance as other healthy young women?"

"Exactly so. I believe more than an even chance, because you are so beautifully, so perfectly formed. Without going into professional particulars, let me tell you: you should sit to a friend of mine who is an artist—as our Mother Eve—for your figure is the perfection of all that is desirable for the procreation of the race."

"Oh, you wicked serpent! But seriously, is that your solemn declaration? Much may depend on your reply."

"It is, my Eve, my most serious opinion. Which you may have confirmed any day you please."

He had placed me in his easy chair. He now came and sat beside me. His face wore an anxious and dejected look.

"So you are going to be married. I might have guessed that so beautiful a girl with so much self-possession, forgive me for saying so, with so much force of character, would not be long without the choice of husbands."

"You may be right, but what then? We are already good friends."

"There, my darling, we are already good friends and if I could think—well, let me explain—if you would not give me up altogether, but if you would come to me sometimes, I, well . . . I should not be jealous."

I felt piqued. I hardly know why. He seemed

almost to catch at the idea of my marrying as something to be desired, and yet he was not at his ease. He waited a moment. He evidently saw my perplexity. Then he continued.

"To be plain with you, my sweet little girl, you are the most delicious treat I ever had in all my life. I have always fancied married women. If only you were really married you would drive me mad with lust to enjoy you. Your enchantment would simply be doubled."

"Is that so? If that is your whim, I will not fail to gratify it. You shall have me all to yourself as soon after I am married as I can contrive it. Are you satisfied?"

He took me in his arms. He became furiously indecent. His face, his voice, his movements, all united to betray the desire which raged within him.

"Oh, my darling! My love! You have given me such pleasure. You promise me? You will let me have you after your marriage?"

"I promise."

We were standing face to face. He pushed me towards the wall. He pressed himself lewdly upon me. He covered my face with hot kisses and took me in his arms. In a second his trousers were open and my hand closed on his limb.

"Oh, how stiff you are! What a size! Do you really like married women? Are they so nice? Is it part of your enjoyment to know that you are committing a real adultery?"

"It is awfully delicious to enjoy a married woman. Your promise maddens me. I consider you are one already. Come, let me have you. I must! I want you so badly. What lovely legs! Don't try to stop my hand. Oh, yes, skin back my thing. It is so nice. Your fingers are so warm and soft. Kiss me! Give me your tongue. You would like to suck it? So then, take it between your pretty lips. What a stupid fool your husband must be! I am going to spend into his wife's belly."

He seized me in his arms. He lifted me panting with my lips exhaling the ambrosia of his large tool. He laid me on the sofa. He was evidently madly excited by his strangely lecherous idea. I determined to encourage it.

"But what would he say? I am his property now; I really cannot let you abuse me. Oh, stop! Fie, take your hands away! Oh . . . you are strong, so cruel to me."

He forced me down. He pressed his long and powerful form upon me. My thighs were easily parted. His stiff limb wagged between them. I felt him divide the moist lips. The next moment he was into me.

"Oh, Christ, what a lovely girl you are! How tight it is! There! There! Now take it quite in. Does that please you? Is that better than your husband's? What a fool! I am going to spend into his wife."

"Oh, shameful! Let me go . . . you must take it out. You must not finish. What would he say? Don't you know you are committing adultery?"

"Yes, that's it. Adultery! Ah, how tight you are! My little married friend. No! No! I shall not take it out. I shall spend into you. Do you hear? Right into your delicious little womb."

"Oh, my poor husband. You are killing me with your great thing. What will he say. Oh!

Oh! You are going to spend. You are coming. Oh, so am I."

*   *   *

A few hours later my wedding was fixed to take place in a few months. Lord Endover left me in a transport of pleasure. He declared his intention to come very frequently if I would allow him to do so. I was most amiable. He received every assurance of my affectionate consideration.

I think I have already demonstrated that I am a hypocrite. The difference is only in degree; the necessity is universal. I never care to do things by halves. I am therefore a very great hypocrite. The higher your position in Society, the more consummate must be your hypocrisy. The attribute begins with the highest. Is not every evasion of the truth a smooth, a plausable hypocrisy? Nobody believes it all the same; that is the strangest part of it. It is offered and accepted. Everybody excuses it, weighs it at its own fictitious value and passes it on. "Tell the truth and shame the devil," that somewhat shabby proverb goes. I think, after a careful study of the subject, that Society would be much more ashamed, in spite of its usual regard, or rather lack of regard of that sentiment, if it had to tell the truth. Weighing one opinion with another, I fancy His Satanic Majesty is decidedly in the background. He could set to work to render his own Society so much more select if he only would—there being so much material to choose from.

A just sense of the value of hypocrisy, of

its judicious use, is absolutely necessary if you would shine in the flickering light of Society. Yet I am not afraid of criticism. I defy criticism to do me any harm. It would certainly not do me any good. No more than Marie Corelli herself. But I have no necessity to rack my brains to produce Demons and Divinities. I find in my exalted position enough of both in Society itself. I meet in every salon, in every boudoir, the saintly who cannot keep his fingers off his choristers; the elderly lordling who apes the vices of a Domitian or a Nero; the minister of religion who ministers to the lambs of his flock in more senses than one; and the blatant, pretentious man-about-town who divides his time and attention between his exaggerated shirt collar and his simpering partner. He would delight to be the very devil himself, if he only knew how. There are, too, the lonely, loving hearts, who, in the never resting vortex, watch long and sadly for the coming of the one they dreamed of the sad long days ago, or who mourn unceasingly the one who will never return, whose hopes never flag, whose faith is intact beneath the false mask they must wear and who will be as constant as I shall be to give up all, to submit to the inevitable when it comes.

CHAPTER 3

"At last I have my darling girl with me again. It has been quite a terrible time, my dear Eveline. You are quite right to remain in town as I directed."

"My dear Papa had only to express his wishes. Eveline is always ready to gratify them."

"I hope you got on well in this lonely house, my dear child."

"Yes, Papa, Mrs. Lockett was very sympathetic. John got on too very nicely. I managed to keep things together. He felt acutely."

Over a week passed since the news had reached me. All was quite over now. The house resumed its wonted appearance. Lord L—— had returned. Percy was at the depot. Only our somber costumes which conventional habit enjoins betrayed to outsiders the change which had taken place so recently.

"You have brought Johnson back with you, of course, my dear Papa? How is Gurkha? Does he look after him? Do you know, Papa, I am not over pleased with Jim, as you call him."

"Why so, Eveline? I thought he was rather a favorite of yours."

"Yes, well . . . he was . . . but to tell the truth, I mistrust that young man Johnson. I believe he is inquisitive. I had occasion more than once to be careful when you and I were riding together, dear Papa. He tries to overhear our conversation. I am sure of that."

"Is that so? Then Jim must go."

"Didn't I see your old friend Sir Currie Fowles who was going out to take up his new appointment in Madras?"

"By Jove, yes. And he asked me to look him out a groom. He wants one to take out with him. He knows I am like him, averse to native syces and prefer an Englishman in charge of my stables in India, so he came to me. Johnson would suit him exactly. I will see to this at once."

Ten days later Jim was tending horses on board a P & O mail steamer in the Red Sea, as head groom to the new Vice Consul in Madras. He received a considerable advance in wages and I was well rid of him.

We sat close together. We spoke of the future. I explained the arrangement for the wedding and told Lord L—— that I had fixed the date. He willingly assented to all. He said it had his entire approval, and that Lord Endover had already written to him on the subject. We could not help feeling that we were

49

now thrown together more than ever. The sentiment of mutual confidence had become stronger as he spoke of my forthcoming marriage. I thought I detected a certain feeling of jealousy in it which pained me.

"We shall always be the same to each other as we are, dear Papa. Shall we not? Nothing shall ever change your little girl as regards her love for you, dear."

"My only anxiety is that no harm shall befall you, my dearest child; no awkward contretemps should take place before your future is assured."

"Have no fear on that account, darling Papa. All is quite safe and will continue so."

"Where are you going, Eveline? That black silk bodice becomes you charmingly."

"I was going to my bootmaker, dear Papa. I want some more black kid boots."

"Extravagant little puss! Why those you are wearing are lovely."

"Do you like them? See, they do not fit badly. What do you think?"

I turned my foot about to show him. I raised my skirt sufficiently to show off my dainty calf in its glistening silk stocking as well.

"By heaven, my dear child, you tempt me dreadfully."

He caught me in his arms. He set me on his knee. With a trembling hand he fondled both boot and leg. Our lips met in a long hot embrace.

"What is to stop you, dear Papa? Certainly not your Eveline."

His excitement increased. We were safe in his room. I was sure of him now. I wanted it badly. He could see the flames of lust in my eyes. He drew me still closer. I put my hand on his trousers. His limb was quite stiff. It was so long since I had felt it; so long since it had been my enjoyment. His pent up passion betrayed itself in every muscle of his face, in every movement of his nervous frame. He put me off his knee and stood before me.

"Oh, Eveline child, I must have you at once. We have a good chance. Oh, my God! How long I have waited for your enjoyment. How I pant for the pleasure we shall give each other."

His passion rose as he spoke. He threw his arms about me. I unbuttoned his trousers. I caressed his handsome limb in my new black kid glove. Papa glared at the lewd spectacle as my little hand moved up and down the standing object in my grasp.

"Is this dear thing so bad, dear Papa? Eveline will take it and comfort it. It shall have all the delightful things it wants. We are alone. Let us do all that will give us the most pleasure."

I put my lips to his ear. I whispered so indecent an invitation that with a low exclamation of lascivious frenzy he bore me towards the sofa and raised my clothes. I fell backwards. He fell upon me. I was all aswim with longing for the incestuous encounter. I guided the skinny knob of his thing to my eager parts. The strong and erect instrument slipped voluptuously into me. He positively foamed at the mouth in his agony of enjoyment. For a few seconds no sound was heard but his stentorian breathing and the rustle of my black silk dress. My spasms became delicious. My womb seemed to open to him invitingly. His limb hardened throughout its length. He discharged with a low groan of rapture. I received every drop of his thick seed—the seed from which I was made. When he retired I kissed off the slippery exuberance of his spendings from the end of his drooping limb. I rearranged the disorder of my condition, baptized as I was with his rich sperm.

I made my preparations to go out. I went alone. The cab set me down at the corner of Great Castle Street. I entered the shop of Monsieur Dalmaine. I had made an appointment with the artist bootmaker.

"Good morning, Monsieur Dalmaine. Are my new boots ready?"

"But certainly, Mademoiselle. Am I not always of the most exact? Besides, how can I keep waiting my most beautiful client?"

"Let us try them on."

He led me into the back room beyond which was his atelier. I seated myself in the large chair. Dalmaine produced the boots from a glass case. He held up these for my inspection. His little eyes danced with pleasure as he scrutinized the glossy black *peau de cheveiul* and the exquisite work of his skilled assistants.

"They appear perfect. I trust they are not too tight. Not like *souliers de vingt-cinq*—you know."

"They are the correct fit for your lovely foot, Mademoiselle. I know not what *souliers de vingt-cinq* are. What are they?"

"They are *neuf et trois*, Monsieur Dalmaine: consequently they are *vingt-cinq*."

"Ah, *Mon Dieu!* Now only do I discover you! It is too good—*neuf et tres et trois! Mais c'est splendide!*"

He sank at my feet. He removed my boot. He inserted my toe into the new one. I pushed my other foot against his apron. The cucumber was already in evidence. I could feel its magnificent proportions. Meanwhile, without noticing my proceedings, the artist in ladies' boots became wholly absorbed in the elegance and delicate fit of his darling study. He no sooner had my foot in than he began lacing in the most exact manner, his face beaming with smiles as he drew the laces together. Not a sign escaped him to show that I had ever permitted any undue familiarity. Nothing marked his conduct beyond the most respectful attention to do credit to his employment.

"I think you had better put on the other boot also, please, so as to make sure there is nothing amiss."

He trembled with delight as he held the pair on my feet. He molded them, he fondled them alternately. I pushed my right foot towards the cucumber, now evidently getting beyond control.

"Ah, Mademoiselle. It is too much! You make me so bad. It is not possible to resist. You are so beautiful."

He pushed his hand away up on my leg. He lost suddenly all his reserve. His other hand was engaged in releasing his member. He turned up my dress as carefully as if he were my own maid. I saw him fix his gaze on my thighs. His fingers pressed on higher yet. He met with no restraint. Suddenly he pushed forward and his face was pressed upon my naked legs. He continued until his head was quite buried beneath my clothes. He gained ground and found his way to the central spot of his desire. I felt him seize the coveted spot with an exclamation of rapture. I pressed his naked limb between my feet. I parted my legs to give him room. His large tongue was now rolling on and around my clitoris, already excited and swollen with the previous exercise Papa had given it. He gave me delicious pleasure. I pressed down upon him, continually responding to his amorous caress with renewed effusions. At length I drew back. He raised his streaming lips. He pulled aside his white apron. I saw his huge member, red-capped and shining stiff as a bar of ivory, distended in front of me.

I gloated on the luscious morsel before me. It resembled John's. It was just as handsome. I seized it. I fingered it all about.

"Stand up. It is my turn now."

The excited man obeyed only too willingly. The stiff limb was within a few inches of my face. I examined it thoroughly. I pressed back the thick white covering skin which lay around the glistening head.

"So this is what you go 'crack' with, Monsieur Dalmaine!"

He was apparently too engrossed to reply. He glanced towards the shop door. He saw that the bolt was shot. All was quiet. He smiled. I imprinted a moist kiss on the little opening in the head.

"Oh, *Mon Dieu!* Mademoiselle! You will drive me to the mad!"

I repeated those moist kisses; my pointed tongue took part in the salacious game. The cucumber acknowledged my condescension by stretching its warm length eagerly to my caress.

I delighted to watch the voluptuous effects on my companion. I continued my kisses; my tickling touches; I worked my little hands in unison.

With the instinct of his countrymen he divined my intention. He still further loosened his clothing and drew back his shirt and trousers. He exposed his belly, his thick bush of sandy hair, his large testicles, closely drawn up between his standing member. I noted all. I determined to gratify him to the utmost. My whole being vibrated with prurient exultation at the delicious prosepct. He pushed his loins forward. My lips opened until they engulfed the head of his limb.

"Ah, *quel plaisir!* You are giving me the pleasure celestial!"

The contact, pressure and suction of my lips seemed to madden, to frenzy. To say he enjoyed conveys but a faint notion of his condition. His eyes were half-closed or fixed alternately on my face. His breath came in gasping sobs. He was acutely sensible of the delicious friction I was providing for him. I continued my voluptuous task. He replied with gentle pushes which served to thrust his stiff limb backwards and forwards upon my tongue. My fingers worked steadily along the white shaft. I stopped suddenly. I drew back. It was the pleasure of anticipation. I looked on the throbbing member close to my lips.

"Do you like that? Is it nice? Say if I shall recommence."

"Ah, Mademoiselle, you are so kind! You give me such pleasure!"

"Would you like me to finish like that?"

"Ah, but yes, sweet Mademoiselle! Make me to finish in your pretty mouth."

"Oh, you shocking, naughty man! What! You want to make that thing finish in a lady's mouth?"

"Yes, yes! I will give you pleasure also."

"You have already afforded me pleasure. I shall, if this pleases you, recommence. I am ready to gratify you."

"Ah, *Mon Dieu!* I shall be quick! I shall have the pleasure of the immortal gods!"

Even as he spoke he pushed the broad head of his thing between my lips. I sucked it voraciously while my gloved hand caressed and stroked the shaft. Dalmaine bent forward. He placed his hands on the back of an easy chair. I took all I could manage of his big member. The game was too good to last long. He gave a little cry. He pushed forward. The next instant my throat and mouth were filled with a flood of sperm. I was greedy. The hot spurts followed each other in quick succession until all was over. I rejected nothing. We had mutually gratified each other's perverse desires.

* * *

It rained for the best part of two days. London was out of season. Only the necessity of making preparations for my approaching nuptials kept Lord L—— and myself in town. I began to feel the insupportable ennui and lassitude which causes one only to fly to almost any distraction to escape from it. Papa remarked on my dejection. He attributed it to the right cause. He was always shrewd in care of me. Divining a means of relief, he hastened to make his proposition.

"You remember, my darling Eveline, our conversation at Eastbourne, when I proposed that a pleasure of unusual delight awaited you?"

"Oh, yes, dear Papa, certainly I do. Only our preoccupation has prevented my curiosity from becoming importunate. What is it to be? When am I to make this new experience?"

"We have nothing in particular to do this evening, dear child. I propose we spend it in the indulgence of this pleasure."

"Oh, Papa, that would be lovely. To tell the truth I am dreadfully dull and ready for anything. Besides, you told me it was medicine for me."

"So be it then! We will dine half an hour earlier than usual and sally forth together. All can be in readiness. I will complete the necessary arrangements at once."

"Dear, kind, Papa! You are always thinking of your little loving Eveline. You are feeling dull, too, and not looking so well as usual."

"We will have a dose of sensuality that will rouse us both."

"Indeed we will! I already feel better. I will go and put on my most enticing things to please my dear Papa."

I had time to make my toilet before the afternoon tea was served. John brought it in. Lord L—— had gone out. I well knew his errand. The footman shut the door, drew down the blinds and placed a chair at the table for my convenience. We were all alone.

"It is three whole days since you noticed poor Robin, Miss Eveline."

"So it is, John. Bring him here—pull him out."

In another second John had his limb out. It showed quite red and white against the black hair on his belly. It was half erect already. The perfume of the male organ began to excite my senses. I laid hold of it. I kissed it— I sucked it for a moment. It rose, superb and rampant at the contact of my warm lips. Then I stopped.

"Not now, dear John, perhaps tonight or tomorrow night, upstairs, I will give you a chance. I am not in the humor now."

The man looked disappointed. I thought him even surly. It occurred to me that I might not be wise to continue this liaison. Was it not time to break it off? Mischief might come of it.

John put away his unhappy member. He buttoned his plush breeches. I thought I caught the muttered words: "A reason for that, perhaps?" as he left the room.

Lord L—— had returned in excellent time for dinner. I could see by his cheerful manner that he had reasons to be content with himself and his mission.

"All is arranged and will be ready. We will

be as secret as the stones of Troy. You will see all in good time. How ravishing you look!"

I wore a black satin bodice and skirt trimmed with black lace, somewhat open in the front and exposing the upper roundness of my bosom. My hair was simply caught up with pins and twisted behind. It was well secured. Black silk openwork stockings of a very fine material, black glossy kid gloves, very thin and with very soft and high French heels, set off my little feet and ankles. The rest was duly arranged as I knew he loved to have it.

We drove to a second-rate theater. Lord L—— sent the brougham home. We slipped out again. Papa took me in his arms, then we threaded more than one small street. We made sure we were not observed. Then suddenly we started again. A door opened—we entered a house. I thought I knew the place. I had been there with Dragoon.

We went upstairs. A little woman in black pushed open a door. I found myself in a narrow corridor. About six feet in front was another door. A third door was on the left. The right hand side was apparently a blank wall. Lord L—— himself pushed open the door immediately in front. It gave access to an elegantly furnished chamber. A soft light came from the screened yellow light which hung suspended from the center. There were pictures on the walls. Two rather handsomely carved wood brackets occupied places on the side of the doorway. On them were two heavy vases.

"Here is a delightful little temple of pleasure, Eveline. The place is so secret and retired that it has never yet been disturbed by vestries or police."

I kept my ideas to myself. I waited for more.

"It is here that I have arranged for your medicine. The substantial medicine that you require dear girl, I have ordered. To drop all metaphor, you will meet here a fine young fellow whose very conditions preclude all risk. His actions are circumscribed. He is, as I told you, both deaf and dumb. He was so born."

"Poor fellow. I do not think I shall be afraid of him. Is he—is he very nice, dear Papa? So very strong—you know what I mean."

"My informant is a medical man—a member of my club. In the course of a conversation he related the case to me. He tells me he is possessed with a surprising degree of copulative power. I was told how I might see him nude and I went to a public bath. I soon picked him out. He was a study for a sculpture. And, oh, my darling girl . . . what a lovestick!"

I have the habit of blushing when I like. I did it then. It is not difficult when you know how.

"Here is a luxurious bed, Eveline. I wish you all the pleasure you are capable of in this retreat of sensuality. I shall come and fetch you when all is over. Meanwhile I will not be far off. You are quite safe here. You can make yourself quite at your ease. You have nothing to fear and all to enjoy, my darling. I will send him up. His name is Theodore."

He left the room. I heard him close both doors. Almost immediately Theodore made his appearance. I was at once struck by this young fellow's really and truly distinguished appearance. His seeming awkwardness of manner was evidently due to so unusual an introduction, but his bearing, his personality, were conspicuous. They were more. They were most uncommon.

He was rather more than fair. His height could not have been less than six feet two inches. His hair of rich auburn was naturally curly and glossy. His complexion was clear and bright. His eyes remarkably fine and expressive. Poor fellow! It was sad to think he neither heard a human voice nor expressed his ideas in speech. His individuality, however, compensated in some measure for these defects.

He came straight up to me with a rather weak smile on his face, as if he were shy. So, in truth, I found him. I motioned him to sit down by me. I made room for him on the sofa. I noticed how he watched furtively all my movements and seemed to be impressed by my personal appearance.

"You are a very handsome young man."

There was no answer. He produced an elaborately mounted slate on which was attached a crayon and a sponge.

I remembered my mistake. I wrote my remark on the slate. He broke into an intelligent smile at once. His whole being seemed to awake in response to my sentence. He was evidently vain. Poor fellow! He commenced writing rapidly. I followed his pencil with my eyes.

"Nature has not been wholly unkind to me.

I am strong. I am young. I rejoice in life. I have the means to enjoy it."

I smiled and put my left hand on his shoulder. I wrote:

"Can you make love?"

"It would not be difficult for anyone to love you. I could die for a girl like you. I have never seen a more beautiful woman."

"Are you in earnest? Would you really like to make love to me?"

In an instant his arms were around me. His lips pressed to mine. His breath was sweet as an angel's. His eyes shone into mine with the awakening of uncontrollable desire. He wrote rapidly:

"I love you already, you are so sweet. I want you. Will you let me?"

I took up the crayon.

"We are here to make love together."

Again there was no use for the slate. He pressed my form to his. He thrust his trembling hands toward my bosom. I denied him nothing. He panted. It was plain he was becoming more and more excited. He covered my face, my neck, my hands with burning kisses. Love and desire have no need for words. It is a language quite understood without sound, communicated without speech. He felt its intensity. Its influence brought with it an unsupportable necessity for relief. He wrote quickly on the slate:

"Do I make myself clear? I possess unusual advantages with which to please a beautiful and voluptuous girl like you."

I read. I believed and blushed. I playfully pulled his ear. He kissed me on the mouth in mock revenge. He became enterprising. He essayed familiarities which were hardly decent. I feigned sufficient resistance to flame his rising fancy. Suddenly he released me again to write:

"I conclude there is no need for too much modesty between us to interfere with our mutual pleasures?"

"No. I am here for your pleasure. You are here for mine. We should enjoy each other. Let us make love in earnest."

His eyes shot flames of lust. He took the slate.

"You are no less sensual than beautiful. We will drown ourselves in pleasure. I love pleasure. With you it will be divine."

He threw off his coat. He assisted me to remove my bodice. Soon I stood in my corset of pale blue satin and a short skirt of the same color and material. He rapidly divested himself of his outer things. He caught my hand. He carried it under his shirt.

"Oh, good heavens! What a monster!"

His instrument was as long as John's and it was even thicker. It was stiff as a ramrod and it throbbed under my touches. He pressed my hand upon it and laughed a strange silent laugh. Then he wrote on the slate.

"What do you call that?"

This was evidently a challenge. Nothing bashful, I took it up at once.

"I call it an instrument—a weapon of offense, a limb."

He put his left hand between my thighs as he wrote:

"I call it a cock."

"Well, he certainly has a very fine crest. He carries himself very proudly. His head is as red as a turkey-cock's. He is a real beauty."

The slate was thrown on one side. Theodore drew me on his knees. He tucked up my short, lace trimmed chemise. I made only just enough resistance to whet his appetite. He lifted me in his strong arms like a child. He bore me to the bed. He deposited me gently upon it. He was by my side in a moment, minus everything but his shirt, which stuck up in front of him as if it were suspended on a peg—as indeed it was. Theodore laid his handsome head on my breast. He toyed with my most secret charms. My round and plump posteriors seemed especially to delight him. I grasped his enormous member in my hand. I ventured also to examine the heavy purse which hung below. His testicles were in proportion to his splendid limb. I separated them from each other. There seemed to be something I did not understand. I felt them over again. Surely . . . yes . . . I was correct. He had three! He led me eagerly to the soft couch.

Once there he recommenced his amorous caresses. I seized him once more by his truncheon. It was so nice to feel the warm length of flesh—the broad red nut, the long white shaft and the triangle of testicles which were drawn up so tight below it. It was so strange, too, that this young man could neither hear nor speak. The spirit of mischief took possession of me. The demon of lust vied with him in stimulating my passion.

I slipped off the bed. Theodore followed me. I raised my chemise up to my middle and laughingly challenged him to follow. The view of my naked charms was evidently appetizing. He tried to seize me again. I avoided his grasp. He ran after me around the table which stood at one end of the room. His expression was all frolic and fun, but with a strong tinge of sensuous desire in his humid eyes and moist lips. I let him catch me. He held me tight this time. I turned my back to him. I felt him pressing his brown curls on the hairy parts of my plump buttocks. He pushed me before him towards the bed. His huge member inserted itself between my thighs. I put my hand down to it. To my surprise he had placed an ivory napkin ring over it. It reduced the available length. It certainly left me less to fear from its unusually large proportions. I had already taken the precaution to anoint my parts with cold cream. I adjusted the head as I leaned forward, belly down on the bed. The young fellow pushed. He entered. I thought he would split me up. He held me by the hips and thrust it into me. It passed up. I groaned with a mingled feeling of pain and pleasure.

He was too excited to pause now. He bore forward, setting himself solidly to work to do the job. I passed my hand down to feel his cock, as he called it, as it emerged from time to time from the pliable sheath. Although I knew he could not hear, yet it delighted me to utter my sensation. Women must talk; they can't help it. I was every bit a woman at that moment. Besides, I could express my ideas in any language I liked, as crudely as I chose;

there was no one to hear me, no one to offend, no one to chide. I jerked forward.

"Oh, take it out. Don't spend yet. I want to change. It's so delicious. How sweetly you poke me, my dear fellow!"

The huge instrument extricated itself with a plop. Theodore divined my intention. He aided me to place myself upon the side of the bed. I took his cock in my hand. I examined it avidly. It was lovely now—all shining and glistening, distended and rigid.

"I want it all . . . all . . . all!"

He understood. He slipped off the napkin ring. He presented it again to my eager slit. It went up slowly.

"Oh, my God! It is too long now! Oh! Oh! Never mind . . . give me it all! Ah, go slowly . . . you brute . . . you are splitting me! Do you hear! Oh! Push now . . . I'm coming!"

He perceived my condition. He bore up close to me as long as my emitting spasms lasted. My swollen clitoris was in closest contact with the back of his staff, which tickled deliciously.

I clung to him with both thighs. I raised my belly to meet his stabbing thrusts. I seized the pillow and covered my face. I bit the pillowcase in my frenzy. When I had finished he stopped a little to let me breathe.

"You have not come, but you will soon. I know it. I can feel it by the strong throbbing of your cock. I want it . . . oh, I want it! I must hold your balls while you spend. I want your sperm."

He became more and more urgent. He was having me with all his tremendous vigor. His strokes were shorter, quicker. My thighs worked in unison. His features writhed in his ecstasy of enjoyment. He was nearing the end. I felt every throb of his huge instrument.

I draw the veil over the termination of the scene. I cannot even use ordinary terms to describe it. My whole nervous system vibrated with voluptuous excitement. My senses deserted me.

When I recovered consciousness, to my astonishment, my companion had disappeared. Papa was standing over my prostrate form. How he had been occupied I shall never know. His face was turgid with satisfied lust. His hands trembled. His dress was disordered. He held in his hands a towel with which he was bathing my aching parts.

He assisted me at my toilet. As I passed out with Lord L—— I noticed that the door on the left of the little corridor was ajar. I peeped through. It gave me access to a little cabinet, not larger than the inside of a double brougham. In the partition which separated it from the chamber where my adventure had taken place, there was one bright point of light which shone from a round hole the size of a wine cork. A hasty glance explained all. The carved fretwork of the bracket on which stood all vases was perforated just under the shelf and quite invisible from that side. I understood all.

Lord L—— had witnessed the activities that had taken place. I hastily followed Papa, who had already descended the stairs. He waited for me. I am not a fool. I kept my discovery to myself.

CHAPTER 4

Wedding bells! The usual bustle and fuss. The usual ceremony. The usual lies on both sides. The usual hypocritical admiration of everybody for everybody, and behold, the day had come! In fact, was half gone when I was made the Countess of Endover.

The marriage ceremony was necessarily a quiet one. It was made as short as possible. A few intimate friends appeared at the church. The dear old Duchess of M—— insisted on being there. She was one of the few whose compliments were not all flattery.

Lord Endover really looked almost handsome in his uniform as Lord Lieutenant of the County. Papa and Percy paid him the honor of acknowledging his military standing as Lieutenant Colonel of Militia by also arraying themselves in their state panoply of war.

The three sisters of the husband were present, of course. The honorable Maud, a confirmed old maid; the next a widow, Lady Tintackle; the youngest, plain, spiteful and nine and twenty, yet a spinster, with every chance of remaining so—Margaret by name. She had begun life with one or two notorious escapades, from the results of which nothing but her brother's influence and position had saved her. The wave of disdain with which Society overwhelms offenders flagrantly transgressing its unwritten laws, and been detected, never seemed to quite unruffle her future. The men were all shy. All three sisters regarded me with little favor, jealous already of a new influence asserting itself between their brother and themselves. I foresaw great need of caution in my intercourse with my noble connections.

We were all relieved to get home. Lord Endover and Papa were closeted in the latter's study with the family solicitors. The ladies were whiling away the half hour before breakfast in the big drawing room. I had found an excuse to escape to my room. I bolted the door and sat down in my favorite chair before the looking glass. I was engaged in admiring myself in my beautiful wedding gown. I was glad to be alone. I wanted to think. I had many ideas to arrange.

We were to spend our honeymoon—how I hated the word!—at Endover Towers. The state rooms had been specially prepared. The place was said to be arranging a festive reception for the Earl and his young bride. The village was *enfete*. It was all to be very gorgeous and gay.

I was still before the mirror. Five minutes had not gone since my entry. Already there was a tap at the door. I rose and opened it. My brother Percy pushed his way in. He immediately locked the door again.

"Now I shall at least have a private view."

"What do you mean, you naughty boy?"

"Oh, it's no use riding the high horse with me, little Countess. Your Ladyship will please descend to the level of ordinary life."

He had seized me by the wrist. His other arm was around my waist in an instant.

"Oh, Percy, please, please, leave me alone! Someone may come!"

"I'm going to give the new Countess of Endover her first lesson in—why, you have no drawers on!"

"You really must not tumble my dress, Percy! For shame!"

He had put me before the large armchair. Before I could prevent him I was made to kneel in it. He had begun raising my skirts from behind. All protestations were in vain. I was horribly in fear someone would want to come in. Still, nothing was more natural than that my brother should come to offer me his private congratulations. He had only seen me once before that day in the church. We had scarcely exchanged a word.

"Oh Eve! Eve, dear! I've sworn to have you first after your marriage. I will not be denied. You looked divine at the altar. Like an innocent angel of light. I declare I could hardly keep my buttons on my trousers. Turn your head, dear Eve, and look."

I did as I was bidden; all power of resistance seemed to pass away. What I saw fired my hot blood.

"Oh, Percy, you wicked boy! It is bigger and bigger. Make haste then. I shall have to go downstairs in a minute."

He pressed his belly to my bottom. My wedding dress and underskirts were thrown over my head. In another instant he was in me up to the balls. There was no time to lose. He knew it. He worked fast to arrive at his climax. My own arrived quickly. With a low groan I sank my head on the cushioned back. His weapon straightened, hardened, and with a sigh he discharged.

Ten minutes later I entered the drawing room. Breakfast was announced. Lord Endover was complimented on all sides. He disposed of my beautiful bouquet on a side table. There was no fuss. There were no speeches— only our healths and champagne.

That evening at 5:30 we entered the village and drove to the towers. The local volunteers with their band bade us welcome at the station. All was in readiness for our reception at Lord Endover's noble country seat. It was a grand old pile. The family had bought it some two hundred years before from the original noble family that had held it since the time of William.

I pass over that portion of my history which relates to my early married life. I am not a hypocrite from choice but from the necessities of my position. Lord Endover never relaxed his fondness for me. I became disgusted with myself. Incapable of reciprocating his passion, I sought a retreat in our beautiful country seat in Cumberland. The Autumn season of Parliament had been started. There were weighty political issues in the balance; my husband had to be present.

It was then that I heard sad tidings from my old home in —— Street, Mayfair. Lord L—— wrote often. In one of his letters he told me that John, the footman, having been sent to St. John's Wood on an important message had met with an accident. He had been run over by a cab and was badly hurt. Conveyed to a hospital, he never quite recovered consciousness. All that could be made out was a ceaseless cry for "gingerbread nuts." Papa bought the poor fellow some pounds of these, but all they got from him was "gingerbread nuts," and so he died.

* * *

It was in the strong, bracing air of the country that I reveled until the obligations of my position necessitated my return to London. Lord Endover had gone to Scotland where he had taken a moor. I had decided not to accompany him. The weather had turned cold and wet. A week's visit to my old home would be enjoyable. Papa received me with a transport of delight.

"My darling Papa is always in the thoughts of his little girl."

"My sweet Eveline! You are more beautiful than ever! You have become rounder and fuller in your figure. The country air has been most beneficial to you. I have had no news from you recently of a private nature. Tell me, darling, has Lord Endover any hopes that . . . "

"I know all you would say, dear Papa. He has none, nor do I desire he should have. It is never likely to be as you suggest."

"I am not surprised, my dear Eveline. It is then as I thought."

"I am determined, Papa, never to perpetuate the race of Endovers. It is bad blood. If ever I had a child, a son, my offspring should have a father capable of procreating a new and healthy race which should endure—otherwise I am content to remain as I am."

He took me in his arms, mingling our kisses in tender sighs of ineffable enjoyment.

"Oh, my darling Eveline, what pleasure you give me!"

"My sweet Papa, you drown me in ecstasy. I am yours . . . yours only! What sweet adultery!"

"Oh Eveline, my child . . . incest is sweeter still."

In lascivious whispers we expanded the ideas which served to whet our ardent passion. Monstrous perceptions of enjoyment floated through our minds. They added poignancy to our lusty fuel to the fire of our already heated temperaments. We paused in our fierce and ravenous enjoyment. We lingered even as the epicure delights to taste to the full of a sumptuous repast, that we might enjoy each separate sensation. We worked ourselves almost to the point of consummation. Then we broke off only to recommence. I excited my darling Papa with every lewd suggestion my prurient imagination could devise. He made such proposals under his breath that only demons of lust could have prompted. We were both drunk with desire, overwhelmed with the intoxication of this renewal of our intimacy.

I made no secret now of my discovery of his peephole. I went further; I asked him if he had enjoyed the exhibition, whether it had kindled his lust. Yes, and whether he would like me to act the scene over again—or another—a more obscene and outrageous one, in which there should be three actors.

In this way we laid our schemes. Thus we invented plans of voluptuous gratification which we determined mutually to carry out. In the midst of our transports, while our imaginations ran riot in a red whirl of Satanic excitement, we rushed together in the final spasmodic struggle. With a volley of erotic expletives, Papa drove his swollen limb and flooded me with a volume of his seed. Exhaustion followed nature's overwrought efforts. A sweet languor followed by a refreshing slumber in each other's arms restored the vigor we had so recently expended. Our fixed determination alone remained. We would indulge our voluptuous inclinations in the future as we had already proposed. We had invented a new pleasure, a lewd distraction of no ordinary kind.

*　　*　　*

Lord Endover came up to town. It had, no doubt, strong inducements for him. I knew him too well to suppose he would be firm enough to free himself entirely from the early allurements that fast life had woven around him.

All I feared was some lasting taint, some loathsome encounter which might entail ruin upon myself as well as my husband.

He would return home very late, or very early, rather, in the morning, from the club, of course. Always the club! If not this club, then that club. It was necessary that he should show himself in the House of Lords also. I grew quite accustomed to these excuses. I received them all with the imperturbable good humor of common sense. I only ventured to remark that I thought he worked too hard for an ungrateful country, but I took care to provide myself with a separate room; one that suited me well in every respect and communicated with a boudoir beyond.

There is no more ill-treated an institution than a man's club in London. The poor thing has to stand all the responsibility and receive all the vituperation of that large section of Society women who suffer from the husband who returns with the milk in the early morning. It is certainly remarkable how many of them believe, or pretend to believe, in the power of that select circle of men of good standing, which spreads its blandishments in the form of whist, cigars and brandies and sodas to the extinction of all natural desire to seek the warm and genuine embrace of the loving and still fresh wife at home.

The awakening comes soon and with it, in too many cases, the natural impulse of revenge by an angry woman surrounded by temptations, to carry her charms to a more profitable, if not more congenial market.

Lord L—— was naturally a frequent visitor.

I drove him in the park. He took me too, on several occasions, to the opera. When the opera season was over we visited the theaters. My husband was rarely at the party and Percy was quartered at Scotland.

* * *

"Tonight, Eveline, in accordance with your wish, I have arranged our little diversion. We start precisely at nine. You are still determined on the adventure?"

"I am ready, dear Papa. Indeed I long for the fun. We will do all we talked of and you will, I hope, be near. You will look on and enjoy it too, will you not? Oh, it will be delicious, if only I know you enjoy it through me."

We drove to our quiet street. I wore a veil. Lord L—— was also unrecognizable. He took me from the cab and we walked a short distance. We were absolutely alone. We turned a corner and stood at the door of the same house. He turned a handle and we passed in. A tall, fair young woman received us in the hall as if by appointment.

"The young men are here. Will you walk upstairs, please?"

I heard all she whispered to Papa.

"They quite understand everything; the lady will be pleased with them. I know they will amuse her. They are only too glad of the chance."

We followed the loquacious woman upstairs. She ushered us into the same room. The two carved brackets were in their places. On them stood the somewhat meaningless Chinese vases as on my last visit. Papa made haste to disappear. Presently the door opened again. Two young men entered. They closed the door and we three were left alone.

My first inclination was to laugh. We must have all looked a little awkward. They were fine, handsome young fellows, stout and broad shouldered, with what Lord L—— would have called plenty of "grit" in them. They were evidently well-to-do. Just the sort of men Eveline would love to enjoy. They promised well. She would not be balked of her pleasure nor, to judge by their look of pleased excitement, were they in any danger of being disappointed. A few words and we were soon on a social footing. They never took their eyes off my person. I sat on the sofa. They came uninvited and sat by me.

"You are not afraid of me, are you? You can be quite at your ease. You both know what a young woman is, don't you?"

"Yes, of course we do. Don't we, Tom? But we don't often see one like you. You're a beauty, a perfect one."

"She's a lovely bit, Bill, she's . . . oh my! I can't say any more. I'm longing for it already."

"How nice you both look. What are you longing for? Give me a kiss."

They vied with each other in snatching kisses from my hands, much and many from my lips and cheeks. I let them pull me this way and that as they wished. I shut my eyes. I let my imagination wander. My attention was quickly called back. One young fellow had insinuated his hand under my clothes. His companion was kissing me on the mouth. I laid a hand on each side of me. I encountered their thighs. I had no difficulty in discovering the position of their privates. Both were already violently erect. They moved excitedly under my touches, which I made pointedly indecent. My right neighbor put his arm around me. He pulled me towards him and I kissed him on the lips. The other man put his left hand on the top of my bosom. I kissed him also.

"Let us be at our ease. Take off your coats; take off everything that is in the way. I want to see you as you are."

They rose quickly. In an incredibly short time they stood before me stripped to their shirts. Their trousers were flung into a chair.

My spirits rose. I was consumed with longing for the game to begin.

I raised their shirts as they stood before me. I grasped their stiff hairy members in my little hands. I determined to be as plainly lewd as possible. I was well aware I was overheard. I desired to make rich amends to the listener for his sacrifice. I knew he would appreciate every indecency, every salacious incident.

"What sweet pricks you have!"

They were in reality splendid, fine specimens of vigorous manhood. Their members confronted me menacingly as I commenced to finger them in turn. I bent down my head. I tickled and kissed them. I played around the soft warm things with my hot tongue. Both became furiously excited. They assisted me to undress. I slipped off my skirts and my bodice. I then stood in my chemise and stockings, retaining my pretty kid boots. Then I threw off my corset and gave them my warm body with which to play.

"What a lovely girl you are! I am longing to get into you."

"See, Tom, what a bottom she's got? Isn't she awfully well-made?"

They felt me all over. Tom went down on his knees. He divided my legs. He kissed my thighs all over. Then he pressed his face forward. He tried hard to arrive at my orbit. I put my hand down and shielded it. Resistance made him more eager.

"We both must have you, my dear. How would you like us to do it?"

"Say, which of us will have you first. I'm sure you're a dandy one when you've got a man up your sweet little belly."

I delighted in their rough indecencies. I knew someone else would also be enjoying them, someone of whose proximity my companions were both ignorant.

"Will you lie on your back, my fine girl? On the sofa first and let me put it into you?"

I pretended to become a little frightened.

"I don't know. I'm sure your things are both so dreadfully large and stiff."

In another second I was on my back on the sofa. It was exactly opposite the china vase to the left of the door. I gave a despairing look in that direction as the young fellow called Tom bent over me. He inserted his knees between my thighs while the other, with the greatest good humor, arranged a soft pillow for my head. Tom lay prone on my belly, his hairy chest pressing my soft breasts. My parts were in no condition to resist him, potent as was this monstrous rammer. I was actually swimming in the moist exudation which kindly Nature produces in such an emergency. Already I felt the broad head of his instrument thrusting itself within my slit. With steady pressure he continued to penetrate.

"Put your hand under her bottom, Bill, I'm held in already. She's . . . she's . . . oh, she's awfully nice!"

"Make haste and give it to her. I want my turn."

Tom began a gentle undulation, supporting himself principally on his knees and hands. He raised his head. He looked into my face.

"Oh, my, you're into me! Oh, ah! Pray go gently. You're so strong. You're too bad!"

Bill's broad palm was still under my buttocks, which he raised up in unison with his friend's movements.

"Is that nice now, eh? Is he stroking you nicely? Hasn't he got a fine tool?"

It was impossible to answer. I stretched out my right arm. My hand encountered Bill's stiff weapon, only waiting the other's vacation of my parts to be itself inserted in the same place. I gasped with pleasure. Meanwhile, the act was proceeding with utmost vigor. The young fellow was in up to his balls. His rough belly, covered with an awfully black growth of curly hair, rubbed upon my satin skin with an exquisite sensation of lustful friction. I felt his limb vibrating with the delightful thrusts with which he was laboring my poor body.

"I've got my finger on the line between his

balls. I think he'll spend directly. You'll get a lot."

"Oh, Bill! He's up to my womb now."

Here were two men assisting in a single act. It was a new sensation. I found it delicious. My flexible parts were stretched around the stiff instrument like a glove. The other's finger seemed to act as a spur upon the other's genitals. He drove up and down furiously. He worked away with incredible energy. I felt the short spasmodic thrusts which precede the discharge. I came. He lay on me, pouring out his rapture. His sperm came from him, wetting my longing parts in rapid jets. When all was done he withdrew with reluctance, but urged thereto by his friend. Before I could even rise Bill sprang upon me. He got between my legs. He contemplated my naked body, red from the rough contact of his companion, as a hawk might gloat over its tender quarry. He lay down to his work, stretching my thighs open to receive his loins between. He pointed his strong limb to my body and my already reeking slit. He drove it into me until I felt the crisp hairs on his belly chafing my mount.

It was a new sensation for me. I found it exquisite. The heat, the slippery condition I was in, the knowledge that the young fellow would spend and thereby double the flood I had already received, wound up my imagination to fever heat.

The big member of my second ravisher seemed to swell to an enormous extent, caused probably by the fervent temperature of my own parts. He seemed very long in bringing the lewd business to a climax, though his limb hardened until it resembled a truncheon of wood. He worked away with frenzy. At length I felt him spend. He spouted a second emission into me. He was so long in doing it I thought he would never finish. At last the final drops were exuded. The human cascade had run dry. My chemise was saturated with their sperm. Even the holland cover on the sofa was marked with a big wet patch. I rose hastily. I made my toilet behind the screen which covered the position of the necessary furniture. We all three then reposed on the sofa pressed together like sardines in a box. Each of my new friends vied with the other in their indecencies and their suggestions.

How I passed the entire hour during the time which these two fine young men kept me wantonly at their service, it is impossible to record. I only know I experienced a round of voluptuous enjoyment indulged amid smothered cries of intense nervous exultation. At last I believe I slept.

I recollect a quaint triangular adieu and a long silence. Then the voice of Lord L——— sounded in my ears and I threw my arms around Papa's neck. He had been a witness to all that had passed. He explained the secret of the little cabinet. He showed me the interior. I looked out at the opening. It could be effectually closed with a wine cork. There were two of these peepholes arranged for seeing and speaking through. Securely screened among the carved foliage of the bracket and immediately under the shelf on which stood the large china vase, no one would suspect their presence, which was rendered doubly unlikely by the blackened corks when not in use. The partition between the two rooms was only a thin paneling of wood.

"I should like to be with you, dear Papa, and share your curious pleasure by witnessing someone else. Could we not see someone on another occasion, just as today you have seen us?"

"I have no doubt it could be managed. I will make inquiries. Money, my dear, will buy anything in London."

"No, Papa dear. No money could buy off the love—the wicked, willful, ardent love that Eveline holds for you."

"Well spoken, my darling. However, it will serve our purpose in this matter. Next week, if you have time and an opportunity, we may bring off an exhibition of a peculiarly interesting character."

CHAPTER 5

How sweet is the country air. How lovely the blue water of the lake which sparkles in the sunlight beneath the shadows of the trees. Yet winter is upon us—winter in Cumberland. I have no taste to remain and encounter the snow and the cold. Chitterlings is delightful in the summer. It is not altogether such a residence as I would choose for the winter months. Endover is still away in the North shooting. I feel also much inclined for a little sport, though I fancy I would be on more congenial ground were I to be shot at and become a target of some gallant gun.

I reached the great gate which gave entrance to the avenue. Mrs. Hodge, the gatekeeper's wife, ran out all wreathed in smiles to open it, a buxom, good looking woman of some seven or eight and 20 years of age. After her came toddling a chubby lad of some three summers. A second held on by the lodge post, just getting firm on his legs.

I looked on, well-pleased to pause in my solitary walk to regale my sight with the picture so rural, so natural, so unobtainable. No; money cannot purchase all. There are gifts for which Nature refuses such dross; blessings which are sometimes unobtainable for all that wealth may have to offer.

"Good morning, Mrs. Hodge. Why, bless me, what fine boys. Are they both your own?"

"Well, yes, My Lady. They are mine—and my man's too. This is my eldest. Yonder one's my second. That's all, My Lady. All at present."

"Ah, Mrs. Hodge, you are a lucky woman to have such splendid children. They are perfect."

"I don't know about that, My Lady, but this one's christened Christopher. The parson gave us the name of a merchant captain who sailed over to America. Christopher Columbus his whole name was. That's Columbus standing by the door. He's just a year old last week, My Lady, and can walk and run till it's all I can do to catch him. But Lord bless him! He's a good little lad."

"I quite envy you. I fear such happiness is not for all the world. Have you a good husband, Mrs. Hodge?"

"Lord bless you, My Lady, that I have. My Jock is never so happy as when his work's done and we sit inside together of an evening. He reads a lot then, all aloud to me, for you see, My Lady, he works hard in the woods, cutting timber all day on the estate out yonder, and he takes his supper hearty, he does, and then he sits and smokes and reads."

"How long have you been married, **Mrs. Hodges?**"

"Nigh on to four years, now, My Lady."

"You've not lost any time, I see."

I laughed. The good woman joined my merriment.

"Lord, Ma'am—Your Ladyship, I mean—I beg pardon—if you only knew how rampageous my Jock gets! Why, I had all the trouble in my life to keep him decently quiet when we were courting, and since we've married there's no holding him. He's like a mad horse, he is."

"And what age is your husband, Mrs. Hodge?"

"Jock's nigh on a year younger than me, My Lady."

"Younger, is he! That is rather unusual in these parts is it not?"

"I don't know, My Lady, but saving your presence, his parents were both dead and gone. He had no home. I had saved up a bit of money here in the dairy and so they gave me the chance at the lodge if we chose to marry and look after each other."

"You're a happy woman, Mrs. Hodge?"

Something in my voice seemed to raise all the woman's tender sympathy. She looked at me inquiringly.

"I hope, My Lady, you won't think me too bold, but we've all of us on the estate been hoping as how My Lord might have an heir."

I pretended not to understand.

"I always thought hares were unusually plentiful this time about Chitterlings.

Mrs. Hodge looked nonplussed.

"I don't mean hares what run, but heirs."

"Oh, I see! Yes, now I see. It is very kind of you, I'm sure. At present, Mrs. Hodge, we must be content as we are."

The good woman drew closer. There was an air of mystery in her open, honest, good face, a look almost of trouble. She shook her head as she slowly uttered her next remark.

"I shouldn't. No, there's something wrong somewhere. Saving your presence, My Lady, and Your Ladyship'll excuse me, but a lovely beautiful well-grown young lady like Your Ladyship has no call to be childless. You may send me off for my impudence or turn us out of the lodge, but after being brought up on the estate, and it's now nigh on 29 years ago I was born on it, I do say now, Your Ladyship ought to have an heir."

There was something in Mrs. Hodge's kindly meant comments which touched me. There was even a dimness in her eyes as her broad, good-humored face looked into mine.

"No, I shouldn't be content. I know there's a difference in the living and the ways of great people and the like of us poor folks, but if I were the Lady of the manor without an heir, I know all the village would want to know why. I can keep my mouth shut, My Lady. I'm not a woman to go about gossiping about what don't concern me. I keeps to myself; but if Your Ladyship heard all they said you would find they knew it wasn't your fault."

The woman looked so kindly sympathetic that I suppressed a natural inclination to resentment. It rose in my throat. What! The Countess of Endover, Lady of the Manor of Chitterlings in my own right, to be thus spoken to and pittied by a peasant on my own estate! No, but it would not do. I broke down. The position was too strained. The tears rose to my eyes. Mrs. Hodge saw my distress. The kindly woman's own sweet nature came up beaming in her sympathetic look as she took my hand and kissed it.

"I know, I know, My Lady. My Lord takes his shooting—takes his hunting. He can do a long day in the covers perhaps, but he's—he's not to be compared to us poor folks under the sheets."

"What do you mean, Mrs. Hodge? My husband, Lord Endover, is all that is kind, all that is . . ."

"Ah, no, My Lady, you must excuse me—I mean no wrong. I only talk as I feel for Your Ladyship. It's not your fault. It's his."

I withdrew my hand. An angry light must have shown in my eyes. My red blood flew to my cheek. I drew myself up. This woman's insolence should not go unpunished. I was mad enough to have been accosted in this style, but to be an object of downright pity—no, this was too much.

"You are angry, My Lady—and no wonder! I am only a poor ignorant woman. You are a great lady. I hope you will forgive me. I meant all right for the best. I could tell you more . . ."

I hesitated. There was an air of reality about the elderly woman I could not mistake.

"Come in here, My Lady. I will explain all. I will tell you all I have to tell. The Lord knows I have no reason to hide it. It's too well-known already."

I entered the comfortable dwelling. Mrs. Hodge carefully dusted a chair with her apron. I sat down and she dropped on both knees in front of me, holding her bony face in her hands. Suddenly she looked up. Her confidence seemed to return. Her cheeks were wet with tears, red and mottled.

"I want to tell you all about it. I always said to myself I would. It was not all my fault. He was old enough to have known better than to take advantage of a poor girl without experience. He was educated and rich, with ladies all around for his asking. I was taken in with his winning ways. I was foolishly proud of his noticing me. He did what he liked with me. More's the pity. He said it was all a bit of fun and nonsense and that he would take care of me. Father came to hear of it. Mother was dead then. The village all heard of it. They sneered at father. It broke his heart. He beat me and turned me out of doors. An old neighbor took me in out of charity like. It killed father. I was left alone. The Countess was kind to me. The last dowager, I mean. She's dead now, and he—can you guess who he was? Yes, I know you do, My Lady."

Down went her head again between her hands. I heard a low sobbing moan. Then she spoke again.

"Fortunately nothing came of my wrongdoing. I lived it down. Then Jock came my way.

He was always a good lad. A bit studious like. Clever at farm work, strong and cheery. I took to him. We married. The dowager Lady Endover had directed them to take care of me. They gave us the lodge. Jock is keeper, as Your Ladyship knows."

Mrs. Hodge looked all around. Seeing that we were quite alone but for the two children playing on the floor, she went on.

"It was then I knew why nothing had come of my wrongdoing. He was not like my Jock. He had not the way of doing what men who take up with young girls ought—I mean are expected—to do. He was weak. Almost without any force at all after the novelty of Jock. It was different with my Jock, my goodness, yes, My Lady. Why I couldn't hold him. He was like a cage filled with lions under the blankets. There wasn't no stopping him. Under ten months my baby was born. My second was planted the first time ever he touched me after I was through with the suckling of the first. And, My Lady, I don't mind telling you my third is coming the same."

Mrs. Hodge rose to her feet. She was quite dramatic in her excitement. As she unfolded her narrative the truth had gradually come to me. It was the old story—like a penny novel. But there was more to it than that. This view struck me also. Every word was obviously true. She had told me at least one fact I recognized only too well. Very naturally she had fallen into an error in her knowledge of only half the facts. Very possibly, as regards my matrimonial affairs, there existed a DOUBLE disqualification. I felt angry at having been deceived. I had been married only a year. I felt I was looked upon all around as a failure —a disappointment. In a flash it suddenly occurred to me why the three sisters of the Earl had commenced a course of subservient patronage towards their cousin, the heir apparent to the title. It was even said the youngest was going to marry him. Many things hitherto hidden from my understanding now became clear. If the cousin, a worthless, idle creature obtained the title, Chitterlings would one day be hers. My woman's instincts were aroused.

"Go on, Mrs. Hodge, I am much interested. Alas! I think it is much as you say. But still I fear there is nothing to be done. I must be content to be as I am. You are blessed with two beautiful children, boys fit to be kings. You have a fine young fellow for a husband, replete with health and strength, while I . . ."

The good woman dropped to her knees again. She came closer and gazed into my face with a puzzled look I could not decipher.

"I shouldn't My Lady. No, not in your place —I shouldn't! It ain't in Nature. What! Let all go to nobody knows where! A fine title! A fine estate! When all might be for you and yours but for the fault of a certain person who has passed his time in ruining his faculties. Look on my boys there. My Jock's the man that knows the trick. Oh, my dear Lady, try my Jock!"

Mrs. Hodge clasped my hand, took it between her own and slobbered kisses on it.

*   *   *

"What, my darling Eveline, you are in town again! So unexpected, too. I thought you had intended remaining at Chitterlings sometime longer."

"So I did, dear Papa, but I have changed my mind. Ladies are apt to be fickle you know."

"But you are not fickle, my dear. You stick to your old love, my sweet little girl. Or your little hand would not be in mine now."

"Do you like to feel your little Eveline's hand right *there* Papa? Is it nice? Does it make you feel you love your own little girl? Do you still like my kisses? Do they give you pleasure? Is my tongue warm and soft? Is it all that which makes this sweet thing so stiff and long? Let me caress it, dear Papa."

"Oh, my God! Eveline! You kill me with pleasure. Your tongue and lips are maddening me. Take care or I shall fill your mouth!"

"Well, Papa, and what then? Do I not love your sweet sperm?"

"Oh, stay! You drive me mad. Not again! Oh? It is in your mouth. You are rolling your hot tongue round the nut. Oh, there, there! Take all—all!"

"You and I shall sleep together tonight, dear Papa, shall we not? You will make the bed go crickey-crack when you are on top of your own little girl, will you not?"

"There is a ball at Lady A——'s in Eaton Square. You had an invitation, I know. It is for the day after tomorrow. Will you go, Eveline? A dance will do you good. If you say yes, I will take you myself."

"Then I will go, dear Papa. Endover is

coming to London. I have sent for him from the North."

"What can be the matter, my darling? I hope nothing is wrong."

"Nothing is wrong in the ordinary sense, but I have come to a decision. I am not satisfied with the state of my health; not altogether sure that things might not be set right as regards my—my present condition, Papa."

"Eveline, you alarm me. One would fear you are not well."

"I am quite well—and quite resolved. One thing is certain: I have been married over 12 months. Endover is becoming more morose. He has given up, domestically. He goes here and there. He writes after every weary interval we pass together, if I have any news for him. I understand what he means."

"My poor darling!"

"You remember our conversation, Papa? Who knows what may be the cause of my sterility? For such it is. I have decided to consult a London physician. I have sent for my husband to hear his opinion after a proper examination. I should like you to be with him on the occasion, dear Papa."

"I think you are very wise. The stake is an enormously important one. It is worth playing for. I will not disguise from you that the Earl has already lamented the loss of all his hopes, in my hearing."

"We shall see. At any rate I will not leave this chance untried."

*   *   *

"Are you ready, Eveline? The carriage is at the door. Although you will not want for partners I should not in your place be late. The supper is arranged, they tell me, for an unusually early hour. Lady A—— likes her guests to dance, as sailors say, with the champagne all aboard."

"How dreadful, dear Papa. I want no such stimulant. I have not danced since my marriage. You must give me a square dance."

"Never mind, as Percy would say, let's make a night of it. But I must leave you early. I have an important engagement to meet the new Viceroy at the Club."

"Yes, I mean to make a night of it, Papa. I may not have such a chance again. But come and take me home."

Papa laughed. I could see that my humor made him nervous. He changed the subject.

"How superbly beautiful you look, my dear child. How lovely your dress, and yet so simple. It does not look good enough for the Countess of Endover, though. But still it is very becoming. What gloves! Your long white gloves are absolutely ravishing. They look so infinitely delicate and soft. They fit like the skin they are, but then, your darling hand is perfect. Your bracelets, too, are selected with perfect taste, so simple and yet so chaste."

"Let us go then, dear Papa. You kill me with your kind hearted flattery. Endover cares nothing now for all the points you mention."

The dancing had been in full swing for some time when we arrived. I found a chance to give Papa a quadrille. Several young men were introduced to me. I selected one—an old acquaintance. We waltzed together. He danced well. The music was good, the time perfect. I thoroughly enjoyed myself. The strains of the melody died away. The dancers stopped. Supper was announced. My partner thought himself the happiest of men to lead me downstairs to partake of it. I was thirsty. The champagne was grateful to my feverish palate. I left the table at the first opportunity. I wanted air. My head ached. I found myself in the entrance hall. The house door was open. An awning had been erected down to the curb. A solitary footman stood in attendance just below the steps. The night breeze was refreshing. I looked behind; I was alone. I advanced a step or two beyond the doorway. I drew the hood of my opera cloak over my head.

"Looking for a carriage, Miss? Shall I find it for you?"

"Oh, no. Thank you very much. It is not here. I felt faint. I want to breathe the fresh air. It is so fine a night. The heat inside is oppressive."

"Yes, Miss. A lovely night. Would you like a quiet turn around in the carriage? Do you good."

I took a rapid survey of the man. He was of the ordinary type; tall, good-looking to a certain extent, and wearing a livery which I did not recognize. It was evident that he knew me.

I flashed such a glance at him as I flatter myself Eveline knows how to give with effect. He caught its intensity.

"It would perhaps be nice. I suffer so, but . . . well, just take me around half of the square at a walk. I think it would do my head good.

The footman whistled. A large closed landau and pair came up out of the darkness. He held open the door. I swiftly stepped in. As I half suspected he would, the man followed. He closed the door, giving a quiet direction to the coachman as he did so. The footman sat himself opposite on the edge of the seat with his back to the horses.

"I still feel faint. My head aches badly—the heat of the room was dreadful."

My self-imposed companion promptly whipped out a fan from the pocket behind him. He began agitating it gently before my face as I reclined on the comfortable cushions. The horses were going at a walk. The night was moonless. The gas lamps alone shone an uncertain streak of light into the carriage at intervals as we passed. By their aid I furtively summed up my neighbor. He was evidently much agitated. His whole bearing betrayed an eagerness hardly compatible with his innocent employment. He bent forward in order to fan me. The better to steady himself, he rested his left hand on my knee. He pushed one of his sturdy legs between my knees. I felt his calf against mine. I was exhaled from myself in the close atmosphere. He evidently inhaled it. It seemed to madden him.

"There, you're better now, Miss. It'll soon pass off."

I could see that his eyes were intent on my face which had emerged from my hood. He stole fervent glances at my bosom, also particularly on the gloved and delicate hands with the left of which I held my cloak not too tightly closed. The right pressed my lace kerchief to my lips. An irrepressible feeling of the absurdity of the situation possessed me. I had difficulty restraining my inclination to laugh. He advanced his left hand a little farther. He even pressed closer with his fingers. He moved his leg at the same time more boldly between mine.

"Oh, you must not do that. You are shockingly indelicate."

There was only coquetry in my voice; only an invitation in my glance. The man noted both. He grew bolder still. I felt quite as wanton as he. My position was exceedingly critical.

"I think you have fanned me enough, thank you. It makes me rather cold. Oh, pray, pray do not put your hand there."

He closed the fan. It fell between us. In stooping to pick it up his hand touched my ankle. Instantly I felt it slip up to my calf. Just then we crossed the lamplight. I saw his face all flushed, his lips apart, his eyes dilated with strong sensual craving. There was no stopping him now. I could stand it no longer. I tittered.

"Oh, don't, pray don't! You must not do that."

His hot hand advanced. He touched my knee. His left hand was under my clothes still. I put down my own in a well-feigned effort to stop him. He seized it with his. He caressed it softly. He fondled the well gloved fingers. He stroked the perfumed kid on my wrist and arm. Suddenly he drew my hand towards his.

He pressed it down on his person. He was fairly aflame with passion. My hand, retained in his strong grasp, detected his condition. Within his garment I felt his limb. It was evidently a fine long one—stiff as buckram and very thick. The contact excited me further.

"How delicious you are! Don't take your lovely little hand away."

A gentle squeeze was all my response. He took care I should not leave off my inspection. It fired my blood. He slightly jerked his loins. I bent my body nearer his own. I repeated the squeeze even more suggestively. He pressed and squeezed my hand on his person.

"Do you feel so naughty then? Let me look at it."

He released his grasp. He quickly unbuttoned his trousers. He pulled up his shirt. A big red-topped member started out. Oh, how long it was and how dreadfully stiff! Curving slightly upward, the swollen head was already naked and staring me in the face. I put my gloved hand upon it. I took it in my palm. My right hand covered the protruding knob. I shook it. He could hardly retain his seat. He thrust his eager fingers into the front of my low dress.

"What shall I do with this? What a large one you have!"

I pressed back with both my hands. He tried to raise my dress. I stopped him.

"Oh, no, it is impossible. You would rumple my dress. You must be very gentle. Sit still —Oh, do, pray!"

I love to finger a man's limb when it is of

such splendid proportions. This man's was excellently molded. It stood awaiting my inspection. There was no reserve between us now. Modesty had flown out the window. We understood each other.

"But what can we do? Pray let me put it into you. I won't hurt you. I'll be as gentle as a lamb. I won't tumble your clothes. It won't take a minute. The coachman is a 'fly' — no one will know. Let me pass my hand up. Let me feel all you have got."

"Ah, no, no! It won't do! I must go back. What do you think they would say of me if they saw me enter all tumbled and rumpled? Sit still—sit still! Is that nice?"

I moved both my hands gently up and down on his huge limb. Each stroke covered and then exposed the red gland. He breathed heavily. He ceased his attack. He pushed his loins forward.

"Nice? Oh, yes! My God! It's delicious! You'll bring it on!"

"Bring it on? Do you mean that I should milk you? Is that so very nice? Like that? And so—like that? Do you like me to play with it?"

"Oh, yes! It's lovely—you'll milk me, Miss, won't you? Oh, oh! Do stop a little Miss."

The horses had stopped. The carriage appeared to be drawn up under the trees close to the square railings, in the dark place near the side. I bent my head lower. I examined the man's limb as well as I could by the uncertain light. It was a model of manly health and vigor. I stooped lower still. My wet and eager lips touched the purple lips below. How soft they were. How delicious the masculine flavor. I kissed them repeatedly. A second later it slipped into my mouth. The man seemed to resign himself. He sighed with delight. My tongue was thrust below the velvet plumlike nut. He pushed the head and shoulders quite into my gullet. I sucked all I could. My gloved hands tickled and pressed the long shaft. He commenced to wriggle on the edge of the back seat. He held his legs straightened wide apart. He threw back his head.

"Oh, my God! Stop . . . no . . . go . . . on!"

I obeyed. He thrust forward. I received a mouthful. He spent furiously. I held on. I caught it all to the last drop. I was half-mad with erotic pleasure. He groaned aloud in his spasmodic discharge as I drew spendings from him. I wiped my lips with my lace handkerchief. He sat up and rearranged his clothes. We listened; then my companion cautiously opened the door. He got out and I heard another voice. The door was closed but the window was on the last button.

"What have you got inside, Chris?"

"Oh, don't ask—a regular stunner. It's a young lady from the ball at No.——. She's all right—she—oh my! I can't speak yet, I've just done it. I've had such a time!"

"Well get out of the way. Keep a lookout for the sergeant. He won't be back along this way just yet."

The door opened again. A strong light was flashed in my face.

"What's up here? What's up?"

The carriage opened wider. A policeman thrust himself in and sat on the front seat.

"I don't know that I oughtn't to run you in, Miss (they all called me Miss) there's been a fine goings-on here. Well, I never! A handsome, beautiful young girl like you. What have you two been doing of? I think I know. He's a nice chap is Chris, but he's clumsy, that's what he is. I should like a go at it myself. Give me a kiss, my beauty. There, don't be shy. It's only my way, you know."

"Oh, please, you mustn't put your hands there. You hurt, you are so rough. You will tear my dress. Let me alone. I say! Oh! pray don't . . . don't do that."

"Sit quiet. I'm in with these chaps. Why they couldn't do nothing without me. It's on my beat you see Miss. Sit quiet, I won't hurt you. But I mean to have you like Chris did."

All this time he was pulling me about with his right hand. He was engaged in unbuttoning his clothes with the other. He had no shame. He pulled out a long white member. He shook it at me impudently in the uncertain light. He was a tall, strong man.

"Now, Miss, just keep quiet or I shall have to do my duty."

"Oh, my goodness, policeman, how dreadfully naughty you are. But, oh dear! What shall I do? Tell me, are you a married man?"

"Yes, I am that. I've a missus at home and three kids. But she ain't a patch to you. You're just to my liking. A real beauty. But what do you want to ask me that for?"

"Well . . . I don't know . . . but if you really are married, and if you are very, very gentle . . ."

"Oh, shut up! I can't wait! Here, turn up your skirt. I want to see your legs."

The wretch put down his hands. He begged me to help him. I did all I could to save the dress. He saw my stockings up to the knees. His truncheon was stiff enough in all conscience now. I saw it plainly sticking up in a wild erection. He pulled me forward to the edge of the seat. He slipped on his knees. He had showed me one of his hands up my clothes. His other arm was around my loins pulling me towards him. His eager fingers were already in contact with my private parts. Secretly I enjoyed his rough toying. My skirts were now up until he could see my white belly. He rudely pushed my thighs asunder.

"Oh, Christ! What a fine little bit you are! You make me awfully randy. Here, take this in your hand. Come! No nonsense now! I can't wait, I tell you! Put it in yourself!"

He forced me to take his truncheon in my gloved hand. I squeezed it. It was level with the place he sought. He thrust forward. I let it slip in. He no sooner felt the hot contact than he pushed it up into me, dragging me close to him. He thrust it in up to the balls. He began to move.

"Now, I'll do the business for you. How do you like that, My Lady?"

"Oh, policeman, how you do push!"

The man worked violently up and down my vagina. He was too excited to be long over the job. He seized me in a vise. Almost immediately I felt him spending. I went off also. I was in the agony of sensuous delight. His sperm was thick and hot. He waited a moment to recover his breath. He drew his limb out and got up. As he did so I noticed a face against the window. It was the footman. He opened the door.

"Come out. I know you've had the young lady. I saw you through the glass. I'm awful randy now. There's time yet. There's no one about. Look out a minute while I have a go."

He entered the carriage and closed the door. He let loose a huge member. It seemed stiffer and bigger than before.

"Now, Miss, I can't help it. He had you and so will I."

"Oh, you beast, what are you doing! Let me alone! Don't thrust my legs open. You'll kill me! What a size it is! Why . . . you're right into me!"

He had already penetrated. He forced the huge thing into me until he seemed to be right up to my womb. He uttered no words. He only breathed hard. And pushed up in his strong excitement. Then his head fell on my shoulder. I knew he was spending. He emitted in short spasmodic jerks. Like his friend, he made haste to escape.

Before he could close the door I heard the flick of the whip. And then a new and very gruff voice said:

"Here, I say! What the hell are you fellows about? I'm going to get down. The old box is shaking about so awful I can't hold the bloody horses."

Just then I heard a scramble. The policeman rushed across the road. The footman got turned rapidly about and then went slowly back toward No.——. I adjusted myself as best I could. I pulled my large opera cloak over my head and was set down once more. I passed hastily in and gained the ladies' retiring room. There I found myself alone. The wild strains of a lovely waltz were filling the air. I took care to repair the damage and changed my gloves.

"Oh, my dear Eveline, I have been looking for you."

"Poor Papa. I had a headache. But it is better now. Have you been making a night of it? I have enjoyed myself thoroughly. Take me home now. I have danced enough."

* * *

Doctor Brookstead-Hoare was a dapper little man. He came of a medical family. His father had commenced life as an assistant to an apothecary and subsequently practiced as such himself. The doctor's brown curly hair, already tinged with gray, was crisply combed around his small and shapely head. His finely-cut features presented nothing in their repose which betrayed his exalted opinion of his own powers, or person. When he spoke, however, his animation increased noticeably.

His mode of expression was adapted to the circumstance of the case. He was obsequiousness itself to the wealthy and the noble; short and terribly decisive to the meek and lowly. He emphasized his opinion with a sort of professional superiority which contrasted with the quaintly careless garrulity of his ordinary conversation. His self-conceit was enormous, and although a valuable adjuntcy in his pose before his patients, it raised a sort of hilarious resentment among his professional confreres, who saw through it.

Dr. Brookstead-Hoare possessed a large practice as a specialist for the treatment of women and children. He was altogether a professional pet of Society in his special department. His fees were immense, but only commensurate with his consummate complacency. He delighted to talk of the notabilities whom he counted among his patients. The pains and sufferings of royalty were all subservient to his skill. If his communications concerning them were not always correct, that at least served to extend his importance as a specialist.

"I have made a most careful examination in this case—ahem!—Her Ladyship—the Countess of Endover—yes, aided by my friend Dr. Archer, who is, I believe, your family adviser. A most thorough and careful examination. I find—ahem!—I find that there is no possible chance of Her Ladyship ever becoming a mother—ahem!—in her present condition. I have, however, ascertained quite beyond the possibility of a doubt, that a trifling . . . let us say . . . a very trivial operation would remove this . . . this disability. There is a small ligament which interferes with the proper position of the organs relatively, which interrupts the . . . the natural sequence of events. I cannot very well demonstrate this to the lay mind, but Doctor Archer and myself are in accord that it could be easily and safely removed. Our dear Countess is in every other way so beautifully and—ahem!—so perfectly formed that I have no doubt, if she be willing to submit to this slight operation, she will have no cause thereafter to disappoint her Lord. Do I make myself clear? It is for Her Ladyship to decide."

Here the little man struck his hands together and placed them under the coattails as he balanced himself in front of the fire, reminding one strongly of a bantam cock contemplating crowing.

Our own family doctor looked anxiously towards me. My husband and Papa looked at one another in mute astonishment.

"The necessities of the case would, of course, entail a little sacrifice of time and comfort on the part of Her Ladyship. There would be the usual antiseptic and anesthetics to adminster, which Dr. Archer would undertake of course, and, then the slight operation to undergo—ahem!—let us say a week's rest and all would be in order again."

The Earl looked immensely relieved. He regarded me wistfully. Papa wore an expression of anxiety mingled with doubt. I put an end to the suspense.

"I am ready to undergo the operation as soon as the arrangements can be made. Tomorrow, if you will; the sooner the better. I have made up my mind. I will take my chance."

My husband actually shed tears of delight. He pressed my hand. The two doctors beamed graciously upon me. Papa hid his emotions behind a well-affected compliment to my courage. Dr. Brookstead-Hoare hastened to reply.

"Be it so—tomorrow at noon—ahem!—I will

be at your mansion. Oh, yes, I know the address. Leave all the arrangements to Dr. Archer. He will, I know, have all in readiness."

The little medico made an entry in his notebook. Then he pompously bowed us all out.

A vision of dissappointed sisters, of a cousin remitted to his pothouses and his scum of Society, flashed across my mind as I took my seat in the carriage, though none the easier for the disturbances caused by the exhaustive examination I had undergone.

* * *

I had now great reasons to be satisfied with the resolution I had formed. The earlier intimation I had received from my medical friend proved without doubt to be correct. The operation, I was informed by both physicians, had been perfectly successful.

"Dr. Archer says I may sit up today, Papa. And I may have what I like to eat."

"I have sent for oysters, my dear Eveline, and Mrs. Lockett will send you up a roast grouse, also a custard pudding of her own special make."

"How kind of you! Today I shall have fare like a queen; but oysters, you know, are supposed to stimulate other nerves than those of mere digestion."

"Yes, that is so. I believe I have felt the influence myself, especially when near my dear Eveline. No doubt they have a certain effect. Certain kinds of fish have the same result. The skate, that nutritious and much neglected fish, is one of them."

I could not help smiling at the serious professional air he assumed while thus lecturing. I let him see the twinkle in my eye.

"You mustn't eat oysters, and you mustn't eat skate, dear Papa, when you come near your little Eveline. She has a certain resolution and she intends to keep it."

He drew a face of such abject misery that I could not repress a little laugh at his expense.

"You are too cruel. Eveline, my child, but perhaps you act for the best. You will always have a will of your own which has hitherto led you to avoid pitfalls."

"I did not mean to be so terribly severe as altogether to exclude those delicacies from my dear Papa's diet . . . only that . . . only . . . you see, Papa . . . Well! We must be careful how we go about things now. At the same time, my great Charlemagne is a great conqueror. He cannot be expected to go altogether without the reward of his victories."

"I do not understand, my darling, quite what you mean."

"I will try to explain myself, dear Papa. When the Emperor Charlemagne first indulged in the luxury of a debauch with his daughters you may be sure he was not long in arriving at a complete enjoyment of their charms. Then came a time when the pleasures of dalliance succeeded to the hot lust of passionate desire. No doubt those recipients of the great man's favors were early taught those auxiliary delights which go to make up the full pleasure of sensual gratification. Do you follow me, dear Papa?"

He nodded, drew his chair closer to my bed and I saw my opportunity. I was not slow to take advantage of it. I only dreaded his terrible disappointment.

"We must be careful. I have fully determined there shall be a direct heir to the Earldom of Endover. I believe in myself. In so doing, I have already won half the battle. But I will have no weakling or ailing offspring of a race which has groveled in all the vices of the Georgian period, whose blood is as tainted as their morals are degenerate."

"My dear Eveline! Are you not a little hard on the Endovers?"

"Hard on them! If you only knew all I have learned concerning them! The men, I mean the father, grandfather—the progenitors of this noble, unadulterated family—why, had the grandfather of my husband not had the good fortune to have hit upon a French millionaire and married the pork-slaughterer's vulgar daughter, there would not have been an acre left, nor a hearth to warm the vapid blood of his son, let alone his grandson. No, Papa, and the estate, if I bear a child to succeed to the title, shall at least revert to one of sound, strong English blood. You may leave the rest to your little Eveline."

"My God, you are right, my child! I have unbounded confidence with you. But how will you compass all this? How carry out your idea?"

"As I have said before, dear Papa, leave it all to me. I believe I shall succeed in all. I have faith in myself—we shall see. I am going down to Chitterlings. Endover goes with

me. We are to have a second honeymoon, he
says. There will be at least the horns of a
new moon for him, and very little honey for
me—the less the better."

"You frighten me, Eveline. I trust all will
turn out as you hope."

I indulged in a little quiet laughter. I put
forward my lips to be kissed. He bent over
me; our lips met. For a second my tongue
touched his. His eyes lighted up with passion.

"You must not let me change my position,
dear Papa. Pull your chair closer yet . . . so,
that will do."

I gently thrust my right hand from out of
the bed. I had arranged a little diversion for
him which I knew would exactly meet the ex-
igencies of the case. My beautiful white kid
glove covered my hand, and half my arm,
fitting like my own skin. On my wrist sparkled a lovely diamond bracelet, his own gift.
He looked down. He beheld the snakelike advance of the little gloved hand and the glistening sheen of the perfumed glove itself.

"Oh, Eveline, all that for me? How deliciously inviting is that beautiful little hand!"

He seized it, covered it with hot kisses.

"We must be careful, dear Papa, how we
handle things now. Come, let me handle yours.
Do you understand better now? Let me give
my dear Papa all the pleasure my active little
fingers can bestow. I am to remain still, but
Dr. Archer says I may use my hands and
arms. I want to avail myself of his kind permission. How stiff it is already! How delightful to feel its long white shaft. Oh, how I long
to kiss it! But no! I want—I want to see your

sweet sperm come out. I want to bathe my new gloves in it. Let me have this pleasure, dear Papa!"

I knew him so well. I was quite aware of his peculiar lechery. I grasped the erected member. He leaned over me. I whispered the old indecencies in his ear—the old invitations in so many crude expressions. I bade him not to spare my nice new glove. He flushed; his lips grew dry and hot. The door was locked, no one had a right to disturb us. I slipped my nimble fingers up and down on his darling weapon. I squeezed it, I bore back the loose skin.

"Oh, my child! Oh! Ah! You give me an ecstasy of pleasure!"

"Is that nice, dear? You wicked Papa! You will spoil my beautiful glove! You will be coming directly—I know you will! You cannot help it—there! Do I rub this big thing as you like? Oh! see how red the top is now! What a contrast with the satin white of my glove! Oh, a little drop already! Quite a beautiful pearl! Oh Papa! there will be a quantity of it, will there not?"

He breathed hard and bore up toward me. He held back his clothes to avoid the consequences of his discharge. I had my handkerchief ready. His lovely member was rapidly manipulated by my hand. How I doted on the big, impudently obtrusive thing as I shook it up and down! His delight was evident. Enjoyment gave expression to his hard respiration, his open mouth, his upturned eyes. I knew by all the symptoms he was on the verge of his climax.

He arrived. He straightened himself. I grasped my victim firmly. He discharged. The hot, thick semen came slopping over my hand. My glove slipped about in the steaming flow. He pushed up towards me to meet my rapid movements until he had emitted the last drops. Then he sank back exhausted in his seat.

"Go at once and get a glass of wine, dear Papa. I must not have you reduced so much again for a long time to come."

* * *

There is no change so beneficial for a convalescent as the sweet country air of the lake district. The bracing breezes of Chitterlings would, I hoped, do much for me. Perhaps I expected their influence to be seconded by more potent agencies. The Earl was with me. Endover was in his gayest humor. The day had been a long and fatiguing one. I begged him to excuse me. I retired early. I told him I felt worn out and tired. He wished to join me in my chamber. I again begged him to excuse me, asking him to be reasonable because of my exhaustion. Tomorrow perhaps, yes, tomorrow night he should share my bed. My loving arms would celebrate our second honeymoon. They would reward him for all his forbearance. There would be no reason to complain of the coldness of his little wife.

I lay awake that night. I resolved in my mind about the many instances of the Earl's indifference; his utter neglect when first, after so brief a period, he had treated me as he had so many other women before me when the novelty of possession had worn off. I felt a disgust, a loathing for him I could not shake off. I thought of his low amours, of all I had heard, of those I knew only too well were his present companions. I remembered the pitiful history which poor Mrs. Hodge had revealed. As I did so, a thought came to my mind of her tearful, honest face. Did she contemplate a secret and terrible retribution? Was she capable in her apparent simplicity of such a double scheme? I would know more tomorrow. I would satisfy myself ere I went further in the matter I had in mind.

Poor Mrs. Hodge, simple Mrs. Hodge. What a cruel fate had left its stain and its memories with her. Only saved from the mire of moral degradation, from absolute destitution, by her strong common sense. She had made her escape into marriage which, if it was not one of absolutely deep affection, afforded her at once a protection and a home. To her ignorant nature, born and bred among the peasantry of the estate, imbued only with the lowest perceptions of the moral sense, she looked upon her rustic spouse principally as a fine animal who had been the means of giving her two equally fine children, and who was a sober and suitable companion in her quiet home. Like a certain class of dependents, becoming fast extinct, her destinies were bound up in those of the great family whose service, and under whose tenure, she and her progenitors had been born and brought up. They made themselves and their interests one with the noble house they served, and in reality looked to the prosperity of their Lord as a necessary assurance of their own.

Mrs. Hodge was delighted to see me. We had frequently met since my first and memorable visit. The anxiety of the good woman on the subject we had discussed had by no means subsided, but she abstained from any pointed reference thereunto, merely contenting herself with a sign and shrug of her broad shoulders, as if to deplore the fact, and my want of appreciation of her views on the subject. But on this occasion she was particularly communicative.

"Ah, My Lady, those big towns like Liverpool and London! The smoke and the fog and the bad air are not doin' you any good, Your Ladyship. If I may make so bold, Your Ladyship is thinner and paler than when you went away. Nothing like the fresh air here, My Lady. In a week you will be a different person indeed."

"I am not satisfied with myself, Mrs. Hodge."

"I don't wonder at it! Why, how can you be? And it's not your own fault either. Ah, dear me, what one has to put up with. Now my Jock—why Lor' bless you, My Lady, there's no holding of him when he's on!"

She had sunk her voice to a whisper. She shut the door of the lodge. She came back and placed herself on her knees before me. It was her favorite attitude. There was something comically irresistible in the semipleading attitude she assumed. I laughed softly.

"Why, Mrs. Hodge, your Jock must be a terrible fellow from your description. I should not care to be in your place."

"Wouldn't you, My Lady? Sometimes I think you would, though. He's not much to look at; only an honest plain-spoken lad, but he's true as steel and—and he can hold his tongue. He's as silent as the night. That's what he is! Don't tell me Your Ladyship is content. I've told you already what I think. It ain't in nature—a beautiful sweet creature like Your Ladyship and wedded to . . . to . . ."

"Oh, Mrs. Hodge! What's done cannot be undone, you know!"

"No, but it can be mended. Do you think I'd waste all my young days if I was in *your* place? Not I!"

"What would you do, Mrs. Hodge?"

"What would I do? Well, if I found my husband was no husband to me, but had deceived me into thinking him a *man*, I'd get one in his place. That's what I'd do! So should you, My Ladyship."

She came up close to me in her excitement. Her volubility seemed to carry her away. She laid her hands caressingly upon my knees. She brought her face closer. She felt more confidential—she grew bolder as she saw me smile. I laid my hand softly on hers. She was about to speak again. I motioned her to remain silent.

"I will not disguise myself from you. I do not attempt to deny my great disappointment. That which you related to me on the occasion of my first coming here, Mrs. Hodge, has made a great impression on me. I am young. As you say, I am in perfect health. You are a woman and you know what a woman's nature is. There should be no reason on my part why I am childless."

"No, I am sure of it, My Lady. I know the cause. It is no fault of yours—why should you continue so? I should not be content in your position."

My blood rose to my face, my eyes flashed, I half-rose. The good woman recoiled, half-afraid. I was in ernest now.

"I will not be childless if it depends upon me to prevent it!"

I clenched my hands and stamped my foot imperiously; my breath came short and angrily. Mrs. Hodge clasped her hands together as she knelt.

"Oh, bless Your Ladyship for that! Now you speak like the great lady that you are. Keep to that. Oh, keep to that, My Lady, and . . . try my Jock!"

CHAPTER 6

The night came and also My Lord. After a long drive across the country, we had dined, or rather supped, at half-past nine. The champagne had done its work and my husband was sufficiently lively. As for myself, I was too careful of the part I had to play to allow myself any liberty with the exhilerating beverage. I pass by all details of that unpalatable nuptial couch. Suffice it to say that my wiles succeeded in giving my husband a complete enjoyment of his marital privileges, while my precautions rendered it perfectly impossible for any consequences such as he hoped for. The Earl left my bed charmed with my warmth and vivacity. He was actually proud of himself and his virility.

I cannot say I shared his sentiments. His weak and languid attempts had only succeeded by my assistance, but they were sufficient to convince him of his prowess in the lists of love. The night passed for me almost without sleep. I was restless, excited and uneasy.

The following morning we had arranged a dinner party. It was a hunting reunion. Only gentlemen were invited. I retired early, left the men enjoying themselves over their wine and cigars. I had been the only lady present. No doubt my absence was the signal for the real revelry to commence. I retired to my chamber, pleading fatigue to my maid, and having dismissed her, locked myself in for the night.

My bedroom was on the ground floor. Three long windows opened upon a wide veranda. One had only to step out to enjoy the scent of the roses and jasmine. My object in doing so on this occasion was different. Just as the clock struck nine I stood outside on the tesselated pavement. Someone was crouching in the shadow of the wall. A whispered word, a cautious footfall on the lawn, and I was beside Mrs. Hodge. I wrapped my long cloak around me closely. I drew the hood over my head and silently followed her across the dark lawn through the shrubbery and along the path under the double row of elms which bordered the avenue. Not a soul stirred there after dark, save only coming or departing guests. We kept together in the deep shade of the spreading foliage. We reached the lodge in silence. I followed my conductress through the portal. She shut and barred the gate and door.

A dim light was shed by a small lamp upon the table. Mrs. Hodge took me by the hand. She led me forward. We passed into the room on the right. I stood beside the bed. All had been arranged. I slipped off my cloak and my skirts. I stood in my light chemise.

I had anticipated the adventure with eagerness. Every detail had been planned with scrupulous precision. My feelings were intensely excited. A restless longing for the embrace of a strong man had troubled my thoughts all day. I had been aroused by the faint efforts to which I had submitted on the previous night. I determined to surrender myself without reserve, at least on this occasion.

The stake was immense, the game was well worth playing. No gambler ever felt more enthusiasm as he staked his pile upon a single chance. I had brought all my wits to bear. There is an enormous power for good or bad in a strong will and I devoted mine with all my naturally strong energy to this object. The second title had long lain dormant. There were three sisters, all secretly plotting, jealous of me from the beginning. The dissolute cousin, to whom the usurers were becoming more accommodating as time rolled on, brought no news to lessen his pretensions to the succession. Lastly, and by no means least, there was my natural womanly pride, the instinct of maternity unsatisfied, and the galling feeling that I would be eventually supplanted in the enjoyment of the property for which I had risked so much.

Mrs. Hodge put her fingers to her lips. She held the bedclothes open. I slipped backwards into the feather bed. Two strong arms entwined themselves around my slender waist. They drew me down into contact with a man's hirsute body. I felt alarmed in spite of my resolution.

"Oh, Mrs. Hodge! Pray do not leave me—oh, pray!"

"Hush . . . hush! Be silent . . . he's a lamb compared to what he is sometimes."

I noticed the change in her intonation—the respectful distance, the conventional mode of address were gone. This also was a part of the comedy.

A rush of hot desire passed through my nervous system as I felt the warmth and solidity of the man who held me. That it was a *man*, there was not the slightest doubt. My back, my buttocks, rested against his belly and thighs. Already his parts protruded viciously. His instrument began to insert itself between my thighs. I interposed my hand.

Mrs. Hodge was still beside the bed. I could just see her outline in the darkened room. She held my left hand. My right encountered a monstrous limb. My hand mechanically closed upon this object. It responded to my exciting caress. I felt a bush of curly hair and a muscular pair of thighs. I remained thus for a few minutes. Not a sound was heard. Then the right arm which had held me was softly removed. A large hand inspected my charms. My bosom, my belly, my mount, and lastly the central spot of a man's desires. If my assailant's passion had been already aroused, my own responded to it. A sudden movement served to turn me on my back. At the same movement Mrs. Hodge assisted by a rapid jerk of my left arm. I raised myself in a half-real, half-feigned effort of modesty. Immediately my bedfellow was upon me. In dragging me towards him my nightdress had been turned up. My body lay naked to his attack. He was not slow to take advantage of the position. The fortress lay open. He had to march through the portals.

"Oh, Mrs. Hodge! I . . . do not let him . . . oh, pray . . . oh!"

There was no response from the good woman who had not released my hand. Instantly I was helplessly extended beneath the weight of a man's naked body.

Under such circumstances a woman never complains of the inconvenient pressure. It is true that the elbows of the operator take on themselves a certain part of the load. For all that the position appears to be a normal one. It is certainly the best—the one particularly adapted for the exchange of enjoyment, for those emotions which accompany the act of copulation; those tender emanations of passions stimulated and excited to an almost insupportable pitch; those outbursts of intense ecstasy which are wrung from the yielding female form vibrating beneath the efforts of a vigorous male.

I had seen Jock on several occasions when visiting the lodge. Usually he made himself scarce by slipping shyly away by the back door. I had rarely, however, exchanged more that a simple salutation with him. He struck me as a particularly fine young man whose face displayed more intellectuality than fell to the lot of the rustics around. His wife took pleasure in repeating her commendation of his intelligence, his industry, and his constant endeavors to instruct himself in the principles and practice of agriculture.

He thus became an object of interest to me, especially after the extraordinary invitation the simple woman had extended to me. In short, I had made my observations. I had matured my decision.

If ever I was in a favorable condition after a forced abstinence to fulfill the requirements of perfected copulation, to relish the joys and participate in the animal pleasure of the act, it was now. My feelings were worked to a frenzy. I remember little of the scene that followed. I received the huge organ of virile manhood with gasping sighs and little cries of mingled pain and pleasure. My assailant lost no time. His arms were around my light body; his own was in determined conjunction with my own. He seemed anxious to incorporate himself with me. He worked with vigor. He did not spare me. He seemed incapable of controlling his emotions.

Mrs. Hodge remained beside me. A few whispered words of encouragement came from her parted lips as the significant sounds and movements progressed beneath her. Then there came a time when I held my breath, when the long pent up forces of nature seemed about to give away. Suddenly I knew the climax had been reached, the end attained. I received a copious outpouring of the prolific balm. Then my companion lay still as death, save for the fluttering of his breath upon my cheek.

I discreetly draw the veil over the remainder of that night's pleasure. It was already late when, guided by my conductress, I again found myself within the precincts of my own chamber. I awoke in the broad sunlight to a new sensation, to a new hope.

*   *   *

"My sweet Eveline is looking all the better for her stay in the delicious air of Cumberland. I quite envy you that lovely little paradise you have there."

"Indeed, Papa, I feel much stronger. It is the air, as you say, which has done me so much good. I have, I am sure, derived much benefit from my visit there. Endover has gone to his moors again."

"You have not forgotten your promise, my dear child? We were to repeat our experiences of the peephole. Will you join me there this afternoon? I have arranged something for your gratification."

"Do tell me what the nature of it is, dear Papa!"

"Well, it is rather a peculiar affair in which the actors will have no knowledge of the presence of witnesses whatsoever."

"And we are to be the witnesses?"

"Yes, my dear, there are two convenient apertures through which we can enjoy together the interview which will take place. I have reason to believe it will be of exceptional interest to us."

"You quite raise my curiosity, dear Papa."

"I must first say that it is no ordinary thing at all. It appears that a certain gentleman, whose name and personality are both unknown to me, takes a young girl to this place. I am told by my informant who conducts this very private establishment that she is very young, in fact, a mere child, although a very charming and beautiful one. It appears that the gentleman is suspected of a close connection with this pretty child. We shall probably know by and by. Anyhow, it is not the business of my informant to trouble himself about such matters. She is discretion itself."

He well knew my perversion. My passion was all in accord with his own. It was evidently his desire to play upon it, to afford another practical example of the amiable weakness so lightly recorded by Voltaire in the case of the great Charlemagne.

"Do you mean to say, dear Papa, that the gentleman is a near relation? That it is—in fact—a case of incest?"

"I believe it is. Yes, we must certainly see that."

"You charming, darling Papa! How our views agree! How closely our tastes and passions coincide. Yes, we must certainly see that."

"Listen, my child, while I tell you more of this subject which engrosses us. The crime, if crime it be, is as old as humanity. At least as old as the Biblical account of it. Did not the children of Adam and Eve, brother and sister, copulate and procreate? The Bible is full of instances of this original and entrancing weakness. Not to quote the example of Lot, the brother-in-law of Abraham, whose two young daughters, for want of male, as the version goes, but in reality from strong lasciviousness, played with the paternal sugar-stick and made their father jolly with fermented juice of the grape. Then they excited him to such an extent that the vigorous parent laid them both, and all three united in an orgy of lust."

CHAPTER 7

That same afternoon, Papa and I duly ensconced ourselves in the snug little closet on the left of the narrow passage which led to the chamber I already knew.

We had not long to wait. Our door was bolted and the apertures uncorked. We had found that each commanded a more complete view of the bedroom. Our heads were not six inches apart. We had chairs on which to sit, with soft cushions on them. I noticed that the legs of these chairs were covered with India-rubber pads, so that no sound would be audible if they were moved. They were like the caps for sticks on crutches. A soft carpet covered the floor and a padded rest was fixed above each peephole on which to rest the forehead.

Everything was luxuriously complete. Presently I heard the sound of footsteps in the corridor. The door of the bedroom opened. A voice in gentle accents murmured:

"This way please."

The door was closed again after the ingress of the two individuals. Then there was silence, except for the gentle breathing of Papa behind me.

The first who came under my view was a short thick-set man of some five and 40 years. His hair was already turning gray; his closely cut beard and heavy moustache were the same grizzly shade. His features struck me as being ordinary without vulgarity, and he possessed a look of ardent sensuality which, to my practiced eye, there was no possibility of mistaking.

The second comer interested me more. She was a young girl, a mere child, whose age could not have exceeded 13 or 14 years. Indeed, from the youthful face and unformed bust, she might have been a year younger. She was far from being either full-grown or fully developed. What struck me most, however, was her extreme beauty. She had a skin like alabaster, white and soft. She was fair and plump for a child of her age. Her features were regular and good and bore a close resemblance to those of her companion. I noticed that she was dressed in the usual childish fashion of her age; she had very short skirts and wore socks, so that her calves were without stockings, showing the naked legs above the tops of her perfectly fitting high and delicate little boots.

Having carefully bolted the door, the man threw himself upon the lounge. The girl set herself with the curiosity of a child to examine and take note of the apartment. He watched her every movement as a cat watches those of a mouse. I thought I already detected a flash of obscene desire in his liquid eyes as he rapidly scrutinized every change of position. Then he threw off his waistcoat, opened his inner coat, deposited his watch and chain on the adjoining table, and removed his tie and collar.

"Do you see her boots?"

"What nice legs she has! What is he going to do, I wonder? She's very small and young."

"Yes, and so pretty too. Do you notice the likeness, dear Papa?"

We could distinctly hear every word they said.

"Come here, Lucy."

The child obeyed with an air of indifference which appeared to me to hide a certain amount of fear. The man put her on his knee.

"When did I do it last?"

"It was last Wednesday—a week ago—the day mother went to Liverpool."

"What did I promise you this time if your temper was good?"

"You said you would give me a new photographic album and a whole pound of chocolate fondants."

"What! All that? Well, I suppose I must be as good as my word. Now then, Lucy, let's see if you are going to be a young woman."

"Oh, I wish I was already a grown-up young woman!"

"It will come in time—you are getting on fast."

While this edifying conversation was progressing the man had let the girl slip from his knee. She stood between his legs. His left arm encircled her tapered waist. His right played with her ankles, her calves, her knees. Then he advanced his eager hand a little further. Suddenly he bent forward and pressed his lips to hers with a fervent embrace which spoke volumes to us witnesses. He sucked her long and ardently at the lips, with the lustful avidity of a satyr.

"Who told you about kissing, Lucy?"

"That girl at school. She said men knew best how to kiss."

"She was right, my dear child. What else did she say?"

"Oh, I don't know, but she said men like to feel girls about . . . well, you know . . . under their clothes."

"Yes, I think she was right, dear girl. So they do!"

Suiting the action to the words he slipped his hand further up between her thighs. His eyes glowed.

"Oh, there it is! What a nice little slit it is!"

"Oh Father, don't! That hurts!"

We looked at one another for a moment. The secret was out.

"Give me your hand, Lucy. What did you say you might call it?"

"I remember—you said it was a prick."

The man had loosened his clothes.

"What did the girl at school call it?"

"She said some other name. I think she said it was a 'diddle.' It was then she pointed to the statue of Mercury on the staircase. But it was not at all like yours. It was very small and hung down. Yours is always upright, Father, and so big!"

He threw aside his shirt. He exposed his naked member with the child's little hand in contact.

"Isn't that nice, Lucy? Oh, so nice? We are all right and quite alone here. You have only to be quiet and play with my prick."

"Yes, I know. Now Mother's at Liverpool we'll not be found out. Oh, my! If I was! How she would beat me! But . . . you won't forget the album will you Father? I'm promised several photos to put in it already."

"No, my darling, certainly not. But come take off your clothes. I want to see you naked. I want to see all your pretty things."

"Oh, Father, must I take them all off?"

As the pretty child stripped I feasted my eyes on the very lascivious exhibition. She was as fair as one of Watteau's beauties and far more comely. A lovely little Venus, with limbs like the most delicate ivory. The man sat at his ease, contemplating the process of disentanglement from the manifold tapes and laces which hindered the operation. His member was exposed in its erected state beneath our full gaze. He had evidently no shame but on the contrary showed rather a Satanic delight in all the indecency he perpetrated.

"Ah, that's right. Now come here, Lucy. What a delicious little slit! Let me feel it. How soft and warm it is! How my finger slips in between the pretty lips! You must never let the boys touch it. You must always keep it for me."

"Mother says that someday I will have hair on it."

"Yes, I dare say. Unless you let me take care of it for you."

The child went down on her knees. She clasped the man's member, a large and long one, with both hands and imprinted a fervent kiss on the livid gland. He pushed forward towards her.

"Now, suck it a little, Lucy. Think of the chocolate."

The young girl opened her lips. The man pushed forward. The big head entered Lucy's mouth. She sucked to order.

"Oh, that is nice! That's delicious . . . stop now! I must suck your little slit. Put your feet on the sofa. Bend over my head . . . so!"

The satyr held the delicate child close to him. He parted the rosy lips of her peachlike slit with his fingers, then he applied his eager face, covering her belly and mound with humid kisses.

"Oh, how stiff you are, dear Papa! This erotic scene is too much for you. Pray keep calm."

The child was on the bed. The man was kneeling over her naked form.

"You won't hurt me again like the last time, will you, Papa?"

"Of course not, Lucy. Only hold still, put your pretty legs apart. Now raise your knees up so. I must lie down on your soft little belly and feel how warm it is."

"Oh, but you are pushing it into me. It's . . . it's . . . oh, my! It's too big! It hurts!"

"Be quiet, I say, you young she-devil. You were not making all that noise when I caught you with young Symes."

"Oh, no, but his thing was not as near so big as yours, and he was very gentle."

"Well, if he could have you, so can I. Lie still, I say! It's going in now . . . there! It's half in already. How tight you are, Lucy . . . you young harlot. I'll tell your mother if you cry out. Lie still, I tell you! There, there, now you've got it."

The man began to move up and down. Lucy took a big mouthful of the bedclothes and half shut her pretty eyes.

"Oh, Father, you hurt!"

"Nonsense, Lucy, you must have it all. I'm too stiff to stop now. Hold up! Let me put my hands around your bottom."

The child groaned. The lascivious satyr commenced to move up and down with a regular cadence. It was easy to see that he was in absolute possession. From our hiding place we could see his weapon moving in and out between the girl's plump thighs. I began senselessly working Papa's limb in my warm hand as we looked on. The man stopped occassionally as if to prolong and linger over his pleasure. The girl lay utterly passive, her hands convulsively clutching the sheet as if to fortify her to bear the process of disapportionate coitus with less suffering. Suddenly her father took himself to his libidinous operation with more application. A few rapid strokes—thrusting, straining movement with his little victim, and it was easy to see that his climax was at hand. It came. He fell with a gasping cry upon Lucy's little form and lay bereft of all motion, save for the heavy breathing with which he accompanied the overflow of nature.

"He has done! He has discharged right into her little belly!"

My hand grasped the erected staff—it pushed itself forward. I worked quickly—decisively. A plentiful stream of hot sperm gushed over my tightly fitting gloves. Papa sighed with pleasure and his head reclined on my shoulder. He had succumbed to the pleasure of the scene.

The voices of the strange couple in the bedroom at length aroused us both.

"I want to know what else that girl at the school told you, Lucy. Didn't she say she had two brothers? Now don't hide anything from me, my girl. You know I'll not tell your mother and you had better tell me about it."

"Well, so I will, Father, if you won't be cross. Amy says she has two brothers, both older than she is, and that they taught her all she knows about . . . diddles . . . and things."

"I suppose they had nice little games between all three."

"Yes, but not at first. It was her younger brother, Fred, who began it, she says. He got her into the woodshed behind the house. They live in the country, you know, and there he pulled up her clothes and made her let him put his finger into her slit. Then he showed her his thing and she found that it got big and stiff when she touched it. After a time the elder brother found them out and wanted to play at it too."

"Well, Lucy, and then, I suppose they began in earnest."

"Yes, they did. The elder brother had a much larger doodle than Fred. He was 17. One day he got Amy in a quiet corner of the garden and I do believe he would have pushed it into her pussy but it started to rain and while they were sheltering in the greenhouse the gardener caught them. Amy says she is sure he saw what they were doing. Alexander was the name of her big brother and he ran away, but the gardener stayed. He explained to her why Alex should not push his diddle into her slit. He said she had an egg like all very young girls and that she ought to have that egg broken. Then she would be quite a woman and be able to play with the boys and even with the men. She was very much pleased for having him explain all about it to her. She told him she was very grateful to him, so that when he offered to break the egg for her, she thought it was kind of him. She told me that the gardener locked the door of the greenhouse and put her on some hay in a wheelbarrow. Then he let down his trousers and showed her his diddle . . ."

"You mean his prick, don't you, Lucy?"

"Yes, it must have been his prick—like yours. Well, he let it out for her to look at, she says. Oh, such a whopper! And all red on the top. He took her in his arms and pulled up her clothes. Then he pushed his diddle—I mean his prick—up between her thighs and right into her little slit. Amy says he was not long doing it, but that it hurt dreadfully, she is sure that he broke the egg because she

134

felt the yolk all running down her legs when he had done."

During this very edifying history, Papa and I had found it very difficult to restrain our laughter. We were quite relieved when the tender parent began once more to tumble and caress the child.

Her naive and innocent story had evidently had its effect, for his limb stood wickedly up in front of him as he pulled the girl from the bed. He was especially attracted by the rosy little buttocks. Bending her face downwards on the side of the bed, he pressed himself against her back. We saw his rampant member protruding beneath her soft little belly. Slowly and carefully he conducted his outrageous assault, till at last he contrived to sheath the greater part of the instrument in her vagina. Regardless then of the child's complaints, he pushed in until the spasmodic vibrations told that his climax was attained. Whether he had broken an egg or not, we had no means of ascertaining. Certain it was, however, that poor Lucy's legs were covered with something which might have passed for a very pale yolk.

CHAPTER 8

Lord Endover was always on his moor in the North. I was again at Chitterlings. It is true the fine air had done me good, but my residence had not been productive of unmixed advantages.

On the contrary, I suffered from a nausea for which I could only account in one way. The maids in the laundry, I thought, eyed me as I passed. I even caught two of them exchanging remarks about what evidently concerned myself. The old housekeeper took an unusual interest in my movements, I thought she looked upon me with a more patronizing air than ever. What did it all mean? True, there was an irregularity on my part—a certain period had passed—I knew there was an overlong extension of that interval which marked the inheritance of Mother Eve. I admit I was frightened as doubt became certainty, so that one morning I sat down at my writing table and penned these lines to the Earl:

"You have so often and so pointedly asked for news—news which might very naturally be joyful to us both, and I have so often disappointed you, that I tremble and hesitate on the present occasion lest I may raise hopes only to have the mortifying need to dispel them in a future letter. It will, I know, be a source of keen satisfaction to you, my dear husband, to hear that I have the strongest possible reasons for believing that your wishes are likely to be gratified. That in fact I am in a condition at length to become a mother. So you see, gallant man that you are, you are a dangerous bedfellow. How shall I forgive you for the mischief you have wrought?"

My letter brought a prompt reply. The Earl returned. The local medical man was consulted. It was soon an open secret that the Countess of Endover was likely—after all—to provide her husband with an heir, or at least an heiress. At first the news was only whispered through the house. It spread through the domain. It reached the country town. At last it fell with a crash upon the expectant cousin and the three sisters of the Earl. They fairly groaned with vexation. They fell upon one another. At length they all three turned on the unhappy cousin.

What might have happened, I don't know, but fortunately a paragraph in the *Society Peeps* made the matter no longer a source of private inquiry. The necessity for the exercise of dignity they really did not possess obliged them to show a bold front. They received the sarcastic congratulations of the crowd with calm. If they inwardly raged at the disappointment, they were too well-bred to let it appear.

The only one who could not be persuaded to open her lips to the outside public or to show any particular interest in the coming event was Mrs. Hodge, but she returned the warm pressure of my hand with a satisfied shake of the head, accompanied by an expression of stolid conviction which was irresistibly comic, as she whispered softly:

"I knowed it, I did! Your Ladyship did right to try my Jock!"

*   *   *

"Ah, my lady, I am so very glad to see you! You do me too much honor. And your excellent Papa, Lord L——, also! Well! so you have come to hear all the interesting facts— all the truths, I fear—between ourselves. A fair, or unfair proportion of lies also, at Bow Street. You will both stay and take a chop with me when the Court rises—a loin chop, of course! Not a chump chop! Ah, you are both so good—how jolly! So glad to see you! Here, Williams, go off to Mrs. W—— at once and get six best loin chops. What! not eat two! Well, to be sure, but your unexpected visit has given me quite an appetite!"

"Really, Sir Langham, it really refreshes one to see you so sprightly and gay—it does one's heart good!"

"Ah, my dear young lady, you are too kind! Pardon me, Lady Endover. I don't think there is much crime on the list today. Some of the ordinary kind: a wife pounded to death. Then there's a sad case, a young fellow charged with forgery. Then let me see—oh, ah—that won't do for you. It's a nasty case but it won't take two of bigamy. Ah, Lady Endover, if they were long. My clerk tells me the evidence is very strong and I think the culprit will plead guilty. You must not be in Court while that one is in hearing. I'll tell them to put it first on the list. It's a way I have at times to disappoint that objectionable class of fashionables who come down here to listen to just such outrages as this."

Sir Langham Beamer drew Papa aside a little, putting a fat finger into a buttonhole of his coat. Then he whispered hoarsely—so hoarsely that I could hear what he said plainly.

"Case of indecent exposure; fellow has been at it for months. His plan was to stand at the entrance to a yard in a quiet street and then when a chance offered he lugged out his . . . hum . . . you know, and wagged it at any likely woman who passed."

"Did he really! How dreadful!"

"Oh, we have a lot of that kind here. Why only last week I had a really serious case before me and sent it to trial. It was a woman who strapped an unfortunate fellow down and then deliberately amputated his . . . well . . . his, you know—*the whole bag of tricks*! The man died, so there was no difficulty in the case, which went to the Assizes as murder."

"I remember that case. The wretched woman gets 20 years penal servitude."

"The Court is open now and the chief clerk

is hearing the night charges. They will not interest you much. There is a case, Lady Endover, I want to dispose of and then you shall both come and sit with me."

Just then the door of the magistrate's private room was opened. A buzz of voices sounded across the corridor. A police sergeant was whispering to the dear old man and Sir Langham took himself away with a courtly apology for his absence.

A short ten minutes passed. Then we were summoned to take our seats. Just as we passed into the Police Court a man was leaving the dock. A warder held the iron gate open for him to pass down the steps which led to the cells below. He stared vacantly into my face. All power of recognition has passed out of that besotted gaze. As I looked, my mind went back to the timber yard and the man in the cloak. It was undoubtedly he.

"A very bad case. He's one of those fellows who are old stagers at the game. He pleaded guilty and got six months—lucky for him! He'd have had two years more if he'd been sent to the Assizes."

It was the police sergeant. He spoke to Lord L——. While we were still in the throng another voice whispered close to my ear:

"From all the rowdy cousins, scheming hags and wicked spinsters, good Lord deliver us!"

Almost before I could rejoin an "Amen" the voice continued but in a tone utterly different in its respectful intonation from the strong nasal drawl in which this invocation had been whispered:

"You have saved that man 18 months of imprisonment."

"How so? What can I have to do with it?"

I turned. It was a tall man in a baker's fustian suit. I knew the voice, the figure. It was Dragoon.

"Just this. The chief clerk advised the solicitor, the solicitor advised his client. He pleaded guilty to save the time of the Court. He enabled the magistrate to convict him instead of sending him for trial. He would certainly have had the two year sentence as a previous offender at the Old Bailey. What brings Your Ladyship here?"

"If you will be at B—— Street today at six o'clock I will tell you. I want you to execute a confidential mission for me—for the benefit of another."

"Your Ladyship honors me too much. Always at your service."

*   *   *

I must not allow myself to forget that these notes are written for my own perusal and reference. No one else will ever read them except him I have designated as the custodian. They contain no more than rudimentary sketches of my intimacy with many of the actors herein. I care nothing for any critic; indeed no such a one will ever have access to opinion of the public, who know me only as what I am not.

My time came at last. All that wealth can do to minimize the agony of maternity I had in abundance. My child was born during the night. Next morning, Endover was ringing with the news that there was at last a male heir to the Earldom, interests and estates. Little Lord Chucklington (the second title had been lying dormant), lay crowing and kicking in the nurse's lap. How I took him to my bosom, how I flouted all idea of a substitute for his own mother's breast, how he thrived and waxed a big and healthy boy—all these things are matters of history now. The Earl of Endover was enraptured. I was an angel. Little Lord Chucklington was a "cupid" and the experienced nurse nearly drove my husband off his head with joy when she reminded him that his infant lordship was "the very spit of himself."

Everyone followed suit and congratulations poured in. The village was illuminated that night. Bands played, drums banged and trumpets rang out as the revelers dispersed in the small hours, sending the faint echoes of their joy on the wings of the wind to my delighted ears in the distant castle.

Eveline had arrived at the zenith of her ambition, but at what a sacrifice! My figure, that fresh, youthful beauty which drove men mad with desire to revel in it, was gone forever. As time went on, I discovered other changes; a transformation which only dawned on me by slow degrees. What may have been a cause will always remain a mystery. It is a fact, however, that all sexual instinct, all desire, had departed from me forever. Possibly some derangement of the nervous tissue had taken place in parturition. It must remain a matter for speculation and conjecture. I never disclosed the fact to anyone. From that time forward I devoted my life to my beautiful boy.

I have yet a few notes to jot down.

"Dragoon" has always been my true and trusted friend.

Mr. Josiah and Mrs. Hodge have emigrated to Canada. They possess a huge farm on the Western prairies. They are rich in the possession of five sons, the elder of which is the mainstay of his father and mother in their agricultural work. Mr. Hodge is reportedly wealthy and all they touch is said to turn into money. Once a year a letter comes, always in the constrained, illiterate handwriting of bony Mrs. Hodge, dutifully assuring me of their happiness. This is as regularly followed by the advent of certain hams and cheese with which my husband is regaled.

A certain tall and fair-haired young medical practitioner one day received a letter informing him that if he chose to make application for a valuable appointment under the Charity Commissioners he was *more than likely* to obtain it. He did so—and succeeded. A second stroke of good luck fell in his way. Another and more desirable appointment soon followed. His keen and corrective powers of diagnosis were soon known and appreciated. His able treatment of his patients brought him renown.

Dr. Brookstead-Hoare did not live to obtain the baronetcy he coveted. His death left a vacancy in the ranks of those members of his profession who as specialists devote their talents to the treatment of women and children. The opening was immediately taken advantage of by the fair-haired aspirant, Dr. A——. He

143

had found time and worked for his M.D. in London and was informed in a certain mysterious manner that the lease of Dr. Brookstead-Hoare's house could be had by him for the asking at a merely nominal cost. He took the hint, also the lease. The aged Duchess of M—— sent for him one day. On the broad flight of stairs which led from the entrance hall, Dr. A——, as he descended, heard a visitor announced.

"The Countess of Endover. Will your Ladyship pass this way, please?"

A moment later a lady passed him going up. In her hand was that of a little boy, bright as an angel, a great favorite with Her Grace. For a second the lady's glance and that of the physician met. A civil inclination of the head and she had gone. The doctor staggered against the wall. He seized the silken cord of the balustrade—or he would have fallen. That which he divined when he reached his new home in the fashionable West had opened his eyes. He knew now, as he buried his honest, kindly face in the cushioned chair, and allowed full vent to his tears of thankfulness and gratitude, who his benefactress had been, and that the world was not all quite one of lust and selfishness.

THE END

Venus Remembered

CHAPTER ONE

If Madame Benoit shrugged her shoulders with a knowing look when the purity and austerity of my manner of living was discussed, she had good cause for it.

Madame Benoit was an old friend, a friend of my childhood. About twenty-four years ago she married a tax collector in the little town of N—, where I made the acquaintance of the gentleman whom I called Monsieur Benoit at first, and who simply became Benoit to me afterwards.

My dear friend had the weakness to confide everything to his wife, even to his old love scrapes, which were familiar to her, and that is why Madame Benoit shrugged her shoulders when my wonderful qualities were enumerated.

Benoit had died some years previously and being somewhat lonely in my bachelor quarters, I took an apartment near my late friend's widow.

There was a good deal of whispering to be sure, but Madame Benoit was forty-two years old and I was forty-eight. The fire of youth was probably soon to be extinguished for my neighbor but as for myself, the older I got, the younger I felt.

My time was spent in dressing, eating, and visiting. I rose late. However, if I was in bed even five minutes before eleven A.M. I was up at eleven sharp. It was my rule at five minutes past eleven every day to be in my bath, as I usually took a cold bath in winter as well as in summer.

Fifteen minutes after eleven, I jumped out of the water to be rubbed down by my faithful

Jean. This operation lasted ten minutes. Then, warmly enveloped, I gave myself up to the delightful operation of touching up my beard with a dye brush and as I was almost bald, the work was not arduous.

My lady friends only saw me at night when I lit up to great advantage, adding to this that when I was not under the scrutinizing eye of Madame Benoit I was very lively, even adventurous, as you will see when you read on.

At noon my toilet was completed and as the clock struck twelve I might have been seen every day rapping at the widow's door.

I generally found one or two callers, not too old, however, to have deserted the ranks of the armchair maids and widows, still on the qui vivre for a husband.

I would chat for a quarter of an hour, and Madame Benoit would give one of her shrugs when fat Mademoiselle Rosalinde would say between two languishing glances: "Ah, how well does Monsieur Dormeiul carry his forty years. It is the effect of regular habits; a well spent existence will bear its fruit."

Naturally I would stammer some polite answer but when Madame shook her head with an 'Ough!' I slipped out of the room. How, I could not say. Far from being timid, heavens knows, I cannot yet understand the terror which seized me when I was in the presence of my terrible neighbor and her friend.

I always took my first meal of the day on the corner of the Rue Montmartre where I read the morning papers. This took one hour and a half altogether.

About two o'clock I strolled along the boulevards and there, in a little shop, I sought my

sweet scented correspondence. Mademoiselle
Hortense, who kept the little shop, was an old
acquaintance of mine.

Ah, Hortense was a queer girl! If just for
fun, you had a fancy to stoop down near her,
and while her handsome dark eyes gazed fix-
edly into yours, you slipped your hand dexterously under her petticoats, you would find a
firm and well shaped leg in a nicely gartered
stocking. Following the stocking, which led you
far, you would have found the contour of a
thigh still half covered by the stocking, but as
to the other half—oh! you ask me the feeling
one has on such occasions? Oh, nothing, but
the devilish sensation which always seizes me
when I come in contact with the warm, soft
palpitating flesh of a woman!

And Mademoiselle Hortense's flesh was so
soft in its firmness! You proceeded to pass your
hand gently around her thigh, when all at once
to your surprise, you could get no further. It
was merely her other fat thigh which pressed
closely against this one. And there between, a
little upwards, was one of nature's marvels,
with a tuft of curly hair hidden away in the
midst of the soft silky bush you would find it
a little more moist than it had been a moment
before.

I touch the slit with my finger and Mademoiselle Hortense's looks grow more and more
sensuous. My finger moved gently upward and
inward, when she would open her thighs widely . . .

My trousers become uncomfortable. Mademoiselle throws one arm about my neck and
presses tighter and still tighter as my finger
moves faster and faster. I feel it slip all the way

up the passage, which is in an amorous blaze. It becomes wet!

What is going to happen? Why nothing, it is all over. Mademoiselle Hortense would straighten up all at once and tap on my hand for form's sake. Her look was no longer intense. Pretty soon boxes would be quickly opened. I used to buy in this way, every fortnight on Thursdays, a pair of gloves. I had at one time many pairs of gloves.

It is time that I should return to my deliciously perfumed correspondence. Some days I found it quite voluminous, other days I had none. The day on which I started these memoirs, I found a tiny note awaiting me.

One Thursday for the reason just given, I remained later than usual at Mademoiselle's. On other days I only took the time to get my letters and exchange polite salutations with her.

Happy possessor of a loving message, I left the shop and walked with a quick step as far as the Rue Coq-Herron where I had a small room.

There, lying back in an easy chair, I could, without fear of interruption, devote myself entirely to the charms of a somewhat hazardous literature inspired by a little god called Cupid by some, but whom others insist upon calling Mammon.

Although each day seemed to repeat itself, yet it was always new to us and it was with the same trembling hand that I tore open the delicate envelope, and always with the same kind of emotion that I plunged into the perusal of a dear, capricious letter. I enjoyed at that time a pleasure that no doubt many persons would fail to understand. I unfolded the letter which read thus:

My dear Friend,

I will need you this evening at the Hotel X—. Do not forget your promise of the day before yesterday, or I will pull out—you know . . .

Truly yours,

PAULINE.

Pauline was a handsome girl but I could not obtain anything from her but correspondence for a long time. I accepted writing to her with the hope that I would gain my point some day, but in vain. You will see later on how I succeeded.

Although it was too early to keep my appointment with Pauline, nevertheless I directed my steps in the direction of the Hotel X— simply because it was my regular hour. When the sweet little maid opened the door, she said mockingly, as she looked at the clock: "I could have guessed it was you!"

The roguish remark was worth the five francs I placed in her hand as I familiarly walked into the little parlor, whose open doors seemed to tender me a pressing invitation. And then I heard the melodious voice of a siren: "Julie!" said the voice, "if Monsieur Lorille comes, bring him in at once."

Julie had no time to answer, as I was already in the room. A splendid blonde was half sitting, half lying on a sofa. I remained standing before her with bowed head. I have always been gallant and I was humbly awaiting when a peal of laughter caused me to start.

"I have not called for a mirror, you are mistaken!"

The little woman was indulging in a hearty laugh at the expense of my bald head. A novice would have been confused, but I answered:

"What, Madame, such charming beauty as yourself, could not do better than admire her own image, she would then imagine that all around her was beautiful."

"Upon my word, Monsieur."

"Monsieur Dormeuil, at your service."

"Monsieur Dormeuil," continued the blonde, "you must forgive me. I like to laugh but I am not the worse for it. Be seated."

Before the charming creature could finish her sentence I was by her side.

"Never having had the happiness to meet you before, Madame, would it be an indiscretion on my part to ask your name?"

"Yes, sir, at least until I know you better."

"To know you better, Madame, is my dearest wish."

"Monsieur Dormeuil," answered the blonde, "men are ungrateful wretches. There is M. Lorille for instance, for whom I have sacrificed so much, but who does not even come as he promised to."

"Adorable blonde, just make half of that same sacrifice for me and . . ."

"What would you have then? I find you rather—what would you call it?" said the little woman impatiently.

"Call it ambitious, that is all!" I replied.

She gave me a look that sent a thrill through my flesh.

By degrees I got nearer to my charmer, I admired her earrings and found her dress in good taste; I wanted to see her shoes, but she refused. However, a well-turned compliment on her dimpled cheeks gained me a smile, which made me notice her beautiful teeth. I tried to kiss my way to them but unsuccessfully.

"Ah, what a beautiful little hand, let me kiss it!" and I obtained permission to do so. Her arm was not withdrawn when I covered it with burning kisses. Little by little, the pretty blonde laughed oftener and easier. Her eyes lighted up; very soon I could see her foot and her ankle —afterwards I was allowed to kiss her cheek. Shyly, I tried to put my lips on her mouth but without success. Finally, on trying again, I not only had a kiss but it was returned.

Liberties now fast succeeded to more serious liberties. I unfastened her waist and feverishly pulled at the fine linen which covered the most beautiful breasts that I had ever seen. My lips wandered from one to the other, and when I had taken off the corset, I seized successively between my teeth, the two little nipples, pink as strawberries.

How good it was to feel those tiny points in my mouth. I leaned over to snatch up the skirts and she offered no resistance. I opened her drawers. Heavens, what beautiful curly hair, and just enough too.

Suddenly I found a little hand trying to find its way into my trousers and with astonishing dexterity my instrument was drawn out, the use of which she seemed so thoroughly to understand in all its details. She gently pulled, and lowered its cap . . .

"I beg of you my dear, stop! Do stop, or I

will spend!" I cried as I felt the intense excitement getting the better of me.

"Make haste then and get at my little pet!" she replied, as she pressed my pizzle into the opening of her fragrant bower.

Ah, what a sensation, it was little tight but how good and soft. I passed my hands under her bottom, voluptuous to the touch, as it rose and fell in my grasp.

Her mouth clung to mine; my tongue caught hers and found it. My little blonde heaved and fluttered and quivered; her tongue pressed harder against mine. Her beautiful breasts, of which I did not lose sight for a moment, palpitated convulsively.

"Oh, go on, it is coming! Not so fast! Faster! Now kiss me—wait—now, there. How good it is! All the way in—all the way in—oh—oh—oh!"

She lifted her bottom, her mouth was glued to mine, the little beauty's body and mine were made but one . . . Then one long shudder with a sharp movement of her buttocks, saying . . . "I am coming . . . go on! quick! Oh, heavens," and she spent. Finally she fell into a spasm of voluptuous rapture. She was beautiful as she lay in her amorous disorder; her hair slightly disarranged, her skirts well raised, showing the wonderful whiteness of her skin.

She remained in this position a moment longer, then rising, she moved towards the door with an unsteady step, unbolted it and passed out of the room without once turning around.

She was probably going to repair the disorder of her toilet and I did the same on my side.

The hall clock struck five when the young

woman re-entered the room, sat down in a chair opposite me and looked calmly at me. After a short silence, I said:

"Mademoiselle, or Madame, sit a little nearer and forgive my silence. I am still under the spell your charms have thrown over me."

As she approached, I took her hand and drew her down onto my lap.

"Have you any family, Monsieur Dormeuil?" she finally asked.

I shook my head. "No," I said, surprised at her question.

"I see—you are a horrid old bachelor!" she said with a pout. I bowed, a little flattered.

"Not too old though," she soon added smilingly, "or you might have come off worse than you did. You love to spend your nights in debaucheries, I suppose, like Monsieur Lorille. I must introduce you to that gentleman, he is a dear friend of mine and has related some of his adventures to me.

"He has had many and knows many more, but the one which follows is one of his most entertaining."

"Not far from the Varennes, on the banks of the Aire," she began in a dreamy way, "stands a convent, in a little valley nestling among the mountains.

"The good nuns there spend their lives in prayer and in sewing for the orphans of the village. Their number, when the convent is full, is about forty. The little church, situated in the middle of the village, counts among its flock the inhabitants of the country for ten miles round and includes the convent in question.

"The officiating priest being old and feeble, was assisted by a young Abbé who had arrived only a few days previous to the opening of this story. The young Abbé was of such modest demeanor, that even the oldest bigots of the parish took him for a saint in swaddling clothes.

"The young girls all remarked that he was undeniably handsome and when they went to the confessional, each one went early to be sure to get a chance to confess during the day.

"The old curate was not sorry to be relieved of his arduous work and it was only right that the poor man should have some rest. He now only confessed the nuns at the convent every fortnight, when they sent their old coach for him.

"It was always a treat at the convent when the venerable priest visited them. They dined in the great refectory and he seemed to bring with him an odor of out-of-doors, which always touched the hearts of the novices, who sighed every now and then under its influence.

"One day, however, the old vehicle brought the young Abbé to the convent. The old curate was ill and had sent his excuses to the Lady Superior. The latter received the young man in the parlor on the ground floor and was quite charmed with his modest bearing. They conversed at first about the curate, then about the crops, then the church. They had been repairing the chapel of St. Anthony, etc.

"The Lady Superior finally assembled the nuns in order to present them to their new pastor, and one after another they passed before him and curtsied without raising their eyes to his face. Why should they, since he was only to speak words of peace and comfort to them from behind the wooden grating.

"Three novices were the last to enter. One of them had examined the young Abbé through a crack in the door before coming in, and her cheeks became crimson as she curtsied to him.

"After the presentation the Lady Superior made a little speech and then accompanied the Abbé to the chapel, followed by the whole party of nuns.

"The young priest opened the center door and closed it carefully after him a moment later. A slight rustling told his auditors that he was slipping on a white surplice that was hanging inside the door, then came the noise of a stool sliding across the floor, and all was silent.

"The nuns were all present except those occupied with the household duties. They had glided into the chapel more like shadows than like human beings. Two of them knelt in the confessional.

"Presently the sound of a deep voice, followed by soft whisperings was heard. The murmur ceased, then commenced again. Then came a long silence. The arms of the sinner moved restlessly as she pronounced mea culpa. The Lady Superior rose with a bowed head, her arms crossed on her breast, moved towards the little chapel of the Holy Virgin.

"All the nuns in turn came and knelt on either side of the confessional. Finally it was the turn of the youngest novice.

"Trembling with fear and yet impatient to hear the Abbé's voice on the other side of the grating, she knelt down on her little wooden stool. By closing her eyes and stopping her ears she tried to examine her conscience. The image of the Abbé, however, would rise up before her. She waited until the rattle of the little window warned her that he was ready to listen to her, and the confession began!

" 'Your blessing, my father,' etc., etc., until the solemn moment arrived when her most secret thoughts must be unveiled.

" 'My child, have you sinned in thought; have you longed for the world and the pleasures thereof?'

"She gave no answer.

"Then the Abbé whispered low: 'Have you ever had any bad thoughts? Did you ever commit any sinful deeds?'

"Still she could not answer.

" 'Have you listened to the demon tempting you to sensual actions? Speak without fear, my child, God is good and will forgive.'

" 'My father,' stammered the poor little novice, not understanding and yet trying to see the priest who was plying her with these terrible questions.

"She could only distinguish, however, through the grating, two flashing eyes which stirred her very soul with a magnetic influence, which the poor little novice would have been unable to define.

" 'Yes, father!' she replied at last, forced to say something.

" 'Have you sinned in thoughts and deeds, my child. How many times?' he then inquired, his voice trembling slightly. 'Did you commit these sins alone or have you a companion in sin? Speak, my child, to obtain pardon, you must confess all, as you can only obtain peace after a full confession. Have you given yourself up to Satan by day or by night? Be careful not to commit sacrilege. I shall be obliged to refuse you absolution the next time if you do. Meanwhile examine your conscience carefully. Pray for help. Then you can approach the communion table. Pray every night with a contrite heart. Go, my child!'

"With an unsteady step she left the chapel. That night the young nun, Sister Clemence by name, could not sleep. She tossed restlessly on her narrow bed, and could think of nothing but the words the Abbé had spoken.

" 'Sinned in thoughts—yes, often I have longed to leave the convent and enter the beautiful shops in the city. Then there was Mr. Ernest, who used to come to my aunt's house. I have often thought how delightful it would be to ramble through the woods with him alone. But are these bad thoughts—sensual thoughts?' she said.

"She finally closed her eyes and fell asleep and saw Satan! Yes, it was Satan. All at once, however, he assumed the form of the Abbé.

"He took her hand and placed it between her legs. Oh, what a delicious sensation, how delightful. 'Mr. Satan, Mr. Abbé, please, please go on . . . don't stop . . . ah, this is delicious! . . . oh! . . . Mr. Abbé!!'

"Sister Clemence awoke suddenly, trembling like a leaf, weak and tired. She felt numb between her legs. Placing her hand there, she found it was wet . . . poor little novice, she could not understand.

"Daylight appeared at last, but Clemence was unable to rest. She threw back the coverings and raised her long white chemise. She wanted to see, but there was nothing but the little stain of blood which surprised her very much at this particular time of month.

"When the great bell gave the signal for rising, Sister Clemence, usually so quick and lively, crept out of bed with difficulty and dressed herself slowly. She was the last to enter the chapel and kneeling down, joined her hands mechanically for the morning prayer.

"In the refectory she was unable to eat. When the Lady Superior arrived she questioned her. She was a sort of physician but she perceived nothing extraordinary in the symptoms of her subordinate and advised a few days of rest.

"During the eight days that Sister Clemence remained in her cell, she did not seem to improve; on the contrary, she grew worse and worse. She could not sleep and if she happened to fall into a feverish slumber, the same vision pursued her, accompanied by the same temptations. It sometimes happened that even half awake, her hands would seek the mysterious spot, center of such delightful sensations, and unconsciously her fingers lingered there.

"Finally, entirely awake, the same irresistible power drew her fingers to the same place, but then it required a longer time to reach the point of supreme enjoyment.

"At first the novice's thoughts were not fixed upon any particular object. Then she thought of Mr. Ernest, and lastly of the Abbé What a sacrilege!

"If you had seen this little childish hand buried between those white thighs, smooth and firm as marble, her lovely eyes partly closed and those ripe red lips slightly parted, you would have seen her body motionless at first, become slightly agitated, then the legs move further and further apart, the little finger slip in and out of the rosy mouth, until with a deep sigh, she sank back, powerless to move hand or foot.

"Two weeks had elapsed and the Abbé returned to confess the nuns. The Lady Superior called on the invalid and asked her if she wished to confess. She even said that the Abbé had kindly offered to come to her cell as she was not able to rise. How to thank the Abbé for such a favor!

" 'Certainly, Mother, I should like to confess,' dutifully replied Sister Clemence.

"The Lady Superior left the cell and soon returned with the Abbé who entered with that bearing of humility he habitually assumed. He appeared most concerned at the illness of the novice and insisted that a full confession was the best possible remedy.

"Sister Clemence did not dare look at him, she was so confused. The Lady Superior retired, and the Abbé took a chair by the side of the bed.

" 'Have you examined your sinful heart, my

child; are you ready to make a full confession?'

" 'Yes, my father!'

"The confession began. The poor little Sister did not know how to reveal what had happened. The fear, however, of not receiving absolution and communion gave her courage. She disclosed everything.

"The Abbé drew closer and closer, until she felt his breath upon her face. Her eyes were closed.

"Suddenly she felt his lips pressing hers in a long kiss. Unconsciously, a timid little kiss from her lips answered his. Then she felt a warm hand upon her body, which gradually seemed to move downward towards that spot where Satan had placed her finger on a certain night.

"The Abbé took another kiss, his hand passed gently over her thighs and slipping under her bottom, forced her to turn over on her side. Now he slapped her gently and pushed his finger into her slit between the two hills of her bottom, and it finally found its way into what appeared to be his desire to reach.

"But his hand set everything on fire on its way. With the other hand he unbuttoned his robe, undid his trousers and pulled out a prick whose erection was fully justified by the beauties his hand had explored and was still exploring.

"With a sudden pull, to throw off the cover, he laid himself down on the edge of the couch, close to her. Then, pressing her in his arms he covered her lips with kisses and taking her hand, placed it upon his god of love, firm and rigid as a rock.

"The contact caused the novice to open her

eyes. He called her by the most endearing names: 'My love, open your eyes—kiss me. Open your eyes—receive my tongue—give me yours—so! Do you know what you are holding and squeezing so hard, my dear? It is the tree of life that you have so often heard about and desired so ardently without knowing the reason why. Place it where you put your finger sometimes. There! Not so quick! Open your legs . . . one minute . . . there it is!' and the enormous instrument presented its head to the little pussy as she instinctively drew nearer to the Abbé.

"He pushed gently, then raising her chemise, he uncovered her breasts and sucked them, bit them, then returned to her lips and with a shove he pushed his prick into its rightful place as he smothered a scream from the poor little novice. Now they are enlaced in the closest embrace and when his pizzle seemed to come out, she clung to him; when she seemed to recede, he boldly followed her up.

"He came out and went in; the action became accelerated; in her amorous transports she crossed her beautiful legs over his back and wriggled about like a dear little eel.

" 'Go on, darling!'

" 'Not so quick!'

" 'Do you feel as if you were coming?'

" 'Yes—it is coming!'

" 'Quick!—your mouth—your tongue!'

" 'Father—oh, how delightful it is. I am coming—heavens, how big it is once more.'

" 'There!' said the Abbé, panting, as he gave a last shove. His engine disappeared in the tiny opening.

"Sister Clemence held him in a close embrace

and covered his face with grateful kisses for the good he had done her.

"From this day on, the Abbé, who had found means of corresponding with the attractive novice, succeeded in introducing himself into the convent many times and Sister Clemence often found herself amorously wriggling under the vigorous pizzle of the priest.

"She received a thorough education in the Art of Love and soon recovered her health. However, this state of affairs could not last much longer. The Abbé was no more to be made a priest and reside forever in the quiet little village than was Sister Clemence to remain in a convent.

"The old aunt who had brought her up had been an invalid for years and finally died, leaving her a handsome fortune. From that time, the whole convent busied itself in trying to persuade her to take her final vows and give up her fortune to the community.

"The Prior even condescended to come in order to preach to her and the poor little novice was about to accede to their wishes, when the Abbé proposed that they should elope.

"One night he came to the secret door of the convent, carrying under his arm a bundle containing a complete suit of boy's clothing, together with a long cloak. Sister Clemence quickly put them on and together they slipped out of the place unseen.

"The novice looked fairly bewitching in her new costume. She spread her legs however a little too much in walking, and after hurrying along for a couple of miles, the Abbé proposed making an examination to see what the trouble could be between those beautiful legs of hers.

"He made her lean up against a tree and unbuttoned her trousers for her. To handle the lips of her little secret mousetrap was his only object, as you may imagine. He soon had her so excited that he was obliged to put his mouth down to it and with his tongue play a thousand amorous tricks.

"In her voluptuous transport, she sought with feverish hand the Abbé's fiery monster, which was only too gratified at being set at liberty. Seizing it, she stroked it vigorously.

"To describe that scene would be impossible. The Abbé's tongue was well educated. Sliding between those rosy lips of her slit, it suddenly came out to circle itself into a multiple of tongues, so rapid were its movements.

"Meanwhile Sister Clemence shook his wand furiously, convulsively, and the movement of her bottom indicated that her delicious moment was coming.

"The Abbé's tongue went slower but pressed harder, and when she gave him a great shove accompanied by a warm rub on his immense cock, a superb jet spouted from the latter, while he received her little amorous dew upon his tongue, the deserved tribute of conscientious labor.

"That very day the Abbé cast his robe to the four winds of heaven and carried little Sister Clemence off to Paris. Once in possession of her fortune, she took pretty lodgings and furnished them nicely. She made up her mind to have a good time between theatre-going and her amorous sports with the Abbé, who had also a comfortable income of his own."

* * *

"The story of Sister Clemence is excellent, Mademoiselle," said I, "and I would give much to make her acquaintance as well as that of the Abbé. Unfortunately, it is only fiction!" I added.

"On the contrary, it is a story of real life, M. Dormeuil, the true history of a person to whom I can introduce you, if you like," replied the little woman.

"Truly I would be charmed to know her and shall await an introduction with impatience," I answered.

"You will not have long to wait," was the unexpected reply of the blonde. She then rose and making a timid curtsy, her eyes modestly cast down, her hands joined, she said:

"Allow me to introduce to you Sister Clemence, Monsieur Dormeuil," and she broke into a merry laugh.

I was amazed. "And the Abbé?" I inquired.

"You have heard me speak of Monsieur Lorille? He is the Abbé," she answered quietly.

I had a good laugh over the whole adventure, and then we conversed pleasantly on many subjects until we were interrupted by the arrival of Pauline.

Pauline was certainly a very handsome girl, very tall and graceful, with rich brown hair, large full, frank eyes and tiny hands and feet. She was Pauline for everybody here but Madame L. de Portiera for Parisian Society.

There were only a few privileged persons at the Hotel X— who had seen her face. This house was a particularly exclusive one, and only frequented by the elite.

Indiscretion was unknown there. Amuse yourself as much as you like and as long as you like but never overstep the boundaries of good society. Such was the motto and the rule of this remarkable house.

A Minister, a Senator or a Prince could come here, give his name as Mr. Toto and if he wished to remain incognito, he never would be anybody else but Mr. Toto while he remained there.

A mask to conceal your features was equally respected. A great many persons wore them, especially the ladies. That is why, as I said before, Madame de Portiera had only been seen by two or three privileged persons.

A few widowers and old bachelors like myself allowed their own names to be used because they had nothing to hide; and they never had cause to regret it.

Pauline (we will use her nom de guerre) wanted to see me to request that I would serve as sponsor to a new guest. I accepted at once and to the usual observations concerning the person, she merely said that he was a Russian.

That was all that I wanted to know. Being near supper time, I took leave of the handsome brunette and strolled over to my restaurant in the Boulevard and afterwards dropped into the Cafe Parisian where I met some old friends, and someone being always ready to play backgammon, we were soon deeply engaged in a game.

It lasted until nine o'clock, when after a few minutes walk on the Boulevard, I returned to the Hotel X. The company was numerous although there was no particular reason for it, and I was soon quite at home with the joyous band. It is true that I often gave the signal for the craziest games and this was perhaps the reason for its popularity.

They were waiting for me. Pauline left a corner of the main parlor and came to meet me, followed by an elegantly dressed man, who at first sight attracted my attention.

A perfect blond, with soft expressive blue eyes, he was my protegé for the evening and I introduced him according to the prescribed rules. He was received at once with boisterous acclamations.

The conversation of the Count, as he was called, had a rare charm that evening, and he spoke our language with great elegance.

In a few words I put him au courant with the few things he did not already know, and he gave me an idea to propose to the assembled party which seemed to me so amusing that I at once communicated it to the party. The ladies then surrounded Count Alexis and tendered him their congratulations.

It was some time since we had an entertainment and we were most grateful to the newcomer for the idea, which was as follows:

The next night there would be a ball and supper in full evening dress, and the ladies were to dress in gentlemen's attire. It was absolutely forbidden, however, for any one to wear trousers. A light gauze was the most that was allowed for the ladies' covering of the lower parts of the body. Everyone was to disguise his or her identity in the most ingenious manner possible and a mask was obligatory.

After arranging the details of the new entertainment, we separated and sat talking in groups and couples, the latter to give themselves up to the pleasure of fingering, almost always followed by a voluptuous coit in a little room next to the parlor.

34

CHAPTER THREE

The moment arrived at last to cross once more the threshold of the Hotel X—.

All day I had been as impatient as a child who had been promised to be taken to a play. I felt very queerly in my dress coat, with the tails flapping against my bare bottom, while my prick rose and fell as though it suspected that something unusual was going to happen.

How strange that, on entering the parlor, no one called me by name. It was simply due to the fact that I had succeeded in disguising myself better even than I had hoped. How few persons there were present. Heavens, what a beautiful cunt! Who could be the beauty who displayed such beautiful thighs and such a lovely mount of Venus? My soldier-like instrument stood at 'Carry Arms!'

Look at the pretty doll of a girl over there, and who is that big fellow who has just passed his hand between her legs and tried to carry her off. By George, he is strongly built! What a prick he has! Aha! She kisses him for fear he might let her fall, she holds him fast by the prick and takes the liberty of shaking it.

All the organs of creation are in erection! Who could help it!

"Ladies and gentlemen," began a tall, slender woman whose well defined notch made me wish to fuzzle her on the spot, "I have taken the liberty of inviting two intimate friends to this reunion. I thought that as we were all masked and in disguise beyond recognition, there would be no harm in so doing. The ladies will be here at midnight!"

"It is twelve o'clock already," exclaimed a

fat man with a broken voice who knelt down
before the beauty and kissed her bower of bliss.

She bent over slightly and raising her coattails, displayed the most beautiful bottom in the
whole world and forced him to kiss it. After this
was done, he held her in spite of her struggles
and went on kissing and biting gently.

The beauty soon began to enjoy herself immensely and it was an easy matter to induce
her to lie down on the carpet and receive a rod
long enough to make a monk jealous, into her
handsome boudoir.

At this juncture a beauty with luxuriant
black hair on her pussy bent over to have a better view of the performance and the 'Big Fellow' before mentioned, took advantage of the
opportunity and coming behind her, raised her
coat and began to rub his stiffener between the
dimpled cheeks of her behind.

But the brunette caught him quickly by the
tool and pulled him all around the room, much
to the amusement of the company. Suddenly
she released him and threw herself upon a sofa,
with her legs spread wide open. He understood
the invitation at once and shoving his arrow
between her thighs quite up to the hilt, he
placed his hands under her bottom and picking
her up, walked with her all about the room as
he futtered her softly.

A sigh of pleasure was soon heard as he
made with her body the motions she would have
made herself. Then he augmented her voluptuous excitement by inserting his finger in the
hole of her arse; she wriggled and held him
tightly round the neck and in the delirium of
pleasure called him all the sweet names imaginable, until he showered her with sperm.

Then he laid her gently on the sofa again and still under the influence of this particular fuzzing, she continued to move her beautiful legs as if in perfect bliss.

Suddenly the door opened and two masked ladies stood on the threshold. Their dresses being only slightly low in the neck, a murmur of disappointment was heard on every side. Being the first to find words to express the general sentiment, I said:

"Ladies, you have made a mistake, you are masked, it is true, but you should have complied with all the regulations of the evening."

"True, sir," replied the smaller of the two, "but you must excuse novices who could not make up their minds to appear in a costume so primitive, yet so civilized."

"There is no excuse for you, ladies!" answered the Big Fellow, "and you are condemned first, to be whipped according to the regulations, then you must submit to a quarter of an hour's sexual connection with whoever is selected for you, and the rest of the evening you must appear in the costume of Mother Eve!"

The two women looked at each other for an instant and appeared undecided.

"Don't be afraid, ladies," I said, "we are all kindly disposed toward you and will do nothing whatever to displease you."

"This is not the reception we expected," answered the smaller one, in an impatient tone.

Before any more could be said, the ladies found themselves between two gentlemen, whose pricks were in a magnificent state of erection; seats were placed as though they were to assist at an entertainment and we were invited to take our places.

The Big Fellow, armed with a birch, prick erect, approached the taller of the two, whose ample form excited my admiration, and began thus:

"Madame, I have been commissioned to administer to you a whipping. It is a great honor which is conferred upon me. I will not insult you by asking you to undress, a long experience on my part facilitating this proceeding which is a most agreeable one."

"Sir, if you are a gentleman, you will not carry out this odious threat," she answered in a low but firm voice.

The Big Fellow whispered something in her ear and it seemed to reassure the beauty by some promise. Then he began to undress her, turning to the audience:

"Ladies and Gentlemen, this waist is in the latest fashion and somewhat difficult to get off but we will succeed finally." Suiting the action to the word, he removed the garment and our beauty appeared in her corset.

Her alabaster bosoms which were heaving with emotion, appeared like two hemispheres. He kissed them ardently, then passing behind her, he untied her skirts and raising the lady in his arms, lifted her out of the mass of clothing which had fallen around her feet, leaving her in her drawers and corset only.

He had no need to recommend that she remain perfectly still; she did not attempt to make a movement. He finally took off her drawers and corset and the contour of an admirably beautiful form was seen through her only remaining garment, a fine cambric chemise. It showed a superb bottom and a pair of magnificent thighs.

Seizing her by the middle of the body, he gently laid her across his knees on her belly and raised her chemise. Between the slightly parted legs could be seen a thick mass of blonde hair. Her white thighs were as smooth as satin and as firm as marble.

"Oh, sir, be quick, I beg of you, or I shall die of shame!" she murmured. For answer, he struck her arse with the switch and she gave a piercing scream. He struck again but she struggled so that he could not hold her alone. Two gentlemen rushed forward, seized her arms, and the Big Fellow struck again. The beauty twisted and turned her bottom in every way in her agony and rage, to avoid the strokes of the switch which still fell upon her.

Her handsome arse was soon covered with red lines and the Big Fellow, considering the punishment sufficient, had an ointment brought him, with which he rubbed the lovely buttocks.

In doing so, however, he found an opportunity of exploring the treasure hidden between her legs and it soon appeared that the beauty had forgotten the whipping and was giving herself up to the pleasure of being rubbed. Her behind rose and fell voluptuously and she was on the point of 'coming' when the Big Fellow asked:

"Who is the happy man who is going to enjoy connection with this lady?"

I was selected by common consent and presented myself before the altar of love, ready to enter from behind. Requesting two gentlemen to hold her slightly raised, when I was about to enter her, she murmured:

"Quick, I beg of you, I am burning with desire!"

With my prick in one hand, while with the other I felt my way, I introduced myself into her warm garden, while she returned the attack with a vigorous movement of her soft white buttocks.

With what ardor she goes on, what happiness it is to me to feel my prick in that region filled with voluptuous moisture. From time to time she squeezes her thighs together, as though to extract the juice quicker from my balls.

The movements of her bottom follow each other with great rapidity and my beauty seems to wish me to penetrate into unknown depths. I am about to attain the supreme point of bliss, when she gives a little cry of voluptuous satisfaction, as she spends with me.

I remain a moment longer with my prick in the yoni of the beauty and it seems as though a little hammer is tapping right upon the end of my tool, a kind of palpitation of the flesh in the interior of the charming retreat. Finally, I withdraw and several ladies carry the beauty to a sofa to rest.

Now comes the turn of the smaller of the two ladies. They were obliged to hold her while they were whipping their companion. Seeing that it would take too long to undress her, a young man, slender and distingué, tied her hands behind her back and dexterously placed her head between his legs.

His prick must have tickled her neck agreeably but nevertheless she did not cease insulting us. In order to get through more quickly he took her skirts and raised them over her back.

The beauty wears drawers which are very

wide open. It is an easy matter to whip her
without taking them off. He raises her chemise
and her arse appears amidst a cloud of laces,
not large but round and dimpled, looking like a
lovely peach.

Slap! Slap! The young executioner does not
think it necessary to use the switch; he merely
gives her a whipping with his hand. No use for
her to wriggle, she cannot escape a single
stroke. Slap! Slap!

"There, Madame, two more than your friend
received, because you have been so naughty!"

It is easy to see throughout his performance
that the young man does not try to hurt her
much and the victim soon begins to understand
the farce, not knowing at first whether to laugh
or grow angry, but finally she takes it all in
good part and laughs heartily.

As a reward for her better behavior, the company gives her the privilege of choosing the one
who is to perform the second operation.

The clear, piercing eyes beneath her mask
go slowly round the room, resting an instant
on each of the gentlemen. I feel them lingering
upon me with some hesitation. They pass on to
my neighbor.

Finally the charmer selects a gentleman who
is tucked away in a corner near the mantlepiece
to be the happy mortal. He is the only one whose
thigh finger is not in erection.

Two ladies rush forward to undress the little
lady. She allows them to do so with the best
grace possible. They strip her completely; she
has the form of a child, how charming!

Her little bosoms are scarcely formed and
her thighs are slender but round. She is like a
charming doll. The gentleman she has selected

comes slowly forward and asks what position she prefers.

"Lie down on your back on this sofa," she answers laughingly, "I will get astride of you and do all the work."

At this moment some one tapped me on the shoulder and as I turn, I see that my neighbor is a lady with abundant, curling, golden hair between her legs.

"Monsieur Dormeuil!" she says.

"Yes!" I answer, not suspecting the trap laid for me.

"Ah, I knew it was you!" and then I recognize Clemence. It is too late to retreat.

"Little Sister Clemence, how charming you are in this costume!" I put my hand under her coattail and over her firm, round bottom, slipping it down to her rose garden and allowing my finger to wander in her silky hair.

"Stop, you naughty pirate! I only wished to introduce you to Monsieur Lorille, the Abbé. It is he who is about to offer up a sacrifice to Venus, but poor man, he is dreadfully tired. He gave it to me seven times already tonight and it was so good!"

"Ah, that is the Abbé! Sure enough, he does seem rather worn out," I remarked, "and the little blonde over there seems to be tiring herself out rubbing his cock without great success."

The Abbé seemed to rally, however, and soon he was stiff enough for the little siren to introduce him into the tiny slit that she opens with her fingers. He is now in and leans forward, first to kiss her red lips, then the pink tips of her bosoms. Ah, how well she works! The little woman rises and falls on his mighty organ with the regularity of an amorous machine, rubbing the Abbé's prick delightfully.

Little cries of pleasure escape from time to time, which thrill me with desire from head to foot. At the moment when he is about to spend, she changed her position so as to make it last longer.

I could wait no longer so I put my prick between her two globes and pressed with my fingers her small child-like bosoms.

Those little titties were very firm and her movements led me to think that very shortly I shall flow into her little arse. At any rate, she is about to spend. Oh, there, one . . . two . . . her plump bottom rises and descends more quickly, she breathes hard, her hand seizes the Abbé's tool and seems to wish to push it up to the hilt. Then comes a shiver that shakes her whole body. I feel that she spends with me and that the Abbé follows suit.

The little woman is all perspiration, and they hasten to her and wrap her up in a cloak.

I now perceive that the Big Fellow has warmed up little Sister Clemence and from the movements of her bottom, I know she is going to get it for the eighth time. I am astonished to see them come towards me and still more to recognize in the hero of the evening, the Russian Count. I was very much pleased and complimented him upon his success.

"Have you discovered Pauline, Count?" I inquired.

"Certainly. She is the tall brunette who announced the arrival of the two ladies, her friends. There she is, talking with the gentleman who so gracefully performed with the little blonde."

Pauline was superb with her majestic limbs, her beautiful bottom that I had admired so much and her handsome retreat so rosy and adorned with a luxuriant hairy covering.

I could not resist the temptation of going to finger her a little. I come up behind her and press a kiss upon each of the globes of her behind. She turns, but not considering the attack dangerous, continues her conversation with Monsieur Lorille.

Her behind is just at the proper height and the temptation being great, I place my tool in the deep rut very gently while I pass my fingers through the curly hair of her treasure.

There is a little sensitive point between the lips of the 'beauty' and every time I touch it she gives a slight start with her arse, which excites me more and more. Now my finger penetrates between the moist lips and moves about in the interior of her boudoir.

She pays no attention to it at first but little by little her buttocks move slightly, and then the movements become more accentuated as my finger moves quicker. Judging that the propitious moment has arrived, I quickly introduce my lance, but the beauty tries to make me lose my hold. I cling to her bottom and hold it like a vise, and the more she tries to throw me off, the more excited I become.

Finally the Abbé comes to my assistance and holds her hands as she throws up her backside with a movement like a bucking horse.

"Ah, you want it!" she says wildly. "Then take this!" Then comes a punch from her plump behind. But she does not succeed in dismounting me. At last the friction of my pizzle in her shrubbery begins to excite her and with head thrown forward on the Abbé's shoulder, she exclaims:

"Push harder—harder!"

Her hips rise and fall and she would not let me draw out my cocked rod now for anything in the world. Her lascivious movements are now so exciting that I can hardly maintain myself in position. Excited to the highest pitch I give three or four good shoves and drench her with my sperm at the very moment when she spends herself. When she has recovered, I whisper softly in her ear:

"When will you give me another—your friend Dormeuil!"

She answers, half angrily: "I wanted to keep you waiting six months longer. Now the second will be whenever you like."

I kiss her hand and rejoin the Count who says he has enjoyed the scene immensely. The two little ladies who were whipped are now walking in the parlor entirely naked, their bottoms shaking prettily as they move about.

I take advantage of the situation to smack them both as they pass by. The music for the dancing has been playing for the last half hour and it is really a charming sight to watch those half-nude women pass before my eyes. After the dance comes the supper. I am seated near a brunette whom I do not recognize and I give myself the treat of investigating her beauties with one hand under the table.

She touches my stick from time to time to keep it awake and we drink and eat heartily.

A wild gallop terminates the whole performance and as the light of day begins to show itself, we conclude that it is time to put on more presentable costumes. The ladies leave first and I go home to seek a much needed rest.

Jean stuck his head into my room to tell me the time of day but I did not hear him. It was five o'clock in the afternoon, before I got up and began my toilet. Jean does not utter a word. He probably thinks he has a new master.

"Has any one been here?"

"Yes, sir, a tall light haired gentleman who left his card. He has been here three times."

"Where is the card?"

Jean handed hit to me; it is the Count's. He writes on the card with a pencil that he will return at six o'clock. Evidently Mademoiselle Hortense will not see me today.

The bell rings and Jean introduces my new friend. He comes to invite me to supper at his country seat. I accept with delight. Before leaving, however, I must go and say goodbye to my neighbor.

"Good morning, neighbor!"

"Say good evening, rather; it is late enough for that," answered Madame Benoit with a severe look.

I was holding the knob and as I closed the door, I heard the murmur: "Old Bachelor!"

CHAPTER FOUR

The Count's carriage is at the door and we are soon on the way to his villa, which is situated near Poissy. It is a pretty, modern, cheerful place with gardens on three sides, the other side sloping gently to the Seine, wooded, with narrow paths through it to the river.

The sun is setting and it is one of those beautiful autumn days that remind one rather of spring than the commencement of winter.

A butler does the honors of the house and if there are any other servants they do not appear.

There is a pretty parlor on the first floor, very richly decorated and furnished with sofas and armchairs and mirrors. I am much surprised at the style of the room, to the great amusement of the Count, who passes his arm through mine and leads me to the dining room.

The table is ready and a stroke of the bell brings the butler, to whom he gives orders for serving our meal.

After an excellent supper I stretched myself out in an armchair and the conversation begins.

The Count, who is a good talker, tells many personal adventures, which are all new and hail from all parts of the world. With a large fortune at his command, he has been able to satisfy every whim, and has traveled through America, Asia and part of Africa.

There is no country in Europe with which he is not perfectly familiar and he speaks several languages fluently; in fact he is a charming fellow.

"I had just been traveling in Switzerland,"

began the Count in his now familiar and well modulated voice, "and I had enjoyed the trip so much that I was tempted to extend my travels further south. I visited all the principal cities in Italy, and the occasion presenting itself to make the trip from Naples to Marseilles with an English family, I accepted the invitation with pleasure, and we set sail.

"For four days the vessel glided smoothly on the Mediterranean and I was almost sorry at last when we arrived at our destination.

"During the trip I had made the conquest of the younger of the girls, who had proposed the most embarrassing things to me: to elope with her or to marry her on her arrival at Marseilles. I got out of the difficulty by promising to go to Manchester the following season, which of course I was careful not to do.

"After taking leave of the Anderson family and thanking them for their kind invitation to visit them in England, I was taken with a severe attack of spleen and hesitated between following the little Miss—which I thought would be ridiculous—and returning to Moscow.

"I do not know what notion possessed me to visit Algiers, which the French had just conquered, but I took passage on the best steamer of the line which was then beginning to run every fortnight.

"The first meal on board the vessel brought together all the passengers around a long dining table. During the first part of the meal I could not fail to see that my neighbor was doing his best to start a conversation with me, and I would have ignored his overtures longer had it been possible. But giving me a nudge on the arm, he said:

" 'This is excellent roast beef, sir, just what we have at home!'

"I turned, and for the first time saw his features. He had a good natured, big round face—simplicity itself—was about forty years of age, and showed that he belonged to the class of well-to-do merchants.

" 'Yes, sir, an excellent roast,' I answered at last.

" 'You are doubtless going to Algiers on business, like myself,' he continued.

" 'No,' I replied, 'I am going on a pleasure trip.'

" 'On a pleasure trip!' cried the good man in amazement.

" 'Certainly, to see the country, hunt, kill time. I cannot kill anything else.'

" 'You are a Parisian,' said he with the air of a man who thinks that only a Parisian could conceive such an extravagant idea.

" 'No, I am a Russian, from Moscow,' I answered.

" 'And I am from Carpentras,' he returned proudly. 'I am going to Algiers on business and I am taking my wife with me. The poor little thing would not be separated from me, so I took her along. We have only been married for six months, he added confidentially with another nudge as he laughed his great big laugh.

"I was undecided whether to continue my conversation with him or to go and take a stroll on the deck, but my companion was a regular sticking plaster.

"Once on deck he talked loud enough to be heard a mile away. I was obliged to listen to the history of his fortune and count it over with him several times.

"His name was Theodore Paillard. At about eleven that evening, we retired to our cabins. My cabin was next to his and before I went to sleep, I heard him relating to his wife a lot of things about me of which I was totally ignorant but which he found in his fertile Southern imagination. I then heard Madame Paillard tell him to stop, that she was sleepy, but he would not be quiet, he wanted it, he said . . . he had not had it for three days.

"She said: 'No, it is not convenient in this little box.' I then heard her scold him. " 'You are too big, Theodore. I assure you that you hurt me. Then you are so heavy, you smother me. Let me put it in myself, you are so awkward. Now go ahead, easy. Oh . . . I don't feel anything. Get it for yourself and be quick about it. Don't pinch me like that, you hurt me, I tell you! How long you are . . . You have been drinking, I am certain.'

"Then all was silent for a moment until Madame Paillard's voice rose once more, but this time in anger.

" 'You are always the same, you satisfy yourself and leave me full of your stuff. You are selfish! I have really only had it once since we are married. Ah, now you are going to sleep and I must get up and wash.'

" 'My dear, I am very tired. I promise you that I will give it to you in the morning,' replied he in a pitiful tone. Then I heard the noise of a syringe. Theodore was snoring like a satiated beast. I dreamed all night of Madame Paillard and when I awoke during the night I got to wondering whether she was pretty, or if she were only passable! One is easily satisfied on board ship.

"Early the next morning I was on deck. I was not alone, however; a young woman was walking up and down, stamping her tiny feet from time to time to warm them.

"When she turned I was literally dazzled. An Andalusian beauty with the delicate features of a Princess. This beautiful lady had a superb skin and large black eyes as soft as velvet; she was, moreover, a blonde. I never saw a more beautiful woman in my life. She passed me, smiling, and apparently wholly ignorant of her beauty, which added to it an irresistible charm. I was stunned, fascinated!

"When she turned to walk back I was still in the same spot. I could not lift my eyes from her. All at once a familiar voice fell disagreeably on my ear. It was that of the man from Carpentras, Paillard, whom I was going to send to the devil, when the beautiful lady suddenly took his arm and said coaxingly:

"'Theodore, please walk with me, I am so cold.'

"Was this Madame Paillard, then; my head was in a whirl.

"'Come, Virginia, let me introduce you to my friend from Moscow,' he cried in his big voice.

"One must have been very deaf not to have heard him, and advancing towards the illassorted couple, I saluted the young woman in my best possible style.

"She received me most gracefully, and turning to her husband, reproached him for not giving my name. I presented my card to her and as she found my name hard to pronounce, she said:

"'I will call you Mr. Alexis, if you will allow me.'

"We then all three walked the deck for a while, talking and chatting. Theodore was still looking at my card, trying to make out my name. The breakfast bell was a welcome sound as the sea air had given me a ravenous appetite.

"When Madame Paillard was relieved of her wrap, I perceived a full bust that made her tight dress look tighter still. She was twice as pretty, and many curious thoughts rushed through my brain.

"I could scarcely eat. On the second day I became more intimate with the lady and on the third, as we were nearing the Balearic Islands, the sea became quite rough, so she remained in her berth.

"The exuberant nature of Theodore needed more space and air; he could not live closeted in these cabins, he said.

"He came to me to explain the situation and asked me to go down to reassure his young wife, who was terribly afraid of the rolling and tossing of the ship. Lying on a little sofa in the cabin, she looked lovely in her negligee. She got up to meet me and I could see her firm bosoms, entirely without support, like two soft spheres, shaking with every movement.

"We talked of a thousand different things and little by little our conversation turned on burning grounds. She told me that she had come to marry Mr. Paillard who had been so kind to her mother! She said this with a sigh, and I felt a rush of desire go through me.

"I could see under her thin dress, and between that dress and her flesh there was a chemise. Attracted to her by an irresistible force, I drew nearer, and as I did so, I had an intense desire to feel that woman's flesh against my own. I could not tell you what I talked about and very likely she did not hear a word.

"Suddenly we seized one another by the shoulders and our mouths formed one, our lips were glued together, my eyes plunged into her and we drank without reserve of the voluptuous bliss of love, that fiery passion beyond compare. There seemed to be a communicative excitement in the very feel of her bare skin, which intoxicated me.

"We would certainly have been surprised by the husband had it not been for his incorrigible habit of loud talking.

"He found me standing by the door. He had not come to remain, he said, but only wanted to see how Virginia was, and finding that she looked well (I should think she would, under the circumstances) he tapped her on either cheek and forced me to sit down on the edge of the bed. He seemed quite delighted to find me so obliging, the poor man. Pshaw! It was his own fault. Why did he want to take advantage of the gratitude of this poor young girl. She was really to be pitied.

"Once more alone, we did not know how to resume the interrupted conversation. Our eyes, however, spoke for us. I went back to my seat at her side and her hands were soon between mine.

"I pressed her voluptuous bosoms with both my hands and carried the license so far as to unbutton her dress and kiss them.

" 'Virginia,' I said, 'let me kiss those treasures. Let me admire this skin, so soft and white!' and I held up one bosom which filled both my hands.

"The little pink tip, hidden at first in the flesh of the globes, all at once appeared triumphant, I seized it between my lips, then between my teeth and sucked and bit it. I then sought the vermillion mouth of my beauty; her moist lips were trembling, they seemed to invade mine, and when my tongue entered her mouth, I thought she was going into spasms.

"Her whole body quivered, she was almost delirious. What would you have done in my place, with a tool as stiff as an iron bar in your trousers? I carefully raised her dress and as I supposed, there was only a long linen chemise to defend her virtue.

"The obstacle was soon removed and as her legs were parted, it was an easy task to introduce my prick and penetrate into the grotto of love. It was as narrow as that of a maidenhead. She felt a slight pain when I pressed further in but feeling my stiff prick in her tiny, moss covered bower, she became furiously agitated and seizing me by the neck, would have smothered me between her large bosoms, had I not freed myself.

"To maintain my position in this retreat, I was obliged to pass my hand beneath her bottom and moderate the hysterical leaps she made, due to a desire so long repressed.

"I now slipped my tongue between her teeth and ran my weapon of war up and down along her little furrow. She suddenly seemed to quiet down and enjoy calmly my amorous embraces.

"Nothing could indicate that she had attained the supreme point of bliss when I was about to spurt my provision of sperm into her retreat, except a slight shudder, followed by complete exhaustion.

"I left her undisturbed for a few minutes while I admired her magnificent thighs, her superb body, so round and firm, and her little pussy of hair like that of a child of sixteen. I proceeded then to wash her, remembering the reproaches she had addressed to her husband the night before.

"The contact of the cold water brought her to her senses. She opened her eyes in astonishment, until she remembered all, and then, jumping down, she threw her arms around my neck and pressed her lips passionately to mine.

"The same scene was renewed the following day amid long talks. She regretted the separation which must come at our landing and it also worried me, for I really hungered after the woman, I had not possessed her enough. I promised to accompany her everywhere but when she thought of how she would be obliged to submit to her husband whom she did not love, burning tears would roll down her cheeks. I was kissing them away gently one day when an idea struck me, and I resolved to communicate it to her and convince her of the success of my scheme whereby we would not be separated on landing.

"I communicated to Virginia my idea whereby we could continue our relationship but she refused to listen at first. The more she refused, the more feasible it seemed to me and I insisted. At last she laughed heartily and was ready to put it into execution. I explained the intrigue to her in every detail.

"Soon after our arrival she was to appear unhappy. Theodore was to find her always gloomy and two days before the departure of the steamer she was to propose returning to France.

"He, stingy, and going to Algiers for the purpose of making money, would not think of consenting to go back with her, and would not allow her to return alone. I would advise him to let her go alone, and the journey being short, the Captain and stewardess would take good care of her.

"By degrees he would become accustomed to the idea, then I would whisper in his ear that without his wife, he could take advantage of the innumerable chances which were never wanting here. Ah, if he should only find a Moorish beauty! One of those ideal women which exist in novels at home, but which are here in flesh and blood.

"I was certain of the success of the scheme. She was to go on board of the steamer, excuse herself a few minutes and go into a cabin where she would find a Moorish costume which I would provide for her. When the first bell rang for the departure, she was to go back on land and leave the rest to me.

" 'But you see, Alexis, the thing is impossible! When I go on land I will find my husband with you. He will accost me and then what language will I speak? I only speak French as it is, and no other language but this and Spanish.'

"This remark disconcerted me for a moment but I soon found a solution. At a pinch we might speak French; there would be nothing extraordinary in a Moorish woman speaking French, but we would have less liberty. He might recognize the voice and a familiar expression might spoil the whole game.

"However, I remembered that when at college in France, the pupils had a way of conversing by adding a termination to each monosyllable, article, etc., being careful to make it accord in sound with the words used. You finally got an outlandish jargon, which no one could understand who did not possess the key.

"Madame Paillard was quite sure that her husband, who was somewhat of a simpleton anyway, would not understand such a language. So everything was settled.

"The young woman, in ten minutes understood the whole system and I left her, recommending that she practice speaking in this manner when alone, feeling that in two or three days she would speak it with facility.

"A few days after our arrival in Algiers, according to program, Madame Paillard became very gloomy; her husband seemed quite uneasy and one day when I told her that a steamer sailed within forty-eight hours, she declared to Theodore that she wanted to return to France. She was dying with ennui, she said.

"Everything happened as we had foreseen. I became really eloquent in the cause and Paillard decided to let her return alone. I arranged everything with the Captain and Stewardess. Madame Paillard's trunks were to remain in Marseilles until further orders.

"We accompanied her to the steamer and at the last moment, the husband would go with her, but the magic words 'Moorish Beauty,' whispered in his ear, decided him to remain. The young woman excused herself and disappeared down the companion way, smothering her laughter.

"At the first signal for departure, Theodore

wished to rush down and kiss her once more good-bye but at that instant a woman, heavily veiled, showing her two handsome eyes, passed by as light as a butterfly and brushing by our friend on the way, she gave him a burning glance.

" 'There is a Moorish woman!' I said hurriedly, 'come do not let us lose this chance, it is a rare one, I assure you.'

"He instantly forgot wife and all, and trotted breathlessly after the woman who was walking a few steps ahead of him. He overtook the beauty and was talking to her when I joined them but, of course, she did not understand a word of French. 'She does not understand French, Mr. Alexis,' said he in such pitiful tones that I could not help bursting out laughing.

" 'Do not distress yourself,' I said, 'I understand her language and will talk to her,' and there I was, chattering away with the Moorish woman in the language I had taught her in ten minutes.

"I was obliged to translate M. Paillard's propositions, which were businesslike, and I made him understand that being in a foreign country, under no consideration whatever to attempt to raise the woman's veil for that meant instant death.

"He promised faithfully not to try the experiment and I felt no more uneasiness on that score.

"I had rented a little villa about five minutes walk from the city, surrounded by beautiful gardens. I explained once more to Mr. Paillard that Moorish women never uncovered their faces; that they always eat and dress alone. To seek to uncover their face is a crime. He was easily convinced.

"'Do you think I could sleep with her?' he asked eagerly.

"'Certainly! Nothing easier!' I answered. 'You will certainly succeed on that point.'

"Everything passed without mishap. I talked all day to the young woman (Madame Paillard), and when it was time to retire at night, she hung on my arm and gave Theodore to understand that she would prefer spending the first night at least with me.

"Theodore retired to the room next to ours and was soon snoring the snore of the just. Left alone, I seized the young woman in my arms.

"She was lovely in her somewhat original costume. I helped her to undress and for fear of a surprise, we concluded she had best sleep with the veil.

"The night was warm and I persuaded her to sleep naked. I felt a foolish desire to view her charms, and took off her chemise in spite of her remonstrances.

"She was a mixture of strength and weakness; her neck was slender and I have already spoken of her handsome bosom. Her luxuriant bottom was enough to make the Colonel of the Tenth Cuirassiers jealous, as they say in Russia.

"I did not know what to handle first; I went from her cunt to these two beautiful globes, which stood out as firm as marble. I felt like eating her up and when I put my face between her admirable thighs, she held my head tight enough to smash it.

"I took her beautiful body in my arms and laid her on the bed; then, placing myself over her, I began to explore her sweet little cunny with my tongue. My prick was placed just above her face and in her excitement she took hold of it and rolled it with her hands. My tongue was shooting a thousand strokes into her vagina and she would lift up her body in her passion, then give a sudden pressure of her legs on my head which nearly sent me wild.

"The very tip of my prick was burning with ardent fire. I put it into her mouth. Oh, how she sucked it! Her tongue gave me an indescribable sensation; my ardor became double and I sucked and bit the lips of her little cunny in a perfect storm of passion.

"Feeling that I was about to spend in her mouth, I withdrew my prick and pushed it between her beautiful bosoms, telling her to press them against my prick as I tickled her two little strawberries.

"This sensation, added to the sensuous lingering of my tongue in her voluptuous vulva, soon threw her into the wildest spasms of delight, and with true cries of delirious joy, she inundated my tongue with her delightful fluid.

"Her cries had awakened Theodore and suddenly I heard him jump from his bed to the floor.

"I had neglected to lock the door and he walked in without further ceremony. Fortunately the light was out and we had time to prepare ourselves. He said his prick was in such a state of erection that he absolutely must have the Moorish woman. What was to be done?

"She did not want him in the least, and he was bound to be satisfied. I made him believe that it was bad form to enter into the vagina of a Moorish woman at the first meeting and that he must content himself with rubbing his prick between the cheeks of her bottom; that she would agree to it, I guaranteed.

"He was so excited that his teeth chattered and he agreed to accept anything that we proposed.

" 'Tell him to make haste,' said the young woman.

" 'You must move your arse so as to hasten matters,' I suggested.

" 'I will,' answered the poor boob.

"He was soon astride her bottom and placing his immense prick between the two hillocks, he began to rub and she to wriggle. Sometimes she raised herself and rubbed her behind against his prick so that he touched her cunt.

" 'It is strange but this backside reminds me of my wife's,' he would say almost out of breath.

" 'Do not talk that way!' I said boldly.

"He soon began puffing like a porpoise and lay down on the young woman's bottom.

"She complained that he was smothering her and I was obliged to raise him up and tell him to be more lively in his movements. She rubbed him a little while longer and when finally a jet of sperm inundated her back, she gave a sigh of relief, which caused him to ask her if she had spent.

" 'Oh, yes, yes,' she replied, and he went away quite satisfied to resume his snoring. I washed her, poor little thing, and fatigued with such hard work, she fell asleep.

"Ever after that I locked the door carefully.

"This went on for a month and only once during that time was he allowed to even rub his cock between the buttocks of his wife. He was far from suspecting her of being his own wife and everything went well with one exception.

"Then it happened in broad daylight when he could not possibly contain himself any longer. I unfastened the full, Turkish trousers of the beauty and held her head between my legs. She took advantage of this to suck me gently while her husband agitated his prick between the cheeks of her bottom.

"This time it rather amused her. She did not pretend to help him and he kept asking me to tell her to move her arse more. He had to spend, however, and I advised him to catch the sperm in his handkerchief. I did not care to receive the charge.

"To tell you of the delightful nights I spent with that lovely woman during that month would take me a very long time and become monotonous, so I will end by saying that all went well.

"It did not surprise Paillard that I should take the beautiful woman to France with me. On arriving at Marseilles, I pretended to leave her at the Hotel until she could be dressed as other women dress in Europe, and she started at once for Carpentras; her mother was to say that she had spent a month with her and everything would be settled all right.

"I parted with her reluctantly but she promised to see me again some day. I detained her husband a day in Marseilles in order to give her time to have everything settled.

"Thus ends my story.

"Ah, you want a conclusion; well, here it is!

"After leaving the husband at the station, I started for Paris where I remained some months and as I was about to leave the city, I received a letter from Theodore, announcing the birth of a boy whom he had named Alexis, with the full consent of his wife.

"Dear old Paillard—this act of courtesy was really due to me."

* * *

The Count had been very animated as he related this adventure, but now he became grave and melancholy and seemed pensive, shaking his head as though to cast off some thought.

"My dear friend, thrown as I have been for the past fifteen years amid pleasure, with no time to study the exact moment for my conquest, I have certainly committed acts which sober people might call indelicate.

"If indeed I have sometimes gone too far in my mad career, if I have brought grief to some hearts and pain to some young slits, at least once in my life I have had scruples.

"Let me confide this strange adventure to you; it will be a relief to me. You have made a study of mankind and I feel certain that you will not laugh at me but will understand my feelings in the matter."

CHAPTER FIVE

"Three years ago, and about eighteen months before my trip to Algiers, I was on my estate, a few miles from Moscow. The winter was very severe and I went to the city as seldom as possible, even when it was a question of sensual satisfaction. Aside from one or two large landowners like myself, I saw no one, and spent the time looking after my servants, hunting wolves and reading a few erotic books, which were not calculated to calm my passions.

"I soon noticed the daughter of one of my farmers, a handsome girl, and the only one who appeared to be modest among all the girls and women with whom I was thrown in contact night and day.

"It was a rare thing to see her smile, but when she did, she showed beautiful teeth, and two dimples would make two deep holes in her rosy cheeks.

"She had luxuriant hair, as black as jet, which she wore in a braid that hung far below her waist; the short dress, which came just below her knees, displayed two handsome legs, round and firm, while her large black eyes were shaded by heavy lashes. She was beautiful, very beautiful, and just fifteen.

"As she was extremely modest, I did not know how to make propositions to her which many of the others would have quickly accepted. Several times I tried to enter into conversation with her. I questioned her first about her parents in a careless, indifferent manner, then I laughingly asked her if she had a betrothed. She looked at me quietly, surprised perhaps at such a question, but she did not answer.

"For a whole month I remained in this embarrassing position. Sometimes I would wake up at night after dreaming that I had her in bed with me, that I had fully possessed her, and I would turn over and find myself alone with my prick at full stand. I would then make up my mind to fly from the spot that very day or force her to surrender, but the day would pass just as the preceding one and nothing came of it.

"Sometimes I surprised her looking at me, but the look was so frank, so innocent, that I did not dare to speak.

"I do not know how or why, but her mother perceived what was going on, and coming to me with tears in her eyes, told me the farm did not produce enough to support the family. Praising her modest daughter, she begged me to take her into my service. I was delighted with the proposition but was careful not to show it, and dismissed the woman without making any promises.

"A few days later I had a visit from the father and finally I consented to take the young girl.

"One day, a theft having been committed in the house, all the accusations fell upon the young girl and I had her summoned before me in order to question her myself.

"She scarcely deigned to defend herself. She had not stolen anything and suspected no one of the deed. This was all she would say. At the head of the female department of the household I had a dragon of a woman who was extremely strict and whose devotion to me was, without question, devout. She advised me to have the girl whipped to make her confess the crime. I was obliged to consent and ordered the whipping to be administered in my presence.

"The girl looked on calmly while the preparations were made for the torture, but what amazed me was to see her quietly undress herself, throwing to the floor one by one her articles of clothing until she was naked to the waist.

"Her back was turned to me. Ah, when the woman struck her on the back with the strap, I almost cried out, and ordered her to stop and retire.

"I got up, took the young girl in my arms and gently drew her on my knees as I tried to reassure her—it was only then that she burst into tears. I tried to draw her hands away from her face, which she had hidden in them; I wanted to see her bewitching eyes bathed in tears.

"She was so beautiful thus that I lost my head, threw her brutally on the sofa and rushed upon her like a hungry wolf.

"I kissed her tiny bosoms furiously. They were firm as marble. I stuck my head under her skirts and there was the peculiar perfume of a clean woman which made me delirious with lubric passion.

"Like an animal, I squeezed the firm, rosy lips of her hidden parts and rubbed my face against them. I was intoxicated by the delicious odor. I stuck my tongue between the lips of her little pussy. I drew out and licked it like an amorous animal, for I too, was an animal then in my sensuous desire.

"Suddenly surprised at not feeling her move, I disengaged my head from her skirts and was not a little bewildered to find her sobbing as though her heart would break.

"I took both her hands in mine and placed my fiery lips upon hers. The tears streamed down her cheeks and dropped one by one on my breast. Her mouth seemed insensible to my caresses.

"Finally calmed by the sight of so much grief, I suddenly awoke as from some horrible nightmare, picked up her clothing and covered her nakedness. This seemed to calm her somewhat and when my paroxysm was over I got her to talk.

"She swore on the image of the Holy Virgin that she was innocent and she gently reproached me for my conduct. It had hurt her so much that she began sobbing again.

"I was ashamed of myself and begged her pardon. I felt vile, degraded before this pure young girl and promised not to annoy her any more. After talking about half an hour, I sent her back, consoled now, to her occupation, and told the other servants that I was convinced of her innocence and would not allow anyone to be wanting in respect to her.

"I was not myself for several days after this incident. I dreaded to meet the young girl and took a thousand precautions to avoid her, and yet I was happy in knowing that she was in the house.

"Naturally, we often came in contact and she met me with the same beautiful smile. I felt the passion which I had for her growing stronger and stronger and it was then that I determined to leave Moscow and go to St. Petersburg.

"I attended all the society balls, and one night as I was helping the Viscountess Xenia on with her furs, she invited me to accompany her home. I sent away my sleigh and slipped into hers.

"Leaning against each other during the ride, I responded to the coquetries of the beautiful woman as best I could. When we arrived at the house, she invited me to come in, which I did with pleasure, not suspecting for a moment that I was to possess that very night the most sought after woman in St. Petersburg.

"I was shown into an immense, well-lighted parlor and requested to wait a few moments. I stretched myself in an armchair and was thinking of nothing in particular, when a servant informed me that he had been ordered to take me to to Madame's apartments. I followed him and we soon reached a sort of boudoir, hung in white satin, with sofas and chairs to match, and a huge mirror.

"Words cannot describe the comfort and elegance of the room. The mistress of the house soon entered, wrapped in a black silk dressing gown without any trimming; the garment became her complexion admirably. She invited me to sit down on the sofa beside her. She wore little golden yellow slippers, with black silk stockings, embroidered with yellow and was tapping the floor with her tiny feet, and continuing the coquetry begun in the sleigh.

" 'They tell me many curious things about you, Count' . . . she began.

" 'What do they say, Madame?'

" 'Oh, they say that you are a fast man, for one thing.'

" 'Where is the man who has not had that said of him?'

" 'True, but there are some little scandals

here and there. In Vienna, Paris, etc., with ladies of good society.'

"'It is proof then, Madame, that I have succeeded in finding favor everywhere except in St. Petersburg. As yet I have not had that good fortune here.'

"'You are so seldom here,' she said, pouting.

"'It rests with you alone, whether I stay or not!' I whispered, taking her hand.

"'Really, sir?' she responded with a look that was a challenge.

"I seized her round the waist and tried to kiss her and during the struggle somehow or other, the dressing gown suddenly became unfastened and flew open from top to bottom, displaying her goddess-like form entirely naked.

"It was only an apparition, however, as she rushed out of the door and closed it after her. Then she made me the most delightful promises if I would undress and put on the costume she would hand me through the door.

"I had long been accustomed to any proposition, however strange it might be, so I took care not to refuse. I waited, and in a few moments, the door was slightly opened and a lot of clothing fell at my feet.

"At first I had some trouble in making out what I had picked up from the floor, but at last I found that it was a very pretty wrapper, handsomely trimmed with red lace, and a pair of woman's drawers and stockings long enough to reach to my thighs.

"'Are you ready?' asked the Countess impatiently.

"'Not yet, Madame, but I will be presently,' I replied.

"I had got into the drawers and stockings

when she entered quickly. I thought it was a saucy little boy who stood before me and the sudden erection of my member betrayed the emotion produced upon me by the lascivious costume of the charmer.

"She had on black velvet breeches fitting her superb figure tightly, little socks reached just above the ankles and her tiny feet were encased in black velvet slippers. The upper part of her body was clothed in a fine shirt, puffed round the waist, a short jacket reaching to the middle of her back, while a broad lace collar covered her shoulders. Added to that, were blonde curls falling in ringlets around her neck.

"I rushed forward to seize her, wishing to add the sensual pleasure of touch to that of looking at her but she stopped me with an angry gesture and offered to assist me in getting into the wrapper. She passed her hands several times over my cock on purpose and I took those occasions to steal a kiss 'on the fly.' I was soon dressed and she commanded me to sit down in an armchair and listen to her with undivided attention.

"'You are going to have a very bad opinion of me, Count, but if I have determined to indulge in this caprice, it is because I have heard your discretion praised as much as your gallant adventures, and I feel very certain that you will banish this evening's experience from your memory entirely.'

"'I will forget it for everyone else, but I can never forget it for you, Madame,' I replied.

"'That is quite sufficient, sir, and now let us abandon ourselves entirely to pleasure . . . come!'

"She now dragged me along a little passage

which led to a chamber below. I will not attempt to describe the luxury of this room. She disappeared in a secret closet and brought out an enormous dildo. I was then obliged to play the lady and she made all the advances and caressed me in every possible manner. She slipped her hand under my wrapper and petted my bottom; she kissed me, but would not allow me to touch her. However, she told me to whip her if she behaved badly and as her big bottom was very tempting in her velvet trousers, I contented myself with giving her slaps on top of her trousers to begin with.

"Her manners became worse and worse, however, so that at last I threw her across my knees, hastily unbuttoned her trousers and gave her a great whipping. Her beautiful buttocks were so fat that in passing my hand over them, near the thighs, the whole compactness moved into a solid block but she held her legs so tightly closed that it was impossible to take the liberty of touching all the beauties which were in that near vicinity.

"After a goodly number of well applied smacks, the beautiful bottom became quite red, and no doubt considering that to be sufficient, she ran away, but her face expressed more passion than before, and returning to me, she raised my wrapper to my waist and fingered my cock for a moment.

"Then laying her head on the edge of the bed, she gave me a cat-like invitation by presenting her handsome behind to me. I rubbed my now thoroughly stiffened member between the beautiful cheeks of her bottom. Then she seized my hand, but would not allow me to put it anywhere near her secret parts.

" 'Not yet,' she said, 'be patient,' and she rubbed her backside against my appendage. A moment later she let my hand go so as to pass her hands slyly under my balls.

"She finally used her handsome behind so well, that I spent at the moment she was fingering me 'a little all over,' as she called it, to accelerate the matter. Then, turning round, she saw my instrument hanging down. She gave me a malicious look and going after the big dildo, she tied it round my waist. She then used a little ointment on it, and presenting to me her superb doorway, whose proportions I was obliged to admire, asked me to introduce the big thing into it.

"I thought that would be impossible, but she wriggled and pressed against me until she got it almost all the way in. This performance took place on the edge of the bed; she unbuttoned her waist and I could see her alabaster bosoms, white, firm, well developed and nicely separated. I gently rubbed her handsome slit with the enormous tool and she seemed absolutely delirious with pleasure.

" 'Open the valve when I tell you,' she murmured, as she continued to play upon it. She had with a sudden movement wound her legs around my waist and seemed to wish to push the dildo up to the handle.

"I never saw so much passion in my life. With her eyes half closed, she seemed to be lost in another world. I stooped over her, squeezed her bosoms which appeared to excite her still more, and finally, as if in agony, she cried out:

" 'Let the valve go—let it go!'

"I did so, and a copious flow of tepid fluid

inundated her handsome cunt. She was still slowly heaving and enjoying this internal 'coit' as I continued the frigging movements with the enormous dildo. Little by little she became more excited and it seemed to me that my pizzle attained the proportions of the big dildo itself. I then slowly untied it and making believe it had slipped out by accident, I introduced my instrument into her loins.

"Her cunt was large but full of voluptuousness and as I shoved my wedge in, I kissed her delicious bosoms, her neck, her belly and then her lascivious mouth.

"She sustained this second assault admirably well and it lasted long. When she cried out again to let the valve go, I was on hand with a new supply of sperm which appeared to satisfy her.

"She remained unconscious for a few moments, then got up, her face crimson, and her body exhausted. I advised sleep and she answered with a smile that indeed she thought she needed it.

"I dressed myself and took leave of the beautiful Countess after taking a voluptuous kiss from her moist coral lips.

"She offered me her sleigh for my return but as my house was not very far off, I preferred to walk there.

"Two days after this I was awakened by a terrible noise at the door of my room. My servant answered the bell and returned to say that a young girl had introduced herself into the house and refused to leave without speaking to me. I ordered that she come down and to my astonishment, I saw, once more, my little servant girl.

"She looked like a beggar and her garments were in shreds. She finally told me that after my departure she had been so unhappy that she determined to follow me. A little money allowed her to travel in a sleigh part of the way, then her purse being empty, she was obliged to walk the rest of the journey.

"The tortures of all kinds she must have suffered gave me an idea of the strength of her will. The poor little thing acknowledged that she loved me and that she would surely kill herself if I abandoned her. I felt an emotion which was entirely new to me. It was impossible to place her with the other servants and the only thing I could do was to persuade her to go to France with me, where I could put her in a school for a few years.

"Three years have elasped now and I have had occasion to appreciate the progress which my protégé has made in every possible way, in learning and in accomplishments of all kinds.

"When my thoughts turn to her it is like balm to my heart. However, she could not remain in school any longer. The Superintendent wrote me lately that she had nothing more to teach her and a few days ago I gave orders to have her brought here, where she is at present.

"I have had two interviews with Wanda— that is the name I have given her—and her love for me is so intense that I dread to see her. When I propose to find a husband for her, she goes into hysterics and I had to promise to make no more allusions to her marriage.

"Such is my position, M. Dormeuil, what would you do in my place?"

"I really cannot say, my dear Count. It is

most embarrassing. You cannot marry her and you do not wish to make her your mistress."

He seemed for a time lost in a profound reverie and did not reply for a few moments.

"She wishes to see me this evening and I am afraid I may weaken," he said at last. "Let me conduct you, dear friend, to a closet, near her room and if passion should get the best of me, come to my assistance, I pray you."

The greater part of the evening was already spent and we had to hasten our visit to Wanda before she should retire. The Count preceded me and made me enter a closet next to the room, at the door of which he knocked.

"Who is there?" called a fresh young voice.

"It is I, Alexis."

"Ah, at last," she cried, and I heard her run to the door. "How glad I am to see you, I feared you would forget my request."

"You see, do you not, that I have not forgotten it, since I am here."

There was a little hole in the door of my hiding place which seemed to have been made on purpose. I peeped through it and saw her on her knees before him. She implored him to keep her with him; she would be his slave.

She is as handsome as the Count has described her, but taller and more distinguished looking in her white wrapper. As she holds his hands and kisses his face, her expression denotes sincere love. She pulls him towards a large armchair and innocently sits on his knees, as she would have done with her father when a child; while with all the grace imaginable, she tries to extract a promise from him that he will not leave her.

It was too much for my Russian friend to

withstand and naturally he seized her head and covered her face with kisses. They are entwined in each other's arms. Their bodies are like one. It would have seemed a crime to me to disturb them, notwithstanding the request made by the Count.

How she twists herself like a snake; now they have fallen pell-mell on a beautiful white bearskin on the floor, and he passes one leg between her naked thighs, and she, following her natural instinct, rubs herself against him.

I could not blame him. As I looked at them, I felt my own prick stiffen up like a poker. When he placed his instrument between her beautiful thighs, I thought he only did his duty, for she was breathlessly wishing for it.

The jerks of the young girl's body became less marked, and all at once she gave a cry of pain! It was only transitory, however, for she entwined herself round the Count more closely than ever. She literally covered his face with kisses and laughed and cried in the same breath.

It is impossible for me see her body with the exception of her thighs which escape her drawers, but that is enough to convince me of the beauty of the rest.

She must have spent several times, although she does not wish to let him go. She has turned over on her side and shows me her back. Her drawers are slightly open and as she pushes with her bottom, I can see her crack with the Count's lance-like prick imbedded in it.

Her backside must be enormous, for it almost splits the delicate envelope that confines it.

The Count has just spent but she still remains sticking to him and does not allow her mouth to leave his for an instant.

I judged that the amorous combat was at an end and in order not to receive any reproaches from the Count, I pretended to be asleep. When he shook me, I begged his pardon for having fallen asleep. He excused me politely and conducted me back to his room without saying a word about Wanda. The next morning the Count came to wake me himself and had been thoughtful enough to have my breakfast brought to me in bed.

I rose and he conducted me to his bath. We talked of a thousand and one things and his conversation was very animated; he seemed much happier and livelier than was his wont.

"Come," said he, "I am going to show you my library."

He led the way to a room whose style was most severe, but where all the erotic works of French, English and Spanish authors were arranged on shelves.

While I admired the handsome collection, the Count pressed a spring and a little drawer flew open which contained some volumes carefully wrapped in silk. He took them from their hiding place with the greatest care and handed them to me one by one. I read their titles:

A Youthful Adventurer
The Comtessa Marga
The Perfumed Garden
Venus in India
Adventures of Lais Lovecock
A Spanish Gallant
Memories of a Voluptuary

and numerous other works of a similar character.

The British Museum contains some of these works, which are not only very rare but also masterpieces of erotic literature.

The collector who could obtain any of them would be fortunate and find their perusal most entertaining. They rank high in their line, and will make many a one stand.

"I must absent myself for some hours," he continued, "but you can spend your time here pleasantly and read anything you like."

As soon as he left, I began to read the rarest of these works. The rest were already known to me, at least those in English and French. *The Horn Book* is a remarkable work and also *The Open Chamber*.

When he returned it seemed to me as if he had only been gone a few moments, so much was I interested in my reading. He announced that he had prepared everything for an agreeable evening, but he would not tell me anything more. He expressed his regrets at not being able to spend the rest of the day with me and added that he had to go out and make a few calls.

I had forgotten Paris, Madame Benoit, Madame Cuchond and the rest! I must go too, or they would send out a general alarm. The Count held me back, smiling, and assured me that everything would be all right, as he would go himself to see Madame Benoit and the others and explain everything.

I preferred it so and agreed to remain. I resumed my erotic reading which caused the remainder of the day to pass very quickly. When five o'clock struck and it began to get dark, I had devoured a large part of the contents of the secret drawer.

The Count returned a little before six o'clock and soon we partook of an excellent supper.

After supper—we took our supper in the parlor—I perceived that my friend was in the best of humors. He had been to Madame X—, had seen Pauline, Clemence, the Abbé, and a few others. They did not know what to think of my absence; he had given them some kind of an explanation and they were convinced that I had gone on a hunting expedition some miles away.

The parlor, I now perceived, had been robbed of its furniture, and there was an open space in the middle of the room. The Count invited me to be seated on a sort of ottoman, low but delightfully comfortable, while he on another, just opposite to mine.

The atmosphere is perfumed, while the light is so arranged as to be of every imaginable color. I feel that my friend is reserving a surprise for me. What can it be?

In answer to his call, Ivan, his faithful servant, brings in two Turkish pipes with their long stems. I would have preferred a good cigar, but for the novelty of the thing I accept the pipe.

We are sitting quietly, when the curtain over the door moves and a woman or girl with a musical instrument enters the room. I say woman or girl, for she is so wrapped up that I cannot see her face. The Count smokes on without manifesting either surprise or curiosity, and I do the same.

The woman begins the entertainment, and sits down on a cushion and commences to play a lazy, monotonous air. Two other women enter the room at this juncture and their dance, monotonous at first, becomes more animated as the music becomes faster.

They turn round each other in the middle of the room and all at once appear to me as if enveloped in a coil of tulle. Sure enough, they have loosened their muslin robes and as they dance, they unwind them. I can distinctly see their legs through their thin single skirt. The dance becomes more and more exciting; the two girls soon become entwined in each other's arms and seem intoxicated.

Suddenly they tear off their veils and I can see their forms which are admirably molded. Both are brunettes and apparently sixteen or seventeen years of age. They each wear a small jacket, open in front from the middle of the body to the cunt, while a many-colored belt, encircles their waists. Besides this, the only garment for each is a gauze skirt.

They must, however, have something else for an undergarment, for it is impossible to see their flesh clearly. They embrace and, still retaining their steps, kiss each other feverishly. Each in turn passes her head beneath the other's jacket and kisses the snowy white bosom beneath.

They soon unfasten their short skirts and throw off their belts. They are bewitching in their unique costumes, a little waist reaching scarcely down to the hips and a light yellow scarf covering their bottoms and hidden places, now complete their outfits.

They continue to excite one another, and the music seems to make them frantic with passion. Hastily they snatch off their clothing and now contemplate each other in almost total nudity.

They roll on the floor like playful kittens, their fingers tickling each other's private parts, while little amorous cries escape their lips. They handle each other's bosoms and tongue their lips. The youngest seems to be the most excited and while she kisses her companion, she puts her tongue far into her mouth; her bottom moves like lightning and when her companion touches her with her fingers between her legs, she starts as though it actually burned her.

She wishes to be played with and yet seems to evade the touch. She jumps astride her friend's bottom and rubs her little cunt on her, and while she fingers her pussy, the other turns her head to receive a kiss, and the music plays on.

At last they have reached the desired degree of excitement and each now feverishly places the head of the other between her own legs, while they caress each other with rapid strokes of their tongues.

The tallest one has her back towards me, and shows me her arse with its little pink hole. Beneath her I see the tongue and lips of the youngest. The little hole seems to open and close as the enjoyment becomes greater. The one underneath her sustains her, and her beautiful bottom looks like a split hemisphere in pink satin.

I never witnessed a more exciting scene, and my prick, as a proof of my feeling, is swollen to its utmost. The Count is still passive. The two young girls are about to spend and their bodies are quivering with passion. The beautiful behind which fascinates me, rises and falls, opens and closes with marvelous rapidity.

Suddenly they both spend and the smaller seems actually to want to eat the little cunny which she has between her teeth. She bites it in her amorous delirium.

My prick makes a movement at the very moment that the girls spend and I have just time to introduce my handkerchief into my breeches to receive the discharge.

They are still stretched upon the floor to recuperate their strength, and their beautiful bodies give a voluptuous tremor from time to time. I turn my head towards the Count and when I look for the erotic pair, they have disappeared.

My friend's eyes are a little more brilliant than usual but that is all. The servant enters with two dressing gowns and the Count invites me to lay aside my ordinary clothes, and sets the example.

"When I traveled in the East, I used to adopt the Oriental costume and now and then I like to indulge in it again. We are going to have a change of scenery," he added as he rang the bell.

A little girl about twelve years old suddenly springs into the room, as light as a bird, her small body almost quivering with modesty in her costume—which is that of nudity.

At a sign from the Count, she approaches me and places herself on my knees. Behind her comes a little boy, somewhat older, his face as sweet and beautiful as the girl's. The Count coolly invites me to take my choice. I retain the little girl, not knowing what was expected of me.

A soft, delicious music now comes from the next room. The child takes my hand and places it between her tiny thighs. Her little aperture is hairless. It seems odd to touch those lips which are so naked. She herself places my finger in her little retreat and seems to know perfectly what she does it for. With her other hand she grasps my prick and rubs and presses it.

I feel a kind of indignation at so much vice but a look from the Count reassures me, so to speak. I pass my hand beneath the naked cunt of the little Bacchante, who begins to agitate her hand vigorously upon my prick, which she has well moistened and wishes to introduce under her Mount of Venus.

She amuses me now, I feel, as if I were playing with a doll. Her little bottom, plump and round, twists about in my hand and moving further, I am surprised to find a body quite developed. She shows me her little breasts, and gives me two little bosoms to kiss, about as large as billiard balls and nearly as firm.

Still she has not succeeded in making my enormous prick penetrate into the depths of her white belly. She soon tries to get astride of my head and thus gives me the lips of her little cunt to kiss. It is with no little pleasure that I use my tongue which seems to excite her immensely. She can scarcely press her little boudoir hard enough against me. She is not very heavy, so I pat her tiny bottom and when she thinks she is excited enough she returns to my prick, which this time she succeeds in forcing into her body.

Ah, how she wriggles! It seems as if there are a million demons or cupids all along my prick; with consummate art she tickles my tool and while I hold her on the end of it, she wriggles and commences to spend. At that moment I take a look at the Count.

He has placed his boy in a kneeling position with his head thrown on an ottoman and has stuck his enormous prick into his behind.

The boy moves his round and dimpled backside with as much art as the most skillful grisette. He knows all the fine points and with the movements of his behind puts the Count into ecstasies of delight. I see his tremendous prick move in and out of those two rosy hills and the pretty little behind gives a shove to make it enter still further, then recedes to let it come further out, and so on.

During this time the Count fingers his little prick, which stiffens and becomes about the size of my finger. This sight, added to the efforts of my little charmer, throws me into the final spasm and as I inject a spray of sperm into the cunt of the little girl, she seems to feel the same voluptuous pleasure as I do. She kisses me and continues the movement a little longer, in order to give me the full enjoyment of it and probably to satisfy herself, then she too, disappears as she came, scarcely giving me time to see her little bottom disappear behind the curtained door.

The Count finished first. He now gave an order in Russian and Ivan entered with a tray and two glasses and a little flask containing a bright red liquid. Two little pieces of fruit, nicely cut, accompanied the liquid. I was served first and put the fruit into my mouth after seeing the Count do so.

"When you feel a little hard substance," he said, "swallow it without uneasiness. It is a preparation which invigorates you."

I had just come to a sweet substance and according to instructions, swallowed it. Ivan presented me then with the glass of liquor which I drank. The liquid seemed to instil new life in me; I felt its warmth pervade my whole being. I had not before noticed a large handsome woman standing before me. She wore Turkish trousers of black silk, while between her thighs was a large mass of silky hair. She holds an enormous dildo in her hands and her bare bosoms, large, well separated, and as firm as marble spheres, seem to shiver in voluptuous anticipation.

At this moment she smiles at the Count and seats herself astride of a chair, after tying the dildo to one of her heels. She now introduces it into the lips of her cunt, while with a movement of her legs she puts it in rapid motion.

It soon appears that she enjoys this game immensely, when suddenly, not finding her legs agile enough, she unties the dildo and throwing herself on the floor, spreads her legs wide apart and shakes the enormous affair about inside of her.

In her passion she throws herself first upon her belly, then on her side, sometimes working fast, then again slowly, very slowly. Sometimes she holds it motionless and with the movement of her arse, presses it in; then again she places it upright on the floor and after letting her trousers down around her feet, she steps over it and forces her cunt open with its large end. Her great round arse rises and falls like a voluptuous machine, as she pushes it up to the hilt.

Her buttocks rebound faster and faster, and finally she throws herself upon her back and reaches the last great paroxysm of enjoyment by gently rubbing with her cunt, as she squeezes the dildo between her powerful thighs, which seem to be made of stone.

Thus, almost nude as she was, she resembled an antique statue and as she displayed her magnificent treasures, my prick fairly ached to take the place of the dildo which she was moving gently in her palpitating organ.

A slight sign from the Count aroused her and she retired slowly, her enormous arse, between whose cheeks I would willingly have disported myself, shaking as she walked away.

CHAPTER SIX

The Count suddenly began laughing; I felt the same desire, gradually creeping over me. I laughed and keep on laughing, unable to stop.

Lights seem to flash before my eyes, but I imagine some one is tying me; a bright light approaches me suddenly. I am in a delightful garden. It is immense—it seems to be a conservatory.

Delicious music is heard, first in the distance, then nearer. The scene changes like a flash. I am now in a room all hung in black; the music changes, a lovely woman enters and undresses herself. The scene is familiar to me. I have seen it somewhere. I finally recognize it as a scene in the passage of a book entitled *The Exposition,* which I have been reading. After having enjoyed reading it, I have the pleasure of seeing it. Then all is dark again, until another flash of light illuminates the next scene.

Two brigands have seized a magnificent woman; she begs for mercy and offers them money but I can see in their eyes that they will only be satisfied by assaulting the beauty. One of them is a strapping big fellow, but handsome withal; he cuts the laces of her bodice with a single stroke and begins to feel her bosoms. She struggles vainly, and the other man raises her skirts and lays bare a glorious bottom; she turns and twists in every direction and to punish her, he unbuckles his leather belt and lathers her handsome arse furiously.

The poor woman weeps, but instead of appeasing him, her screams seem to excite him all the more. The other robber after feeling her bosoms, finally draws them out and admires them, and taking an enormous prick out of his trousers, rubs it gently between her snow-white legs.

At last she quiets down and her struggles cease. The second robber leaves off whipping her and he, too, draws out his prick and placing it first in her arse, at last presents it at the entrance of her handsome portico.

The beauty again resists, but two or three slaps bring her to reason, and she allows him to introduce the haughty head of his prick between the shuddering lips of her cunt. His need must have been great, for he had scarcely given two or three shoves before he spends.

At this, the other robber raises her skirts and putting her in the desired position, enters also by the front. The poor traveler overwhelmed them both with insults and renewed her struggles, but now the tall fellow inserted his instrument, and the more she wriggled and twisted, the more she excited him. He holds her two hands in one of his and applies his mouth to hers.

He kisses her beautiful titties and discharges at the very moment that she spits into his face. It is only after satisfying themselves five or six times apiece that they tie her to a tree, whip her again and leave her at the mercy of other brigands, or some passerby.

Scarcely have they disappeared when a monk passes by. He crosses himself as he perceives the handsome cunt so well exposed. The woman implores him to untie her and he does so, when she relates her story to him. She is about thirty-five years old and from her story he learns that she is the Lady Superior of a convent not far distant, but she does not give its name.

She had donned a costume to preserve her identity while on a visit. The coach was stopped by two brigands, and she was made to descend. Being the only woman in it, they ordered the driver to continue his journey and leave her with them. No one, not a single man had the courage to interfere, but allowed the robbers to drag her to the woods.

As the Abbess finished her story, her eyes assumed a strange look. The nudity which she was unable to cover was beautiful in the extreme, so dimpled and so white. The monk does not dare look at her but she looks at him and I soon perceive that this poor St. Anthony is having a rude trial to support.

With no thought but of the passion which has been awakened by the repeated assaults of the brigands, the Lady Superior suddenly throws herself on the monk, seizes his enormous prick, which would have filled her two hands, and quickly raising his robe, straddles him, planting his big tool in her burning orifice before the monk can interfere.

She does all the work, holds the instrument in one hand and supports herself with the other resting on the grass. She belabors him with her lower pouting lips in great style and at last, spends, manipulating the enormous prick much as the instrument she hides so carefully in the convent, and uses every night when going to bed.

The monk supports the attack admirably; his prick is still as stiff at the moment when the Abbess writhes in the act of spending, as at the beginning of the amorous battle. She spends, but is just warmed up to thorough lasciviousness. She also desires to satisfy him and not knowing what to do, her slit being bruised and sore, she presents to him her big arse and allows him to satisfy himself.

He runs his long prick against her arse cheeks while the skin rises and falls on the extremity. Finally, the Lady Superior gives a movement or two of her backside and an enormous jet spurts out.

The scene changes again and I find myself upon a lawn sprinkled with flowers, amid a crowd of boys and girls at play. A young girl hides the face of a youth in her lap, while he has one hand behind his back. The other girls advance on tip-toe and with little screams of terror, they cautiously give the hand a slap and then await, blushing and breathless, for the young man to turn, and guess who gave the slap. After watching them a moment I am satisfied that the forfeit of the one who is caught is not an ordinary one.

When it is a boy they take down his trousers and each gives him a slap, not on the hand this time, but on the naked bottom. He must catch the last one who strikes him and that person must take his or her place until someone else is caught again. It is now the turn of a mischievous little girl to have her dress turned up. She buries her face in the lap of one whose office it is to hold and hide the eyes of each one who is hit.

They raise her skirts and expose her pretty little arse, while a little lower down can be seen a little pink cunt surrounded by its auburn fringe.

Whack! Whack! and the rosy skin takes on a deeper tint. The girl rises, and scans the circle but does not guess rightly and once more they hide her head and again the pretty bottom is exposed. This continues until a tall blonde is caught.

They hide her head, unbutton her drawers, raise her chemise, and, as she is tall, her little cunny is more exposed. I can perceive the rosy entrance as a mischievous little girls sticks her finger in the opening. The blade does not move and the little girl continues to rub gently with her finger till the blonde gives unmistakable evidence that she likes it.

At this point a boy draws the girl's finger away and inserts his standing prick. The blonde perceives the difference and gives evidence of the fact by becoming more excited.

This is the signal for a general debauch such as I have never witnessed since or before. Each little mischief unbuttons a boy's trousers and sucks his little tool; she caresses it until it is stiff enough to enter her little cunt.

There are forty couples in the greatest diversity of positions. They all spend once and spend again; then, with shirts up and pricks in the air, they have a game of Ring Around the Rosy.

The girls, with one hand on their neighbor's tools, the boys with one finger in the girls' cunts, either from the front or from the back. Then things become confused and finally I see nothing more.

"How long have I been asleep?" is the first question I ask the Count, as he enters my room.

"Thirty-six hours," he says, "or at least so says Ivan, for I have slept just as long myself. My dear Monsieur Dormeuil, I wished you to become acquainted with the strange sensations and visions caused by hashish!"

This explained the fanciful dreams I had had. I remained a few days longer with the Count and then returned to Paris to resume my old habits.

I reached my apartment at ten o'clock and surprised Jean in conversation with a chambermaid living in the neighborhood. I was able to approach them without being heard. She was just showing the boob how to do it.

"Great Idiot! Wait until I rub that tool of yours," said she, and began rubbing his prick and shaking it, too. "Take my titties, John dear. Not that way, you hurt me. There, that's it. Now tickle the nipples. You see, you begin to grow stiffer. Put your hand under my skirt—there—feel my leg. Wait, you are too rough; you hurt me with your big fingers; now there, what do you feel? Is it wet? Now put your finger in—not there, you are too far down. How stupid you are. I tell you, that is my arsehole. Ah, now you are stiff as a Grenadier. Now is the time—what are you doing—that is the right place, but you are hurting me; take your hand away and you will see."

She takes his prick and puts it between her thighs. "There—shove, John—not so hard—don't you see you keep slipping. There it is—now push. Easy at first—wait, I will get it in myself!" And at last she gets it into her cunt.

The amorous combat commences and lasts for some time. Several times she is about to spend but the idiot allowed his prick to slip out. Evidently it is his first experience and that is why she displays so much patience. Finally he spends, and I hear him say to her, "I did not feel anything much, did you?"

"Yes, I did, it was ever so good; you are a ninny. Do you want to have another one?"

But I thought that another one would be too long, so I began to cough and called Jean as loudly as I could. I heard a rustle of skirts and then Jean appeared, as red as a poppy.

He was very glad to see me back and for that matter, I was not sorry to be at home again.

I soon pay my respects to my terrible neighbor and am delighted with my reception as I found her quite improved in manner. She has changed her style of dressing her hair and looks much younger. She wears a close fitting dress which displays her still slender form to advantage.

Our conversation becomes quite animated. She asks me a thousand questions.

I next go to our restaurant and next to Mademoiselle Hortense whose little cunt I explore of course, since it is part of my Thursday program. My correspondence is scant and uninteresting. I go to see Madame X—, but I do not return there in the evening, for I feel the effects of the days spent at Poissy.

The next morning I receive a letter from the Count announcing his intention to start for Russia. Wanda desires him to take the trip, so he will go. He sends his compliments to me.

This departure grieves me; I have really taken a liking to this peculiar individual, and for some days I feel out of sorts. I spend a great deal of my time in the company of Madame Benoit and find her decidedly more interesting than formerly.

Two weeks have elasped; I only go to see Madame X— at intervals, and I have not purchased any more gloves. I lie in bed and think of the past, and have day dreams. I no longer have the same love for women. I do not feel the same regard of gratifying my passions. Another fortnight passes away and brings me tidings from the Count.

I am more and more in Madame Benoit's company and . . . shall I acknowledge it? I have made a proposition of marriage to her.

Who would have thought that one day I would be a husband and Madame Benoit my wife?

Now and then I kiss the lips of my betrothed and I dare not attempt a liberty, but tomorrow night I shall have the plump body of my wife entwined in my arms in this bed or hers, whichever she may like better.

The wedding takes place as arranged. It is midnight, and all the guests have retired. The women have kissed the bride and whispered to their hearts' content.

Naturally, Madame Dormeuil blushes lightly every time she meets my eyes, which becomes her very much. I take her on my knees and try to assist her to take off her waist. She will not allow that.

"Stop! I beg of you," she exclaims.

I take a kiss, then another, a third . . . a great many. However at last I find myself in my own room. She would not grant me the conjugal bed tonight. She denied me so charmingly that I could not insist. I go to bed feeling cross and out of humor. Several times during the night I feel like forcing the other door that separates the cruel one from me. But I am afraid of the noise and the scandal.

We spend the next day in the suburbs of Paris. The weather is so beautiful that we decided to go to the country. My wife is quite lively and eats and drinks with appetite.

We return at nine o'clock and as I take off her shoes, I take the liberty of examining the commencement of round, well turned leg. Madame Dormeuil will not shut the door in my face tonight! We have a lengthy discussion on that point, but she will do her duty as a wife. She says that I am to be forbidden the sight of her disrobing, so I am banished temporarily to my own apartment. Twice have I gone to the door but have not been admitted. At last I am able to turn the knob. The lamp on the table is turned very low and the room is so dark that I can scarcely distinguish the bed, the curtains of which are drawn.

It does not take me long to undress, then I slip in between the sheets where a slight warmth alone betrays her presence. I wait a few minutes, but my wife does not show any intention of beginning a conversation.

"Dearest!" I venture to say then: "Gertrude! Gertrude!"

Perhaps she is asleep, and I touch her gently on the back. At the contact of my finger she doubles herself up and draws close to the wall, but I become bolder and in my title of husband, put my arm about her waist, and draw her to me. I forcibly turn her face to mine and impress a burning kiss upon her lips.

I feel her big bosoms and press them close to me; I turn her quickly in my arms, but she begs me to let her sleep. It appears so ridiculous to her to have me in her bed, she has become so accustomed to consider me as a friend, as a brother, and so on. As she speaks, she hides her head in my bosom. I cannot stand it any longer. Little by little I have raised her chemise.

I pass my hand over her legs, her large bottom, and press it gently. Then I suddenly thrust one leg between her thighs, explore her legs, the knees, then further up. As I feel the luxuriant hair against my leg, I grasp her pouting pussy, then again I feel her bosoms. They fill my hands, firm yet so soft. Now my hand descends to her great cunt. What a beauty she has! Surely she must feel my prick; it is like a great club against her body.

"Anatole, I beg of you, not tonight, tomorrow night if you like!"

"No, my darling, tonight, now!" I say passionately and I succeed but not without some difficulty in getting between her legs; then I immediately try to place my tool at the entrance of her big pussy. On pressing a little, I enter with ease. I give a vigorous shove and I am there! I begin to rub softly and put one hand under her bottom. It does not take her long to respond.

"Anatole, kiss me," she murmurs. Presently I kiss her again, her tongue responds to mine and her arse moves, keeping time as I enter and leave the little grotto of love. I kiss her voluptuous bosom and I move still faster.

"Anatole, how good it is. Not so fast! Ah!

Ah! Ah! A little faster now. Faster!! It is so delightful. Ah-h-h-h!!"

And now her big bosom goes like a steam engine and she squeezes my tool and plays with my balls. I take good care not to stop her. She is coming! I feel it—there it is!

"Anatole, I am coming, my darling! Oh, I love you, my husband, my darling!" and her great bottom falls heavily on my hands. We spend once, then spend again, and I am still ready to spend the third time.

After three successive assaults, we go to sleep in each other's arms, but before closing my eyes I calculate how many years my wife had to remain without having relations with a man and admit that fate is indeed hard on a woman.

The next day, when I look at Madame Dormeuil I remember my reflection of the night before and I give her a hearty kiss without telling her why. Things go on pretty much the same after the first night, but without any struggle on her part.

I had been happy in my new existence for a month, when I received a letter from Count Alexis.

In order to give you an idea of the effect it had on me, I will reproduce it.

My dear Dormeuil,

My dear friend, you must either have thought I had forgotten you or that I was dead. My silence was caused by much work and great uncertainty of mind.

Do you remember Wanda? She is here with me. I was sick and she took care of me with wonderful devotion. Many admirers, young, rich and titled, have asked for her hand in marriage. She refused them all and seems happy only by my side. Before so much devotion, I, the high-lived, have succumbed. My heart has spoken; I am going to marry Wanda.

According to the French custom, before my marriage, I intend to give an entertainment to all my friends. It will be my last bachelor's dinner and I cordially invite you to attend. My next letter will give you the date. I shall count upon you and we will be sure to have a good time.

By the way, I have a confidence to make to you. You remember when I visited Madame Benoit, your terrible neighbor. When I told her I was sent by you, I found her in a bad humor. One of my little jokes at last, however, made her smile, then laugh heartily.

Unintentionally, a naughty word or two would creep into the conversation, and I remember that she made me repeat them. Her hearing was not so very good perhaps; to be frank with you, I took a few liberties which were not badly received, and one thing which you will certainly not believe, my dear Dormeuil, is that Madame Benoit's skin is very soft and that her bosoms are magnificently firm.

Once warmed up by the coquetry of your neighbor, I raised her skirts and presented you-know-what, at the entrance of her retreat.

Plenty of beautifully curling hairs and big thighs, on my word!

You doubt the fact I am sure, and think me insane, but it is true for all that; I shall always remember that glorious mount. It was one of the best I ever had.

Your neighbor fucks well; I should never have dreamed of such a thing, and it was in your interest that I carried matters so far. That is undoubtedly the reason of your charming reception on your return; now good luck to you; use this little confidence as you please. Try it yourself; she is not as terrible as she looks. Let me hear from you pretty soon. I expect your visit shortly.

With cordial good wishes, I am your friend,

ALEXIS.

Who would have thought such a thing! Oh, Madame Benoit, the prude. But I reasoned with myself. After all, Madame Benoit was free at that time to do as she pleased and I was a fool.

A week ago, I myself broke our marriage vows. I received a letter, giving me a rendez-vous at 37 Rue de l'Ecoille. It was Miss Anderson, whom Count Alexis had met at Naples. She was still in love with him and asked me news of him. I have revenged myself on the Count with this young English girl.

I pressed her so hard that I laid her on the bed, and, raising her skirts, introduced my tool into her reception room before she had time to refuse. She worked well and vigorously, and I soon gave her a reserve of sperm which I had saved up, as my wife was angry with me.

She is a very loving and lovely thing, this little auburn-haired girl. She really spends with the finesse of art. I see her often and she has promised to stay here another month.

I have abandoned the idea of going to Russia, neither will I be angry with Gertrude, who is quite enough—more than enough for me now!

II

CARESSES

PREFACE

Old castles harbor many curious things, sometimes hidden away in the priceless antique furniture. And often, one is almost forced to ask himself how many secrets have slumbered quietly throughout the centuries, before they were discovered by sheer coincidence . . .

Till one day while browsing through an attic, or opening an old chest of drawers, one stumbles upon some yellowed documents, a bundle of letters, or a carefully written diary, left there, Lord knows how long ago, by some respectable ancestor.

This is what happened to me when I visited the old family castle. I don't know why I decided to make the trip, nor can I precisely remember what made me rummage through the old chest of drawers. But I found an old, yellowed diary, carefully bound in moroccan leather, bordered with red silk, written by the galant, beautiful Marquise whose portrait I have always admired since I was a little child. She seemed so far away, this long-dead ancestor of mine; her slight, knowing smile, hiding secrets of which she knew the answers while I could not yet formulate the questions.

Was my finding your diary perhaps the reward for my secret devotioñ to you, oh Jacqueline, or was it a mere coincidence? I want to prefer the first, and believe that the hand of fate made me discover your innermost secrets.

You have always been my favorite, hanging in the heavy gold frame between my other ancestors, the whole gallery of which I would happily trade if I could only have a word with you.

They are all there . . . your father and his, his great-uncle, the ArchBishop who looks so stern in his purple mantle, but who, I know from history was a devoted pupil of Pavillon and almost shared prison with the Jansenist Abbot of Saint-Cyran.

And now, through a miracle, you have suddenly come to life for me. Complete with all your charm your daring exploits and your almost incredible passions. They are all there, jumping at me from the yellowing pages of this little red book.

I hope, by publishing your memoirs, that I may be able to immortalize you with all the other great lovers of your time. Oh, darling Jacqueline, shameless and charming, barely blushing while dropping your beautiful clothing and rustling silken finery. A girl of a century past and gone, but immortalized by gallantry and freedom of customs!

CHAPTER ONE

I want to write down, upon these pages, the happiest moments of my love life, the most exciting episodes, the most gallant adventures.

I do not know what has brought me to serve Eros and Venus so wholeheartedly throughout my life, but I am convinced that the immortal goddess stood by my cradle and that Amor has smiled down upon me ever since my early childhood.

The way of life in the ancestral castle, as dictated by my father, was one of strictest austerity and severity. No matter how far I try to think back into my childhood, I cannot remember ever having seen a smile upon my father's face.

He was always sad, and in mourning, which was easy to understand, since my dear mother died while very young, only two years after I was born.

My father was more than twenty years older than my mother, and the old nobleman never was capable of recuperating from the severe blow fate had dealt him. Strictest devotion and austerity regulated his life from the day of mother's death; when I was ten years old, he followed his older brother and entered a trappist monastery. In the white habit of the followers of the Abbot de Rance he spent his life, and ended it without ever having spoken a single word since his entrance into the monastery. I was given into the care of my aunt.

This aunt was my father's younger sister. Quite contrary to both her austere brothers, she had a vivacious, one might even say, loose, character. She consorted with the most brilliant minds of her time, the most famous artists, authors and philosophers. I remember having seen, upon more than one occasion, the gnarled figure of the old Monsieur Voltaire . . .

I loved my dear aunt very much. Her open mind, her consideration for me, her free education which did not bother with old-fashioned prejudices, have all contributed to my becoming what I am today.

*   *   *

The old family castle was witness to my first love affairs.

Our lordly mansion was famous in the entire neighborhood. My father had barely left the front door when my aunt decided to do a lot of remodeling in the fashion of the time. The home lost its austere character. Marble nymphs and fauns were placed in the gardens, cascading fountains and waterfalls were designed and a labyrinth of bushes were artfully arranged. The living quarters were furnished with beautiful furniture and the latest conveniences.

I was delighted with the changes my aunt brought to the ancestral estate; my vivacious nature had always wanted to live in such a place. The shrubbery reverberated with my singing; I ran through the beautiful lanes with the gorgeous flowers, and I frequently bathed in one of the basins with marble nymphs, offering my naked body to the cooling, streaming cascades.

My senses awakened early and rapidly, and I was soon acquainted with the game of love, at least in theory. I would experience actual practice somewhat later.

But I already knew every exciting detail from the many beautiful books, adorned with fine engravings, which were distributed throughout practically every room in the house. My aunt, who loved this form of literature, never tried to hide her passion for it and it was therefore very easy for me to acquaint myself with the contents of those beautiful works.

More than once I took one of these little books, in prose or in verse, to my bedroom with me, and I learned from them about everything I wanted to know.

I often stood in front of one of the large mirrors and compared my own body with those of the heroines in the books, who were drawn by some of our finest artists. I discovered, according to these artists, by the simple process of comparison, that I should be considered very pretty. I also discovered something else. I tried out some of the detailed descriptions of the various caresses on my own body. It was not very difficult to find the sensitive spot which was hidden in the middle of my young, barely discernible fleece. And my nimble, quick fingers gave me my first joys.

I had just turned fifteen years old.

When I think back to that time, it seems to me that I must have been a fairly delectable young lady. I was tall and slender; my neck was graceful; I had two small, marvelously graceful breasts; my pretty, well-formed legs were supported by tiny feet, just like the marble nymphs in the garden. This body supported an oval face with blue eyes, simultaneously impish and passionate, a little mouth with dark red, full lips and two rows of regular, pearly white teeth. My golden blonde hair cascaded down my slender, softly sloping shoulders . . .

I now fully understand that in those days I was an extremely desirable woman. Therefore, I am not surprised at the adventures I was about to experience. To be honest, I must add that I called them upon myself with all the fervor of my passionate nature.

* * *

My dear aunt had seen to it that I received a good elementary education. I was soon able to read, and also to write with fairly good skill. I was also instructed in the most liberal philosophy which is indispensable for a young and free spirit wanting to fight the horrible prejudices of a bygone age.

But my aunt was convinced that it was about time to further my knowledge in all fields, and to give me the brilliant instruction which is absolutely necessary for a young lady of my rank and standing. With incredible skill she selected the proper man to be my teacher.

The young man in question was originally destined to become a member of the clergy. A brilliant student, he had completed his studies in short time, but then he left the Seminary. He had become interested in the New Philosophy and its morals, and he absolutely refused to be consecrated into the priesthood. It was for this that his family had severed all ties with him. Since he was a member of a noble family, my aunt was very happy to be able to take him under her wings.

The young Baron, Francois de B— was several years older than I. He was extremely brilliant and his knowledge of Greek, Latin, and ancient and modern literature—sacred as well as profane—was astonishing. I was especially interested in the worldly, modern literature and he made a perfect student out of me.

He was also very proficient in many other things, but I will reserve that for a next chapter.

CHAPTER TWO

I was quite apprehensive when the first day of my lessons approached.

My aunt had given my new teacher living quarters in the right wing of the castle. He now occupied the rooms on the second floor, which had been empty ever since my uncle retired into the monastery.

The apartment consisted of three rooms, two of which were living quarters for Francois, and the third one was supposed to be our classroom. I did not like this room at all, since it had retained the austerity of the days past. Rows of books were standing upon the shelves on the wall, and the portraits of monks and stern philosophers seemed to stare disdainfully down upon the small sofa, the only elegant piece of furniture in the entire room. And, indeed, this little sofa became the focal point of a little pastime which the noble people in their black ebony frames would have frowned upon, if not downright condemned!

But this room with the large windows which opened up into the estate's park was soon to become one of the most pleasant places for me to be.

*   *   *

I had noticed that very first day that Francois was a very good-looking young man. He was extremely shy that first morning, when I entered to receive my instruction. He blushed and stuttered when he began to ask me the first, innocent questions.

But soon he grew bolder and looked at me

with penetrating eyes which seemed to be more concerned with my looks than with his thoughts about how to teach me philosophy. I was well aware that I had made a deep impression upon my tutor, but I was not about to let him know immediately that I had guessed his innermost thoughts. I therefore sat down beside my teacher like a nice, obedient little girl, allowing him to glance down my neckline which plunged rather deeply, as far as nice little girls are concerned.

Francois trembled slightly, and it seemed to take all his will power to avert his eyes from my firm little breasts whose nipples strained against the body-hugging silk of my blouse.

I could not help myself, but my desires were awakened by this good-looking teacher of mine who, himself, had great trouble to hide his increasing passion for me!

During this first lesson we did not talk much. All he did was to review briefly my existing knowledge of Latin and the few other subjects I had taken.

After we had taken our meal, Francois and I went into the park for a little stroll. This was part of the daily curriculum which my good aunt had worked out for us.

Francois is walking next to me, from time to time taking my arm. It seems that he has become a little bit more sure of himself. I hope he has recognized the fact that I am a precocious girl. I aim to find out shortly.

We have approached a beautiful marble statue. Leda is leaning back and the swan, white as fresh-fallen snow, rubs its long neck voluptuously between the legs of the goddess, caressing her with its bill.

I stand still, admiring this beautiful grouping. Leda has a marvelous expression of satisfied passion, and looking at this passion which one can only guess and which I have been hungering to experience, always excites me.

Francois also has stopped walking, and he is standing right next to me. I innocently ask him many questions about Leda and the Swan. Does he believe my hypocritical innocence, or has he discovered my little game? He blushes, his hand presses my arm tighter, and quickly we walk away from the statue, continuing our stroll.

On our way back we again pass the statue of Leda and the Swan. Again I ask him, smilingly, to explain the mystery of Leda's facial expression. Finally Francois offers to explain to me the whole story of the divine Leda and her mysterious partner.

He puts it in such a way that I have reason to believe he has understood me . . .

* * *

Two days have gone by, and Francois still has not explained the mystery of Leda. I do not dare to ask him, or to remind him of his promise. The Latin hours are monotonous and boring.

* * *

One day, it seems that Francois has made up his mind. He looks rather tired and strange that morning. Like any other diligent and obedient pupil, I sit down in front of my little lectern and look up at him, awaiting the morning's first lesson.

But he remains standing behind me, and waits till I start writing. I am well aware of his glances and I know that he is looking down my neckline and feasting his eyes upon my little, well-formed breasts. I can feel that, this time, he is terribly excited! Suddenly he throws his arms around my waist and presses a light kiss upon my shoulder.

I shiver, and get up from my seat. I walk around the desk and stretch myself out upon the little sofa. Francois follows me with his eyes. When he notices that I do not put up any resistance, and it becomes apparent to him that I desire him as much as he does me, he walks over to me, and kneels beside the sofa, murmuring softly.

"Oh! Jacqueline, Jacqueline, is it possible . . . ?"

"Francois, oh . . . my Francois!" I whisper, offering my lips to his. His panting mouth comes closer.

The kiss lingers on and on, Francois slowly lifts my dress, his hands slowly caress my legs. They instinctively close around his hands. But he still succeeds to reach my little drawers, pulling them down over my knees. Not long afterward, my foot kicks them impatiently to the floor. The only obstacle left is my thin, silken chemise which, too, is quickly removed. My teacher indulges himself with me in some of the most marvelous caresses I ever experienced.

Of course, custom demands that I put up token resistance. And it is exactly this resistance which makes it easier for Francois' hand to more fully explore the area. He has found the curls of my little blonde fleece under which this very secret and also very sensitive little spot is hidden. Then he, too, finds that little spot, and his caressing hand lingers there.

Francois continues his caresses for a long, long time. I am beginning to pant, and my hand automatically goes out toward my teacher, rubbing along his legs, trying to find the corresponding spot on his body.

Alas, we have no time to continue our little game. The sound of the dinner bell interrupts the magic, even before my nimble fingers had succeeded to unbutton that part of his breeches which are hiding the object of my intense curiosity.

Mealtime has been announced and we have to make haste bringing our appearances in order before we can walk to the dining room where my dear aunt is awaiting us.

CHAPTER THREE

I have checked the position of the sofa in my classroom very carefully, and to this end insisted that we take our afternoon stroll in the garden past the right wing of the estate. I could establish to my own satisfaction that the place of our mutual pleasure which had not been put on the planned curriculum, was invisible to any viewer from the outside.

We had barely returned into the classroom when I asked Francois to continue the lecture he had started upon the sofa. I wanted to make sure that we would have enough time ahead of us and that we would not be again so rudely interrupted before we had started anything of real interest.

The good start of that morning had given me a foretaste of possible pleasures and I did not want to lose a single precious moment. I take off my drawers myself, and begin to unbutton the leg coverings of my charming teacher. I had never done anything of the sort, and my fingers were not as nimble as I thought they were. Moreover, Francois had taken my hand, and guided it into the opening I had made, before I had finished unbuttoning him completely . . .

Francois kneels in front of the sofa upon which I am stretched out, and he only has to come a little bit closer so that I can see his thing, the object of my desire and curiosity.

There it is! I am holding it between my fingers and I can feel it jerk! I touch it, I caress it, and I look upon it with great, unexplainable desire . . . I also notice that it is heavy; much, much heavier than those of the statues in the park. And it is quite long! But it does not seem to be a mistake—on the contrary . . .

I also notice that it is getting harder and harder; it feels very warm and it is beginning to throb. It seems to be very happy with my caresses, because it is jumping for joy. I think that that is very sweet. I admire it, my eyes devour it and I bend myself so close to it that my face almost touches it . . .

Suddenly I know a name for it: Francinet! Little Francinet, delicious Francinet . . .

But suddenly my Francois—the tall one—stands bolt upright. He makes Francinet disappear into the depths of his breeches . . . Why?

That was the entire lecture for this afternoon.

*　　*　　*

I do not know if I am making any progress at all in Latin, but I have learned a lot in the art of caressing.

Francois has taught me how Francinet wants to be caressed. And I have tried. Obviously, the first time I was rather clumsy, though it seems that Francinet enjoyed it very much. It is, by the way, much easier than I had thought. Francois helps me and I take Francinet between thumb and index finger, closing them as if they were a ring.

And now Francinet is a prisoner!

He is beautiful, very beautiful. I can feel that Francinet is tremendously delighted; so is Francois. Soon Francinet swells to enormous proportions and then, all of a sudden, he becomes tiny, very tiny . . .

116

Francois is of the opinion that I have done it too quickly, and he patiently explains that tomorrow we will proceed at a much slower pace. He has promised me that Francinet will be able to remain large much longer and that the pleasure will be greater and more beautiful.

* * *

We were again in the park, standing in front of Leda. And Francois explains:

"Jacqueline, my dearest, when I caress you with my fingers, it seems beautiful to you. But you should know how much more beautiful it is when I caress you there with my tongue, much like the swan is caressing Leda with its bill . . ."

"Oh, Francois!" I feign surprise.

* * *

"Oh, Francois, quick, quick, I want to feel the caresses of your tongue . . ."

Francois puts me down upon the sofa and shoves a pillow under my buttocks. I lay down upon the sofa as if it is an altar, and I feel as if I am about to be sacrificed. Shivers of anticipation run up and down my spine. Francois kneels now in front of me, and spreads my legs carefully apart. He tells me to cross them over his back.

My treasure, framed by my curly golden fleece, is moist and warm. It is also opened and awaiting the promised caresses. Francois' greedy mouth approaches.

"Oh . . . !" I feel his tongue kissing me, I feel it caressing my curls softly, I feel it enter slowly between the folds of my buttocks, pushing upward in between my thighs . . . I groan and trample my legs, knowing that this is only the preparation; the tongue carefully exploring its way to the most secret spot.

"Oh, Francois . . . !" Now he has reached it and this time I can feel his tongue slowly penetrating me, it works around deep inside me and, while his lips press firmly upon my fleece, I can feel his tongue work its way to my most sensitive spot.

"Oh!" How beautiful, how delicious it feels. I feel him licking me, slowly sucking me, and I can feel his spittle mix with the juices of my love.

Suddenly I scream out loud, and a tremendous spasm jolts through my body.

"Oh, Francois! Francois!"

I fall back upon the sofa and I feel satisfied, deeply satisfied; every nerve and fiber in my body is completely relaxed. I had never felt anything like it, the excitement of the moist caresses, the voluptuousness of those kisses that were imparted upon the most secret part of my being . . .

But I have become so terribly tired that I can feel myself sink away into a deep sleep. I have never slept so completely, so utterly and so deeply. It is an entirely new sensation.

When I open my eyes again, the first thing I see is Francois. He is reading a book. I call him, and he is near me instantly.

"Oh, Francois, my dear, dear Francois . . ."

Our lips met and mingled in a long, deep kiss, under the stern eyes of the portraits in their ebony frames on the walls.

CHAPTER FOUR

The atmosphere in my classroom begins to become positively charming—as a matter of fact, so are the lectures. The hours we spend here are full of joy.

I am making progress, and I know how to conjugate the verb 'to love', without making any mistake. I can do it in latin and . . . in practice.

But the lectures mostly take place upon the sofa! That is also the place where I made closer acquaintance with Francinet. I have looked at him much closer, and have spent much time kissing him. But, tell me, what else could I do after the delicious hour Francois provided for me yesterday.

Perhaps my kisses were a little bit too shy in the beginning, but the cries of joy, uttered by my teacher, encouraged me and made me more bold. I believe that I have accomplished the entire affair to a satisfactory ending. At least, Francois has assured me that I did.

We had barely arrived in our little classroom when Francois laid himself down upon the sofa, in exactly the same position I was in yesterday.

I understood immediately and freed Francinet from his prison, caressing him carefully with my fingers.

How sweet that is! I feel him grow between my lips, warm and velvety. Then I caress him slowly with my tongue, press down upon him and moisten him as much as I can.

Aah! Francinet . . . He grows, stretches and builds up to an enormous size, much larger than when I was caressing him with my fingers only. Finally he has become so big that I wonder whether my mouth will be big enough to envelop him.

But Francois, groaning, pulls him a little bit back, only to push him in much deeper! He moves Francinet deliciously back and forth between my firmly closed lips. I follow him all the while with my tongue, carefully licking him on all sides.

Suddenly Francinet announces the climax of his lust by flooding my mouth with a warm fluid which is so rich that I have to swallow it down.

Did I do that right? At first the question did not enter my mind, and I did it without hesitation. I think I must have acted correctly, because it was delicious, delicious . . .

But Francinet rapidly dwindled in size and with a groaning sigh, Francois pulled it softly out of my mouth. Like I did yesterday, Francois remained totally exhausted on the sofa . . . he fell in a deep faint. I pressed a kiss upon his lips and let him rest.

I walk over to the window. The weather is marvelous. The whole world shares my joy. The large trees in the park bend their branches under the caresses of a soft wind, and the nymphs under the waterfall seem more beautiful than ever, smiling their knowing smiles . . .

Francois has promised a very interesting lesson for this afternoon.

He carefully closes the door, locking it with the big bolt, and he undresses himself till he is stark naked. He tells me that I should do the same.

I hesitate slightly, but Francois is becoming impatient. He opens my dress and it falls to the floor. While I am unhooking my bodice, my teacher has knelt down in front of me, removing my garters and—in passing—he slowly kisses the insides of my thighs.

Now the last cover has fallen to the floor, and, instead of blushing, I smile with extreme satisfaction, especially since Francois seems delighted at the sight of me. He is extremely overjoyed with my youthful beauty and charm. Francinet, too, expresses his admiration by becoming extremely hard and stiff.

Francois pulls me quickly over to the sofa upon which he stretches out. He orders me to do the same. I want to lie down, but before I have a chance to do so, my teacher has grabbed me and forces me to sit down upon his face. Without hesitation he puts his nimble tongue to work.

Aha! Now I understand . . . I remember that I have seen this curious position in one of the books I read secretly. I lay myself down upon Francois, my breasts pressing warmly upon his belly. A sweet tingling penetrates my body. And what is that? Oh, beautiful thing, right in front of my eyes. Francinet is standing there, a lonely sentinel, proud and erect, directly under my face, stretching out toward my lips. And he is jumping, the little darling, he is begging for a soft caress.

I hurry to take him between thumb and index finger and to shove him into my mouth. But suddenly I have to sigh deeply. At the same moment, Francois shoves his tongue into my secret slit, hitting the center of my passion which, as I now discover, is precisely down upon his face.

Oh! It feels so good . . . A very strong feeling floods through my body, penetrates into my deepest being, overtaking me completely. Jolting spasms shoot through my entire body, and I am thrashing around upon the body of my teacher. I never let go of Francinet, though, who seems to enjoy the wild movements I am making with my head.

My arms and legs tighten up, my back arches, my mouth works quickly and I am caressing Francois and Francinet with lips and moist tongue.

Suddenly . . . ooh, incomparable delight . . . a warm balsam fills my mouth. Francinet is jumping up and down, and Francois is mixing his spittle with the warm dew that is sprinkling my fleece.

I fall into a deep swoon, and I am in the grip of an extraordinary passion. I can feel that my lover feels exactly as I do; I can feel him twitch under me, and I can hear him groan.

Floating, our limbs feel crushed, we loosen our embrace. We slide next to one another, tired but happy, and our lips find each other in a passionate and long, very long kiss.

* * *

My aunt has allowed us to take a stroll in the park after dinner. Francois has expressed the wish to show me the stars and to tell me the name and the nature of the constellations.

What a beautiful night! We reach the marble statue where Leda is swooning under the caresses of the swan. The moon throws its faint rays upon the marble grouping, and this light makes it the more sensuous and mystical.

Francois embraces me and tells me beautiful mythological stories about the love life of gods and goddesses.

We stayed long in the bushes, sitting on the grass, our hands playfully reaching for our secret parts. Francois' fingers grope my golden fleece, and mine find Francinet who playfully reaches toward me.

And our lips come together again, melting into one of those passionate, endless kisses.

CHAPTER FIVE

Something unexpected happened which cut short my lessons, and which kept me separated from Francois for several days.

One of my cousins, Alain de Cambelousse, who serves in His Majesty's Navy, had just earned his first epaulets and gold stripes.

Through a messenger, who arrived one day at the castle, we learned that his ship had anchored in Bordeaux and that it would remain there for several days.

My aunt used the opportunity to drive into the city where it seemed she had a lot of things to do. She suggested that I accompany her.

I did not like the idea at all, and at first I was tempted to decline her invitation, trying to find some good reason to stay home. But then it occurred to me that it was not fitting for a young girl to remain alone with her male teacher, and the last thing I wanted to do was to create suspicion in my aunt's mind.

For better or worse, I had to play along, and I decided to go with my aunt into the city.

* *. *

Bordeaux is several miles away from the old family estate, and in less than a day the wheels of our carriage rattled on the quays of the Gironde River. We were the guests of a dear, old friend of my aunt.

The next day we went to the harbor, and I liked the multicolored spectacle. There were ships from all parts of the world and the lusty songs of the sailors filled the air. Throngs of people were there to look at all the marvelous things that were unloaded onto the docks, and to amuse themselves with the funny-faced monkeys and colorful parrots which the sailors had brought with them. There were a lot of people in the harbor, and the sound of drums, the music, the laughter and the screams, reminded me of a yearly fair.

Finally we reached my cousin's ship. It was an imposing structure and the lily flag of His Majesty proudly flew from the top.

A narrow gangplank went from the quay to the ship. With the surefootedness of an old sailor, my aunt climbed the plank, motioning me to follow her. I was surprised to find out how well she knew her way around on the ship and even more that she seemed to know everybody, from the captain on down to the lowest cabin boy.

She introduced me to her nephew whom I had never seen before. He was a beautiful naval officer, and his uniform made him look positively gorgeous. Dark curly hair framed his good-looking face with its perfect nose, thin lips and blue, dreamy-looking eyes.

We remained on the ship for a considerable length of time, and, while my aunt conversed with the captain, my cousin offered to show me around. It was quite exciting to see the insides of this big ship and we walked through a lot of corridors and crossed a lot of decks. I breathed deeply; the smell of the salty air and the pitch of the ship was new to me, and very exciting. I followed my cousin, who was obviously very proud to show a girl around in his domain. We walked down one of the rickety stairs into a large room where spare sails were kept. It was fairly dark in there; the only light came from high up through some holes in the ceiling.

From time to time my cousin looked at me, and he seemed very pleased with what he saw. Even though it was half-dark I could see him blush when he was peeking down my neckline.

The beautiful officer was clearly excited, which pleased me immensely. As a matter of fact, I was so pleased, that I did not watch where I was going and I fell from the last rung of one of the ladders. I fell down upon one of those large rolls of sail cloth, in a most uncomfortable and ridiculous position. My legs were up in the air, and my skirts fell about my waist.

I soon had recuperated from the first scare, and I began to laugh, especially since my handsome cousin had put his hand between my thighs and started to tickle me.

This unexpected situation in the bowels of the ship, on top of a roll of sail cloth, seemed priceless to me. And, instead of defending myself, I encouraged Alain with his voyages of discovery. I trampled, moved my legs into a better position, to facilitate his finding that spot which men are usually after.

My cousin was quite surprised, especially since I stretched out my hand toward that spot in his breeches where I had discovered a considerable swelling.

But he was as stupid as he was handsome, and he did not seem to be aware that I offered him a splendid opportunity. He got up, helped me up, brushed off his uniform and mumbled a few inane apologies. I think he suddenly became afraid; I do not know why . . . I assume that he was afraid we might be discovered. He started to climb the ladder again, telling me to follow him.

I was, at the same time, terribly disappointed and also happy. Disappointed, because a little adventure with my handsome cousin would have enhanced my self-esteem, happy, because I had not been unfaithful to Francois. But, despite all these worthy feelings, I had to do something about the desire which my cousin had awakened, and that night I sought solace in solitary satisfaction.

* * *

The next day my aunt visited the priest of Sainte-Croix who was an old acquaintance of hers, and from there she went to see friends in the Rue Sainte-Colombe. Before dinner, we took one last stroll through the main streets of this beautiful town.

It was very pleasant to visit the many shops and to admire all the beautiful window displays. On the esplanade I watched the gorgeous officers of the Royal Guard, my heart pounding when I noticed the way they looked at me. We also went to a bookshop, bought some maps and a few illustrated books. Then we returned to the home of my aunt's friend, who was waiting for us with dinner.

The next day we took leave from our charming hostess and went back home to our castle, where we arrived before dark.

The first thing I did was to lock myself in with Francois to tell him about my trip and my adventures. I obviously remained silent about what had happened between myself and my cousin in the ship; but the memory of it gave me a desire which could only be satisfied by giving and receiving many caresses.

I got fully compensated by the poor Francois who had to bear the full brunt of my failure in Bordeaux. He was not at all mad about this, which I noticed from the behavior of Francinet who, that particular evening, became tremendously powerful and mighty between my lips, and who jumped deliciously around in my wide opened mouth.

CHAPTER SIX

I have, it seems, to learn a lot of things, and our lessons are becoming more intensive. Both in my study room as well as in the Park.

Leda and the nymphs are alternately witnesses to our games. The wild caresses to which we give ourselves in the bushes, yes, even upon the green meadows, surpass anything we have done till now. It is especially delightful at night when the tall branches of the trees in the park filter out the moonlight.

Truly, the memory which I will keep of my ancestral estate will be one of the most beautiful of my life. I will never forget the hours which I spent in the arms of my dear teacher. I snuggle up very close to him, my body presses against his, and my mouth reaches for his. Oh! I wish that time could stand still and that we could remain locked in each other's arms for eternity, without any other sound but the sweet nothings we murmur into each other's ears.

I bless the lucky coincidence which brought us together without either one of us having planned it. Oh, yes, a thousand blessings for all those hours, all those minutes which kept us in a tight embrace.

* * *

A new lesson!

This morning Francois told me to take off my drawers and to kneel down upon the sofa, my elbows stretched forward.

I cannot recall ever having seen this position in any of the books I read . . .

What are the plans of my dear Francois? Ere

I can ask him, he has lifted my skirts, baring the two half globes which start to twitch under his penetrating caresses.

He is kissing and caressing me alternately. Now I feel the warm skin of his hands, and then the moist coolness of his wet lips.

Suddenly—aah! Darling!—I feel his very warm, very nimble tongue which insistently searches for a certain spot and softly penetrates me.

Ooh! It feels delicious! And my pleasures are doubled, because my darling lover caresses me simultaneously up front with his searching fingers . . .

My entire body trembles, I cannot stand it any longer . . . The prickly sensation, the tingling, and especially the moist caresses excite me so much that I collapse with a tremendous jolt in an indescribable cloud of lasciviousness.

* * *

Has my dear aunt become suspicious?

It seems that during dinner time she is looking at us with a curious glance in her eyes. She is about to open her mouth as if she wants to ask something, and her eyes shine with curiosity . . .

I do my best not to blush and look at my dear Francois out of the corner of my eye. He seems so sure of himself that my shyness gradually disappears. He begins a long discourse about the eating habits of the ancients, through the Middle Ages, into our modern times. The cause of this sudden discourse on table manners is the baked capon which had just been served, and which also happens to be my dear aunt's favorite dish.

My self-confidence returns slowly, and I look admiringly upon my beloved teacher whose lecture becomes more vivacious with every bite, his words a firework sparkling with wit. My aunt smiles happily, and my lover's words seem to please her as much as the bits of juicy capon she is chewing.

I am now completely at ease, and when Joseph, our major domo, serves dessert, she allows me to have coffee with cognac! Now I am sure that my dear aunt is in a marvelous mood!

* * *

Last night a batch of new books arrived from the city, and we are supposed to go through them this afternoon. That means that we have to be on our best behavior.

We are slowly strolling through the lanes of the park, and I am thinking of the many hours of hard work ahead of us. It seems to me that Leda and her swan give me a glib smile! By God, no! This day shall not pass without any lovemaking! And, since we have to work hard all afternoon, I decide right then and there that we shall have the pastime in the park which we usually reserve for the sofa in our study.

The weather is beautiful, and the shadow in the bushes inviting. I soon direct Francois toward a cluster of them.

Just smile, you mysterious nymphs! My dress is soon up around my waist, and the hands of my lover caress between lace and silk. My own hands do not remain idle, either.

We are bedded down upon the soft grass, the

leaves of the trees form a green ceiling above us, protecting us from the sun's burning rays and at the same time silencing our heavy sighs.

Now we abandon ourselves to our desires with a wildness that would have wrecked the sofa in our study. We savor the many caresses of tongues and fingers. We are bucking up and down, from time to time uttering soft cries of pleasure. My breasts strain against the silk of my bodice, the nipples are incredibly hard. I loosen bodice and blouse; it seems as if Francois has waited for the moment. He bends over, takes a nipple in his mouth, and starts nibbling it furiously. Then he shifts to the other one, licking, sucking and nibbling.

I am going wild . . . I don't think I can stand it much longer! I grab for Francinet with both hands. He is enormous! Hard, thick and incredibly stiff. Oh, how lovely! My soft fingers give him deep satisfaction which he indicates with wild jumps. Soon his balsam squirts with gigantic spurts which quickly quiet down both of us.

* * *

We walk slowly back to the castle, tired and happy.

Joseph has carried the books from Bordeaux into our study; full of curiosity we start leafing through them.

There are very nice ones among them, with charts and maps, and beautiful etchings showing natives in their colorful state. The volumes of Louis Antoine de Bougainville's world travels are remarkable because of their enormous size. Francois points out the natural happiness of the island dwellers, and he directs my attention especially to the delicious liberty in their games of love.

They are not, like us, hampered by thousands of ridiculous conventions. One of the etchings shows us happy island girls, as naked as our mother Eve, adorned only with a crown of flowers in their hair. They dance! If we, in our civilized France, were to dance that way a *lettre de cachet* would put us in prison for utter lascivious behavior in public. To the island girls it seems natural and harmless.

My Francois is reading passages where Monsieur de Bougainville tells about the reception his sailors received from these delicious and innocent children of Nature; he interrupts his lecture frequently to press his burning lips upon mine.

My dear teacher leafs hungrily through the travelogue. I, meanwhile, crouched upon the sofa, am reading a book which is equally as interesting. It is full of beautiful pictures: The stories by Restif de la Bretonne . . .

CHAPTER SEVEN

The last few days I have come to a most curious discovery!—yes, indeed! Despite our wild caresses, our kisses, and the knowledge of our most intimate secrets, Francois and I do not seem to completely belong to one another!

And why? Could it be that a certain, lingering shyness keeps Francois back from this last, all-important step? Might he be afraid of something which prevents him from completing the lectures that began with so much promise. There seems to be an invisible roadblock preventing me from reaching the final delight experienced by all those beautiful women in the etchings from the books which Francois and I read day after day. It seems to me that Francois has peeled off petal by petal the tender leaves that protected the beautiful flower I am; and now he seems to be afraid to pluck the flower.

I have asked Francois about it; I have told him as frankly as I could that I would be more than happy to satisfy all his wishes, provided he satisfies mine.

". . . because I love you, my dearest Francois, I want to belong to you completely, with soul and body . . ."

My darling teacher smiled and lifted one hand as if to say, "Patience!" But I threw my arms around his neck, embraced him hotly, pressing my lips firmly upon his.

*   *   *

I am now very sure about it. I am deeply in love with Francois, and I can no longer doubt that my hot desires for him are without bounds, without restraints, and—above all—unquenchable.

I love him, I love him; it is unfair of him to deny me the thing which can only make our love grow deeper and stronger. It could be possible that sex is not necessary to love, and I know that I could live without it. But, I simply do not want to.

But I cannot deny that the demands of my body are stronger than those of my heart.

I do not care, I have realized that there is more lust than love involved! I can no longer stand it; my entire being reaches out for him, everything within me cries out, "Take me . . . take me completely!"

* * *

Today I am nineteen years old. Between two kisses I told Francois and I also made it quite plain what I wanted for my birthday.

I soon noticed that this was going to be the big day and, filled with joy, I ran off to the study.

To make things simpler I took off my clothing and lay down upon the sofa. Soon, Francois joined me, but I detected that he was far more serious than usual. He embraces me, but he does not smile as usual. Instead, his eyes shine with desire and lust.

I lie down full of anticipation, and remain silent. He covers my body with hot kisses. I shiver under these moist caresses.

Suddenly he places his hands under my hips and lays down upon me, his lips pressing against mine, his tongue slipping into my mouth. I can feel Francinet make its way between my thighs, searching for my already moist fleece which is hiding the narrow entrance, now burning with hot desire.

Ouch! I yelled out loud, feeling a sharp, stabbing pain. But, I am not afraid, because the pain is mixed with a strong passion. Francinet jumps up and down within me, and now he begins a wild movement. The pain becomes more stinging, almost unendurable, but my passion increases at the same time, finally taking the upper hand.

Francois is groaning, too. I kiss his lips passionately and I stammer, delirious with joy, "Darling, darling, I love you . . . Oh, my darling . . . lover!"

Now I scream out loud and collapse into total relaxation. I can feel Francinet squirm deep inside my belly, spurting jets of deliciously hot balsam which seem to fill me up completely.

Francois groans louder, and collapses on top of me. We remain motionless, our eyes glazed. I see a big splotch of blood slowly soaking into the sofa's upholstery. Proof for all the stern faces in their ebony frames to see that today, my nineteenth birthday, I have become a woman.

But whoever told me that love-making was tiresome? I haven't noticed any slackening of my desires. On the contrary, a true spirit of discovery has been awakened in me, and I am, so to speak, raring to go and find out more.

"When are we going to do this again, my darling? When? Tell me, tomorrow?"

This time my dear aunt must have guessed everything. She looked at us with a mysterious smile while we were having dinner, and the little twinkle in her eye when she gazed at me, told me that she knew my secret.

Francois and I must have looked completely different.

There was no longer any doubt in my mind when I looked in the mirror. The deep joy which I had tasted this morning was still visible in my eyes. My entire face had changed and everything about me seemed to proudly tell the world what I had lost upon the sofa that morning.

Even the way I walked was different. I noticed that when I saw my own reflection in the tall mirrors in the corridor on my way to the park for my nightly stroll with Francois.

He had changed, too. He took my arm more firmly, more proudly and when we walked past Leda I knew that I no longer had to be jealous of her. She might have the bill of her swan, but didn't I possess for the satisfaction of my passions the lips and tongue of my lover? And not only those . . . I had Francinet, wonderful, marvelous Francinet, who swelled with pride at my touch and who could do things which made me happier than the goddess who could only get the bill from her swan.

CHAPTER EIGHT

Today my darling teacher received my aunt's permission to accompany me outside of our domain to give me lessons in botany. Francois was filled with the ideas of that curious Monsieur Rousseau and he thought it most important that I studied Nature closely, all the plants and flowers which cover the fields.

My aunt, who shares Francois' enthusiasm for this philosopher, thought it a splendid idea that I would get a first-hand look at the virginal fields and forests as Nature had intended them, rather than getting used to the artificial surroundings of our park.

We left early in the morning. Francois carried his little botany box, and I carried a little umbrella.

The fields that surround our castle are positively charming. There are many ponds and across their quiet waters flit dragonflies and butterflies, their wings like little jewels glittering in the sun.

We started to pick flowers and soon Francois' box was filled with a variety of plants and flowers of which he told me the names, explaining how and why they were classified.

Slowly we approached a thicket and Francois embraced me so passionately that it became very clear to me that he was about to pick a flower of an entirely different kind. We forgot our learned talk, and walked slowly into the forest. Our lips met; the only witnesses were the majestic trees. We bedded down upon the grass which was soft and cool and perfectly charming for the games we had in mind.

I lay down, flattening the soft grass, and

with a triumphant smile I took off my panties.

My dear Francois followed my invitation to a sweet game of love and stretched out next to me. His lips pressed firmly upon mine and his hand strayed into the opening of my blouse, squeezing and stroking the roundness of my breasts, whose rosy tips hardened and swelled, jumping out of their silken prison to catch a breath of fresh air.

Suddenly Francois mounted me, pushing his hands under my hips. Now I knew how to help him and to make his task easier. I spread my thighs wide and my hand guided Francinet through the curls of my fleece till he had reached the opening of the rosy center of my passion.

"Aah! My sweet Francinet . . . He is quite erect and stiff, the little darling." For the second time I can feel him penetrate me, diving into me as deep as he can, mixing his warmth with mine.

And then he starts to move deep inside me. At first slowly and softly but soon more persistent, quicker and harder.

It is beautiful, fantastic! With every move the sweet, moist feeling permeates my entire being. It is pure revelation, because this up and down movement exceeds anything I have heretofore experienced.

The feeling which engulfs me, which envelops my entire being is enervating and precious. There are no words to express it; one must have experienced it to form a proper picture of the situation.

Aah! Now I understand that even the wisest people will do the most foolish things to play this marvelous game. How truly do I pity the ones who cannot participate for whatever reason!

Ooh! Francois, my darling Francois! . . . We kiss without stopping, our legs are entwined; they cling together, loosening occasionally, keeping up with the rhythm of our hips.

We groan and moan, we scream, smothering those screams in our endless, passionate kisses. We do not, for once, interrupt the grinding motions of our bodies.

Suddenly—Ooh, greatest of all delights!— we both, simultaneously let out a deep moaning scream. A warm liquid flows, spurting, deep inside my belly. Francinet rears up and spasms; I can feel it clearly. We both have reached the climax of our passion and now we sink back in a cloud of indescribable happiness. We just lie there, together, our bodies closely intertwined, tumbling into a deep sleep.

But Francinet wakes me up; he has recuperated and is throbbing and pulsating in my hand. His pressure becomes insistent, as if he is begging for new caresses.

I am very tired, but the darling is responsible for the great pleasure I have had, and I do not want to disappoint him. I grab him playfully and now we begin all those various caresses and darling little games which bring about our passion and lust. I spice them with new variations and combinations of old ones.

My mouth kisses Francinet wildly, I suck the throbbing knob with ardent passion. Francois, meanwhile, has sunk his thirsty lips in my moist fleece and his trembling tongue works violently on my rosy triangle. I groan and shiver, trampling upon the soft grass with both feet. It is too, too much! A jolting spasm rattles through my body, and I suddenly relax; I capitulate unconditionally, sinking away into a feeling of unhampered happiness . . .

*　　*　　*

When I regain consciousness, I see that Francois is examining the flowers we have picked. My legs look like two, long stemmed, fleshy flowers resting upon the grass. I begin to put on my stockings and push away my teacher who has put his hands under the lace of my petticoat, pretending to help me with my garters.

We begin to struggle; Francois grabs me and I resist, laughing. But I am too tired. I cannot put up enough resistance, and Francois is victorious again. He pulls my thighs apart, and I am obliged to offer him my still dripping triangle for further sacrifices. He kisses the rosy lips with ardent passion, his tongue playing around with my secret parts. Francinet meanwhile has swollen to enormous proportions and now petulantly demands entrance into what has become his domain. I faint again in a delirium of happiness . . .

CHAPTER NINE

We abandon ourselves daily to the Great Game. That means, we no longer are satisfied with the variety of caresses which we have been giving to each other for such a long time. Of course, we have not abandoned them . . . on the contrary. Either before, or after, sometimes even during, we invent new positions, new variations, and our lustful fantasies are never at a loss for trying our utmost to do something we have never done before. But regardless, we wind up doing the one thing that gives us true fulfillment.

I have gathered all the frivolous books in the house, and I force my darling Francois to possess me in the manifold positions which are portrayed in the many etchings.

Today I tried a completely new one. I don't even remember ever having seen this position in one of the books . . .

How I got in the position, I don't recall either. Our legs were intertwined, and suddenly . . . there I was, sitting on top of Francois, resting upon his knees. One thing I know for sure. Sweet Francinet was pulsating and reaching impatiently for my lower belly. He almost shouted his impatience and wanted to rest in his hide-out.

I suddenly decided to lift myself slightly, and then to sit down again, but not before I had grabbed a hold of Francinet and guided him with tender hand in the voluptuous hiding place of our mutual pleasure.

It feels as if I am riding horseback, and I move up and down as if I am proudly in the saddle. Francois is very helpful, and I enjoy the game tremendously.

Occasionally Francinet slips out of my moist sheath, but the sweet little darling knows what is good for him, and jumps right back.

I am enormously pleased with myself, and Francois, who also seems to be very happy, encourages me and tries to excite me even more. But suddenly I have to hold on to him, because my horse starts bucking wildly, and I have trouble remaining in the saddle and keeping Francinet in the warm grip of my sheath.

Finally the jumping begins to wear me out, and with a turn of my hips I force Francois to follow my example. Now he is on top of me and a series of tremendous jolts brings us to a satisfying climax.

* * *

Nobody exists for me in the entire world, except Francois. I am totally disinterested in everything else, except for loving and being loved.

The soft words spoken by my precious teacher, and his constant caresses, are worth more to me than all the jewels and gold in the world. Ooh! My eyes light up when I hear him call me, 'his little darling, his treasure, his joy' . . .

I will never forget these precious hours during which I am supposed to learn Latin and Greek grammar, but which are mostly spent upon the sofa.

We have a world globe standing on the table, but Francois prefers to lift my dress and put his hands upon my own soft globe which, he says, allows him to discover a new world, giving him all the pleasures he can think of.

His trembling fingers glide across the velvety skin, his inexhaustible tongue explores every nook and cranny, lingering upon the folds and crevices ultimately loosing itself in the depths of my golden forest.

Those are precious moments indeed! Our happiness is complete, and we discover many pleasures during our explorations, especially since I do not hesitate to go on some explorations of my own. Francois has offered me his forest in the middle of which Francinet stands like a giant tree trunk, robbed of its branches.

The firm stem resists my onslaughts, but I shake it so firmly that it becomes more pliable. I go further, touching it from beginning to end, till it finally collapses, a victim of my insistence . . . not without having thrown out its life juices as high as a geyser.

*   *   *

My aunt had a surprise for us during dinner. She announces that my girl cousin will visit us for a month. Aunt has decided that she will also take lessons from Francois so that her stay in the country will also be beneficial to her education.

Francois does not seem to be overjoyed at the prospect, but I put him at ease by telling him that my cousin is a very charming and beautiful young lady . . .

"And, above all, she has a beautiful name, my darling. A name that sounds like the smell of a field with flowers. It is Amaranthe, a beautiful flower, waiting to be picked."

We laugh heartily while we are walking around in the park under the soft light of the moon which is reflected by the nymphs and fountains around us.

CHAPTER TEN

As usual, we took our daily afternoon stroll in the park.

After we had said hello to Leda, who, also as usual, was dying under the caresses of her swan, we wandered into the lane with the nymphs. We always like to look at those marble nymphs who laughingly and playfully surrender themselves to the lustful fauns.

Looking at them gives us a thousand voluptuous ideas, and soon we leave them to their eternal games and go into the bushes to play a few games ourselves, always trying to outdo those marble statues.

This particular day, Francois began his game by putting me down upon the grass without giving me time to take off my panties. His feverish hands groped under my dress and his nimble fingers loosened my garters and began to take off my silken stockings. He loved to hide his head under my petticoat, kissing my thighs impatiently, working his way slowly toward my curly fleece, where his tongue would be lapping the juices and his teeth put tiny marks in the rosy lips. This game usually drives me wild. I put my legs over his shoulders to make it easier for him to get with his mouth deeper into my love nest and my feet tap the rhythm upon his back. Francois gets wilder and wilder and finally I reach a climax, giving a loud scream and collapsing into a delicious numbness.

Just as I fainted away I thought I heard something rustle in the bushes. I pushed Francois' head away, and though I thought it might have been a bird or a squirrel, I did not want to take any chances. I pulled up my stockings, smoothed my dress and left the bushes, motioning Francois to follow me.

I was utterly surprised. A charming young girl stood before me. Her blue eyes were wide open and expressed confusion, and the wind had disarranged her hair, which was as golden blonde as mine.

When she saw us, she began to blush. But I opened my arms with a wide smile. She embraced me, kissing me upon the forehead. I kissed her ardently, meanwhile looking around if there was someone else present. As soon as I was satisfied that she was alone, I introduced her to Francois.

It was my cousin Amaranthe.

After we had strolled through the park some more we went back to the castle together. Amaranthe told us that she had just arrived, and after she had taken her second breakfast with my aunt, the latter had told her that she would find us somewhere in the park.

My cousin was very vivacious and on occasion her remarks sounded like a pun about what I was afraid she might have witnessed in the bushes. The way she looked at us, I was almost sure that she knew what we had been doing.

Francois did not say a word; he just looked at my lovely cousin who had taken my arm. We must have been a charming couple. Amaranthe was a stunningly beautiful girl, about a year younger than I, vivacious, witty and with a little bit of devil in her.

Despite what had happened, I was very glad to see her again, and I liked the idea that she was going to stay with us for a month. The idea that she would be a stumbling block to our love games did not occur to me. On the contrary! And, since she had not yet indicated what, if anything, she had seen us do in the bushes, I decided to question her about it that evening, and make her my confidante.

. . . Yes! I could even give her a couple of lessons myself! This silly idea flitted across my mind when I felt her warm hand and smooth arm pressed against mine.

This idea made me so happy that I began to laugh, kissing Amaranthe on both cheeks, brushing her lips as if by mistake, but in reality I had planned it that way.

When I turned around to look at Francois, I saw that a curious smile played around his lips.

CHAPTER ELEVEN

Amaranthe's room is next to mine. After dinner I decided to pay my cousin a visit. We have a lot to talk about since the last time we saw each other.

Amaranthe told me about her voyage. She vivaciously described the changes of coaches and horses, her staying at the various inns, and all the thousands of little things that happen during a long trip. She told me that she was as happy as a child having escaped from her home for a while, and she also mentioned that I had changed so much, that I had become so much of a woman . . .

The one question I want to ask her burns upon my lips, but I recognize from Amaranthe's slight innuendos, her behavior, and especially from the tone of her voice when she tells me that she went out in the park to look for us, that she is fully familiar with our secret and that she has watched us in the bushes from beginning to end.

There is no longer any doubt left in my mind when she begins to ask impish questions about my tutor.

It is no longer necessary to pretend that there is a secret. Smiling, while trying not to blush, I admit the truth to my dear cousin.

Amaranthe laughs, and says, "Oh, yes, my dear. I have seen the two of you playing playing around in the bushes. And I must admit that I have seen a lot of things which were very interesting and also . . . a little bit shocking."

"Tell me, my dearest Amaranthe, what did you see?"

"But, darling, why should I tell you! You know much better what you have been doing in those bushes than I. After all, you were a participant, and I was only an onlooker."

"Please! Tell me . . ."

"All right! As you know, I was looking for the two of you somewhere in the park. It seemed to me that those marble nymphs were pointing at the bushes, so I went in to look for you there. When I came closer I heard someone groan and moan; obviously I came even closer so that I could see what was going on. Can you imagine my surprise, darling cousin, when I saw you down on the grass, your legs sticking up in the air, and your dear tutor using his head for a purpose which I had always heard was the task of another part of a man's anatomy. It sure looked funny to see his slobbering face between your thighs . . .

"But I also realized that you were enjoying it tremendously because your sighing and groaning became stronger, expressing the greatest joy. Your fists were balled, your feet drummed upon his back, and spasms seemed to jolt your body and jerk your hips.

"I stood there, not moving, frankly shocked, but against my will. My eyes were forced to stare upon the spectacle in the grass. Suddenly you uttered a loud scream.

"I suddenly came to my senses and ran away, very scared. But then, you came out of the bushes, smiling and happy, and I understood immediately . . . I must admit that I am a little bit jealous of you for having such a fabulous teacher . . ."

During those last words my cousin's eyes were filled with lust and desire, betraying far more clearly than words her true thoughts. I knew that she was burning up inside, and could not wait to be initiated into the joys and pleasures of the game of love.

The memory of that afternoon, plus Amaranthe's vivid description of it, had made me very excited, and I embraced my cousin passionately kissing her upon the lips. At first Amaranthe was a little taken aback, but I kissed her so passionately, and held my lips so firmly upon her mouth, that her lips parted and allowed my tongue to explore her mouth. She was soon panting under my feverish kisses and let herself fall limply back upon the couch.

She began to kiss me in return, which gave me another idea! I suddenly wanted to give her the same caresses with which Francois always brought me to a climax. I pulled her legs slowly apart, pulled down her panties and lifted her skirts. For the sake of appearances, Amaranthe put up a very mild struggle which was not too convincing. Her struggle stopped the instant my lips approached her blonde fleece and my tongue went into her little rosy slit.

She shuddered under my caresses and began to moan slightly when I went on to explore her little secret spot which was so much like my own. I did my best to imitate Francois with hands, tongue and lips and I must admit that I was doing it rather well, because Amaranthe began to groan and buck. I recognized her pleasure, because the little cries of joy were similar to the ones I had so often uttered when Francois was sucking and licking my love spot.

I was very pleased to be able to give my cousin so much pleasure with my caresses. My tongue was very busy in that little triangle, the warm moist flower which I sprinkled with my spittle, mixing it with the warm juices exuding from her love nest.

Suddenly Amaranthe, who had been trembling like an aspen leaf, cried out loudly. She lifted her buttocks high off the couch, her legs and arms spasmed, her entire body shuddered, and I realized that she had tasted a true climax for the first time in her life. She remained motionless upon the couch, and I pulled my head slowly back, covering her marble-white thighs with ardent kisses.

I was suddenly very tired. It had greatly pleased me to initiate my dear cousin in the pleasures of love. I had passionately made love to her with my tongue and lips. It made me happy, though a curious pain was mixed with my joy; I had not had any real satisfaction. I was about to dampen my glowing desire with my own fingers when I suddenly uttered a sharp cry of surprise which awakened Amaranthe from her slumber.

Francois came from behind the Chinese screen.

I did not even have the chance to ask him how he got into the room, and whether he had seen what Amaranthe and I had been doing. He suddenly jumped toward me and mounted me as if I were a dog.

Looking at the throbbing Francinet, I realized that Francois had seen everything and that it had brought him to an extreme state of excitement. He did not waste time on preliminaries, but shoved Francinet deep inside me and began to push with such vehemence that I could feel his balls slam against my buttocks.

—Ooh! It was marvelous. I was roughly

taken before the very eyes of my dear Amaranthe. Soon the passionate glow inside me was extinguished.

I was no longer able to take it, and I pushed Francois away from me. My sweet Francinet left its moist sheath, but it seemed that his excitement was too great because he immediately stretched out and became erect again, as thick and stiff as he had been before entering me.

He went directly toward my cousin; Francois mounted her and Francinet found the way to his satisfaction without any trouble at all. Amaranthe was more than prepared. First, I had whetted her appetite with my moist caresses, and secondly, she was practically under me when I was mounted and taken by Francois. The scene she had watched had more than excited her and her desire was at its peak.

At first I did not enjoy the idea at all. I was aware that my cousin was about to enjoy what I considered the ultimate climax of the game of love, and that she did not have to suffer the long months of preparation which I have had to endure. In short, I felt a tinge of jealousy.

But then I realized that it was, after all, my own fault, and that I had no right to object because of a silly little jealousy. It did not take me long to push those unpleasant ideas out of my mind, because the scene I was about to witness was extremely interesting and I became fully absorbed in it.

I looked at my dear Francois from behind, and could see the muscles of his firm buttocks harden, when he pushed Francinet deep into my dear cousin and began to work her over with tremendous jolts. Amaranthe's charming legs were trampling, sticking high up in the air.

And I heard her moan and groan her little screams of joy, her Oohs! and Aahs! and finally, "Ooh, darling . . . I'm dying . . . oooh, darling, darling . . . it . . . is . . . too much!"

A scream, louder than all the other ones, announced that the thunderstorm of love was over. I got up from my seat and walked over to the couple, who were now relaxing upon the large couch.

Francinet looked just plain terrible after this double attack. And my dear Amaranthe was in about the same condition I had been in only a month earlier. She silently looked down upon the large spot of blood which announced louder than words what she had just irreparably lost.

For a long time the three of us rested in silence upon the huge couch, and then we began to laugh. Our tiredness had passed. The curious situation which had developed was truly amusing!

My dear teacher complimented me upon the effectiveness with which I had demonstrated that his lessons had not fallen upon deaf ears, and he thought it magnanimous of me that I had wanted my cousin to share my happiness. Then he began a long lecture about love between women, pointing out the things that were missing, though he had to admit grudgingly that their mutual caresses could be infinitely more tender.

To round out his lessons for the day, Francois showed us that three people can act out more love fantasies than two.

CHAPTER TWELVE

The day after this memorable evening Amaranthe insisted upon reciprocating my little service of love and showing her gratitude for having been initiated into those precious caresses which had culminated in her receiving the ultimate delight of making love.

Francois had taken his horse and was riding in the fields to get lots of fresh air and to recuperate from his exhausting labors. He wanted to restore his powers quickly.

Amaranthe and I were alone in my room.

As a matter of fact, I was still in bed when my charming cousin knocked on my door. She was wearing a charming night gown of lace and silk, and her clear blue eyes still showed the strain from the previous night. But they looked happy and content nevertheless, and a certain glint betrayed that she was already in a certain state of excitement.

She slipped under the covers next to me, cuddled up, and began with the youthful impatience of a beginner to caress me copiously. She imitated as well as she could everything I had done to her that previous night; instinctively she invented the most refined caresses and I quickly reached a point where I felt an intensive lust.

Even though her rather inexperienced caresses and kisses did not have the expertness of my dear Francois, who was a connisseur in that area, I did reach a very intensified climax.

As soon as I had come to my senses again, I patiently explained to Amaranthe how much her quick approach had spoiled part of the intimacy of my excitement.

And since, by now, we were both naked in the large bed, I could demonstrate my teachings upon her own charming body. I proceeded very carefully and slowly, thereby intensifying her voluptuous yearnings and putting off the climax which she so greatly desired. I carefully went over every part of her exposed body.

I covered every corner with my kisses, the little breasts with the rosy tips, her narrow waist, her flaring hips, the insides of her slender thighs, her flat belly, the blonde curls of her armpits and the delicious fleece which was hiding her moist, warm flower.

I stroked with my hands the soft skin of her belly and legs. I turned her over on her stomach and kneeded and squeezed her firm buttocks. Then I let my tongue slowly penetrate her love nest till it had found the little tickler. I rolled it around till it was quite erect, my nimble hands twitching the hardened rosy nipples of her breasts.

Amaranthe was surprised at the effects. She arched her back, her legs trampled in the air, and her fists drummed upon the mattress. I turned her around again, falling upon her and we rubbed our fleeces together. Amaranthe groaned and moaned, went into a jolting spasm and experienced a satisfying climax. When she had rested a while she noticed that the nipples of my breasts were standing proudly erect and that a hot flush covered my body. The dear girl understood immediately. She kissed them and nibbled on them, her hands searched for my fleece, caressing my thighs; in short, she did to me what I had done to her, and I, too, went into a tremendous climax. Our games went on and on till late in the afternoon, and finally we fell asleep in each other's arms, completely exhausted, but happy.

The dinner bell woke us up with a start and we were rather late when we appeared for dinner. Francois stared at us with a knowing smirk, and he even used the absence of my aunt for making a few unseemly remarks which were designed to make us feel silly, also indicating that our teacher knew exactly how we had spent our day.

Poor Amaranthe blushed and was red as a peony, but I quickly changed the subject by kidding Francois about his sudden urge to be alone with his horse all day, asking him a thousand questions about his ride into the country.

Fortunately my aunt returned quickly and we sat down to dinner. Needless to say we honored our sumptuous meal with great appetite, repairing our strength with delicious bits of meat, fowl and fish, not to speak of a reasonable quantity of burgundy wine.

CHAPTER THIRTEEN

The time during which my dear cousin Amaranthe stayed at the castle was one uninterrupted series of delicious joys. She participated in every respect in my lectures and became an equal partner in our daily strolls through the park.

The botanical excursions in the neighborhood of the castle were continued and expanded, and Amaranthe was surely not the last who gave herself in full abandon to the wild caresses, kisses and other games of our beloved teacher.

My cousin showed, on the contrary, an ardent desire to learn during those games. But her stay here will soon come to an end, and it seems to me as if she is squirreling away a great store of experiences before she has to go back to her dull, parental home. I cannot blame her that she is trying to cram as much experience as she can into the few remaining days. It is understandable that she desires to know as much as she can about the game of love, because after her departure she will be on her own without the superb guidance of our teacher. She will have to pluck the gallant flowers that will bloom upon her life's path without supervision, and taste the joys of lasciviousness guided by her own instincts. It is our holy task to prepare her for the future as well as it is in our power . . .

These are our last outings. The weather is beautiful. The sun's rays are burning the fields golden and bathing Nature in full splendor.

We are searching for the loneliest, most hidden spots to enable us to give ourselves completely and unhindered by curious onlookers to the most voluptuous games our combined fantasies can think of. We wander throughout the entire area; sure of the fact that friendly Nature somewhere has a place for us with a soft bed of grass, with walls and ceiling of thicket and tree leaves. And . . . we find it! The loneliness and the silence of the place are so great that it seems to us as if we are the only three people left on earth. We have no objections to Amaranthe's suggestion to undress completely. In no time Francois, my cousin and I are as naked as the day we were born. It seems as if we were transported back in time to Paradise!

Suddenly the feeling overpowers us and we play the wildest, most delicious games. Amaranthe and I embrace each other passionately, our lips firmly pressed against one another, our fleeces rubbing and our tongues playing a marvelous game.

Francois uses the opportunity to his own advantage. He climbs on top of me and sends Francinet on its natural way. Meanwhile his lips have reached the thighs and his tongue the fleece of Amaranthe; he reaches around till his tongue has discovered her most sensitive spot and Francois begins to buck and slurp at the same time, using both our bodies.

It is marvelous! Excited by the moist caresses, Amaranthe kisses me more devotedly and passionately than ever, and a double joy floods my entire being. I can feel Francinet penetrate me with doubled force. And Francois, too, is enjoying double passion; the glowing passion with which his lips explore the inner secrets of my dear Amaranthe makes itself felt by the double size of the throbbing Francinet who is pushing deep inside me.

We groan and pant, and tumble around and around in the soft grass. Arms, legs and bodies are wildly intertwined. Lips, tongues and hands caress every available part of soft flesh; our fleecy triangles are moist and twitching, Francinet grows harder and stiffer. throbbing wildly with every shove given by Francois. We stay in this passionate embrace, forming a perfect triangle, and each angle is the ultimate passion for the other. Amaranthe and I shudder in this delightful embrace while Francinet keeps pounding unmercifully into me, and Francois' tongue drives deeper and deeper into the fleece of Amaranthe.

Suddenly my cousin and I are in the grip of a long and shaking spasm. Our lips let go of one another to cry out our joy. Our happiness is complete because I realize that the tongue of Francois has given Amaranthe the same climax which I have just been given by Francinet.

* * *

The three of us continue our lessons and excursions till the very day that my dearest Amaranthe has to take her leave from us. My cousin's parents have completed their move to Bordeaux, and she must leave now to return into the fold of her own family.

Before she went into the coach she kissed both of us so intimately and passionately that it caused my dear aunt to raise her eyebrows in wonder. Her farewell kisses were obviously far more than convention demanded.

We agreed that we would use the first best opportunity to see each other again in Bordeaux. From the rest of my memoirs one can see that fate would send me to Paris before I could fulfill my promise to meet Amaranthe on the banks of the Gironde River. Francois and my cousin did meet again, and I will write down the results of that meeting.

CHAPTER FOURTEEN

At the moment of our separation Francois and I felt terribly lonely at the prospect of being without Amaranthe; but that same night we consoled each other with a passionate game of love, performed, as of old, by only the two of us.

For a solid month we had scandalously ignored Latin and Greek grammar, and we now set out to remedy this oversight. In between lessons my teacher admired my velvet soft buttocks, covering them with kisses under the eyes of my stern forebears in their black ebony frames.

Quite frequently we make sure that the door to our study is locked; I then undress and offer myself completely naked to the loving caresses of my darling Francois.

His hands know to find the most sensitive spots instantly; the tickling gives me goose pimples and makes my entire body shudder. But I let him, because these are the precious preparations which excite me to the point where I am willing to do anything.

I must admit that Francois knows how to bring variations to our game. He follows the soft curves of my body with quick kisses, till he reaches the blonde hairs of my armpit. He nuzzles me and licks till the hair is wet and matted. It seems that the smell of that particular spot excites him most of all, because whenever he reaches that point, Francinet bulges so dangerously that I always expect him to burst out of his prison.

Finally Francois proceeds towards my breasts and takes his time to suck and nibble the rosy tips. While he is licking the one, he twirls the other between thumb and index finger. When he finally begins to put little love bites on them, I am so greatly excited that I cannot hold back little cries of joy and pleasure.

When I have reached that point, Francois falls down upon his knees and manipulates a breast with each hand. His tongue slides down from my navel into the golden fleece and hungrily he begins to suck the lips, searching for the little erect bud of my love nest. My back arches and I push my fleece toward his face, holding the back of his head, afraid that he might change his mind and pull back before I have reached complete enjoyment.

Daily we grow more bold with our game of love. Our desire grows and grows and finally we have reached the point where we give ourselves completely to the game of love, forgetting our lessons altogether. We do not care any longer about knowledge, we have become one being.

One day, Francois fell asleep in my arms for the first time. He was utterly exhausted. I, too, was very tired, but I fought off my sleep because I was so happy to be close to my lover and I felt that I had to watch over him while he slept . . .

But when he woke up, we started all over again. It is like wrestling, brutal and loving at the same time. We do not utter a single sound. And suddenly we experience the greatest and deepest joy just by being so close together, even before we have possessed one another.

But now I quickly put an end to it. I take Francinet in my mouth and we both fall back upon the sofa, exhausted. We are asleep almost immediately. It is marvelous. Our bodies are closely intertwined, and when we wake up, we are still in the same position . . . our lips close together.

But, we must beware. Despite the closed and locked doors, we could have been caught during our sleep. And then, who could have doubted that there existed a tender bond between the tutor and his high-born pupil? Ooh, silly conventions!

That night, when we went down for dinner, we received very bad news. The father of my dear Francois was dying, and he had expressed the wish to see his son once more before he left this vale of tears.

For me it was nothing short of a catastrophe! Francois had to leave very early the next morning and we barely had time to say our farewells, and exchange a few quick caresses and kisses.

I was never to see my dear teacher again! His father died before Francois arrived, and then he had to undertake several voyages to settle all the various matters of inheritance.

A month later he took a ship which sailed for San Domingo where he remained for over two years. His father had owned many plantations on the island and Francois who was the oldest son, and now head of the family, had to take over the business enterprises.

During these few years he put on weight, lost his hair and gained a respectable position in his community. Soon he became well-known. Later, when I lived in Paris, I heard that he had returned to Bordeaux and married my cousin Amaranthe.

This is how fate separated us. Aside from

a very short and unexpected meeting our paths were destined never to cross again. I must here take a leap into the future, before I come back to my story. I was happy to hear that Francois and Amaranthe were a perfect love match and that they had many healthy children. I became caught in a whirlpool of adventures in which gallantry and love were always the main factors.

The teacher had retired with one of his pupils into a secure and small place. But the other pupil—me—wanted to explore all the possibilities derived from his teaching, and I was determined to get all the joys I could out of life and high living!

That is life! An inescapable fate rules over it and no power in the world can change the path of life which has been cut out for a person. I could make endless deductions, but this is not a philosophy book. It is a mere diary which might never be read. Before I take up the thread of my own story, and write down what happened after Francois and I became separated, I must report that my poor Francois died under the guillotine during the revolution. Amaranthe died of a broken heart soon thereafter, and the surviving children fled to the islands where they were taken in by one of their grandfather's brothers who had never wanted to leave San Domingo.

CHAPTER FIFTEEN

The coach arrives very early in the morning on the main street of the little village of Rondelles, a few miles from our castle.

Even earlier my dear Francois departs in our coach, and I did not have the courage to accompany him to the village because I did not choose to show the unbearable pain from which I suffered. It took all my will power to keep back a flood of tears.

Now that our separation had become a fact, I wanted it to be over quickly. I know it is unusual, but I want to avoid prolonging the misery which made it almost impossible for me to remain calm and collected. I knew that I could not stand a drawn out farewell.

Ooh! How terrible it was. Since my aunt and all our servants were there, I could not even kiss my poor Francois the way I had wanted to. He controlled his feelings stoically and concerned himself mainly with his luggage. He took his leave of my aunt very ceremoniously and barely touched my forehead with his lips as is expected from a teacher who says goodbye to his pupil. I began to shake and tremble, and needed all my strength not to cry out my misery when my lover got into the coach and the coachman laid his whip over the horses.

I was in a hurry to be alone so that I could cry uninterrupted. I ran up to my room from which I could overlook the road into the village and red-eyed I stared at the carriage till it had become a mere point in the distance, taking my love, my joy, and my very life with it.

I rubbed my eyes, fell down upon my bed and gave myself completely to my total desperation.

During lunch I was unable to eat a single bite. I fled into my study, threw myself upon the sofa, and cried bitter tears. It seemed to me that the stern faces of my ancestors on the wall were leering at me. I buried my face in the pillows and cried, and cried.

During dinner, too, I did not touch a bite. Despite my aunt's good intentions—she was trying to lift my spirits with some inane story—my misery only grew. This was the time that Francois and I used to take our stroll in the park.

I wandered lonely and forlorn through the lanes, remembering the many exciting moments we had spent behind the various bushes. Leda and all the other marble nymphs and fauns were witness to my despair. I went into the bushes, the places of our sweet pastimes. I threw myself upon the ground, rolled in the soft grass, sobbing and biting my handkerchief.

My dear aunt had become worried and instructed the servants to look for me. I went to my room and tried to sleep. The next day I contracted a terrible fever and had to stay in bed for a week.

I was inconsolable and I wanted to die.

I made my misery worse than it was on purpose, because I believed that by doing so I could prove to myself that I could remain true to my lover. My aunt took wonderful care of me, and thanks to her ministrations I was saved from physical illness. But the deep wound that had torn my heart did not heal.

As soon as the weakness which was caused by my immeasurable misery was over, another illness began to gnaw on me. It was the lack of caresses and kisses to which I had become accustomed. This pain took on an entirely different form. The physical symptoms were stronger than the spiritual ones. I made a curious discovery which, at first, I tried to fight. But it was stronger than my will power; the desire cured me from my love which I slowly forgot, giving myself to the joys of the lonely.

This is how I discovered that my lasciviousness and lust were stronger than all my other feelings put together. Time and absence did their duty; I slowly forgot Francois and could only think about who or what could become a substitute for him. The desires of my body were stronger than the wishes of my soul. I wanted daily satisfaction.

* * *

Eros watches over his children, or a lucky coincidence smiles upon those who desire nothing but love.

I found that out for the first time when I became tired of masturbating and playing with myself. I was looking around for some possibility which could give me stronger and better joys.

One day, I was resting upon the grass, hidden by a thicket, daydreaming over the contents of a frivolous book, trying desperately to allow my imagination to give me what my own fingers no longer could do. I had finished one particularly exciting story, and I was about to get up, when I spotted the son of one of our farmers who daily went into the castle to deliver milk, butter and cheese.

He was a strong, healthy boy, about eighteen years old. I never really had noticed him before. He always greeted me very respectfully and I usually reciprocated condescendingly. But I had never really taken any notice of him. Why should I look at him so closely today? I really do not know.

Jerome, dressed in a simple peasant blouse and shorts, came closer, carrying his milk and cheese. He could not possibly have seen me, since I remained motionless in the bushes, and the grass patch where I was hiding was invisible from the lane where he was walking.

Jerome was very close to the bushes where I was hiding, when he suddenly put down his basket and milk jar. He pulled up his blouse and unbuttoned his fly.

I did not dare to breathe; I could see his profile, and it was obvious that he was about to perform a natural function. And without being seen, I could clearly observe him wetting the tree-trunk.

At the sight of it I shuddered with lust. The desire was so strong that I suddenly got up, pushed aside the twigs of the thicket, and was suddenly standing before Jerome. My sudden appearance scared him so greatly that he forgot to put back his thing.

"Jerome," I said to him, "don't be afraid. Take your basket and your milk and hurry to the castle. Then return here to show me that beautiful tool again which, I am sure, you don't know how to use properly!"

I petted the thing, and Jerome caused it to disappear quickly. He stammered some unconnected words without meaning but I recognized from the way he blushed, from the sudden glint in his eyes, and especially from the enormous bulge, that he had understood my desire. And it was obvious that a similar desire had come up in his mind, and that he was more than willing to take me up on my kind offer.

"Hurry! Hurry!" I said to him. "Come back to me quickly!"

The boy disappeared, and I laid myself down upon the grass. I lifted my skirts and took off my panties to give him a reception upon his return which would excite him and cause him to play the game which would satisfy my senses and put out the fire which was threatening to devour me. My new-found acquaintance had only fanned the flames, and I was determined to do something about it.

CHAPTER SIXTEEN

I had laid myself down upon the grass again, pulled up my dress, and openly showed all the charms of my otherwise hidden secrets. I trembled with impatient desire, and spied through the thicket to see if Jerome would really come back to me in the bushes.

Suddenly I saw him. He was walking quickly toward my direction. When he had reached the bushes, he hesitated a little. I called out to him, assuring him that there was nothing to be afraid of, and that I was waiting for him with great longing.

The boy pushed the branches apart and his face covered with a deep purple blush when he saw my nakedness.

Contrary to what I had expected, it seemed that my gallant nudity made him shy and awkward instead of fanning his desires.

Jerome just stood there; his eyes downcast, twirling his hat in his strong peasant hands. It was a very funny sight and I looked at him in amazement. The boy was very good-looking, strong, and the blush on his face made him appear extremely healthy. His short pants reached just below the knees; his calves were firm and strong, his muscular thighs were beautifully molded. He looked very clean and I found that Jerome was not unworthy of me.

"Come on, you dumb boy, stretch out next to me and make yourself comfortable."

I slowly caressed his cheeks, trying to alleviate his obvious fear of me, and I asked him if he was always so shy in the company of a woman.

"Have you never looked at a girl in all her

uncovered charms before?" I asked, taking his hands and holding one against my breasts, which were trying to escape my silken bodice, and putting the other between my thighs which I then firmly pressed together.

The dear boy immediately understood what I wanted! He carefully caressed my breasts till the tips were stiff and hard. He tried to get his other hand free and, in doing so, his fingers fumbled around in the golden locks of my moist fleece.

Now the fire of wild desire began to sparkle in his eyes; his face became redder and his breath was halting. He did not speak, but his silence and his excitement proved to me that this boy knew the rules of the game and could not think of anything else but to put them into practice with me.

My face approached his and I offered him my lips. He kissed them ardently with a long and passionate kiss. My hands slowly slid up and down his thighs, and I could feel that the fabric of his pants was strained by an enormous bulge.

This bulge was for me the ultimate proof of his excitement. My caresses became more insistent, and Jerome unbuttoned himself. Freed from its prison the thing jumped forward into my hand.

Now the boy was quite beside himself. He mounted me, spread my thighs carefully and tried to reach the center of my passion. I noticed that he had a little bit of trouble finding the correct spot and it was necessary for me to guide him in. I squeezed him slightly, trying to make the preliminaries as short as possible.

Suddenly I screamed out loud! His enormous flesh pole had penetrated me up to the hilt.

The poor boy was frightened and he wanted to pull out. But I tried to reassure him as well as I could, giving him charming little names. "Don't worry, my little darling . . . it feels marvelous . . . ooh, it's sooo good and wonderful . . . Go on, do with me what you want!"

He needed no further reassurance. Whipped into fierce passion by my cries of joy, Jerome doubled his efforts and pushed into me with all the strength of his strong, muscular buttocks —he is very quick and extremely powerful. His piston driving up and down is augmented by the swinging rhythm of my hips. My back is arched and I groan with pleasure. The thick head of the heavy monster penetrates deeply into my body and we are so firmly pressed together that we truly form one body.

I make his work easier for him with the various movements I have learned. Our sighs mix together into one; our lips crush each other. We let go so that we can take a deep breath and then our mouths search for each other again in renewed and ardent kisses.

The jolting spasms which now begin to take a hold of my body release an incredible happiness in me. I can feel that I am about to reach an enormous climax. I want to reach it together and I begin to grind my buttocks in the same pistoning rhythm of Jerome's incessant pounding. I pull my lover close to me. Finally both of us tumble into the abyss of all carnal joys and I can feel the warm and benevolent love juices spurt into my body.

We remained upon the grass, our bodies closely intertwined, motionless and sleepy, the fantastic aftermath which approaches perfect satisfaction.

When I came to and looked up, I saw that Jerome was sitting upon his knees between my thighs, looking down upon me with spirited devotion. He caressed me with trembling hands and kissed my thighs and legs.

For a moment it occurred to me that I should take his head and guide it toward my fleece, but I was really too tired and I thought that tomorrow might be a better time to initiate Jerome into the delights of these marvelous caresses.

Finally the poor boy's mouth approached mine, as if he were begging for one more, final kiss. I kissed him, and he was so grateful and thanked me so profusely that it suddenly dawned on me how incredibly naive this boy was.

He covered my hands with kisses. I pulled him to his feet and told him to be at this same spot tomorrow. He gave me one more kiss and left me. I saw him run across the meadows in the direction of his father's tenant farm. I straightened out my dress, and walked toward the castle.

CHAPTER SEVENTEEN

I was overjoyed that night when I went to sleep. I finally had found a successor for Francois and I would no longer lack the caresses and games of love-making.

Yes, I was very flattered, too. Because with Jerome and me the roles were reversed. The boy was going to be my pupil and I would become the teacher.

These thoughts made me very happy. I promised myself that I was going to get the greatest benefit out of the lessons I had received from Francois. By initiating Jerome I could force him to give me complete joy and utter satisfaction.

The next day, and the days that followed, we gave ourselves completely and utterly to the same voluptuous games. I had managed to let my strolls in the park coincide with the time when Jerome returned from the castle.

But then the weather changed, and the temperature went down. This brought us some embarrassment which became worse every day. Winter set in quickly, and it became impossible to meet in the open.

I was looking for an opportunity to smuggle Jerome into my room. My plans were made easy by my aunt—unwittingly, of course—who had to leave the castle for a few days shopping in the city. After Jerome had delivered his basket and his jars, it was not at all difficult for him to meet me in the hallway from where I could smuggle him into my room.

The dear boy was completely flabbergasted at the sight of so much luxury. He picked up and looked at many of the knick-knacks, felt the furniture upholstery, but finally he came over to the couch upon which I was resting. I asked him to take off his blouse and shoes; he gladly obliged.

It was a little bit difficult for me to help him fight his shyness. The poor boy was completely overwhelmed by his surroundings. But I finally managed, and he became a little bit more bold. He covered my hands with kisses, but, since I had stretched out very voluptuously and offered him my body to caress, he suddenly was in the grip of heat and passion.

Without having to help him, he pushed up my dress, and—since I was not wearing any underwear—he took hold of my thighs. I opened them very slowly to make it easier for him to reach his goal. His hand wandered over my fleece, his fingers were playing around in the golden curls. I had no objections, though he was an obvious beginner at this game. I enjoyed it tremendously, especially since he had now reached the moist lips of my triangle.

When he had reached the proper spot, I took him by the wrist to indicate that he had reached the seat of my voluptuous desires. Moreover, the moisture had guided the dear boy to the proper spot and he knew how to give me the preliminary joys by soft stroking on that spot.

I let him play with my love nest for a while; then I took his hand, pushed it away and told him that the same caresses, when done with the tongue and lips, would be far more pleasurable both for him and for me.

Jerome seemed very surprised to hear this but he did not have to be invited for a second time. He buried his face between my thighs, and I crossed my legs around his neck.

It did not take the darling long to find the most sensitive spot, and his caresses, though inexperienced, were very pleasant and sweet, giving me complete satisfaction. Encouraged by my little cries of joy and pleasure, the dear boy labored quicker and more intensively. His strong, smooth tongue hit me with strong jolts, and his lips slurped my love juices which flowed copiously out of my love nest.

When I suddenly spasmed, arching my back and trampling my legs, I could see that Jerome's face was purple with desire, a wild glow sparkling in his eyes. I thought that was very sweet and I told him that I would reward his troubles and bring him to complete satisfaction, similar to the way he had done to me.

I told him to stretch out upon the sofa; I unbuttoned his breeches and his beautiful tool jumped up toward me. The sight of it drove me wild and I thought up a thousand ways to caress it. The beautiful big treasure jumped for joy in my expert hands. I could no longer contain myself and kissed it with hot lips, taking the large knob in my mouth. It smelled delicious, the sweet fragrance of freshly mowed hay.

Jerome let me do with him what I wanted. He trembled with joy and his hands reached for my breasts, kneading them with his firm hands till the buds were as stiff and swollen as his own marvelous tool.

He shuddered with pleasure when I tried to take his whole tool into my mouth. I loved the warm taste of it.

Jerome began to buck, forcing his enormous pole down my throat. I had trouble breathing, and tried to pull away, but Jerome had taken my head and was holding it firmly, pushing his giant tool deeper down my throat. Suddenly I felt the mighty spurts and at the same time Jerome groaned with pleasure.

The boy thanked me with kisses plastered all over my body, and he assured me by all the saints in heaven that he would never forget the most beautiful hour of his life. Since I was not wearing any clothes, he looked at me full of love, kneeled in front of me and began to kiss my moist fleece all over again. I could see that it excited him, because his limp tool began to swell mightily and soon it was proudly erect again.

However, prudence forbade me to let him do it again, because I did not want to run the risk of the servants' guessing what might be going on in my room. I got up from the couch and took my leave of him with a last kiss.

I could see that the dear boy was very reluctant to leave, but I was tired, the sweet tiredness which always follows a good love bout . . .

CHAPTER EIGHTEEN

I notice that I am writing down the details of my first steps into the great adventure of love-making without any shame. It surprises me a little, since I am supposed to keep these things a secret, and, being a young girl from the aristocracy, I have to blush at the mere mention of the word.

But I have always been against superfluous shame, especially since it is the worst form of hypocrisy I can think of. My morals and customs are the result of my birth, my upbringing and education in a time where it was acceptable. I daily thank fate which caused me to be born in an environment which was lenient toward the satisfaction of my needs and desires.

It was very early in life that I became convinced that free morals were the true sign of nobility and elegance and not, as those stern moralists insist, a degeneration of the spirit. On the contrary, nothing is more noble than to bring the spirit into concord with the body. It allows people to live their life in fullness, to offer them a delightful youth, and to make them grow old gracefully without any unnecessary guilt feelings.

*   *   *

I knew that my relationship with the tenant farmer's son had absolutely nothing to do with love. The only thing which bound me to him was my desire for carnal lust and its ultimate fulfillment. Nevertheless, I cannot deny that a certain tenderness in feelings was growing between us. But I realized now that I had had the same feelings for Francois, and that my so-called undying love for him had passed away the day I found Jerome. I was not, therefore, afraid of what might happen to me if anything should come between Jerome and me. I was now convinced that after him I might soon find another.

Besides, our affair did not last long. It was my own fault, because I had become overconfident, and slightly careless. We were soon separated, and my life suddenly changed drastically.

It happened on the day that my dear aunt was expected to return to the castle, and I had not deemed it necessary to interrupt our game of love. As I had done the two previous days, I invited Jerome up to my room. Each day our love-making became more elaborate, and dear Jerome was a very eager and extremely good pupil. Of course, the enormous tool he had to work with, made instruction pure pleasure for me.

I was determined to teach my darling all the positions I had learned from Francois and then some, and Jerome, blinded and happy, announced his pleasure with grunts and groans, which I answered with panting cries and moaning. I was completely naked on the couch, my legs up in the air, offering my golden fleece and all its secrets to Jerome, who was in my moist fleece. He was about to ram his pole deep into my belly when suddenly the door opened!

Jerome, whose face was buried between my breasts did not see anything, but I could see my aunt standing in the door opening. She did not seem mad, though her face expressed certain disgust.

She turned around and shut the door behind her. Jerome and I were alone again. But I got up off the couch, leaving Jerome completely bewildered, and hurriedly dressed myself, telling Jerome to do the same. I explained it to him in one word, "Aunt!"

The poor boy was petrified; he turned pale, and did not know what to do. We looked at one another, not daring to leave the room. Jerome trembled like an aspen leaf.

I was the first one to recover my composure. I dressed carefully, brought my hair in order, applied some rouge to my face, and looked as if nothing had happened. Jerome had put on his blouse, buttoned his breeches and put on his shoes. I went into the corridor; it was empty. I went downstairs, Jerome following me as if he were my shadow; the hall was empty, too. Jerome dashed for the door, and ran out into the park, forgetting his milk jar and cheese basket. It was the last time I saw him.

*   *   *

I saw my aunt at dinner, and much to my surprise, she did not at all allude to what she had seen that afternoon, but, instead, spoke in a pleasant tone about her shopping trip and about friends she had met. I was terribly confused but managed not to show it, and dinner proceeded as usual.

I must admit that I was terribly worried when I went to bed, because I was afraid that this stillness might be the forerunner of a terrible thunderstorm. My mind was racing. I was conjuring a thousand horrible punishments and I was deadly afraid that I would be sent to a cloister.

Finally I fell asleep. The next day my fear grew, when a servant announced that my aunt wanted to see me for breakfast. This had never happened before!

I was very surprised therefore that she did not seem furious at all. On the contrary, she looked at me with a smile! It seemed to me that she was amused about my fear and confusion.

She was sitting in her big armchair in front of her desk, which was littered with papers. She took her ivory snuff box and took a deep snuff. Then she motioned me to sit down next to her.

She took my hand, and said, "Jacqueline, I will not make any accusations. After all, I knew your mother and your father . . . their blood flows through your veins, and, I myself burn with the same fire.

"I have known about your games with your teacher and your cousin Amaranthe from the day they began. But though I have said nothing when you took Francois as your lover, I cannot stand by silently about your affair with Jerome. Your teacher came from a splendid family; Jerome is only a peasant.

"Mind you, my dear cousin, I do not have a prejudiced mind, and I do not look down upon peasants. As a matter of fact, I am convinced that among them you will find more honesty and naturalness than among the great of the world who are bloated with pride and vanity.

"But, dear Jacqueline, it is the way of the world, and you alone cannot fight it. Despite all the advances made by the philosophers, I cannot allow you to continue what you are doing.

To do so would be delivering you to ridicule and shame, and it would be disastrous to our proud family name.

"I have therefore decided that we shall move to Paris to finish your education. We shall find ourselves a nobleman who is equal to you in birth. I think that marriage is the best and most convenient way to extinguish your burning desires in a manner approved of by society."

* * *

This little speech set me to daydreaming. But soon I was overwhelmed by the idea, and became very enthusiastic. I thanked my aunt profusely.

Paris! With its luxury, its easy manners, its many pleasures . . . Everything which I had ever wanted!

That night I danced through the lanes of the park. Goodbye, Leda . . . goodbye swan! Goodbye, oh beautiful place where I was initiated into Eros' games . . . goodbye nymphs and fauns, witnesses to my ever-increasing abilities in the game of love. And goodbye dear bushes, in whose shadows I have tasted the pleasures of the flesh.

A month after the decision was made, my aunt and I departed for Paris.

A new life was about to begin!

CHAPTER NINETEEN

My dear aunt moved into a beautiful home on the rue Saint-Honore, almost directly across from the Royal Palace.

It happened that this house had two empty floors and an empty ground floor. We could not have had better luck. My aunt decorated the home with furniture which not only was luxurious but also witness to her refined taste. She kept the second floor for herself, while the first floor became my apartment. I was very happy with this arrangement, since it allowed me an enormous measure of freedom.

On the ground floor were the salon and the reception rooms. The courtyard had stables, a barn for the coaches, the carrying chairs, and also living quarters for the servants.

I liked it very much there, because we lived in the middle of the city! The Louvre with its beautiful gardens was in the neighborhood, and as I already wrote, the Royal Palace was practically across the street, as were the beautiful promenades where I was to discover a thousand wonderful things!

Our first Sunday in Paris we went to hear mass in Saint-Roch. I was very surprised about this religious devotion of my aunt, who, I knew, was not devout at all. On the contrary, she made no bones about the fact that she was an atheist! But my dear aunt explained to me that it was customary to show up at this place of prayer, which was visited by the best members of society.

I soon found out that she was right. Moreover, when we left the church, I made acquaintance with the Marquis de F— who became my first conquest—and my first lover—in Paris.

* * *

But first I must talk about a gallant adventure which I had with one of my chambermaids.

This tall, nineteen-year-old girl was in our service, and I selected her to be my chambermaid, because I had noticed her beauty and charm. Moreover, she looked a little bit like my dear cousin, Amaranthe.

Her name was Toinette, and she had a marvelous bosom with gorgeous breasts, very well-developed for her age. Her face was pleasant and her eyes were twinkling with laughter, large and vivacious. Her beautiful lips were dark red, her teeth were even and pearly white, but most attractive was her ashen-blonde hair which made me surmise the beauty and delight of her hidden fleece.

I made haste to use this girl for secret and pleasurable affairs and on the evening of our second day in Paris, after dinner, I told her that it was to be her duty to take care of my person, my laundry, my toilette, and my apartment.

The charming Toinette was overjoyed and thanked me profusely. I was secretly very pleased with her joy, because it gave me the assurance that I would not encounter too many difficulties with her in the future. Because, you see, I had fallen in love with this charming girl at first sight.

When I retired to my apartment I called her, and told her to follow me.

After we were alone, and I had carefully locked the door, we began a conversation which I interrupted now and then to caress my new-found girl friend. I asked her if she was pleased to be close to me and if she would be able to learn to love me. Her only answer was a deep blushing and some confused stammering. I bent over and kissed her, first upon the forehead, then the cheeks, finally her irresistible lips, and then I gave myself over completely to my passions. I took off my dress and bodice and sat down. I ordered Toinette to kneel before me and help me take off my shoes and stockings.

The dear little one knelt down, pulling my shoes off my feet, and she began to feel around in my lace and silken underwear to find my garters so she could take off my stockings.

I used the position the girl was in to pull her closer to me and to press her neck between my thighs. I then leaned suddenly back so that my belly slightly protruded. This maneuver brought my panties close to Toinette's shame-reddened face.

I squeezed my thighs closer together on purpose, mainly to force Toinette in the position I wanted; I could feel the warmth of her breath through the thin silk of my panties and I began to shudder with delight.

By lifting myself slightly I could slide down my panties. Toinette instantly guessed my intention and she pulled them down, taking them off. Then she threw her arms around me, caressed my buttocks with her soft hands, and her eager mouth began to explore my fleece.

Soon she had reached the entrance to my love slit and I could feel the warm moistness of her tongue which forcefully penetrated me.

I do not know whether the charming Toinette was used to this kind of service, but she showed certain experience and the eagerness with which she fulfilled her task made up a hundred-fold for what she lacked in finesse. She was not in the least impressed by my screams of joy and the more I groaned the deeper and firmer her tongue would explore my inside. She increased the pressure—her entire mouth had disappeared into my hole, and she began to nibble at the center of my passions. I quickly experienced complete release. I could no longer control my spasms—my thighs opened wide, releasing the girl, and with a loud scream I collapsed in a deep swoon.

When I came to, Toinette was still kneeling in front of me, devouring me with her eyes. Her very soft hands stroked my thighs and legs, she murmured soft words of endearment, and she called me her darling mistress.

Her large eyes burned with a voluptuous desire and lust overcame me again. I got up, pushed Toinette down upon the bed and made her put a pillow under her buttocks. She did, and also lifted her legs high up in the air.

I quickly grabbed her thighs, spread them wide apart and ravaged her secret garden. The sweet darling had a slightly curled fleece and I quickly reached the soft flower of love. I opened the folds with my lips and caressed the swelling bud with glowing hot tongue.

The little one groaned and her voluptuous moaning made me double my efforts. Ooh, I caressed the secrets of my charming Toinette with ardent passion! There was not a single spot between her thighs and her firm, smooth belly which remained unkissed.

The little darling twitched and twisted, spreading her thighs, arching her back, making it as easy as possible for me to penetrate deep into her moist secret. She offered me all her treasures, and my lips and tongue were incessantly busy bringing her pleasure after pleasure.

It took her a long time to reach a climax, which in turn, increased my desire and I gave her the wildest caresses my panting lust could dream up.

Finally she reached the ultimate peak of her lust. I recognized the symptoms. Her back arched higher, her buttocks squeezed together, jolting spasms racked through her body, and the soft flower of her love spot in which I had burrowed my mouth began to quiver uncontrollably.

Suddenly she groaned loudly, pushed back my head, collapsed, and remained motionless upon the bed. Her beautiful eyes expressed great satisfaction, her cheeks were deep red and her lips seemed to me like ripe strawberries waiting to be kissed.

I hastened to do so. Toinette woke up out of her swoon, and she returned my kisses. Our bodies intertwined, and she declared her undying love for me. She assured me that this was the first time in her life that she had reached such a deep and satisfying climax, and she did not stop thanking me for it . . .

Finally I invited her to share my large bed

with me; we took off all our clothes and fell
asleep in each other's arms. But not before we
had exchanged a hundred thousand passionate
kisses.

CHAPTER TWENTY

One Sunday, after we had been to mass at Saint-Roch church, my aunt was in a hurry to leave because she was late for an appointment. I walked a little slower, and upon leaving the church I dipped my finger in the Holy water vessel. I happened to do this simultaneously with a very good-looking nobleman. Our fingers touched, and before I had had a chance to make the sign of the cross, he held my hand and brought it to his lips.

Even though I had already been expecting some bold move from this particular gentleman, especially since we had been exchanging glances in between prayers, I pretended to be extremely shocked about his unseemly behavior in this sacred place.

But it seemed that my face belied my shocked voice because my cavalier was not in the least embarrassed. On the contrary, he offered me a broad smile and his arm. Together we left the church. My aunt was impatiently waiting for me in the coach, her eyes were straying across the people that left the church through its three doors. She suddenly spotted me when I walked down the last few steps on the arm of my unknown cavalier.

My heart beat faster when the beautiful nobleman, whom I greatly admired, walked straight to my aunt's coach and greeted her respectfully.

"Madame," he said, "I beg a thousand pardons. I took the liberty of guiding your charming daughter, because she almost stumbled in the rush of people getting out of church." And he introduced himself. To my great surprise he turned out to be the Marquis de F——. My aunt seemed to be very familiar with the noble name. She received his excuse with a dazzling smile and offered him her hand which he gallantly kissed. She thanked him for the service he had rendered me.

I liked the proud boldness of that young man. I made myself an accomplice to his harmless little lie by profusely thanking him for his help, adding that without it I most probably would have ruined my gown and possibly could have been a subject to ridicule if I had fallen down those steps.

The Marquis helped us into the coach, took his leave from us and walked over to his own carriage. I could see that he followed us through the streets and when we stopped in front of our home, I noticed that he ordered his driver to slow down. He looked out of the window and motioned with his hand.

I understood that he was asking me if this was our home and, since my aunt was already descending from the carriage, I nodded yes.

My dear aunt never policed me and she left me a lot of freedom. I frequently went out alone, or accompanied by Toinette.

The day after I had so suddenly met the Marquis de F——, I was not at all surprised to see him stroll up and down the promenade of the Royal Palace, watching our home from the corner of his eye. He was the one who was surprised to see me all alone, and he was hesitant about talking to me. But I took the lead, walked up to him and asked with my most charming smile, "Dearest Marquis, what has happened to yesterday's boldness?"

He laughed and kissed my hand. Then he

asked me about my aunt, whom he mistakenly had taken to be my mother. And, above all, he wanted to know how a girl of my age and standing, managed to walk the promenade alone! I laughed again and assured him that my aunt was a philosopher and absolutely disinterested in stupid prejudices. I also made it quite clear that I was even more of a freethinker and could not care less about the ridiculous conventions of society.

The Marquis was slightly stumped by my little speech and it took him a minute to recuperate. Then he asked me, "My dearest young lady, does that mean that you would have no objections if I invited you into my carriage for a ride?"

I thought the question was very funny and countered whether he thought there should be anything objectionable to it. "Try me, and ask the question."

During this conversation we had reached his carriage, and he helped me get in. Then he sat down next to me and, while the carriage sped away, he told me that he was overjoyed about my freedom which allowed him to be alone with such a charming girl. He paid me a thousand compliments about my looks, my gown, my face, my hair, my eyes and my lips. We had not even reached the gate of rue Saint-Honore when he put his arm around my waist.

When we drove through the gate, our lips met for the first time and when we were outside of the city I allowed him to lift my dress so he could rest his hand upon my knee, stroking me softly, obviously trying to reach my thigh.

I resisted slightly, making sure that during

this little struggle his hand was clamped between my thighs. I could see to my great pleasure that my gallant had become extremely excited. He grew more daring and through the fine silk of my panties he began to caress my fleece. The bulge of his virility, which stretched his breeches to the limit, was a sight to behold. It made me very, very happy.

There was no doubt that we understood each other. The bold, good-looking cavalier realized that my mood was equal to his desire; pantingly we slowed down our caresses. He happened to mention that he owned a little cottage in the neighborhood of Auteuil, and that it would be sort of nice if, one of these days, we could go there and pass the time away with a few games and conversation.

I answered that he better make his horses run quicker, because a passionate desire was devouring me and it needed to be extinguished.

The Marquis was utterly surprised, but I did not have to ask him twice. He had obviously intended to possess me one of these days but he had not in his wildest dreams expected such a quick success.

His cottage was the scene of our first hours of love. The pleasant cavalier knew how to satisfy me completely and he was more than surprised to find out that I knew certain rules of the game, myself. I proved to him beyond the shadow of a doubt that a young girl from the noble classes could be as adept at the game of Venus as the best and most expensive of the courtesans.

On our way back to Paris we reminisced about the way we had met at the church. We were both very happy about that meeting, and we promised that we should meet again frequently to repeat our games of this afternoon. It had been a most delicious and satisfying pastime for both of us.

CHAPTER TWENTY-ONE

The Marquis had invited me to visit him in his small but comfortable apartments which were near our home. The apartments were part of a mansion which belonged to his parents, and, since they were extremely severe and moralistic, my lover had to employ a thousand different tricks to get me into his rooms without their becoming suspicious.

He decided that I should dress as a chambermaid so that I could reach his apartments without any difficulties.

Of course I had some misgivings and did not show too much enthusiasm for the idea, but the Marquis was so absolutely enthusiastic about his brilliant idea that I finally decided to give in. I had also discovered a certain peculiarity. It seemed that the idea of smuggling me into his apartments as a common chambermaid had a certain added excitement for my Marquis. This latter consideration prompted me to borrow a dress and overcoat from Toinette, and I walked over to the home of the Marquis.

It was so extremely easy to see the young Marquis that it seemed as if he had bribed his parents into consent. My lover received me into his home and covered me with kisses. The decoration was charming, the furniture was tasteful and very comfortable for making love.

A little table had been set. We ate a few sweets and drank some chinese tea. Then the Marquis offered me a few glasses of delicious liqueur which set my entire body afire.

After those few drinks he did not have to implore me long to enter his bedroom. I had become very excited and was impatient to begin the games of Eros and Venus.

The Marquis repeated his declarations of undying love. He carefully undressed me and I stood naked before him; only my stockings and shoes were not removed.

The young nobleman was overjoyed with the charming sight. He told me that he had never before seen a girl who was so well-developed, who had such a beautiful figure, and such a smooth skin without blemishes. He took his sweet time to explore my body extensively, kissing every part of it, fondling my breasts and nipples.

The young man went about it very tenderly and I was very grateful to him for this as well as for the honorable way in which he treated me and the many compliments he paid my beauty and charm.

He employed some exciting caresses which fanned my desire and I could hardly wait for him to pick me up and carry me to his bed. He finally decided to do just that. He took me in his strong arms and put me down upon the pillows. Then he began to take off his own clothes without taking his eyes off my charming form.

He was already standing in his undershirt and I could admire his muscular form and the tremendous bulge which indicated his waxing desire, when suddenly the door was thrown wide open and an imposing figure, dressed in cardinal's red, entered the room.

"Ooh, uncle!" the young Marquis cried out. The bulge disappeared and the Marquis himself stiffened.

"Well, well, that is a curious exhibition," remarked the Cardinal. "How dare you give yourself to these unspeakable things in the very house in which your parents live, nephew! And especially during my visit here, which is a time when you should think about higher things, and when your mind should be occupied with devotions and prayer."

Though the speech was stern, the smile belied the Cardinal's words. But my young Marquis, reddened with shame, had picked up his clothes and ran out of his apartments. There I was, completely naked, upon the bed.

I had hoped that the Cardinal would follow his nephew. He went to the door, but instead of leaving, he carefully locked the door and returned to the bed.

He sat down upon the bed and began to pet me, giving me a chance to look him over a little bit more carefully.

He was tall and strong, still young, with a noble bearing and an almost majestic elegance. His eyes sparkled impishly and his face began to redden till it had almost become as purple as the robe he was wearing.

Suddenly he bent over me, murmuring little nothings in my ear, and he began to caress and kiss me. The novelty of the situation excited me. The adventure had fanned the flames of passion instead of extinguishing them. I looked the prelate boldly in the eyes, and moved my body voluptuously under his careful caresses.

Soon it became very clear to me that His Eminence desired more than anything else to mount me and make love to me. He lifted his purple robe and I noticed a short pair of breeches of the same color with a strong bulge between the thighs.

The sight of this purple bulge increased my desire tremendously and I began to unbutton the purple breeches very carefully. The male member of the Cardinal jumped out toward me and I could not prevent the cry of admiration that escaped from my lips. Never in my life had I seen such a gigantic member. Till now I had believed that Jerome had the biggest and hardest tool which was possible on a man. But the Cardinal's giant made Jerome's look like a little pinkie.

His Eminence mounted me and buried his tool deep in my insides with expertness and without any troubles at all. He behaved like a perfect lover and made me forget all about his unfortunate nephew. I reached the highest peaks of satisfaction several times which flattered the Cardinal tremendously. He was very friendly and asked me about the details of my loss of virginity. He was a very good conversationalist and told me repeatedly that this pleasant affair with such a young and beautiful girl had deeply satisfied him.

When he found out who I was, and that I belonged to the cream of society, his enthusiasm knew no bounds. He thanked me profusely for my company and vowed that we should repeat our sacrifice to the goddess of love more often. He gave me the address of a small home where we could meet as often as possible without creating any difficulties for him or for me.

Beside himself with joy, he showed me that his tongue was as good as his tool when it came to exciting my private parts. I quivered under his kisses and because I did not want to be outdone, I reciprocated by kissing, sucking and caressing his big, heavy tool which had so perfectly extinguished the all-consuming fire in my body. Soon I was floating on a cloud of delight, and when I came out of my swoon, the Cardinal was standing next to the bed, in full majesty and only the deep, dark rings under his eyes betrayed that he had just savored a wild and wonderful journey through the valley of lust.

We said farewell, and he kissed my hand. I glanced in the mirror and had to laugh at the sight of this majestic Cardinal kissing a naked girl. After he had left, I dressed, left the bedroom and tried to find the Marquis.

I was walking through the corridors, trying to find my way, when I suddenly heard a loud groan, and a cry of lust and pain. The sounds came from a little room, the door of which was ajar. I tiptoed toward the door and what I saw made my mouth slacken with surprise! A young page boy was presenting his naked buttocks to my young Marquis, who was pumping his tool into him. This was the way he consoled himself —with a young page boy who served him . . . as a mistress!

I fled the home, laughing, and I thought that this was the way of all flesh. We turned to our own sex, when we could not find an outlet with the other. This is why I turned so often to my own, dear, Toinette.

The Cardinal had given me so much pleasure that I could not be mad at the Marquis about his cowardly flight and his affair with the page boy. At first I was a little bit disappointed that he had turned toward his own sex rather than to me, and when I told him so—later— he was at first confused, but then he, too, laughed about the episode.

It was different, though, when I told him that his uncle had been a more than perfect replacement, and that it would be very difficult to please me as much, now that I had found out certain things which might have remained hidden from me were it not for the Marquis' own cowardice.

"I am very grateful that His Eminence took pity on me, and gallantly fulfilled the desire which you had fanned in me," I said, "because you left me suddenly without caring about my feelings."

The Marquis was furious about his uncle's behavior and he called him all sorts of vile names . . . a dirty old hypocrite and a ravager of young girls. I interrupted his furious monologue by pointing out that he, himself, was responsible for what had happened. He was the one who had left the battlefield, handing over the spoils to his opponent.

"Do you really believe, my dear lover, that your uncle, facing a charming and naked girl in the bed, would have begun a sermon on morals and then asked her to join him in prayer?"

"He did the natural thing which any real man in those circumstances would do. Nature took its course and I must admit that I was more than satisfied. I cannot possibly be disenchanted with your uncle."

The Marquis was still furious, in fact, after my little speech even more so. We quarreled most of that afternoon, and finally I told him that I did not desire to go on that way, and that I thought his jealousy was ridiculous. And I also pointed out that he had taken his pleasure with the page boy.

My last remark quieted him down considerably and he suggested that we retire to his cottage near Auteuil to finish what he had planned for that morning.

The horses were readied, and soon our carriage hurried through the suburbs toward our little love nest. We returned to Paris very late that evening, and my dear aunt was terribly upset. The dinner hour had long since passed and she was friendly but firm in pointing out that, especially in the late evening hours, things could happen to innocent young girls which might mark them for life.

"The dangers," she said, "are many. Believe me, my dear, not every man you meet has honorable intentions."

CHAPTER TWENTY-TWO

The days which followed this episode were for me the most memorable and pleasant ones in the execution of my love-making.

The Marquis was very lazy and usually slept till noon. I therefore reserved the mornings for his uncle who always received me in his bed. The good Father was as strong as a bull and very experienced in the art of love. During his stay in Paris he fulfilled my wildest desires, gave me tremendous joy, and satisfied me completely.

This, of course, did not deter me from enjoying the same games on the afternoons with his nephew. The Marquis did not dare to receive me at his home, so we either tumbled around in my apartment or in his cottage near Auteuil.

And, despite my tiredness from enjoying all this love-making, I gave myself completely, at night, to the ministrations of my beloved Toinette.

My charming maid fulfilled her task with such admirable vigor and ardor that I did not want to deny her my body and its delights for one single night. Especially since it gave me, too, tremendous joy and contrary to common opinion it did not wear me out but refreshed my powers for the love games I would play the next day.

Toinette simply adored me. She could foresee my slightest wishes and she fulfilled them instantly with a devotion that is quite uncommon for people of her low standing. The charming child never takes off my shoes without kissing my feet and legs. Every time she helps me put on a new gown, or undress for the night, her lips linger upon my body and her moist caresses cover every single spot of my exposed skin.

And that is only the prelude to more ardent and passionate caresses. I do not have to tell her about my desires. I simply stretch out on the couch, or sit down in a chair and spread my legs apart. Darling Toinette immediately throws herself upon me, buries her face deep in my fleece and her lips begin to nibble away at my treasure, her tongue eagerly searching for the jumping bud. She affords me the wildest caresses and she keeps it up as long as it pleases me. I am sure that she could leave her lips all night buried in my love treasure were it not for the fact that after several jolting spasms I am simply forced to push her head away.

The sweet girl still is not satisfied. She kisses my nude body with moist lips, presses her mouth against my buttocks and her trembling tongue traces patterns in every grove and furrow of my body. She caresses my breasts and nibbles the hardening nipples, while her tender, soft hands stroke my body endlessly in all the sensitive spots she knows so well. I never know when she is finished because I always fall asleep under her tender caresses. I am always in a state of wild desire when I fall asleep, and in the morning, upon awakening, dear Toinette is there to give me deep satisfaction.

This deep love and devotion of a young girl for another girl surprised me, and one day I asked Toinette for an explanation.

Toinette admitted to me that she had never known the love of a man; that she was still a virgin, and deeply devoted to lesbian love. She swore to me that she would never allow a man to touch her, because no man would be able to give her the deep satisfaction which she experienced from giving and taking female bodies.

This answer made me very curious and I wanted to know more about this. Toinette finally told me about her experiences, and how she was initiated into lesbian lovemaking. It had happened when she was sixteen years old and in the service of the famous Countess de B—.

I was stretched out upon the couch and Toinette had pressed her body against mine. She slowly stroked my belly and breasts, pressing a moist kiss now and then upon the nipples, and she began to tell me her story, now and then interrupting to take a long draught from my moist fleece.

CHAPTER TWENTY-THREE

Toinette's Story

I came from the provinces to this town and entered the services of the Countess de B——. Very soon I became her chambermaid.

My charming mistress was in the prime of life. She had been widowed at an early age, and her new freedom allowed her to be as tender and passionate as she wanted, whenever she wanted it.

The Countess was not severe. She treated her servants well and was familiar with all of them. She was only very strict on the point of cleanliness.

I liked it very much in her home, because the house where I had worked in the province was headed by an old hag with a terrible temper, who paid extremely low wages and punished the slightest mistake horribly.

I was attracted to the idea of going to Paris where, I had heard, the wages were much better, and I wanted to be able to send some money now and then to my poor and ailing mother.

One evening, when I was helping the Countess prepare for bed, she looked at me in a curious way. She asked all sorts of questions about my background and my family and finally she ordered me, just before I was about to leave, to show her my underwear. She praised the cleanliness of it and told me that I should undress completely, because she wanted to know if my body was as clean as my laundry.

I was a little bit confused and somewhat ashamed, but I did as I was told. Soon I stood fully naked before my mistress who showed her satisfaction by fondling my breasts and stroking my buttocks. She also kissed me and said that I was very charming and that I had a fine figure. She praised my cleanliness and informed me that from now on I was going to have another job which suited my cleanliness and my personality much better.

I told the Countess that I was very grateful and, after she had fallen asleep, I left her room.

* * *

The next day the Countess drove to Passy where she owned a country home.

I knew the town, because I had been there twice. What I did not know was that my mistress used to receive her female lovers there.

She, herself, made the preparations for my reception. A few hours later I got into a carriage and the governess, a very witty, elderly lady who was head of the Countess' household, accompanied me to the country home in Passy.

It looked like a huge farm, behind which an enormous orchard stretched out in all directions. The trees were so close together that they formed an impenetrable wall through which the neighbors were unable to spy. Actually, the orchard was a beautiful park with lanes and meadows, and hidden behind another cluster of trees was a beautiful pavilion which the Countess had dedicated as a temple to that famous poetess, Sappho of Lesbos.

A beautiful marble statue was erected in honor of this great female lover of women. It was surrrounded by gorgeous nymphs whose secret parts fulfilled the function of fountains.

I was brought into the temple, bathed, perfumed and my body hair was painlessly removed. I also got a wonderful massage. Then I was dressed in a beautiful silken gown which was very low cut in front and from behind it left my buttocks free. A thin veil covered my breasts, and I was sent into the rooms of my dear mistress.

The Countess seemed to me more beautiful than ever. She was dressed in a long silken gown and she languished upon a sofa. She looked like a perfect statue of exquisite form. Her exposed bosom revealed two large and firm globes, crowned by rosy buds; they invited caresses. Her beautiful belly and her marble-white thighs were clearly visible through the thin fabric. Her firm arms and the calves of her legs were uncovered.

She arose slowly when I entered, and looked at me passionately. In her soft, melodious voice she invited me to sit down next to her. She asked me if I was happy to be near her and if I were willing to love her.

I answered that I was willing to do almost anything to show her my gratitude, and I threw myself upon her, kissing her passionately.

"No, no, my dumb little goose. That is not how one does it! Have you never seen two doves rub their bills with loving caresses? That is the example you should follow!"

She pulled my face toward hers and stuck her tongue into my mouth. A divine, hitherto unknown feeling came over me, and I reciprocated this voluptuous kiss as well as I could.

The Countess stroked my breasts, exclaiming her admiration. "Oh, how sweet! They are so charming and firm! And look . . . the little darlings are swelling and stiffening!"

I kissed her passionately and wanted to stroke her breasts also when she suddenly put her hand between my thighs, discovering my buttocks.

She caressed me, and her nimble fingers played around, coming closer and closer to the center of all joy. She excited me for a long time in this manner and then she pushed me gently back upon the sofa. She admired the beautiful flower in the center of my fleece, bringing her face closer and closer, finally kissing it. I know now what she wanted when I felt her lips press upon my love spot and her tongue insistently penetrate toward the throbbing bud. It was delicious.

She kept covering me with hot, moist, passionate kisses, thereby slowly turning herself around till her secret parts were above my own mouth. I immediately understood and I did not have to be invited twice. My eager mouth sought the fleece, my lips passionately pressed against her organ and my tongue began to explore the soft inside, searching for her innermost secret. It filled me with indescribable joy to cover the moist, delicious flower of my dear mistress with kisses and to caress the inside with my tongue.

We exchanged the most glowing and tender caresses for more than an hour without letting go of our firm embrace. We almost choked on each other's love juices which copiously flowed, mixing with the spittle of our passionate mouths. Finally, jolting spasms overtook us and we sank exhausted down upon the sofa.

The Countess rang and two chambermaids appeared who washed and perfumed us. We then took a copious meal during which my mistress told me all about lesbian love and instructed me in its history and supremacy. She told me that she was a member of a sect called the Tribades, and that she ardently wished that I, too, would become a member.

She added that one had to be a virgin, which I was, and that one had to be convinced of the superiority of love-making between women. I also would have to swear that I would never allow a man to touch me, and that I would forever spread word of the superiority of lesbian love and, if necessary, be capable of proving it.

The Countess took me into her confidence by telling me that she was, as I, still a virgin. Despite her marriage into which her family had forced her, she had managed to remain pure. True, she admitted, her husband had made it easy for her, because he was an old lecher who preferred to consort with whores of the lowest kind. Moreover, as a Marshall of France, he had had the good taste to win many honors for his King and Country, whereupon, mortally wounded, he expired in foreign lands, leaving his bereaved widow with a famous name, a fabulous fortune and full freedom.

My dear mistress also told me that it was a great honor to become a member of the Sect of Tribades and that I had to undergo a series of strict examinations before I was admitted. But she also told me that she was convinced that I was worthy to be initiated into the divine rites and mysteries of lesbian love. That same night the first examinations would take place.

The Countess was convinced that I would be successful because she had an excellent opinion of me on account of our leisurely afternoon. And she also believed that I would be more than willing to sacrifice my life to the delicious pleasure of lasciviousness.

I thanked my mistress profusely and assured her that she would never have any reason to regret her decision, and that I would do everything in my power to prove myself worthy of her trust in me.

After dinner we strolled together through the park for many delicious hours in which I was thoroughly instructed to make sure that I would pass the strict examinations which would make me a full-fledged member of the lesbian cult of the Tribades.

CHAPTER TWENTY-FOUR

When my dearest Toinette had reached this point of her story I was suddenly overcome by an irresistible desire. The vivid description of her love games had excited me beyond the point of control. I suddenly threw my little darling backwards upon the sofa, used her surprise to roughly open her thighs and dive deeply with my hot mouth into her fleece. My tongue eagerly sought the bud and my lips burned passionate kisses upon her secret parts.

I had a wild desire to caress this delightful girl and I also wanted to prove to her that despite my lost virginity I was not unworthy to become a member of the divine cult of Sappho.

The dear child submitted readily to my caresses and soon she was reciprocating my hot kisses. We licked and sucked each other, kissing and tonguing till we both collapsed in jolting spasms, copiously flooding each other's face with our love juices. When we had rested and dried our faces, Toinette continued her story:

* * *

I was led into a very charming boudoir, and the door was firmly bolted behind me. In the center stood a gigantic statue of the god Priapus, his enormous tool threateningly erect in the full power of his virile strength and beauty. The paintings on the wall depicted men and women in the most various and lascivious positions. On the tables were books and etchings with similar positions, describing in vivid detail the many ways in which men and women can play the game of love.

At the foot of the enormous statue burned a fire which I was supposed to tend. The flame was fed by a quickly burning substance and a single moment of inattention could cause the flame to burn out without any possibility of starting it again.

This was a very easy way to find out if the candidate expressed any interest at all in the forbidden ways of love-making. One moment of forgetfulness would extinguish the flame and the honor of becoming a member of this lesbian society would be forfeited forever.

Sometimes these tests lasted for days. In my case it was a mere few hours because the flame burned brightly and continuously since I had absolutely no interest in what the depicted gentlemen were doing with their despicable tools. Three lesbians entered the boudoir and when they saw that I was only interested in tending the flame they freed me of my task.

Then I was brought into the temple. All member lesbians were there, dressed in festive gowns. The full-fledged members wore red tunics with a blue waistband, and the novices wore white and pink. The necklines were very low, so that the breasts were free. The tunics were short, showing the thighs, and the back and front were split, giving free access to fleece and buttocks. All the ladies present had beautiful figures, marvelous breasts and wonderful thighs and buttocks. It was a feast for the eye!

A large fire was kept burning in the middle of the great hall; novices threw incense in it from time to time, and a light, aromatic smoke circled toward the ceiling.

I had reached the front row of the membership, where the ruling committee was sitting.

I had to kneel in front of a beautiful woman—
I found out later that she was the Duchess de
R—, and my mistress, the Countess, gave the
following short speech:

"Honored and dearest Madame President and
you, my charming and beautiful lady friends.
I have the honor to present to you today a young
candidate who, I believe, possesses all the necessary qualities to become a welcome member
of our little circle. She is, as you can see for
yourself, a beautiful girl, and I can vouch for
her inclinations, because I have tried her myself. I can also vouch for her eagerness and her
sense of duty, and beg of you to initiate her
today as a member."

I was told to get up and take off my tunic.
I had to stand fully in the nude so that the
members of the committee and the other sisters
could take a good look at me. The President
was first. She patted my buttocks and squeezed
my firm breasts, her hand slid down my belly
and her fingers caressed my fleece. She stuck
her index finger suddenly quite deep into me to
satisfy herself that I was still a virgin.

I was a little bit ashamed and shy during
this examination, but it turned out that this
shyness was in my favor; the ladies proclaimed
their satisfaction unanimously and acknowledged my charms and beauty.

Accompanied by two attendants I was led out
of the temple to give the membership a chance
to discuss me and cast their ballots. A few minutes later the Countess entered the anteroom,
embraced me passionately, and told me that I
had been unanimously accepted. When I returned into the temple all the lesbians kissed

me profusely, and I was dressed in the tunic of a novice.

I then swore solemnly that I would forever abjure physical contact with men, that I would abide by the rules of this true lesbian society, and that I would never reveal the secret rites, and mysteries of our sect.

The night ended with a mutual pairing off. It was my task to satisfy the lusts of the members of the committee and the President. But I kept my most devoted caresses for my mistress to show her my gratitude for having introduced me to this marvelous society of refined ladies.

After a short novice period and after having undergone several severe tests, I was accepted as a full-fledged sister of Lesbos. Then something terrible happened. My beloved Countess had an accident and died. I will never forget her and I will forever honor the principles, the secrets and the oaths of this beautiful society of lesbians.

* * *

Poor Toinette had cried when she remembered her early benefactress, but I kissed her eyes and lips and soon our mouths were glued together. Her story had made me very hot and passionate again and my desire to possess her knew no bounds. That night my dear Toinette received climax after climax under my passionate kisses. I worked hard at it, because I had resolved to spare neither toil nor trouble, and make Toinette love me as much as she had her former mistress. We united our bodies according to the rites of Toinette's lesbian cult, which my little darling had explained to me after I had solemnly sworn never to reveal anything of what she had told me. It had become a point of honor to me to replace the late Countess in Toinette's affections. I fully believe that I have been quite successful.

Toinette would like to see that I stop all activities with the other sex. It is more a matter of principle to her than jealousy, but I do not think that I am completely ripe for this form of sexual exclusiveness.

Even though I do not deny the voluptuous charms of my dearest Toinette, I simply cannot go without the stronger satisfactions that only the male of the species can give me. And just as I managed, back home at the ancestral castle, to divide my attentions between Francois and Amaranthe, I can manage the same here, in Paris, between my Marquis and my chambermaid.

And, as far as men are concerned, I have a greater selection to choose from, especially since the Cardinal returns quite frequently to Paris. As a matter of fact, I pride myself that he does not return because of church business, but because he cannot stay away from me for any prolonged period of time. It drives his nephew into fits of jealousy because the Marquis, despite my assurances that I love him deeply, is a very suspicious person.

But, I manage somehow. Everybody has his own charms which are capable of satisfying my lusts. And I have decided to make it my exclusive pastime to discover as much as I can.

CHAPTER TWENTY-FIVE

The Marquis told me about a group of people of both sexes, freethinkers, who have devoted their lives to the cult of Priapus and who worship the God of sexual lust in the same manner as the ancients. I was terribly curious about these people and I did not stop pestering my lover with questions, though he was very reluctant to talk to me about them.

But finally, one evening, after an especially satisfying love bout, my darling promised me that he would introduce me to this group, and that I would be able to participate in one of their sessions. He warned me, however, about a special custom of theirs, so that I would be prepared as to what might happen: it was customary to search for a partner in a fully darkened hall.

My lover explained to me that this rite was followed by many cults in the ancient world. The system, he said, afforded the greatest voluptuous feelings and gave tremendous satisfaction. The love games and sexual struggles could be extremely exciting and rewarding. When I hesitated because, as I explained to him, I did not want to run the risk of being embraced by ugly and senile old men, he reassured me. Only those who were deemed worthy of Eros and Venus were selected by the membership. The Marquis added that I, too, had to undergo this examination before I could be admitted as a member of the Adamites. That was the name of the club, commemorating the founder of all mankind who lived the early part of his life in blissful nudity.

* * *

I had completely forgotten about this discussion till one night in his cottage in Auteuil something happened which rather forcefully reminded me about the existence of the Adamites.

We were both in bed, busily making love when suddenly three noblemen appeared from behind the heavy curtains. I screamed out loud and was terribly embarrassed by their ungallant behavior. But my lover reassured me, telling me that the three gentlemen were good friends of his and also members of the Adamites. They had watched our performance, which was part of the preliminary examinations, and I was glad to hear that I had passed this part with flying colors.

The gentlemen apologized for their seeming indiscretion and they retired into another room. When the Marquis and I had reached complete satisfaction, we went into the dining room for a little bite to eat. Can you imagine my surprise when I found those three gentlemen still there, as naked as the day they were born. The Marquis, too, wore nothing but his Adam's costume while I was as nude as the mother of all mankind.

I was slightly embarrassed to sit at dinner with four undressed gentlemen, but I had decided not to show my confusion. I tried to be a charming hostess, pretending that we were all fully dressed for a gala dinner.

When dessert had arrived one of our guests stood up and proclaimed that it was about time to bring a sacrifice to the gods of love just as we had sacrificed so copiously to the gods of food and drink.

We enthusiastically agreed and the table was

cleared, except for the flowers and the candles. The gentlemen lifted me up and laid me down upon the table. My body was to become the altar and I was at the same time goddess and sacrifice.

My lover got up to be the first one. He had filled his cup with wine and lifted it high, while he gave a long and beautiful speech. Meanwhile his friends caressed my thighs, my breasts, arms, legs and buttocks. My lover poured the wine over my body as a first sacrifice in the rite that followed.

This heady bath only served to increase my desire. I embraced the cavalier who was closest to me. He got up on the table, his strong arm whisked the flowers and candelabras away, and he began to satisfy me in a hearty and solid manner.

His powerful, swollen member which swiftly penetrated deep into my belly caused me to cry out loud with screams of deep passion. He pumped quickly and deeply; the moment he had satisfied himself, he pulled out and left me for the next partner who was ready to mount me.

My second lover made me enjoy the trip through loveland as much as the first one. He squirted his warm juices deep inside my belly, then gave way to number three, who plunged his powerful member into my overflowing love nest.

The Marquis wanted to honor the goddess of love also, but he was very drunk. He turned me on my stomach and he penetrated the lake of lust through the other passage, similar in manner to the way he had used his little page-boy. It was quite a different experience, and, though it is not accepted by many, I must admit to my surprise that this extremely virile way of love-making gave me a deep and lasting satisfaction. I can now understand that there are not only lesbians who can exclusively satisfy one another, but that their male counterparts are as numerous as willing women.

CHAPTER TWENTY-SIX

Before I finish these memoirs of my youth I want to write down one more memory which is very dear to me. It was a very exciting one, too.

Ever since I entered the Society of the Adamites I have remained true to its members and their principles. Aside from the pleasure of being able to associate with freethinking people who are remarkably without prejudices and other ridiculous notions, I found that the element of surprise was a powerful spice in the game of Eros, and it increased the satisfaction tenfold.

Our meetings take place in a small palace in the Rue Servandoni. It belongs to the Duke de B—, who is an excellent and charming leader of our select little group.

The place is well-hidden and the towers of the orthodox Saint-Sulpice church overshadow the charming little building. A large park with beautiful trees hides a small temple which is dedicated to the god Priapus. The decorations and the furniture of the large hall in which we celebrate our orgies are totally dedicated to the game of love in all its various forms.

Huge wall paintings depict the most famous orgies of the ancients and marble statues which are grouped in the park repeat those obscene scenes very clearly.

* * *

A few years after my initiation in the club we were told one evening that a group of noblemen from the province were to be our guests for the night. As usual the hall would be darkened and we would pair off with an anonymous partner.

Dinner was finished, the servants cleared the tables, we sat down upon our sofas and the lights were extinguished. We could not see our guests and they, in turn, could not see us.

Upon a sign from the President we all got up from our places, groping our way through the darkness in search for a partner.

I was slowly walking around, feeling the size of some of the available tools, and also checking their state of readiness when someone put an arm around my waist and a very soft hand began to caress my breast and nipple. I immediately lowered my hands to feel the thighs of my partner and grabbed his member which was very big and extremely stiff.

We fell down upon the pillows on the floor. I could feel the weight of my anonymous lover fall upon me and suddenly I cried out loudly because I tumbled into a deep abyss of delight when he sank his enormous tool deep in my belly.

I felt as if I had been drilled down to the floor and pinned forever upon the pillow like a little butterfly. The divine tool of my partner was trampling around in my insides and his expert hips were grinding away slowly. He was guided by a strong desire and soon we were both drawn into the delights of pure physical love.

But my moans were stifled by his hot lips which bore down upon my mouth. His tongue forced an entrance between my lips and explored the cavity of my mouth. The delight of that kiss stirred long-forgotten memories in my brain.

Meanwhile my partner is rutting deeply in my insides. I hear his voluptuous grunts and my passions reach a peak of incredible wildness. My hips rotate, my back arches and I push back with the same force that is driving him into me. I am beginning a long drawn out spasm, and the same happens to my partner. A deep groan answers my cry of joy when our floodgates open simultaneously and I feel myself flooded with a sweet, hot wave.

We remain motionless upon the pillows without loosening our hold on one another. A concerts of groans, moans, sighs and delighted screams, and the heady aroma of rutting floods the hall.

But what do I feel? The excitement of my lover starts all over again. His thing is growing to a tremendous size and begins to pulsate against my body. I take the divine thing in my hands where it grows to an even larger size. It is firm, thick and throbbing with a soft, heavy knob.

Filled with gratitude for so much desire and full of admiration for this big thing I decide to reward it with my special treatment. I turn around and search for it in the dark with eager lips.

Oh delight without comparison: it is sticking between my lips. I know that it loves this particular way of caressing because the darling thing begins to throb and the owner grabs my head, pushing it down.

I shove it with nimble fingers into my mouth. The thing loves it! My tongue touches its warm and very sweet moisture. I am kissing it, my fingers are tickling and caressing it, and slowly I shove it deeper and deeper into my mouth till it sticks in my throat.

The divine thing is very satisfied with this treatment. And it makes that very clear because it begins to move up and down, throbbing heartily. Suddenly it begins to twitch and floods my mouth with a rich, sweet stream which I thirstily swallow.

Now I let go of the limp tool, petting and caressing it while nimble fingers search in the curls of my fleece for my love bud. And the anonymous lover returns the favor by burying his head between my thighs and I soon groan under the kisses of his hot lips and the pushing of his insistent tongue.

Ooh, delightful moments! You are my only reason for living. I shall always remain true to the exercise of passion and the satisfaction of my voluptuous desires. I have devoted my entire life to the delights of pure sex!

I close my eyes and the many scenes of my youth race through my mind. From the very first tender kisses, to my deflowering, my first lesbian experiences, my first conquest in Paris, the Cardinal and . . .

Suddenly the torches are lit and the dark room is now well-lighted. I cry out in happiness.

The anonymous lover lies still in my embrace, our bodies are close together, our lips are still touching. I look at him and I recognize Francois, my dear Francois, the teacher who initiated me into the delights of love . . .

* * *

One evening my aunt suddenly left me. She

died without having shown any sign of illness. It caused me great suffering and still, after these many years, I feel the deep loss. I will always remember my dear aunt with great devotion since I owe her the happiest childhood and youth anybody could wish for.

And now even youth is about to leave me, though only on the surface, because though the years may pass by, true youth is a state of the soul, full of gifts and exquisite privileges to those who have devoted their lives to love and who remain true to the voluptuous ideals of Eros and the immortal goddess, Venus.

Venus
Unmasked

CONTENTS

PROLOGUE

LETTER FROM SIR CLIFFORD NORTON
TO HIS FRIEND MISS CLARA BIRCHEM...

"My dear Clara:

'N incident in my boyish life to-night passes before me in all the tinting of a panoramic view; and as my thoughts run back over the checkered pathway of forty years, which has sprinkled my hair with gray, filled my life with thorns and orange blossoms, to a month that has left its imprint on my whole life, I wish that I possessed the power to reproduce the picture in all its colours, and do justice to the work which, at your request, I undertake to-night. I regret that the favour you ask is one which compels me to write of myself; and in the perusal of this, I trust your eye will rest on the unpleasant character I am, as little as possible.

"I was born 'neath a warm sun and pleasant skies; where the air was freighted with the blended odour of the magnolia and jessamine that heightened the senses; where everything had its bud and blossom almost at its birth; where the dreamy languor of the voluptuary seemed inherent in all; where even in those who here in the North would be termed children, the sexual spark only waited for contact to flame up in its power; where girls were mothers at thirteen and grandmas at thirty.

"My introduction to the pleasures and mysteries that have ever been associated with the couch of Love was not entrusted to a novice; no timid, simpering girl, taking her first steps toward the realisation of the anticipation of forbidden pleasures, but to a woman — a woman of thirty, who being an apt pupil under the skilful manipulations and teachings of a husband for a term of years, had herself become a preceptress in all those delicate points that surround an amour with such delights and rosy tints.

"How plainly do I see her to-night! How much keener is my appreciation of the wonderful piece of anatomy, that time only still deeper imprints upon my memory; the standard by which from that time all female perfections have been gauged. Ah! she is before me again, and this time unveiled. Look at her! Is she not beautiful? Note the poise of her head, from which her glinted golden hair falls in such a wealth. See those amber eyes; those wonderfully chiselled lips, so red, pulpy and moist; her fair cheeks tinted by their reflection.

"See those shoulders—how perfectly and exquisitely moulded—rounded with the same finish as her beautiful, swelling globes, so daintily pinked and tipped. What belly, back and hips ever had the graceful curves of thine? And you! Rounded arms, white swelling thighs and full dimpled knees (in your warm, fond pressures of years ago I feel you again to-night) was the mould broken with your completion? Gone? Yes! Only in memory now.

"My initiatrix snatched me from my little heaven with its delightful anticipations, and chaperoned me through the hot-house of passion, where every beautiful flower was filled with a subtle poison which racked the nerves, sapped the life and deadened the brain; and on that sweet, sighing summer day in my twelfth year, when Cupid threw apart the silken drapery, revealing beauties of which I had not even dreamed, to books I said farewell, and ambition was dead. That was a day of fate.

.. ..

"In a dense shade, where the sun could not penetrate, we sat down on a log; and after she had taken off my hat and run her dainty white hands through my hair, she placed my head in her lap, and, pulling me close to her panting bosom, she placed her pretty lips on mine and held them there, with her eyes shut, until sometimes I stifled and almost lost my breath; then she would take her lips away while her eyes sparkled, and her cheeks reddened clear to her hair.

"There was something about it all that I liked, for I would ask her to do it again; and she, exclaiming: "Bless my little man," would press me to her again, and kiss me until my lips and face were all wet from her lips. Each attack and each pressure seemed to create for me some new and delightful sensation I had not known before, and then, where my little pantaloons buttoned in front, I had a pain and a great hard lump that hurt me, and in my innocence I told her about.

"Let me see" she said kindly; and one of her hands, that had so many pretty rings on her fingers stole, down and unbuttoned my pants; and then, what I had never seen more than two inches long, and soft as a baby's flesh, was standing out full five inches and terribly swollen. I was awfully frightened at the sight and the pain, but she took my young prick in her hand, kissed it four or five times and bit it gently, telling me "it was no matter," and I seemed to get better right away.

"But I was perfectly passive in the hands of my fair seducer, and I suffered my pantaloons to be taken down, and myself to be thrown backwards on the grass. Her snowy hand eagerly flew up and down the dainty shaft of my cock, keeping the glowing head uncovered, and all the thread of the froenum well stretched. She stooped, and her tongue caressed the tip of my penis, while her other hand was making that magic tickling (called by the French the spider's legs) on my balls, and up and down the urethra.

"Suddenly my thighs stiffened out. I trembled violently and felt a strange sickening sensation. I believed that I was about to faint, as the white spunk, flashing out from my bursting knob and bedewing her cheeks and tongue with liquid pearl, fell in a tiny splash on my belly, whilst her swimming eyes were fixed on my spending prick, as it shot the jet forth.

"Then she carelessly unfastened her chemise, and I saw what I had never seen before in that way—two beautiful bosoms at once. How pretty they looked, so white and so round. She rubbed them, panting and heaving, over my face and lips, and then whispered to me to " bite them," and as my lips fastened over the little hard tips, her breath almost burned my face, and I felt a new joy and realised that I was swelling again.

"Then I felt one of her warm hands steal down and take my pego, while with the other she took my hand, rubbed it up and down on the big part of her soft legs, and then to the softest, prettiest thing I had ever felt in my young life, where she left it. Oh, what a plaything I had found, so soft, curly and juicy; and as my hand found a delicate opening, she jumped as though I had hurt her. Then I felt her open her legs wide apart, after which she whispered to me to get in there and lie on top of her, which I did.

"As she pulled my little shirt up, I felt my bare belly fitting close to hers, and that her chemise was clear up to her arms. Oh! How she hugged and kissed me, and how nice her plump bare arms felt to my face and neck. I thought that she would break me in two. Whispering to me to do just as she told me, she reached down and took the little fellow that was killing me with pain, and placed it where I had my finger when I thought I had hurt her. "Now you make it go in," she whispered, and she raised her body with my weight on her, and when she settled back my prick *was* in.

"She gave a great sigh, as I had heard people do who were in trouble. Then she squeezed me and bit me, and seemed to be trying to rock me in a new kind of cradle; and taking me by the hips, she would push me off and pull me back, never letting that little fellow get out of the nest, where she had placed him; and while I felt a tingling sensation in my fingers and toes, and up and down my back, she would roll her head from side to side, saying, "Oh, oh, oh!"

"My initiatrix suddenly locked her legs over my back; then, bending her back, she panted and held me so for a second, trying

— 15 —

to reach my lips, but I was too short. Then I lost my senses and everything got green, and I felt that I was bleeding in and all over that pretty little plaything on which I had been lying for ten minutes. Her arms and legs unloosened, and I rolled off from her, shaking like a leaf; but she kissed me, and whispered that I would feel better in a few minutes, and I did.

"Then she took me in her arms, telling me that I *must never tell*; and asking me if it wasn't awful nice, she kissed me again a few times, made me kiss her, and with my head on her pretty bosom, we fell in the most intoxicating rapture. "Wasn't it awful nice?" Well, I should say it was; the little heaven I had created had all been knocked by the one she had created for me. I smile when I think of my innocence—smile when I reflect what a public benefactor I was at that tender age.

"Imagine—Friend Clara—how exciting it is for a woman of thirty, well-formed and knowing all things, how exciting it is, I say, for such a one to clasp to her full-formed and matured bosom, the slender frame of some sweet child of about twelve; to press the thick golden forest of her curls, and full lips of her cunt, against the hairless shaft and balls of a lovely boy; to watch his first delight, to see the child stiffen himself out and grind his pearly teeth in the ecstasy of a first spend, while she herself is lost in lustful delight at feeling her companion's little hand wet through with the flowing spunk that follows his motions to and fro in her full-developed quim, drenching the thick curls through. It is this pleasure which made my beautiful seducer teach me this exquisite bliss.

.. ..

"Yes, that was a day of fate. In the afternoon, we strolled out into the woods. She was silent for a while, then turning to me she said: "My little man, for you are a man, what we did is what those do who get married. My husband is sick, and for months I have been almost dying for the pleasure your little body has given me so tenderly," and drawing me to her, she kissed me rapidly. I felt very proud of myself after what she said, and immediately asked her if I might do it again; with a smile, she kissed me and said she "would see about it."

"I had a strange desire, for one of my age, to see more, and I said: "Mrs. B—, you have such pretty legs, would you let me see them higher up?" She said: "Why, certainly my little man, I will do anything for you," and reaching down, she gathered her dress, skirts and ruffles, and held them clear up over her face. Gods! What a picture; the tight-fitting stockings, the blue garters above her knees, and the white, bare thighs. Then the skirts went down again, but the picture was left in my mind.

"She who had so delicately taken my virginity knew the power her beautiful legs had brought upon me, and on the way back she revealed them at every opportunity; and when I asked her if I might put my hand on the little beauty-spot, she said: "Yes, but be quick," and I was; but I did, and she liked it as well as I; and the reaching down, and putting my hand up, under her rattling skirts, to the mossy charm, created the same intense thrill that characterised the same attempt in my later years.

"Again I peeped under her little shirt, and saw the white bare thighs that had held me so tightly. How beautiful and fascinating she was as she stooped to unlace her shoes, and drawing the stockings from her bewitching legs, as she stood up again. "I like you," I said to her in a low tone ,and she replied: "You little rascal, have you been all this time watching me?" I inclined my head, and whispered that I thought she was so nice and pretty. "Bless your heart," she ejaculated, "do you think so?" I answered: "Yes," and asked if she wouldn't please take *all* off.

"Looking at me a second, she shrugged her lovely shoulders, and the chemise slipped down to her feet; then I saw her all at once from her full neck to her toes—saw what I had longed to see—that little beauty with golden hair which had almost killed me with joy. "Now are you satisfied?" she asked, and she bent over me, while her bosoms rested on my face; and as I put my hands on them as though to keep them, she put on her chemise—then took it off again—and was less than a minute in getting by my side.

"My initiatrix was a magnificent woman of thirty; her bosoms were of immense size, her eyes beamed with lust and expectation, her thighs and bottom were well shaped, and the thick golden fleece of her quim reached nearly till her navel. She threw herself backwards on the grass, and suddenly opened her legs wide, driving two of her fingers deep into her large and thick-lipped coral slit; then lifting up and bending one leg, she forced one finger (having wetted it in her cunt) right up the corrugated brown hole of her bottom, in which it was sheathed.

"Then she moved her fingers backwards and forwards in and out of both apertures. Soon she lost all control of herself and, grinding her teeth, she quivered with lust from head to foot; she moved faster and faster, and soon the most obscene words came from her lips: "Oh God! oh Fuck! oh Fuck!" she cried, and then with a moan of delight, she arched her body and fell back spending, with eyes, large, dark and bright, fixed on the foliage above. "Oh God!" she exclaimed, as she took out her fingers, and the spunk flowed in torrents down her thighs.

"Oh God! what bliss!" I knew now what she wanted; what I wanted; the ice had been broken. I was an apt pupil, and the secret fire of my youth had burst forth in all its fury. I bit her arms, her belly, her legs; bit and sucked her rosy nipples; kissed her from head to foot; tickled her little beauty with golden curls; got on to and off from her; put my head between her hot thighs, which pressed it until I thought it would split; sported from knees to lips in a wild delirium of newfound ecstasy, her breath burning my cheeks as I rested for a moment with my head on her beating bubbies.

"Then, holding me tightly, my fair enticer put a sudden stop to my gambols, and sliding her hand down to her little friend, who had attained his majority—and was no slouch for twelve years, I assure you—she put me on my back, and bending over me she nibbled him gently with her red, damp lips; and then, falling on her back, she lifted me, as though with iron force, above her.

"Opening her quivering thighs, my lascivious preceptress let me down gently, saying: "All ready," and taking in her hand the pet who was eager for his duty, she gently parted the golden hairs, and having fitted him, locked her arms around my body; then she kissed me, and, raising her buttocks from the grass, pressed gently up; my bare belly fitting close to hers, I pressed down, and she fell back with a smile and glowing cheeks.

"The motion she had produced before in her way, when she had taken my *pucelage,*

I now felt that I could perform it without
assistance, and as I did so she tried to kiss
me, and whispered: "That's right," her voice
fluttering so that I thought she was chok-
ing. I had found the secret of her pleasure,
and hers was mine; and as I alternately
tickled her, briskly, then gently, I remember
a suppressed, fluttering moan, which I now
know was the acme of bliss. But I grew
tired and fell where I lay; and yet linked
together the bliss went on in a delicious
throbbing, that cannot be told.

Soon my ruttish partner gasped: "More!
more!" and I, loving her so strongly that I
would do anything for fer, began again the
gentle movement. She whispered to me, but
I was getting deaf and blind with erotic rapture; and then I whispered to her that it
was coming. She straightened her snowy
legs, drew them together, threw her belly up
against mine, loosened her arms, quivered
from head to foot, gasped: "Now them!" and
as a thick mist gathered in my eyes, I felt
the hot stream go from me to her, and all
was over.

"Oh, you sweet boy," said my handsome
debaucher, as she pulled me up to her lips,
kissing me and biting my neck, "you dont

know how happy you have made me—how you have satisfied my restless, burning fever." As happy as a lark, I ran my hand all over her beauties here and there, petted the little flaxen-haired darling, crawled up to her bubbies and nibbled them awhile, and then, with her kiss upon my lips, I fell asleep. while she was smoothing my hair, and the sun, shining through the grove, was lighting her beautiful, velvety skin with a rosy tint.

"After dinner, we went down to the boat for a ride. She talked to me while I rowed and kept my eyes on hers, and observing that once in a while my eyes glanced towards her little feet, she seemed to know by intuition what was in my thoughts, and up went all that hid what I longed to see. The sight sent the blood to my white face, and, as she put down her skirts, she looked at me and, smiling, said: "My little sweetheart, if you will row to some nice, quiet little spot, where no one goes, and we can be alone, you can lie between the legs you think so pretty and like so much." I pulled up to the point, and we came to a nice little grass plot, on which we sat down, after she had spread out a light shawl.

"Oh! little one, ain't this nice?" she said to me, "what a nice time we will have alone in the lovely shade"; and putting her arm around me she fell back on the shawl, taking me with her. We were both on our backs, looking up among the green leaves. Soon she drew me closer to her, and asked me what I wanted, and as I placed one of my hands on the bosom of her dress, she began to unhook it at the neck one by one, until all were undone, and I saw them peeping out over her chemise, so white and round; then she unclasped her corset.

"By this time, I was on my knees, and unbuttoning her chemise, I turned the corners back and took the pretty things, all undressed, in my hands. Then I bent over them and kissed them, bit them gently, then sucked them, and it seemed to me then, that I would have given my life to have one of them all in my mouth. I was feeling good all over as she pulled me down to her, and kissed me in such a new way that she seemed to cover my whole mouth with her lips and suck it all in between them.

"I felt her hot tongue in my mouth and almost down my throat, while her breath came hot and her bubbies rose and fell. I turned and saw her skirts above her knees, and as with one hand I reached down to pull them up higher, so as to feast my eyes, I felt her hand working into my pants and tickling the little eggs that I thought would burst with pain. I had just got my hand on the little bird's-nest, that was such an infatuation to me, when she said: "Jump up quick and take off your pants."

"As I arose to do her bidding, and unbuttoned my pants from my jacket, what a delightful view I had of her many charms; and those bare thighs! how intensely inviting do I remember them. My pants off, I walked to her and stood over her, the little soldier standing hard and proud. She put out one of her hands and took hold of it, and then raised herself until her lips could touch it. Oh! how she squeezed and bit it, all the time muttering some little words of affection.

"Then, springing from me, my fair initiatrix leant over a log, and I sat on my knees, between her legs widely straddled apart. Thus, just over my face, I had a view of a magnificent bottom, with its corrugated brown hole, surrounded by little ringlets of hair, red shot with gold, and pressed out between her thighs, the thick velvety lips of her enormously developed cunt. I, conveniently placed, pressed my face against the red flesh of her luscious quim, and darted in my tongue.

"Her outrageously lustful passions soon showed themselves; convulsive tremors shook her frame; her crimson cunt opened and shut on my tongue. She supplemented my efforts by frigging herself on the ruby-button in front. Soon the Crisis approached; I heard her murmuring: "Prick—Cunt—Fuck —Spunk," till at last, with a spasmodic contraction of the cheeks of her bottom, a flood of spunk, creamy and thick, shot out, like a man's, over my face and bosom, and ran down her own thighs.

"I kept my head down between her white legs, and kissed little goldy until she rolled and moaned, and said she could stand it no longer. "Do it now! do it now!" she said, and as she threw her thighs apart, I crawled between them, and rested my weight on her belly. Then I felt her warm fingers arranging things; and she had placed her pet as she wanted him, I felt him among the parted curls that were all wet, gliding so smoothly until the whole shaft was all in, and our bodies were fitted close together.

"Oh! what delight!" she seemed to be doing the same thing with her mossy lips that she had with the others, when she kissed me a few moments before; and I felt that she would draw me to her very heart, body and all, as she lay there, murmuring: "Oh, you sweet boy! now, you do it to me nice," as I drew back gently my rampant prick, and then plunged it back quickly.

"I felt her body writhing under me with some new motion of her buttocks, that I had not felt before, which was highly electrifying to us both; but how wet and smooth she was there. Soon she began to draw her legs up, and then straighten them out again, her hands squeezing her bubbies, while, with her eyes shut, she rolled her head from side to side, a gentle moan escaping her half-open lips.

"Now! Now! Quick! Quick!" she said, as she opened her eyes and started suddenly. I felt that I was dying with delight, but I immediately began knocking more vigorously at her little gateway, and as she locked her legs over my back, holding them so tight that I could not move, I felt a tingling, twitching sensation of delight, and in a second her velvet-lined lips were sipping the hot stream of my youthful passion. Her arms fell lifeless at her sides; her legs dropped from my back, and the smile on her beautiful face spoke more than words.

.. ..

"Ah! how that woman, on that day of fate, had crept into my life. I was hers, body and soul; she was my sunshine, my life; no thought that was not of her, no act but that tending to gain her smiles. I could look in her face and eyes for hours and never weary of it. Little did I know then what the heart was; what it could suffer; what it could stand; and yet how short was the time until mine was put to the test. The days came and went, but there was no abating in my desire to see her charms; to know the delightful intoxications that I found in her arms.

"My mistress did not always humour me in my desires, however, knowing that for her pleasure I must have time to recruit to be equal to her passion, but she was always kind and gentle, and outside of the *act*, never denying me a wish in the looking at or feeling what I chose. Yes, the mould was broken after those hips and legs so well shaped. How often, while standing, has she allowed me to stoop down and get under her skirts, and with my arms around her hips, let me bury my face high up between her swelling thighs, until I almost suffocated.

"Then she would lie and lift her legs in the air, bending her knees; my hand was passed between her legs, so that my finger touched her ruby-button enshrined in golden floss; my other hand was passed under her thighs and my finger embedded in the gap which, like a scarlet slash, opened between the golden curls. Swift motions followed, and soon the Crisis came. I saw the pearly drops of Love oozing out, as her frame trembled with lust. It was over; she lay with her head thrown back, her lovely thighs apart, and from between the swollen lips of her vermilion slit, streamed the sweet drops of creamy spending.

"I loved this hot-blooded voluptuous woman who gave herself up to me entirely, and humoured every sexual caprice, and knew every whim and fancy. Her kisses were of fire; her lithe limbs twined round me; her lips wandered over every part of my body; her fingers, with their magic touches on my cock, my balls, my bottom, drove me mad with lust; her cunt, warm, wet, thickhaired, and spending, drew the very life blood from my heart; and as I often died away between her soft thighs, her skilful touches never fail to rouse me again to action.

"What woman could equal my lecherous seducer, who could mount on the top and, engulfing my prick in her quim, exercise that power of internally clipping grasping and squeezing my rod by inward pressure, in the convulsive throbs of supreme lust, called the "Nippers"; not forgetting to vibrate her pretty, rounded bottom, and so draw forth the fountain into her womb? or who, lying upon me, could rub her sweet, fair-haired slit on my mouth, and by hands and lips revive my drooping shaft, till it shot its treasures over her agile tongue? In fact, on my back, with her lustful cunt on my face, her tongue and lips, responsive to mine, could draw forth that liquid bliss, that the *other* lips have failed to elicit.

"In the midst of the luxurious course we were running, she could softly babble such bawdy words as might excite me more; and as she murmured: "Fuck! fuck! cunt! spunk! frig me! fuck me!" urged me to the sweet end. Lastly, when my pego longed for "fresh fields and pastures new," she could even present her bottom, with its soft curves, to me, and, parting its cheeks with her jewelled fingers, show me the rosy and crinkled aperture of Sodom, in which tight sheath I could shoot my sperm, into her inmost recesses.

"Owing to her large and swelling breasts, my fair one could even practise the "bosom-fucking". She lay on her back, and as I placed my stiff and glowing prick between her bubbing bubbies, she pressed them together on each side, so as to embed completely my penis in the warm and snowy crease. Now I moved to and fro, and up and down, the purple head appearing and disappearing before her enraptured eyes, till the sweet Crisis, when the jet of spunk shot out, and the slippery stream deluged her breasts. Her feelings were then so roussed, that a few insertions of my finger or ticklings of my tongue in her burning vagina brought down her magic flow of bliss as well.

"In short, as a woman to please, my lascivious mistress was most complaisant, and *stuck at nothing*. She even allowed me with delight to penetrate her quim, at those periodic times when "the red flag was flying" and when all men know women want it twice as much, and love the man who lets nothing stand in his way, and is wise enough to know his darling is better than ever then.

.. ..

"One day, my fair debaucher wished to go to the city and return in the evening. On her promise to take good care of me, I was allowed to accompany her. On arriving we went to an hotel, and were placed in a lovely room. After closing the lower shutters, she began taking off her clothes, while my eyes were wide with wonder; one thing and then another were taken off, until finally she stood with nothing on but her stockings and chemise. She seemed to hesitate a second, and then taking those off, she threw herself on the bed with her hands over her head.

"How sweet she was, and as I stood looking at her, she said: "Come, my little man, ain't you going to take yours off, and come and lie with me?" I was going to be in heaven again, and I had mine off in half the time she had taken, and was as naked as she, when I stepped up and stood beside her. At last, I had a chance to fuck my darling in a cosy hotel, as a smart dandy does. But I failed, at first, to perform my duty on that particular occasion.

"Yes, I got into bed with her, and I failed utterly, partly, no doubt, from over-anxiety, partly nervousness. Dr. Johnson said that "a woman ought to take off her modesty with her petticoat." My lewd mistress found that such was the case. She pretended to take no notice of it, but by sly touches, many caresses, and exhibition of her lovely naked body in many attitudes, endeavoured to make the best of what was but a momentary feeling, caused by a too eager desire to please her, and a nervous anxiety for the last sweet favours she was ready to grant completely.

"Taking her playmate in her hand, so soft and white, she tickled him awhile and saw him grow, and after nibbling me a little on my belly, she threw her arms around me and tossed me over on the bed, and, straightening me out full length, she drew me close to her hot skin and covered me with kisses. As soon as she loosened her embrace, I had my mouth on one of the nipples of her snowy breast (and as I remember now, that act struck every electrical wire in my body—it does yet).

"My hand was over the little "poulter" nestling in the soft of her thighs, and as my finger found its way in slowly, she rather liked the two sensations. Her cheeks growing redder each moment, she grasped the fellow who, at his full size, was throbbing at her side, then, jumping up quickly, she took the pillows, and throwing them together on the bed, told me how to lie on them. When she had me bent over them to her idea, that, which she was longing to feel wedged in her mossy lips, was standing up hard and proud.

"Then the method was for the fair one to lie on her side, on the bad, as I lay half facing her, and half on my back. Then lifting up her upper leg and laying my face on the lower thigh, Il could see the lovely golden-haired cleft, and press in it my lips and tongue, and as her upper thigh remained raised, I could, whilst gamahuching her, see the lovely curls and ringlets that ran back and fringed her arsehole. This left my hand at liberty to frig fiercely her bursting clitoris, which excited her madly, as it does every woman. As she was tickling my balls with her soft hand, her Crisis soon arrived, and her warm thigh fell on my face. I saw her arsehole throb and her cunt spend enormously, as it shot out in jets, and completely drenched my arm. It was the glorious spending, swimming quim of the full-blown and lascivious woman of free passions.

"As soon as she was recovered, she got over me in the right position. I felt her place my fleshly weapon between the hot velvety lips, and after a gentle motion on her part, it was all in, where she seemed so delighted to have it. "There, now! ain't that nice!" she asked, with a look of mingled joy and pride, and then she began to slide up and down on it (in a peculiar way that I have not known since), her bosoms jumping with every move that seemed to send fire through my veins to my brain.

"I could feel that she was making me awful wet where we were linked, but the sensation was hot and delightful; and as she kept at work, I saw her grasp her bosoms, as though she would crush them. Her motion became more rapid, her lips swelled, she shut her eyes and threw back her head. She flung out her arms and drew them back again, and as she trembled all over, my delight reached its height; and as my love messenger took wings and flew, she fell forward on me with all her weight, almost crushing my bones.

"She lay panting and gasping for a moment, and as she jumped to the floor, I saw that he who had given her so much comfort, also my belly, bore delicate crimson stains. She saw it, and blushing deeply, said it was no matter, and sponging me off, I put on my shirt, and lay with my face to the wall, as she had asked me to do. Soon she came with her chemise on, and taking me in her arms, we went to sleep, my face resting on her white bosom.

"After awaking and imprinting a lustful kiss on the crest of my juvenile cock, my salacious mistress, exciting herself with her middle finger for a short time, threw herself over me, so that she knelt astride of my face. Then lowering herself a little, and throwing herself forward, she presented to my enraptured view her magnificent buttocks, and her corrugated pink bottom-hole surrounded by tiny curls; and beneath, the splendid coral gash of her lovely cunt, with its inner lips spread open, gaping with expectant lust,, and the glorious golden bush of hair covering her mount Venus and running up, as I before described, to her navel.

"My ruttish initiatrix then pressed her luscious quim upon my eager mouth, and my tongue revelled in the moist and lovely scented gap, and travelled round the prominent button, taking it into my lips and sucking the crimson knob of her clitoris, which was of immense size, from so many scenes of love and lust. Nor was she idle; as she took the whole of the head of my prick into her mouth. There, we laid belly to belly, devouring, kissing, licking each other's sexual treasures; each with a busy finger tickling the arsehole I with one hand moulding her breasts from below, she my balls.

"We indulged in the most intoxicating lasciviousness, but this could not last long. Our bodies writhed, her rampant cunt seemed to expand and take in half my face; my bursting penis seemed all within her mouth. With a smothered cry we both spent, and the white sperm bubbled out of the corners of her lips in pulsating throbs, while her thick and slimy spendings deluged my face. We both swallowed all up, and fell apart, gasping with fierce delight. But like Messalina, my lewd mistress was "*lassata sed non satiata*", wearied but still not satisfied. After a last kissing, we arose and dressed, and at nine were at the cottage.

.. ..

"The last rapture, that I ever knew lying between her voluptuous swelling thighs, was on that day she took me with her to the city; and that night my young, boyish heart felt its first aches and trouble. Two days after, she kissed me sweetly at the gate, saying that she would never forget me (it has been mutual). She let me get in her snowy arms, she allowed me freedom with her bosom, but with any attempt to put my hand under her chemise, she took it away, saying: "No; no more." My fevered brain sketched and re-sketched the beautiful life figures, which she had unveiled to my eager eyes; and the spark she had discovered and fanned was burning me alive.

"After long weeks, I was victorious and, when strong enough, returned to school. But ah! in those days, my prurient seducer injected into my veins the sweet poison which has remained for years; and I sacrificed health and ambition. Trusting that in the perusal of this, you will be—Dear

Clara—rewarded with all the pleasurable emotions that you anticipated,—that I have written nothing to burst the front buttons from the trousers of your young gentlemen (1), or bring the dear girls to the use of a long-necked *cologne* bottle to quench the flame in their electric generators,—my task is finished.

---

(1) *Miss Clara Birchem was the handsome and voluptuous governess of a school, at the time she is here introduced.*

CHAPTER I

HARRY

A FINE looking fresh coloured youth named Harry Staunton, the son of a London merchant, sent down to the village of Allsport for the benefit of his health, was passing down a lane skirting the town, when his eye was caught by a young and handsome girl whose fully developed legs were beginning to make the short skirts she wore dangerously exciting to the gentlemen who visited at the house of her mamma, who were obliged to curb their desires and satisfy the excitement of their pricks by closely pressing her to them when they could get her into their arms for a romp.

It must be admitted that the warmth of the young lady's temperament urged her to afford them this opportunity as frequently as possible although she could not account for the pleasure it caused both her and them. They would tickle her round the hips and under the arms and pinch her bottom and occasionally press her lovely bubbies.

Miss Wynne was in the act of fastening her garter when Harry turning a corner of the lane came suddenly upon her. As this was not the first occasion of their meeting, Julia nearly put down her clothes and waited for his approach. He came up and took her by the hand and she with a flushed face expressed her pleasure to meeet him again.

The night before they had been playing forfeits with some companions and as the game went on, it so happened that she was kissed by Harry who without knowing why slipped his tongue in her mouth and kept it there till his young prick throbbed against her so violently that she felt it against her belly through her clothing.

All the evening afterwards they sought every occasion te be together. On one occa sion several fell down on each other and Harry and Julia being underneath, there was sufficient time for him to get his hand under her clothes, insinuate it within her drawers and then to feel her soft warm thigh and afterwards her cunt which was just covered with a soft down.

Julia did nothing that night but dream of feeling Harry's tongue sucking her own as he was kissing her and reproducing the same sensations, she had felt when his finger penetrated just inside the lips of her cunt.

Before morning she had renewed the feeling by the agency of her own finger and only ceased to frig herself, when an emission came to her relief. It was no wonder therefore that she was glad to meet her lover.

Harry placed his arm round her waist and pressing her towards him kissed her and slipped his tongue into her mouth. She met it with her own and as they curled amorously around each other, he not only made her feel his standing prick pressing against her as on the previous evening, but taking her willing hand made her squeeze it.

—"Oh, Harry, what is that," the pretty

little creature murmured pressing her finger tightly around it of her own accord.

—"Put your hand dear inside my trousers and feel," he answered pushing against her as if to make it penetrate her even through her clothes, while she pressed against him with equal force.

Unbuttoning his trousers, she thrust her dainty little hand inside and felt his prick which was so hot as almost to burn her hand.

—"Feel it dear naked, while I feel you," he cried again, and stooping until he got his hand under her clothes, he passed it upwards between her thighs, and seized her cunt preparatory to putting his finger in it.

Prompted by her sensations, the young lady had that morning left off her drawers and Harry on finding the glowing and palpitating flesh all naked to his touch, took his arm from her waist and raising her petti-coats up around her, groped her hips and bottom with one hand while he frigged her gently with the other.

She, lifting up his shirt, had taken his cock in her hand and taught by nature alone, while chafing it, began to place it near the place where his fingers were placed. They were just on the verge of actually fucking when to their chagrin they were disturbed.

Coming towards them from the other end of the lane was Miss Birchem, the handsome and voluptuous governess of a school for young gentlemen. She had espied the amorous occupation of Harry and Julia and had seen the excited youth take up the young lady's clothes, while her white bottom had thus been exposed to her.

The governess had also seen that, which caused still more emotion in her own quim, the prick of the handsome boy fondled by the hand of the girl. The sight had maddened her and for a moment she had been compelled to lean against a tree, which prevented her from being seen by them.

While her legs trembled under her, Miss Birchem had raised her own clothes above her cunt, parting the hairy lips of which she had thrust her finger in it up to the first joint and commenced to frig with rapidity her sensitive clitoris.

This she continued to do, her breasts heaving and her whole body oscillating under the influence of the sensations she was experiencing, until she saw Harry and Julia in that close contact that had the appearance of actual fucking.

This brought her feelings to such a height that with a gasp and a quickened movement of her agile waist the governess spent to such an extent, that she almost shrieked as her spunk issued from her.

At this moment Harry had just placed his prick inside Julia's quim who was lying prostrate and the girl had lost her maidenhead, had not the young man restrained himself.

But just as he had partially penetrated her quivering body and she was kissing him passionately, the Crisis came upon him and he shot forth his spendings on her clitoris, giving her however even thus pleasure to a greater extent than was attainable by her own finger.

This caused Julia to embrace him still more closely, curling her leg around him so as to get him further into her in her desire for a continuance of the pleasure she had hardly tasted.

Miss Birchem however came upon them and thus interruped their amorous sports. This lewd governess had a mad passion for flagellation, preferring first to have her own buttocks well birched by a gentleman while he was frigging her with his finger to assist her in spending.

She next liked to flog the buttocks of a gentleman, watching its effect on his prick, especia ly if he was at the same time fucking a girl, increasing his excitement from time to time and tickling and momentarily sucking his testicles till she at last caused him to spend with a shower of rapture, during which Crisis she would flog him unmercifully.

Seeing the charming bum of Julia when Harry raised her clothes, filled her with a burning desire to whip her while Harry's prick was buried in her own cunt, as copious spending had not quelled the lust with which she burned.

Julia drew down her clothes and Harry tried to hide his prick as the governess confronted them. But she seized them both at once, young Harry by his prick causing its head to erect itself as much as ever at the contact of her pulpy hand, and Julia by her half covered thigh, saying:

—"Oh you wicked children, what are you about together! What has he been doing to you Miss, with this naked cook of his? Do you know it is very wrong of you to let the boys put their things into your cunt until it is covered with hair like mine? See here."

And giving a furtive squeeze to Julia's quim to ascertain if it had been spent into, the governess glancing lewdly at the young man, pulled up her own clothes, displaying to the fascinated eyes of Harry, limbs of surpassing beauty, covered with attractive silk-stockings.

Miss Birchem had thighs actually smooth and white as ivory and belly of ravishing sweetness, below which was a tuft of dark hair which was moist from her recent emission, while in the midst of it could be seen the pink lips of a full but closely shut cunt.

—"There Miss," she said, enjoying the admiration with which Harry viewed her beautiful quim, "you must wait till you have hair like this on it, before you can enjoy the insertion of a prick as I do."

—"It does give me pleasure now," said Julia fixing her eye upon the swollen prick of her lover, rather than upon the handsome nude limbs of the lascivious governess.

—"But it ought not to, and I shall give you a good whipping for your wickedness," said the lewd and sensual woman, her whole form glowing with excitement as she gloated on the lovely bottom of Julia, which she had wholly uncovered.

Miss Birchem then left her victims and gathered a huge handful of birch which was growing all around them, and Julia blushed as she saw her tying it together with some ribbons that she took from her pocket, the bottom of the prurient maid tingling with the mere anticipation of what she was going to receive, a sensation not altogether unpleasant but novel.

The salacious governess now armed with this verdant rod took Julia by the hand, saying: "How I must whip you to correct your naughty feelings, but as you have excited me by allowing me to see you take this young gentleman's prick in your cunny, I must insist on his putting it into mine."

—"When I was your age," continued the libidinous woman, "a gentleman put his cock into me, but he hurt me so dreadfully by fucking me, that I have never been able to allow any one else to do so, nor could I marry for this reason, therefore I am compelled to take lads to fuck me and Master Harry here must do it now."

—"Come to the bank," resumed the ruttish governess, "and sit down so that you can take me on your lap and put it up from under me, while I am taking Julia across my knees to give her a warning, that she must not be fucked again until she is more of a woman. There is no one near or to disturb us while we are doing it."

The lecherous woman now made Harry sit down upon the grassy bank. His prick was erect and hard and throbbed violently with desire to be in the beautiful fornicatress, as she raised her clothes behind her, displaying once more her glorious legs and thighs, with the most superb pair of large buttocks that was possible for a lady to expose.

The lustful Miss Birchem then seated herself with her legs well divided according to the bawdy manner, upon the lad who in his eagerness to thrust his hot burning prick into her dark cunt, seized her around the waist, creating a jealous feeling in the mind of Julia to see how readily he was prepared to fuck another cunt than her own.

The concupiscent governess once more seized the young man's prick and sitting down upon it, guided the moist head—not into her cunt as he expected—but up her bottomhole which Harry found quite elastic enough to receive his tool.

Excited as he was, the youth began to fuck her there violently, as though he was buried in her quim, while the indecent woman taking up Julia's dress all around her, thus unchastely exposed the cunt of the lovely girl as well as her bottom.

The voluptuous governess now made on the spot the virgin lie across her tighs, keeping her between them and holding her victim in this position by passing her right leg over, shuddering with lust as the naked flesh came in contact with her own.

The shameless woman then gently separated the buttocks of the tamed girl and examined with looks of fire the lovely little pink hole which looked like a pouting rosebud. In the clutches of such a Messalina, the unresisting maid quivered with the anticipation of what she was going to undergo.

The debauched woman actually laid her finger flat between the cheeks and gently pierced the pouting rosebud, an action which caused Julia to press violently against the thighs of the governess and contract the muscles of her bottom.

The cruel governess then seized the birch and commenced to flog the pretty girl with sufficient severity to make her plunge and indulge in such contortions as to afford most delicious sensations to the operator.

When Harry's prick was buried in her bottomhole to the very balls, Miss Birchem grew nearly frantic with delight and continued lashing the bottom under her eyes, with a vigour that increased with every subsequent thrust that Harry made in her bottom.

CHAPTER II

MISS BIRCHEM

MISS Birchem when she said that no
gentleman could fuck her was roman-
cing. She had originally been mistress of a nobleman, Sir Clifford, who having
passed a life of voluptuousness in the society
of women who had seconded him in all his
whims and strange desires, had at last required more stimulus to his passions than they
themselves could afford.

At first his *outré* desire was to enjoy her
posteriors by birching them. This she submitted to at first to please him but after-

wards to please herself, because under her correct and modest outward appearance burned a violent fire.

She soon conceived such a mad passion that she implored her lover to administer the birch to her burning posterior, an indulgence he never denied her, no salacious wantonness being sufficiently voluptuous for her.

The baronet's mistress soon became in possession of outrageously lustful passions for flagellation, and the sensations were so delicious that she suffered physically and mentally, when in the impossibility of satisfying her sensual desires.

At lengh her cunt did not seem tight enough round his prick when he fucked her, till on one occasion when he had been severely flogging her, as she knelt on the bed, projecting the cheeks of her naked bottom, all naked as she was, he proposed to fuck her in her inviting anus.

The rod had generated such a heat in all her private parts that she imagined that it must give her pleasure to receive him there and she therefore consented. With his prick inflated to its utmost, he leant over the naked creature whose burning face and palpitating breasts were half buried in the downy bed.

Bringing the point of this prick opposite the orifice he wished to enter, he gave a lunge and succeeded in getting a portion of it into her body. At first it gave her such an exquisite feeling that she encouraged him in his attempt to get farther in.

But as his cock stretched her wider open and appeared to enter with much difficulty, she tried to shrink from him. He was however too much excited to stop, and her extreme tightness and the heat of her posteriors goaded him on.

Sir Clifford had been holding his mistress by both her shoulders, but now he passed one hand under her breasts to feel and move those luscious orbs. The other hand he carried down below her belly and seized her burning cunt.

Opening its velvet lips, the baronet sought and found her clitoris, which he rubbed gently about with his fingers and thus worked upon her venery to such an extent that she was capable of bearing anything.

Thus simultaneously frigging her mistress and driving his prick into her anus, she at length received the whole of his enormous tool fully within her, having thus a double pleasure conferred on her.

Miss Birchem's body now was bathed in blissful heat, their motions kept pace with each other, the room resounded with her sighs and exclamations of enjoyment and the luscious sound so exciting to the ears of the voluptuary. At length her movements grew so rapid as to announce the near approach of the Crisis.

Her lover felt he could no longer refrain from spending. Both gave way to their feelings and the baronet ejected a flow of spunk into her body, while his hand was wetted with her emission which oozed out from her convulsed and struggling quim.

From this time Sir Clifford more frequently fucked her mistress in this way than in any other, until the novelty having passed off to a certain extent, he had an idea that he should like to see her fucked by another, while he stood by and watched the effect on her and the performer who was buried in her quim.

The nobleman had as usual stripped her perfectly naked and for a change had taken her across his lap, in which position she threw widely about her handsome legs under the infliction of the birch. Each time the lash fell upon the crimson cheeks, Miss Birchem cried out:

—"Oh heavens! my bottom, my backside! Oh flog it, whip it, birch it, flagellate me harder, harder, lash me darling more severely. I can bear it as hard as you can lay it on your mistress. Oh you must put your darling prick into me after this."

Wildly excited by her cries, he said: "By heavens! I will, I must!" Throwing the rod aside and taking her in his arms, he laid her on the bed. She turned upon her back, her thighs wide open and her cunt instinct with life, showing such muscular throbbing action of the lips that it inflamed him to the utmost.

The baronet leaped upon the bed and lay on her upheaving form, belly to belly, then with mouth to mouth and tongue clinging to tongue, his marvellous cock entered that longing cunt and she threw her legs around his loins and her arms about his neck. Too full of bliss to speak for a time, she frequently withdrew her tongue from his mouth and asked:

—"How do you like to fuck me like this once more?"

—"Intensely, you enchanting girl," he replied.

—"What would I not do to give you pleasure, anything, everything—for your prick is so divine—but you are spending into me too quickly," said his mistress, as she felt the burning spunk leap from him into her.

—"I cannot help it! Oh God, you are so beautiful and your cunt does throb so."

—"But I want to be fucked till I spend," urged the lewd woman, willing to indulge in the most intoxicating lasciviousness.

—"Will you let William fuck you then while I am witness to the pleasure you will give him," said her lover.

—"Anything that will afford me delight," replied his ruttish mistress.

Sir Clifford got up and dressed himself, while she still lay in the position she was in while he was enjoying her, her lovely limbs stretched out, playing with the rosy nipples of her lovely breast which were standing up stiff and hard.

When he had put on his coat, he stopped first to kiss her cherry mouth, then for a moment to suck her enchanting breasts and then her lovely cunt which she elevated to meet his caress. Then throwing the sheet over her, he left the room.

The baronet shortly returned accompanied by a fine handsome youth in page livery. He had called him into the library when he departed on his mission, and asked him how he got on with the maid and whether any of them had yet taken his maidenhead.

The boy of fifteen blushing like a *pucelle*, said with the utmost confusion that he had never done anything to them or they to him.

—"How William," said his master, "How would you like to be with a naked woman? Would you enjoy her quim, if she would allow you to fuck her?"

William did not know what to reply, but his master perceiving that his prick was commencing to bulge out the front of his trousers, decided for him and conducted him to his mistress who had been frigging her cunt the whole time he had been away, in order to keep her excitement from cooling.

Fastening the door, Sir Clifford led the lad up to the bed, took his hand and carrying it under the sheet, slowly passed it over her legs and thighs and left it on her spending quim, an effect her frigging had just produced.

Seeing that his blood was heated by desire, his master slowly turned up the sheet as high as his mistress'breasts, leaving her face alone concealed. The boy trembled violently, his tongue seemed to grow double its size and he felt a strange sickening sensation.

Perfectly passive in his master's hands, the page suffered his trousers to be taken down till they hung at his heels and himself to be projected on the bed. The libidinous baronet then took the lad's prick which was swollen and stiff in his hand and said:

—"Get upon her, William, I shall put your cock into her for you and she shall take your maidenhead, if you have never fucked a woman."

Miss Birchem did not speak in order that her voice should not betray her, but as she felt the youth getting between her quivering thighs, she raised her cunt towards him and in another instant her lover had plunged within her that which seemed like a bar of red hot iron, as his virile member was so fearfully stiff and burning.

Carried away by his own keen feelings, William commenced to lunge spasmodically at her and he was no sooner in to the root than he was rendered incapable, owing to the intensity of his pleasure, of resisting anything that might be done to him.

His master separated his legs and placed them on each side of his mistress' thighs, who immediately closed hers and thus kept the boy's prick firmly imbedded there. Arranging their relative positions, they both soon ran a course of the most luxurious and salacious enjoyment imaginable.

Leaning over the bed, Sir Clifford watched with looks of wild lust the to and fro motion glide by the side of his prick within the moist folds of his mistress' cunt clung convulsively, her whole belly seeming on fire.

The moisture slowly oozed out at each thrust and maddened by the sight, the baronet commenced to suck the testicles of his page, ever and anon allowing his tongue to glide by the side of this prick within the moist and slipping orifice of the cunt he was fucking.

Very shortly his master found by the swelling of the muscles and the increased stiffness of the prick that the boy was about ready to spend, which caused him to redouble his exertion and when the Crisis overtook them, their mutual spending oozed out and flowed into his delighted mouth.

After a momentary pause, to his great delight the page recommenced fucking the lovely palpitating body below him. Sir Clifing the few days the boy had been with himself with a magnificent instrument. It was a dildoe of the most perfect sort. From a stomacher of India-rubber, covered with black curly hair stood forth an exact model of the baronet's glorious stiff member.

The master carefully covered with cold cream the perfectly shaped and painted prick with balls below, and watching his opportunity he inserted the dildoe in the arse of his mistress, on whom it had an electrical effect. Writhing and tossing herself madly about, she drove the page wild with pleasure.

The baronet seeing his opportunity, now knelt behind him and raising his shirt, presented his own cock and commenced to do to him what he had previously done to his mistress. But for the rapture of the boy while fucking the unknown lady, it would have been impossible for him to bear his master's action.

Sir Clifford had on several occasions during the few days the boy had been with him tried him in vain, when it occurred to him that if the introduced his page's prick into his mistress' cunt he would be able to insert his own prick in his bottom.

Miss Birchem actually did not see what he was about and William fucked her till she spent 2 ou 3 times, the nobleman emitting into him just as frequently, and only after the proceedings were finished and the page had left the room, his lecherous mistress was informed of what had happened.

Like many other lewd women, the relation had the most powerful effect upon her erotic nature, and her lover promised her to repeat the scene the following afternoon, when her face should be uncovered and she could see everything. The following afternoon when they were seated in the drawing room, she reminded him of his promise.

—"My dear," said the baronet, "you so drained me last night that I much fear my prick will not stand."

—"Indeed!" said the Messalina, "then I must birch you till it does," and putting her hand underneath the couch on which she sat, she produced a formidable birch.

—"Come here, Sir," she said, and the fornicatress commenced to unbutton his trousers.

—"Lie across my knees," she added when this was effected, pulling up her petticoats and folding them above her quim so that his belly, prick, and balls should come in contact with her naked thighs.

Even while she was pulling aside his shirt so as to have no impediment to their close contact, his prick began to erect itself, but when he began to lay across her, and his cock came near her quim, it stood so stiffly that with a little guidance its inflamed head was nestling in the soft hair around it.

Then as Miss Birchem birched her lover, his excitement grew so keen that he plunged and struggled, sending his penis gradually into her sideways until it was fleshed completely to the hilt and their hairs were commingled.

Then while his cruel mistress flogged him up to fury, the baronet fucked her quim until it would have been impossible to refrain longer from spending, when he entreated her to stop. She did so, and he arose and quickly adjusted his clothes.

The lustful woman soon threw herself at full length on the couch in a voluptuous attitude, her dress sufficiently in discorder to display the beauty of her legs and open enough at the bosom to reveal the loveliness of her breasts.

Sir Clifford then rang the bell and William appeared. "Shut the door and come here," said the baronet. The page obeyed and having closed the door approached the couch.

At a previous period the lad would have felt abashed at the state in which he saw his mistress, but his yesterday's experience had been increased in the evening, and he had acquired even greater boldness.

The parlour-maid had invited him to feel her charms and he had done so. While so employed the cook had arrived on the scene, but instead of interrupting them, took his balls in her hand and assisted them both to spend. He had afterwards slept with them both.

The effect of all this caused the boy's face to redden with desire. "William, have you ever seen this before?" said the baronet, raising his mistress' drapery and tossing it high enough to display the beauties of her person and bewitching quim.

His master pushed the page towards the couch and his salacious mistress held out her arms to receive him, and buried his face between her soft breasts. Meanwhile his prick was taken out by his master, who also pulled down his trousers and buried the boy's penis in the quim that was waiting for it.

William was soon in the agonies of spending, upon which Sir Clifford took advantage of the circumstance to bugger him again, an operation the pleasure of which his mistress did her utmost to heighten.

For some considerable time the intercourse between the trio was kept up, till Sir Clifford again desired a change, and as Miss Birchem wished to extend her field of amorous operations, a school was taken for her, which she was carrying on, at the time she is here introduced.

CHAPTER III

Mr. SPANKER

ISS Birchem whipped the bottom of Miss Wynne till Harry Staunton spent into her and his prick grew too limp to give her any longer pleasure, and when the governess released the flagellated girl from the position in which she had held her, she herself rose from Harry's lap.

Unsatisfied with the amount of pleasure he had given her,—had they been alone he would have had his prick violently frigged by her,—but seeing Julia's looks of unsatisfied desire raised by the tingling on her bottom she promised that the maid should have some pleasure.

The governess then took the virgin on her lap, taking care that their naked flesh should be in contact, and gradually raising her shift in front, told Harry to kneel before the lovely girl.

Then this lewd woman placed the young gentleman's head on Julia's naked thighs, and instructed him how to gamahuche her and this he did, holding the handsome damsel convulsively by the thighs, while his tongue went in and out, the point of it being directed at her clitoris.

Julia soon was in heavenly rapture, she held his head forward to her burning quim with all her strength, her body quivering with emotion, her eyes half blinded by the humidity that came over them.

While Harry was thus occupied in giving pleasure to Julia, Miss Birchem lowered his trousers and by the pliant use of her busy fingers soon produced an erection, and increased the ardour with which he ravenously sucked the young and moist cunt of Julia.

Shortly the lecherous nymph let her head fall back, her eyes closed and her whole form was convulsed, while her lovely liquor of love oozed forth into the delighted mouth of her gamahucher. As soon as she had recovered, the eager governess took the lad between her thighs and made him fuck her.

While this proceeding was going on, it so happened that Mr. Spanker, a gallant horse-dealer, was strolling through the meadows, thinking of the beauties of young Julia's mamma, whose naked beauties he was accustomed to enjoy in the privacy of her own room.

Behind the hedge against the bank on which Miss Birchem had seated herself, while Julia was sucked by young Harry, Mr. Spanker had witnessed Harry's frigging and subsequent fucking of the ruttish governess.

The scene had been too much for him, for while busy Harry was piercing the damsel's cunt with his tongue, he had spent incontinently. Therefore he feared to make his presence known, as he feared his prick would not second his desires.

Leaving them therefore the horse-dealer went home. But before he reached home, the remembrance of what he had seen caused his prick to stiffen, and immediately on his arrival he was compelled to seek his wife whom he found dressing.

The buxom proprietress of the house was speedily divested of stays and shift, and lay on the bed with her thighs around her husband's neck, who was frantically forcing his tongue up her bottom-hole.

Afterwards Mr. Spanker took himself from his wife's embrace, just as she was commencing to spend from the excitement this luxurious proceeding caused her, and burying his erect prick within her cunt, he fucked her furiously, and she so enjoyed the unexpected attack, that she aided his efforts by every means in her power.

After he had spent, the rake left his unsatisfied wife for the arms of Mrs. Wynne, whose embraces he lusted for more than ever, since he had seen her daughter's naked beauties, and the amorous joy she had experienced. Mrs. Spanker had therefore to be satisfied with a nephew, who was staying in the house and whom she determined to allure, by remaining in the same state her husband had left her.

After frigging herself, she rose with the intention of dressing and seeking Augustus and bringing him to her bedroom under pretences of romping with him, till her young nephew should find himself held between her legs.

Then this shameless matron would tickle the boy's prick and afterwards take it out. Wriggling till her clothes were above her belly, she would force his stiff cock within her and obtain by force the fucking she was dying for.

But at the moment Mrs. Spanker heard Augustus pass her door. Hastily opening it, nearly naked as she was, her white breasts completely bare, her back and shoulders only covered by her long hair, her legs naked more than halfway up, she called him in.

In a few minutes, the ruttish woman was on her bed, her chemise removed, and her legs around her nephew of fifteen, his fine prick within her, and both their bodies vibrated with the throbs of heavenly agony.

Meantime her husband was at Mrs. Wynne's house, but that lady not expecting him had gone out to keep an assignation with another lover, in whose company she was spending her time, between the sheets of a downy bed. Her daughter Julia however had reached their house some time before.

When Mr. Spanker arrived, he found her in the drawing room, scarcely recovered from the confusion of her senses, caused by the novel and delicious occupation, in which she had been engaged. As they were old friends, she was soon sitting on his knees.

Feeling something hard pressing against her, the young puss more knowing than before, since the lesson the governess had taught her, laid her hand upon it, artlessly enquiring: "Oh! what is that?, surely a mouse inside your pocket?"

—"Put your hand in, and feel the mouse," said the horse-dealer. She allowed him to insert her hand inside his trousers. When her naked fingers touched his burning prick, she gave it a squeeze, and then drew her hand out, saying: "It is not a mouse, it has no hair on it."

—"You only felt its nose, darling, look here," and he drew his rod completely out. She got off his lap, her eyes sparkling as if with curiosity to see the little thing. He stood up, unfastened all the buttons, and exhibited not only his stiff prick, but the balls covered with hair.

—"Gracious! what can this be for?", said the little maid artlessly.

—"I shall show you, darling," said Mr. Spanker, and sitting down again with his legs wide open, he drew her between them. He then with little difficulty succeeded in raising her clothes, and placing his finger in her cunt, commenced to frig her deliciously.

Julia kissed him passionately, and seizing his prick, pushed the skin up and down, until he was on the verge of spending, then her lover seized her hand and dragged it away, at the same moment applying his prick to her quim, which was moist with excitement.

The lovely girl let her head fall on his shoulder, hiding her burning face. "Oh, you darling, I must fuck you," he muttered, then repeated the expression with increased emphasis, getting his prick a little farther within her, at each upward heave.

It gave her such delicious sensations, that she assisted him, by firmly bearing down her cunt upon his prick, though now and then she could not help ejaculating: "Oh! it hurts me!", as he endeavoured to make his way upwards within her.

This happened every time Mr. Spanker tried to get his arrow in, beyond the nut. The lustful horse-dealer was indeed mad to take her maidenhead, but feared he could not do it in this position.

There was no one in the house but the servant, and she was quite safe as he well knew. So he said to the luscious virgin: "Let me take you upstairs, darling, and place you on a bed, it will then go quite into you and will not hurt."

—"Take me then," said Julia, "for I want so much for you to do it to me." He took her up to her mother's bedroom, and placing her on the edge of the bed, he again raised her clothes, and could not resist for a moment sucking that lovely panting and pulpy cunt.

Then as the compliant nymph lay there, her whole body palpitating with desire, her lovely eyes fixed on the stiff prick about to perforate her, her adorer placed a pillow under her bottom, and raised her cunt on a level with his prick.

Then spreading her thighs wide asunder, and getting in between them, Mr. Spanker drew so close to her, that his prick touched her cunt. Separating the pink lips with his thumb and finger, he guided his burning rod into her narrow quim, and then lying on her, began the fucking, that was doomed to destroy her virginity.

—"Put your legs over my back, darling," demanded the lascivious horse-dealer.

Julia did so, and with his assistance her pretty thighs formed a resting place for his head, her knees were at his neck, and her legs hung over his back. This position stretched her cunt open to its utmost extent, and every thrust he now gave, drove him deeper within her.

The violated maid murmured: "Oh! your cock! it is too large, and so stiff it hurts, but so deliciously."

—"Bite my neck, darling girl," cried her seducer, "I am going into you, and one more thrust will do it."

The frightened damsel did so, and then prevented herself from uttering a cry during her defloration, as she was pierced to the quick, and her cunt inundated with the hot spunk which rushed from the great prick within her.

Her virginity was now destroyed. She closed her eyes, and lay still when her lover withdrew, her buttocks alone giving an occasionally spasmodic heave, as the white spunk issued forth in precious drops.

Julia then arose and threw herself upon Mr. Spanker's arm, hiding her face in his bosom, while her seducer lovingly caressed her now womanly cunt.

CHAPTER IV

JULIA

EENLY desirous after this to enjoy the amorous girl at full leisure and in a state of nudity, Mr. Spanker made her promise to meet him on the following day at his apartments, when he would take her to a house of assignation and fuck her naked.

Her seducer would not attempt then nor afterwards to fuck Julia under the roof of her mamma, for fond as that lady was of voluptuous pleasure, she might not approve of her daughter being fucked.

He also wished to give her lovely posteriors such a flagellation as he had seen Miss Birchem bestow on her beautiful bum. Julia actually kept her appointment, and assumed an attire more appropriate to her, as she was no longer a virgin.

Her stepfather, for her mamma had married twice, had noticed how the gentlemen fixed their eyes on Julia's legs, and how they evidently lusted for her, on seeing the rounded outlines of her well developed legs.

He had therefore insisted that she should wear longer skirts. New dresses having been made for her, she had put one of them on this day for the first time, but not before the exhibition of her lovely limbs has caused her to have received another fucking.

Towards the evening of the previous day, and after Mr. Spanker had taken her maidenhead, the fickle girl thought she would like to see if Harry Staunton was looking for her in the lane, where the previous birching scene had been enacted.

She therefore wandered thither, and was very near the same spot, close to a gate that led into a field covered with wild flowers. Here Sir Clifford chanced to see her. He accosted her, for the moment being very desirous to possess so beautiful and so young a girl.

The enamoured baronet asked where the path through the fields led to, and on her informing him, he so overwhelmed her with compliments on her loveliness, that her face was suffused with blushes, and she seemed panting with excitement.

The nobleman then asked her to go with him, so that he might not lose himself. Julia readily consented. It was necessary to climb over a gate and the gallant baronet assisted the alluring maid to mount it. As she stepped up, his eyes were gloating on her fine limbs.

When he helped her to throw her leg over the top bar, he not only contrived that her dress should be so disarranged, that a portion of her thigh should be uncovered, but that his hand should slip upwards on her warm flesh, till it reached her quim.

When he touched the warm lips of her quim, her sensations were indescribably exquisite. "Let me get over on the other side to help you, my dear," said this chivalrous man, and Julia blushed assent.

Giving an emphatic pressure to her velvet cunt, the eager baronet leaned over, holding his arms out to receive her. She jumped, her clothes flying up and disclosing her young charms, as he caught her. The grass was tall, and well covered with daisies and golden buttercups.

Thinking he would follow her, the tantalizing girl ran some distance, and commenced to cull the flowers, her face flushing and her bosom rising with sensual emotion. Her admirer was very soon by her side, and pretending to pluck wild flowers also, selecting those apparently that were by her dress.

But as her legs were wide open as she stooped, his hand had little or no difficulty in finding her tempting little cunt, into which he quickly inserted his finger. As he touched her excitedly on the clitoris, she fell forward on his arm, while he continued to frig her.

The voluptuous girl let her fair young face rest on his shoulder, as she acutely enjoyed the pleasure he was causing her. Without any diminution of the activity with which he manipulated her moist cunt, Sir Clifford then took out his prick, and asked her to fondle it.

—"So," enquired Julia, as she chafed his magnificent cock with her dainty fingers, till he was on the point of coming, while her own eyes betrayed that she was fast approaching a similar condition. He would have preferred to check his own and her emission, so that he might have enjoyed her to the full, and ravished her thoroughly.

It was however impossible, and the libidinous baronet was compelled to send his spending over Julia's hand, while she under the friction of his finger gave way to her sensations, spending exquisitely and sighing deeply as she spent.

When they had recovered, Sir Clifford still wished to fuck her, and therefore begged her to come to the farther corner of the field, where they would be altogether unobserved. She readily consented. He helped her to rise, for she had sunk on the grass for him to frig her, and they went away together.

When he had laid the appetizing maid down on the bank, which formed a natural couch, the libertine unfastened the front of her dress, and liberating her breasts, began to tickle and squeeze the nipples.

Seeing how excited she became, the voluptuary gradually raised her dress, and fastening his lips to the lips of her cunt, all wet and moist as it was from her recent spending, this debaucher sucked her luscious quim amorously, and licked her clitoris now fully erect and hard, till Julia again profusely emitted into his mouth.

This caused his prick to become stiff and burning. Placing himself between her thighs, the baronet put the scarlet head of his rod in the rosy opening of her body, and placing both his hands beneath, and parting the cheeks of her bottom, he raised her slightly towards him.

The fornicator sent his prick in up to the hilt, and commenced to thrust it backwards and forwards. Suddenly they heard the sound of footsteps, but as they evidently proceeded from the other side of the hedge, they knew they could not be seen, so continued their lovely occupation.

Sir Clifford and his luxurious companion heard however that the new comers evidently were reclining behind the hedge, and also they were members of the opposite sex. Suddenly Julia whispered : "It is my mother and her nephew."

Mrs. Wynne and her young nephew evidently were bent on pleasure, for after the sound of kissing had been heard, a lascivious sound succeeded, from which it was very evident they were either gamahuching or fucking.

—"It is coming," murmured Mamma. "So is mine," uttered the nephew. This had such an effect on the daughter, that she became frantic, and spent in almost agonised convulsions, bathing the prick of the baronet with the pearly dew.

Sir Clifford and Julia now separated, but the young lady was still more madly lewd than before, and hastened to the house of Mr. Spanker. When she arrived there, she threw herself in his arms, and he placing her in an easy chair, knelt in front of her, and gave her a hasty taste of bliss.

After which they started for the house of assignation, in order that the bottom of the debauched girl might be birched, and she initiated into all the wild excesses of lust, and all kinds of whipping lubricity.

Julia was by now fully conscious of her pruriency. A large number of men and women delight to practise flagellation in all its forms, as an accompaniment or as an inducement to love's paroxysm, cruelty creating an intense sensual excitement in some, when holding under physical domination a creature ot the opposite sex.

There was no doubt for the lecherous maid, that her seducer also possessed this mania, and the pain he was about to inflict upon her, would lend additional zest to their mutual enjoyment, in that house of assignation which they were bound for.

It was in fact a brothel, where rods and whips are kept in reserve, to use on the posteriors of the customers or the delicate charms of the venal nymphs, according to wishes expressed and paid for, while the voluptuary gives large sums to the procuress to ravish tremulous virgins.

CHAPTER V

THE HOUSE OF FLAGELLATION

AS she entered the room in which the operations were to take place, Julia was influenced by various emotions, but her temperament was such, that the lascivious sensations she had experienced already inflamed her lust to a greater extent than would otherwise have been the case.

The chamber of flagellation contained a large bedstead with a bed of down. From the posts and other points were heavy silk-cords, that were used for tying the person to be birched in an extended position, so that the effect might be seen by the operator in the most perfect manner.

There were also velvet pillows that might be placed between the thighs, so that the friction and soft contact of the velvet might assist the victim to spend, while undergoing flagellation. An ardent curiosity and the desire of amorous pleasures drove the wanton damsel almost mad with suppressed expectation.

Around the room were whipping machines of varied construction. One was made in such a manner that when tied up, the back was in a horizontal position, whilst there projected from the lower part a dildoe long enough to reach and penetrate the quim.

Another whipping machine was like a rocking-horse, on which the woman was stretched on her face, her legs embracing the sides of the machine. Every chair was of a different pattern, and had its own special use, being devoted to some special form of lust, and intended for the gratification of a special whim.

Mr. Spanker explained the use of these various things, and his young mistress grew every moment more madly lewd, until at last she was ready to undergo anything. Her seducer now commenced to remove her hat and jacket, and then to unbutton the bosom of her dress, releasing her panting bubbies.

With these he toyed for a while, until she herself proceeded to rid herself of every article of clothing, and was very shortly standing before him in a state of perfect nudity. The horse-dealer followed her example, and seizing her by the lower part of her body, his bare arm between her thighs, he lifted her on the bed.

The debauchee then extended the panting girl on her belly, fastening her hands in velvet bands, which were attached to the silken cords, hanging from the upper end of the bed and firmly securing them to the two posts. He then extended her legs in a like manner, fastening her feet to the lower posts by similar appliances.

Heavens! what a sight was thus presented to him. Her white and palpitating flesh throbbed, and every muscle was strained to the utmost. Her lovely breasts could be seen under her elevated arms, and the distension of her legs enabled the interior of her moist cunt to be perfectly seen, her clitoris quite stiff and red.

The lovely anus too could be seen, nestling between the rounded cheeks of Julia's bottom. Having manipulated it for some time, this salacious man eagerly stooped down, and licked the full white bottom all over. Thrusting his nose into the furrow, he then placed his tongue for a moment in the nether orifice, after postilloning it with two fingers.

After the voluptuary had tongued the utmost recesses of her fundament, and wetted it amply with his saliva, which made her moan with pleasure, he then placed his hands under the beautiful creature. He felt her juicy cunt with one hand and gently frigged her, while he rubbed her nipples with the other hand, till she was on the verge of spending, when he ceased and watched with gloating eyes the spasm that convulsed every fibre of her coral slit.

The tormentor now selected a pliant birch, and commenced to flog her gently on the buttocks and inside of the thighs, gradually increasing the force of the blows, one violent blow after another falling on the damsel's trembling bottom, as the horse-dealer flogged faster and faster, harder and harder, till all began to tingle and grow red.

Miss Wynne bounded at each blow, screaming it was too much and too hard, but Mr. Spanker was merciless and continued the flogging for another minute. He then ceased for a moment and, inserting one finger in her hot vulva, gently frigged her again, while he birched with the other arm, in such a manner as to excite rather than hurt.

Julia was overwhelmed by an unknown delicious sensation. This caused her to undulate her back, and raise her buttocks, as well as circumstances would permit to meet the falling lash. Her tormentor now grew frantic, and increased the force of his blows to such an extent, as to make her cry out: "Oh! you do hurt me, it is cutting into my flesh."

This brought into the room the buxom proprietress of the house of flagellation. He notioned to her not to discover herself, and she accordingly watched with glaring eye and inflated nostril the exciting scene that was being enacted, till she was obliged to raise her clothes and commence to frig her quim.

The procuress was half mad with voluptuousness. Her knees trembled, and her breasts which were uncovered heaved violently. Wriggling her body in all directions, she widened her thighs and heaved her bottom, till throwing herself on the whipping machine with the dildoe, she caused it to enter her vagina, and by the energy of her motions soon covered it with her spendings.

In the meantime Julia cried out: «Oh! flog me harder, kill me, do anything, I am mad with my feelings." She felt no more pain, only the most intoxicating pleasure, and soon died away in all the agony of a final rapture: "Oh heavens! my bottom, my cunt, it is coming, I am going to spend."

With a howl of pleasure, the lewd girl discharged copiously, her lovely pink bumhole opening and closing with each thrust of the loins, in which the cheeks of her bottom hardened with the contraction consequent on the spasm passing through her.

While his luxurious mistress lay half insensible, Mr. Spanker unscrewed the dildoe from the whipping machine, and reeking as it was with the spunk that had just been shed on it, gently pressed it into Julia's arsehole, and fast moved the artificial member backwards and forwards through the narrow corrugated brown hole.

Her whole body stiffened, and the lovely girl seemed like one convulsed, so marvellous was the effect on her erotic nature. While her lover was withdrawing again the magnificent *godmiché,* and placing it up her sweet cunt, she commenced the up and down movement of her body to frig herself with it involuntarily.

The lady of the house of flagellation now begged Mr. Spanker to birch her. She had stripped, and was lying on a couch constructed in such a manner, that the velvet fitted every curve of her body, belly downwards. He advanced to the upper end of the couch, and leaning a little forward commenced to flagellate her violently.

This soon excited her again, and she seized his almost bursting penis, and nestling it between her lips, sucked it luxuriously, contracting the muscles of her mouth around the palpitating member, at the present moment raised to its full length, and pushing her head to and fro, till he spent with the wildest contortions, and a copious discharge sent her into an agony of delight.

The lewd procuress then looked up at her tormentor pleadingly, the lovely drops of sperm still hanging about her lips, and he bent down and kissed her fervently, receiving back into his own mouth some of the dew he had spent in her's.

Mr. Spanker then fondled her firm thighs and curly haired mount Venus, and rubbed violently the glaring red point all smooth and moist. Frigging her luscious fanny with the palm of his hand, he speedily brought on the Crisis. With a spasmodic contraction of her buttocks, she shot out a flood of thick, pearl-coloured spunk over his hand, and lay for several minutes soaking with bliss.

When this was concluded, they perceived that Julia was watching them intently. "Oh!" said she, "do come to me again, do not leave me." «You shall have a new pleasure, darling," said her lover, "and our friend here shall initiate you." Rising from the couch, the *Madame* came and lay on the bed beside the gamy girl in a reversed position, and commenced to kiss her bottom and tickle her clitoris.

Then passing one leg over her prostrate body, her cunt pressed hard against Julia's loins, she buried her head between her thighs and gamahuched her luxuriously, and passing a finger gently up her anus, caused her the most divine pleasure.

After this, Julia was released, and they all sat side by side and partook of champagne and other refreshments. Mr. Spanker then said that he must be birched, in order to make his shaft stand again, and the fair Julia had the satisfaction of flagellating his bottom, till his enormous prick stood like iron.

Then hastily rising, he placed the proprietress in an easy chair, which being unfolded made her fall backwards, so as to lie horizontally with his knees, the chair being high enough to bring her quim on a level with his rampant pego exhibited at full stretch. Her legs were then elevated, with her feet tossing about in the air.

In this position the buxom lady of the house was fucked, till they both spend in the wildest ecstasy, Julia all the time flogging his backside, while a torrent of boiling sperm was shed into the bawd's womb. A lovely waiting maid, who had entered during this occurence, was now seized, thrown on her belly on a chair, her clothes tossed up.

She was fucked up her bottom-hole by Mr. Spanker, while Julia sucked madly at the relaxed quim of the salacious procuress, and then embracing the spending woman forcibly rubbed her excited button and cunt up against hers. She brought on such a spasm of delight, that not only their grottos, mounts Venus and bellies, but also their thighs, arses and buttocks were wetted with their united abundant spendings, till they fell on the floor utterly exhausted.

The horse-dealer and his young mistress shortly after left the house of flagellation. But an appointment was made for the following Monday, when several girls were expected at the house, who had never been fucked or frigged, having been imported from the country by a wealthy nobleman, in order that he might see them debauched and treated in every manner that unbridled and imaginative lust could devise.

CHAPTER VI

Mrs. MINETTE

N Monday accordingly Mr. Spanker and Miss Wynne were again visitors to the house of flagellation. They found the buxom proprietress, Mrs. Minette seated in the room already described, with a flowing robe of silk, lined with swandown. She greeted them warmly and gave Julia a loving squeeze, which made her tremble with desire.

The lewd procuress said : "I shall want your help, as well as that of my two waiting maids, as I shall have five or six young girls and one boy about thirteen, and it might be necessary to use force in order to frig them successfully and make them spend." The horse-dealer and his young mistress were only too glad to tender their aid.

—"As for the gentleman who has arranged to have them sent here," resumed the lady of the house, "he will be in the adjoining room and view all through a hole in the partition, while one of my friends kneels in front of him and sucks his prick." It was in fact Sir Clifford, the libidinous baronet.

Shortly afterwards, the waiting maids, who were dressed in dressing gowns with their breasts uncovered, came in leading a lovely little girl apparently about twelve of age. She was well developed for her age, and a shy and modest demeanour added to her attractions. Mrs. Minette immediately took her by her side.

She told her that she would find her school calculated to make her happy, that she need not fear restraint, but that everything would be done to add to her happiness. The little girl replied, that she was very much frightened at the idea of coming to a boarding school, but felt quite sure she would be happy.

Mrs. Minette gave her a glass of wine and some cake, and continued talking to her, by degrees commencing to fondle her. After she had taken the wine, her face flushed, and she seemed uneasy, restless irritable sensations seemed to be pervading her. The moment the procuress saw this, she eagerly pressed her arm around the little waist and increased her caresses.

Mrs. Minette then pressed her hand against the small breasts, which were already rounded and delightfully firm. The lovely little girl rather resisted this in a half frightened way, when Julia, who had been watching the proceeding with a wild look in her eyes, came on the other side of her, and commenced to caress her also.

At length they succeeded in unfastening her dress and bringing out the little bubbies, when each began to suck one rosy nipple. At this the girl began to struggle and cry out. Mr. Spanker now half mad with a strange feeling of lechery, came in front of them and raised her short petticoats.

A sense of maidenly bashfulness seized her. Her face and neck all crimson with shame, she now shrieked out in real earnest, and struggled with all her might. This but excited him the more, and he forcibly separated her legs and tore open her drawers, exhibiting to his view a lovely little pink cunt entirely destitute of hair.

After he had postilloned her smaller brown orifice with two fingers, the debaucher stooped and grasping her thighs, kissed her smooth belly and tiny mount Venus all over. He then fastened his lips to her vermilion slit and commenced to suck it, forcing his tongue in, as far as it would go, her other two tormentors now holding her fast, in order to facilitate his operations.

The sweet little thing exhausted with fright and strange feelings fainted, and they carried her to the bed, and stripped her entirely naked. They then took thick silken cords, and drawing her knees upwards, fastened them securely under her breast in such a manner, that her bottom was elevated, as she lay face downwards on the bed.

The proprietress then took some *eau de Cologne*, which she rubbed into the charming buttocks, and opening them wide apart, the rosy lips of her small quim were as smooth as her soft cheeks. Mrs. Minette just touched the pouting lips of her charming pink cunt, that lay projecting forwards from the position in which she was bound.

Then the luxurious lady of the house stooped and sucked the cunt, till it throbbed, and swelled out with excitement, then she held her down by the shoulders, and asked Julia to birch her. This she was madly desiring, and commenced immediately to obey such a pleasant command, animated as she was by a strange feeling of lubricity.

She dealt one or two sharp stinging blows, when the victim recovered her senses, and commenced to scream with fright and pain. "Hit her harder," said the cruel procuress. Julia—by now in hysterics—required no incentive, and lashed at the puckered bottom before her, like one possessed. "Oh! you are killing me," shrieked the little one, "Oh! my bottom."

Mrs. Minette, as a true priestess of Venus, eagerly opened the pouting lips of the nymphet's quim, and put her middle finger there, on the top of the little button at the top of the velvet lips. As her hand was moving faster, the sweet creature's perfumed breath came quicker, her thighs trembled, and her flagellated bottom moved up and down, as nature teaches it.

Her cries grew fainter. She struggled to free herself from the position in which she was bound, and from her convulsive movement evidently was about for the first time in her life to spend. With one final heave, she ground her pearly teeth together, and the procuress' finger was bedewed with the virgin spunk, as the little girl spent in ecstasy.

—"We will make you feel more than this," said Mrs. Minette, and signing to Julia in raptures to desist, which she did with evident reluctance, the bawd took a small dildoe, and first inserting a finger in the crevice, that was throbbing under the scarlet cheeks of her bottom, began to tickle again the little clitoris and bottom-hole.

She then withdrew her finger, and gently inserted in the crimson vulva the head of the dreadful *godmiché*, around which the lips of the girl's cunt clung most enticingly. She pushed it backwards and forwards, till the Crisis overtook her, when with a brutal lunge, she forced in the artificial prick to its entire length, breaking the hymen and causing the most acute pain, at the very moment her first pearly spunk commenced to flow from her now womanly cunt.

The lovely little girl screamed and struggled piteously, but this only excited all her tormentors, to fury, and Mr. Spanker seizing Julia fucked her savagely, perforating her corrugated brown hole with his finger as he did so, while his young mistress—by now a ruttish bitch—was squeezing his balls in her dainty fingers.

The buxom proprietress of the house, in the meantime was pushing the dildoe about in every direction, in the luscious young quim she had ravished, so as to thoroughly open it, but had hardly completed her operations when the Crisis seized her, and she fell on the bed by her victim, spending profusely.

Seeing this, the two waiting maids came to her relief. As Mrs. Minette had full and protuberant breasts with prominent nipples, and a magnificent bumhole, one waiting maid alternatively sucked her nipples and gamahuched her anus, as the other maid drained her vagina of every drop of liquor that her amorous tongue could produce, and so drove the salacious procuress half-mad with lust and lasciviousness.

The little girl was then taken into another room and put to bed, being carefully tended, until she was sufficiently recovered to be made to take part in the wildest excesses of lust. After a short interval, other virgins of exquisite beauty were brought in. They were a trifle older than the last victim, and for this reason their lust was still further increased, till they were made to indulge in pleasures, that would fiercely take away their maidenheads.

As had been previously arranged, one virgin was seized by each of them, the two waiting maids, Julia and Mr. Spanker, and carried to chairs, which on being sat on, set the springs in motion, and a piece of ingenious mechanism held fast the legs and arms of the occupant.

The beautiful nymphs were paralyzed with fear, their nakedness, and Mr. Spanker's erect prick filling them with wonderment. Excited by the idea that they were watched by these lovely girls, innocent of everything, their tormentors commenced to put in practice every species of abandoned licentiousness, in which it was possible to indulge.

Julia knelt down in front of Mr. Spanker and sucked his rampant Jack, while the horse-dealer gamahuched one of the waiting maids, who stooped over his face for the purpose, while Mrs. Minette with one finger in her fanny and the other in her arse frigged both orifices, while she was herself operated on a similar manner by the waiting maid.

These lecherous tormentors were very soon rolling on the floor in a confused heap, their forms undulating in the mad embraces of lascivious loves, and in the shuddering crisis of satisfied spending, torrents of boiling sperm dashing on each others'bodies and faces in all directions, their figures soon lying in the soft abandonment of the after-moment.

They then turned their attention to the four girls, and approaching them they commenced to feel their bosoms and unfasten the front of their dresses, afterwards raising their dresses in front, and examining with lustful enjoyment their young vermilion slits, their pretty mounts Venus, on which a soft and silky down was appearing.

Three of the frightened virgins were loud in their outcries, but as they were unable to move, the wantons enjoyed to the full the handling of their private parts, the more so that the attractive nymphs were powerless in their hands. Desires could no longer be hid, kisses were forced upon the panting breasts, and more than one of the girls in torture found eager fingers straying against their hymens. «Away with all ceremony and restraint," said the procuress, "here we are in my bagnio, here we can do all that love or lust dictates."

The fourth girl was flushed, and Julia on examining her dear little vulva, found it moist and throbbing, and on putting her finger in her vagina, found that it entered quite easily. She was evidently of an immensely warm temperament, for in spite of her terror she soon spent under Julia's caressing hand, who with her lips on the spot sucked her long and ardently.

The amorous torturers now provided themselves with scissors, and cut off every particle of their clothing and released them, then bound them to flogging machines in such a manner, that their bellies and fannies were in close contact, and their breasts pressed also against each other.

Then they inserted two well moistened double dildoes in their cunts, so that the knob of the imitation-tools entered just within the velvet lips of their chapels. Then taking up their position on either side, they commenced to birch them at first gently, but growing excited increased the severity of the blows, until they writhed and shrieked with pain.

They then desisted for a time to watch the effects, and placed their hands on their crimsoned buttocks and pressed them, laying their fingers flat between the junction of their thighs, titillating them gently. This evidently had the most wonderful effect on them, for they ceased their cries, and by the movement of the muscles, it could clearly be seen that they were experiencing pleasure.

In a few movements it was evident that the luxurious virgins were about to reach the Crisis, and only refrained from pressing their bellies against each other with their whole force by the pain, which such as an action would cause by the consequent increased insertion of the dreadful shaft of the artificial pricks in their luscious grottos.

The indefatigable tormentors now resumed the rods, and showered down stinging blows. They soon increased the force of their blows to such an extent, as to make their victims half mad with a strange feeling. The flagellated girls could not resist this, and growing frantic, with wild cries they involuntarily forced the double dildoes up to the hilt in their quivering bodies, and mingled blood from their destroyed hymens and pearly spunk both issued forth.

The rods were now thrown aside, and advancing to the girl on whom Julia had previously operated, Mr. Spanker thrust his enormous prick into her bottom-hole with the utmost force, tearing his way in her burning rectum, and pushing his rampant rammer backwards and forwards through her corrugated brown hole, till he inundated her with his boiling sperm.

Mrs. Minette took Julia across her naked thighs, and inserted a *godmiché* in her anus, as she lay with her belly upwards, and then stooping gamahuched her, while working the shaft of the dildoe to and fro, till the lewd wench spent with the utmost delight.

Then seizing the *godmiché* which had dropped from her anus, Julia plunged the magnificent tool of good size and exact shape into the procuress' quim, till it was completely sheathed in the moist gap, and produced a constant in-and-out movement, the effect of which was very obvious, in Mrs. Minette's flushed cheeks, sparkling eyes, and heaving belly and bosoms, and on the pouting and moistering lips of her large quim. Julia fiercely frigged the lady of the house of flagellation, with this giant *Wife's Comfort,* till her eyes closed, and every muscle stiffened, and with a howl of pleasure she discharged profusely in an agony of delight.

This entrancing sight maddened the waiting maids, who flew into each other's arms, and frigged and gamahuched in every position, till they were commingled in a Sixty-Nine posture, their faces buried in the bushy curls, with their bellies pressed on the voluminous bosoms, while their tongues searched out the delicate scarlet cracks of their burning fannies, till the same pleasure overtook them, and all lay in a confused heap, reeling with excess of gratified lubricity.

The raptures all had experienced cannot be expressed, more especially at that particular moment when the four maidenheads of the girls were simultaneously destroyed by their own involuntary movements, amid screams and struggling. Mr. Spanker felt as though he would faint, every muscle trembled and his priape throbbed dreadfully, while Julia was literally maddened.

They now turned their attention to the girls who were still suspended, and perceived to their astonishment and delight, that they were involuntarily pressing backwards and forwards against each other. They separated the cheeks of theirs bottoms, and carefully inserted their moistened fingers within the lovely orifice, and pushed them gently backwards and forwards through each anus, to the hilt in the rectum.

The effect of this was soon evident by the convulsive manner, in which the bottom-holes closed and throbbed on the finger inserted in them. Just as the enslaved girls were on the verge of spending again under the lash, the four stood up behind them, and squeezed the panting bodies sandwiched between them, with all their strength, and assisted them in spending by their lascivious movement.

After they had separated the moaning girls, and licked up their spendings, as their juicy cunts emitted copious discharges, all were now thoroughly exhausted in the chamber of flagellation, and Julia and Mr. Spanker having resumed their clothes left the bagnio.

CHAPTER VII

AUGUSTUS

SOME days later, Julia and Mr. Spanker again visited the house of flagellation. Mrs. Minette told them, that a beautiful boy of about fifteen years of age had been secured for ministering to the lust of themselves. Julia trembled with suppressed emotion, and begged to be allowed to do what she pleased with him.

This was agreed to, on conditions that her operations were conducted in the presence of Mr. Spanker and Mrs. Minette. The latter lady then left the room, and shortly after returned with a well proportioned and agreeable looking youth. He was invited to sit on one of the spring chairs, and was immediately a prisoner.

But Julia did not approve of this proceeding, as soon as she recognized Mrs. Spanker's handsome nephew Augustus, and at a sign from her, the astonished youth was on the spot released. Julia then approached the boy, embracing him warmly, and pressing her lovely breasts against his chest.

The lascivious damsel then pushed Augustus towards the bed, and attempted to put her hand between his thighs, but he struggled to such an extent, that she could not succeed in unbuttoning his trousers, and reaching his prick. Mr. Spanker and the procuress however assisted her, by holding the youth's arms and legs, and she succeeded in unfastening them, and bringing forth his cock with her trembling fingers.

Augustus' shaft was not stiff, but at its top the little very pretty and very smooth projection, like the cup of an acorn, was sufficiently swollen to prove that with discreet manipulation, and the influence of exciting feelings, the boy's pego would soon become erect. Julia now wished him to be placed again in the chair: which was immediately done by the buxom proprietress.

Julia then brought out Augustus'penis and testicles, and let them completely to view. She commenced to fondle his corrugated brown scrotum. The folds of the skin and the veins became very distinct on the pego, and its knob, attached to the shaft by a ringlet of skin, assumed a goodly size. It seemed so smooth, so delicate, so dear, so sweet, that Julia could have kissed it on the spot.

As the blood was boiling in her veins, and a sharp shivering sensation was passing through her body, and the little button between her legs was throbbing more violently than ever, she seated herself before Augustus, and slowly raised her dress. Exposing her plump buttocks and lovely thighs, and pressing them together, the salacious wench put down her hand between them, to stop the tickling feeling in her little fanny, and commenced slowly to frig herself.

Allowing the youth to see every detail of the process, his prick soon began to rise with little jerks, until it stood erect and throbbing. Seeing this, Julia knelt in front of Augustus, and exposing her lovely breasts, she placed his rod between them, and passing her arms around his loins, hugged him to her, and commenced to frig him by the friction of her bubbies, thus pushing his foreskin up and down.

The youth groaned with delight. The blood rushed into his cock, filling it, and making it swell out to an unknown size. The girl's unexpected proceedings, keeping the glowing knob uncovered, and all the threads of the frœnum well stretched, brought his cockey on the verge of spending.

Just as Augustus commenced to spend, Julia darted back, and watched with gloating eyes the foaming spunk, flashing out from his bursting knob, as he moaned aloud. She instantly seized the ruby head of his prick in her mouth, closing her lips around it, and titillating it with her tongue to the intense gratification of the boy. She milked it with such violence that the youth was forced to utter a cry.

The fierce wench however continued until Augustus wholly discharged in her mouth, as the grand Crisis seized him, and he shot forth a torrent of burning sperm. Her sweet tongue directly called forth the liquid of Love, which poured down her throat as she drank his health in his own sperm. Julia was in raptures, but as the creamy spunk threatened to suffocate her, she instantly withdrew and gazed at the limp member.

To her great disappointment, she beheld the so lately rampant weapon, drooping its head and retiring within its shell, while some few drops of the milky white liquor were oozing from the small orifice in its head. It was reduced to a mere shadow of its former self, while she gazed at it, and the foreskin gradually covered the lately so fiery and bursting knob.

The wicked damsel then suggested all should frig him, each in turn, until he fainted from exhaustion. This idea excited each of his tormentors, and releasing him once more, Augustus was extended on the bed, as Julia had been on her initiation in the mysteries of flagellation. There they fastened his hands and legs, in the velvet bands attached to the silken cords hanging from the bed-posts, and they flogged and frig him with actual cruelty, till he became insensible.

Mrs. Minette first approached, and embracing his thighs, between which she placed her lovely arm, pressed her breast against his bottom and balls, which she then tickled until his prick was erect. Seeing that his pego was by now exhibited at full stretch, with a very smooth and brilliant head, she stooped to kiss it.

—"How on earth can that little innocent thing attain such formidable proportions?" said the lewd procuress, while she was slipping under the youth, and directing the tantalizing knob to her eager cunt. Uttering the most frantic exclamations of enjoyment, she spent herself at the same moment as he did, both thoroughly wetted with their united abundant spendings.

Then the disgusting lady of the house sucked his anus, and darted her greedy tongue inside the utmost recesses, at the same time tickling his scrotum and the inside of his thighs. Then slowly drawing the foreskin around his machine up and down, as far as it would go, she said suddenly: "He is going to spend again, I can feel it by the increased size and stiffness of his lovely prick," and frigging him with the greatest rapidity, his spunk flowed.

As soon as she left him, Augustus begged to be released, saying his cock was so sore, and pained him so much, that he could scarcely bear it. Mrs. Minette's lubricity, restrained during the flogging and frigging of the boy, was by now raised to the utmost extent. The procuress actually was wild like a ruttish bitch, to feel a prick in her lustful cunt or greedy mouth, and she replied brutally: "You shall be frigged till you faint."

Mr. Spanker now approached his nephew. The horse-dealer was so fearfully excited from the exhibition he had witnessed, and the idea that he was going to brutally frig a boy, that was already half fainting from his repeated emissions and whose prick and balls were completely bathed in their own spunk, inflamed his lust still more.

Scarcely knowing what he did, he determined to bugger Augustus, and accordingly he squeezed his slippery testicles in his hand and, well rubbing his fingers about them, transferred the moisture to his bottom-hole, into which he placed his finger, all the time fondling his nephew's cock and balls.

Julia now approached, unbuttoned her lover's trousers, and drew forth an enormous prick, at the present moment raised to its full length. She eagerly stooped to suck Mr. Spanker's priape and, when it was well moistened, asked him to put it in the boy's bottom-hole, an operation she was most anxious to see.

She and the buxom proprietress now pulled apart the flagellated cheeks, and the horse-dealer placed the point of his tool just within the notch. Julia now dealt him a tremendous blow, which compelled him to thrust forward, and in so doing he half buried his magnificent rammer in the arsehole in front of him.

This caused his victim the most frightful pain. Augustus moaned and yelled, struggling fiercely to rid himself of the fearful weapon, that had thus penetrated his fundament. All this excited Mr. Spanker the more, and he thrust with greater energy, his young mistress pushing him in, with all her strength, and at the same time fondling his hairy balls, and tickling his bumhole.

Mrs. Minette was frigging the lifeless penis of the boy. "He shall spend," said she " if it kills him." Mr. Spanker now gave a furious lunge, and was buried into the boy up to the testicles. He commenced to push his shaft backwards and forwards with cruel force, while Mrs. Minette in the meantime was frigging the youth's sore cock with both hands with the utmost velocity.

A shiver now passed through Mr. Spanker's frame, and with a positive howl he spent within Augustus' body, and sent down a most copious discharge of sperm into his rectum. The cruel Messalina still continued her operations, till at last the boy's prick slightly thickened, and a few drops of spending came forth. Mr. Spanker's nephew was by now perfectly insensible. He was then released and taken away.

After he had gone, the three operators in this scene of cruelty literally glared at each other, every muscle throbbing wildly. They rushed on each other, and seized each other's private parts, which they handled, squeezed and frigged, all convulsively writhing in a confused heap on the floor. They almost immediately spent in the wildest ecstasy.

Then Mrs. Minette drew Julia on her in the reserve way, and they were speedily gamahuching each other wildly. Mad with voluptuousness, the lecherous procuress slipped under her delighted partner, in a Sixty-Nine posture, crossed her legs on her back, and pressing and clasping her close, wriggled and alternatively kissed and bit her. The lips of both their juicy quims were opened

and squeezed against their faces, quite pushed into each other, in a bawdy manner.

Mr. Spanker, who was witnessing this exhibition with gloating eyes, approached Julia
and inserted his immense crimson arrow dog-
fashion in her luscious gap, while Mrs. Minette sucked her coral clitoris, and occasionally his testicles, and passed her tongue up
the vagina over her, by the side of the wet
and throbbing penis, that was buried in it.
They soon reached the Crisis, and the spunk
flowed from them in streams.

It was then proposed, that Julia should be
tied to the flogging machine which stood in
the room, erect with her legs and arms widely
extended. This was done, and Mrs. Minette
took up a large birch, and commenced to flagellate her lovely bottom. Mr. Spanker knelt
down in front of her, and commenced to
gamahuche her gently, allowing his tongue
to pass lazily over her madly excited clitoris.

As he had intensely toyed with her strutting scarlet button, and she was just on the
point of emission, he desisted and in spite of
her entreaties would not touch her. The
wanton girl was then in quite an extraordinary state of rut, and her lover watched
with intense enjoyment the spasmodic con-

traction on the lips of her fanny, and even of her belly and thighs, so great was her excitement, while the flogger continued her strokes, each one of which heating more maddening desire.

One of the waiting maids was now sent for, and Mr. Spanker was bound in a similar manner to the same whipping machine, facing his lewd mistress. They thus came in contact, lip to lip, breast to breast, and his dreadful shaft immediately opposite that lovely slit, into which it entered at once quite mechanically. The ruttish wench gave a satisfied sigh, and the waiting maid commenced to flagellate Mr. Spanker, in a similar manner to that in which Mrs. Minette was still operating on Julia.

It was a fair sight to see a beautiful girl with golden hair and blue eyes, white as snow, writhing with pleasure and delight against her lover, whose statuesque limbs made him like a bronze statue, his enormous prick buried in her streaming cunt, and the wiry pellets of black wool surrounding it, driving her into a fit of erotic ecstasy, as the root of his splendid shaft rubbed against her fiery and bursting clitoris, and mingled with her golden down.

The consequence of this was that they soon were dissolved in bliss, and both dying away in all the raptures of satisfied desire. After being released, and having indulged in mutual sucking of cock and cunts and breasts, they again left the house of flagellation, in which they had experienced so much sensual pleasure in their bawdy orgies, owing to the strangely salacious proprietress, who preferred a trio to a duo.

CHAPTER VIII

ANNIE

A VERY pretty girl of graceful figure, walking through Jermyn street, was accosted by a gentlemanly young man, who after some conversation of a character highly flattering to herself, and which completely won the confidence of her guileless heart, persuaded her to accompany him to his chambers, which were close by.

When they arrived, he brought out wine and biscuits which he persuaded her to take. Sitting on a luxurious sofa, the influence of the wine and his fascination, she became so enamoured of him, that when he put his arm around her waist and, drawing her closely to him, pressed warm kisses on her pouting lips, she was so overcome as to return them, nor was she able to resist when he began to take further liberties with her.

The young man pressed her to him, and with a little difficulty got his hand inside the bosom of her dress, and pressed the warm and firm globes that nestled there. The pretty girl struggled slightly, and said: "Oh! you must not! Dont, do let me alone." "I dont wish to let you alone," said the young gallant. "You must let me feel this soft and enchanting bosom, you must indeed."

Saying this, he managed to unfasten her dress completely, and actually got out one naked globe in his hand, which he devoured with kisses, and so disordered all her senses, that, while her breasts were fluttering under the wanton encroachments of his hand, which was now moulding her bubbing bubbies into all sorts of forms, he succeeded also in gradually raising her dress sufficiently high, to enable him to place the other hand between her thighs, up which he gradually groped, till he reached the silken covering of the spot where they joined.

This alarmed her at first, and she tried hard to remove his hand, but getting his fingers between the velvet lips of her warm slit, he began to frig her, and this eager action rendered her powerless. The panting girl yielded herself entirely, and lay back in his arms, her head upon his shoulder, her eyes half closed, her lips moving in unison with his, as he kissed her.

The young Don Juan saw she was in no condition to resist him, if he even fucked her. He therefore drew forth his prick, hot and swollen as it was, and throwing one leg over her, he brought his stiff cock close enough to her, to enable him to bring the bursting head, among the floss that covered the entrance, to her juicy cunt.

Now, while maintaining the progress he had made, he shifted her into a better position for enjoying her. Shifting her head to the pillow on the couch, he laid one of her legs on that substitute for a bed, and getting between them, he brought the other up also, and then lay down on the body of the panting girl, whose face was now flushed with the deep crimson of desire.

He, all the time was stopping her entreaties by his constant kisses on her half open mouth, while his arms were pressing around her loins. Already the dreadful shaft was pressing its way to its utmost length, into the luscious gap of her quim, while she was opening and extending her legs of her own accord, so as to enable him to penetrate her better.

Suddenly, the tremulous maid was horrified on seeing the room-door open, and another gentleman enter the room. With a look of such genuine shame, that she could not have imagined it mere acting, her lover disengaged himself from her endearing arms, and rose from her form, which thus became exposed to the sight of the intruder, leaving her to cover as best she could her private parts.

This she could not readily accomplish, as her lover had contrived to entangle his foot amongst her drapery. The intruder was thus enabled to gain her side, before she could recover an upright position, and cover herself up. This he prevented her doing, holding her clothes as she attempted to pull them down, and at the same time pressing her backwards in the position, in which she lay before.

The trembling girl was alarmed, as the intruder's stern voice was heard saying: "So,

Sir, this is the way you bring young ladies here in my absence. Leave the room, Sir. As for you, Miss, I shall keep you here as you are, and send for your friends whom I know, in order that they may see how you behave, when away from them."

The ci-devant lover slunk away, and left the room, and the frightened girl felt as though she could have sunk through the floor, as he still kept her clothes up, when they were left alone. She entreated him to let her go, but he would not, and after gloating for a while on her charms, he said: "How I shall either expose you or give you a good birching for your wickedness, Choose, which it shall be."

After a few moments, she, in her confusion and fright, chose the latter alternative. He then allowed her to rise, and taking a birch from a buffet, that stood in the room, the tormentor sat down and, stretching out his legs before him, he bent her across them, her fair head hanging down as if to hide her face, while submitting to such a punishment, as she was about to receive.

For quite a quarter an hour, the cruel gentleman thus gratified himself by birching her posteriors, enjoying her sighs, which she gave vent to, as the process of the whipping gradually brought back that lustful heat in her quim, which the blandishments of her betrayer had first generated there, and these sighs soon became more expressive of voluptuous passion than of any other feeling.

Before he had birched her up to that point, when the man feels he must fuck the flagellated one, or let his spunk flow in his trousers, the panting maid was as willing as he was, that her flagellator should enjoy her in front, as well as behind. Throwing the rod aside, he took her in his arms, and begged that she would make friends with him, saying, that he could not resist flogging her, when he saw another enjoying her lovely charms.

While she was in this excited state, she could not resist his appeal to allow him to fuck her. When his hand was laid on her cunt, he elevated it with a significance, that her arch smile made still more tempting. Kissing her ardently, he at once placed her on the couch in the same position he had found he, and placed himself between her extended thighs.

His enormous prick speedily entered her, and he commenced to move backwards and forwards, until with spasmodic action they both yielded up love's exquisite stream. He then got off, but would not allow her to rise, sitting by her side, and toying with her beautiful limbs. After some little time, he pulled a bell within reach, and she heard approaching footsteps, begging him at the same time to allow her to cover her nakedness.

This, he refused to allow, and when his page entered, he showed him where his priapus had just entered, and their united spendings still oozing from it. "I must make you amends for having deprived you of your sweetheart, even if it was only for a time. I have been enjoying her, but I cannot even now spare her from my sight," said he, "So if you fuck her, it must be while I watch you. I am sure she will allow me that pleasure."

Being by this time too wanton to object, and in order to carry out their scheme more thoroughly, they took her to a place more calculated for practising lechery. The gentleman was Sir Clifford Norton, and the page the same William, who had shared with him the lascivious body of Miss Birchem, and it was by Sir Clifford's order that William had gone out, in search of a pretty girl, that they might make the victim of their joint lust.

Miss Annie found herself in the bedroom of the baronet. The first thing they did, was to undress her to her corset, and the next to strip off all their own clothing. Annie was asked to sit a the foot of the bed, when they tucked up her chemise and fastened it up, in order that her lovely cunt and thighs might be fully exhibited.

William laid on his back on the bed, and his stiff cock was grasped by Sir Clifford, who was manipulating it, in order that Annie might receive it in her body, while in a state of glorious development. They had taken up the birch, as the lustful maid was by now fully conscious that flagellation creates an intense sensual excitement, and is the best inducement to love's paroxysm, as she had experienced by herself, when flogged by the baronet.

Now Annie was castigating the baronet's posteriors with the magnificent birch, as he leant over the bed, frigging his page. After this had fiercely continued for some time, the lewd girl threw herself on her back on the bed, and they both gloated on her glowing charms, their stiff pricks throbbing and rising, at each pulsation of the blood swelling through their veins.

William then grasped her bubbies, squeezing the erect nipples, until she moaned with delight. Sir Clifford rubbed fiercely her clitoris now crimson, hard and bursting. The page then mounted above the panting and crying girl, and as she pressed him tightly in her arms, the baronet guided William's throbbing prick into her gaping vulva. When the pego was fairly in, the ruttish wench closed her thighs over him, and for a while gave herself wholly up to her lascivious feelings.

Annie was exciting her imagination and looking at Sir Clifford's priapus, whose immense shaft was dreadfully erect, with the glowing red head uncovered, and all the threads of the frœnum well stretched. The baronet in turn watched with the keenest interest the page's rammer, as it now disappeared within fair Annie's labouring body, and now reappeared in all its glory, as he withdrew it from its narrow cavity, only to send it again with still greater vigour and delight, into the utmost recesses of her streaming vagina.

The whim then seized the luxurious maid, that she should like to have them both at once upon her, and like a queen of love whose word was law, she bade Sir Clifford to mount behind the page, that they might both have her at once. The baronet instantly obeyed her, but whether his penis would not reach so far as her cunt, or whether he found a greater attraction elsewhere, it is certain that his giant tool found a resting place, before it reached her greedy cunt.

Annie could see quite well, what was taking place between the nobleman and his page. William's eyes were nearly starting from his head, with a flush of heated lust upon each feature, while Sir Clifford looked as though his lascivious gratification was literally burning him up. The scene continued, till the voluptuous girl felt a flood of hot sperm bursting into her, and found her own passions so affected by it, that she also gave way to her feelings, which utterly overcame her.

They then arose and sat down by the fire. After some lascivious toying, they took off the chemise and corsets which Annie had retained until now, and the libidinous baronet, whose prick was again intensely stiff, took her upon his lap, impaling her upon his upright shaft, and while he fucked her, the pretty girl frigged the cock of the page, and amorously played with his balls, tickling the rosy foreskin and squeezing the hard testicles nestling in his corrugated scrotum.

William was excited to the utmost, and how eloquent of pleasant emotion were the eyes of Annie, as she received the full discharge of the baronet's spunk into her gloious cunt, while the creamy jet from the page spouted forth over her caressing fingers. Once more they prepared to roger the girl, this time on the bed again.

William lay on his back, Annie above him, while Sir Clifford stood by the side of the bed, frigging himself, and watching them in the ecstasy of coition. Then in his excitement the page seized the baronet's penis and frigged him, while still fucking Annie, with a vigour that seemed to increase, as her delightful quim grew hotter and randier.

With a bewitching voice, the lecherous maid gave expression to her wantonness, repeating after them the most bawdy terms conceivable. All this so maddened Sir Clifford, that his body was pervaded with fuck. He then brought out a rod, and lashed the heaving buttocks of the lascivious girl, who in the abundance of her pleasure, challenged him to flog and fuck her to death.

As she goaded them into a fury that could only be quenched by their smothering her with spunk, the page soon made his spendings fly into her belly, and directed the full stream of the baronet's profuse discharge over her flagellated backside. Still their desires for the voluptuous girl were not quenched, although their weapons were for the time incapable of standing.

Annie exerted all her fascination to arouse them, kissing their bodies and private parts, sucking their luscious knobs, licking the threads of the frœnum well stretched, toying with their foreskins and hairy balls, and giving up every portion of her body to them, making them kiss and suck her breasts, titillate her rosy nipples, lick her still nervously throbbing cunt and corrugated brown arsehole.

Lying on her back, Annie showed them all the graceful curves her undulating form and beauteous limbs could offer, while they enacted with her all the voluptuous dalliance, that so exquisite a figure could incite them to. Presently she leapt up and cried: "If you cannot fuck my fanny again, if a naked woman will not excite you sufficiently, show me what you can do together."

"Come Sir," said the salacious maid, addressing the baronet, "place yourself like a woman, and see what your page can do for you, and if he cannot do more for you than for me, I will flog him till he cannot stand." Sir Clifford now extended himself on his belly, opened his thighs and buttocks, and made William mount up behind.

Annie now guided the page's penis into his master's anus, holding the lower part of it, while she administered such a birching to both cheeks of his bottom, as soon caused the shaft to stand as stiff as ever. She watched the pego now gradually make its way, within the narrow aperture between the cheeks of the baronet's bottom, until it was buried to the root.

They then went through that sport, for which Sir Clifford had so keen a relish, affording to Annie the most intense delight. As the nobleman tossed and writhed on the bed, the wicked girl secured his enormous prick, and squeezing it as hard as she forcibly could, she chafed the glowing instrument from root to point, with almost demoniac energy.

The baronet spent with a scream of mingled pain and pleasure, and at the same moment received the spunk of his page in the innermost recesses of his arse, while the girl mad with voluptuousness, grasping the palpitating lips of her fanny, and fiercely rubbing her strutting clitoris, was so indulging in the most intoxicating lasciviousness.

After this bout, Sir Clifford dismissed Annie with a handsome present, and arranged a future meeting, which the delighted girl promised to attend.

CHAPTER IX

WILLIAM

THE narrator is a young lady of ardent temperament, who is in the habit of tasting all the delights of voluptuousness in the arms of an amorous baronet, of whom she has become enamoured. Afterwards, as her desires increase, the nobleman introduces his page, and with him they join in the most lascivious orgies. One day, in the baronet's absence, the young man relates to her his history, which she recounts as follows.

William was the son of a gentleman of good position, in his fourteenth year when the bank, in which his father's money was deposited, failed, and his father was so affected by his loss, that he committed suicide leaving the boy and his mother destitute. Sir Clifford was then in their town, and had been paying much attention to the mother previously, but as William thought without success up to the period of her widowhood, at least his mother subsequently assured him so.

The gallant baronet now instantly came forward, and most liberally placed his purse at their disposal. Of course, this ended in the mother soon becoming covertly under his protection, and the son was sent to College until he was fifteen, when he was brought back to reside with his mother, so as to blind the world as to the connection with Sir Clifford.

William, during his absence, had learnt the secret as to the connection between the sexes, and he very soon discovered the terms existing between his mother and the baronet. He managed to find an opportunity of observing them from a hidden recess, and gloat on the amorous enjoyment in which they were indulging, envying the nobleman the possession of his mother's ripe and luscious charms, for she was a magnificent woman of a warm and erotic constitution, and in the prime of life, being thirty-four years of age.

About three months after the boy's return from College, his governess Miss Birchem had taken his maidenhead, and as he was approaching his sixteenth year, the constant witnessing of the love combats between his mother and Sir Clifford, had wonderfully developed his virile member, and from his hidden post of observation, he used to frig himself, longing all the time to be buried in the beautiful body of his mother.

Doing this to excess, one day he became exhausted, and fell asleep, his hand still clasping his young prick, which was covered with his spendings. The baronet soon left. The mother had finished her ablutions, and was drying herself in a state of perfect nudity, when she was startled to hear a snore close by her.

She approached the recess, opened it, and saw her son with his very respectable cock in his hand. Sleep had reinvigorated his strutting pego, and it was standing stiffly. "Good Heavens!", cried his mother in her suprise at the sight. Her exclamation woke her son, who to his astonishment and delight, saw his mother standing before him in all the glory of her charms.

The magnificent woman seemed to have forgotten the state, in which she was, in her surprise on finding her son in such a condition. In his excitement, William sprang to his feet, and threw his arms wildly about her naked body. She staggered back under his unexpected attack. A sofa behind her tripped her up, and she fell back on it, her son falling on her, whose private parts thus became fully exposed.

While his arm was pressing around her loins, the boy fiercely grasped and opened her vermilion slit, eagerly attempting to thrust his instrument forward. She struggled, and put her hand on her curly haired mount Venus, and whispered: "Oh! William dear, you must not fuck your mother," while her enchanting breasts were squeezed under the juvenile form.

All her movements to escape, only made it more easy for the standing prick, already pressing hard against her frightened cunt, to engulf itself up to the hilt, into the innermost recesses of the motherly vagina, and the youth, mad with lust and the determination to fuck his mother, began working away within her, with all his might, and from time to time sucking the luscious fleshly raspberries enlightening the white globes of her bosom.

William told me, that he thought his mother quickly got erotically excited by his movements, because her efforts to escape and entreaties for him to desist, grew feebler and feebler, and although she did not respond to his forward thrusts, still when he spent and continued to give convulsive heaves forward, he felt her upward pressures close on his rampant priapus.

Her womb had been stirred with so many thrusts, when her rosy cheeks became of a deeper dye, her eyes swam, her lips parted, and her sighs of pleasure were instantly echoed by his, as he felt a delicious baptism of moisture on his shaft, the gathered sperm of his prime gushing from his crest so profusely, that he seemed completely transferred with waves of rapture into his beautiful mother, and about to mingle his being with hers.

When he had finished, William found that his mother was weeping bitterly, her hands hidding the short, thick hair, coral clitoris and streaming slit, where her warm, smooth belly terminated. The boy strove to comfort her, but she now easily pushed him away, and then throwing herself on her belly, sobbed as if her heart would break.

Her son knelt by her side, and endeavoured to console her, but she still sobbed on. In his attempt to soothe her, he could not help casting his eye on the magnificent bottom, which was thus fully exposed to him, as she lay on her belly, with her plump buttocks wide apart revealing a pouting, corrugated, brown arsehole, where the deep furrow terminated.

The bewitching spectacle of these glorious globes, for she was particularly well developed in those parts, combined with incestuous thought that it was really his mother, instantly reawakened his lust, and his cock became as stiff as ever, with the foreskin gradually uncovering its fiery and bursting head, when the youth made his kisses rain on the luscious neck and shoulders of his mother.

Her right leg was now drawn up, so that on shifting his head towards the bottom of the sofa, the whole of the fat and pouting lips of her cunt, all foaming with his own young sperm still oozing out, lay exposed to his gaze, and madly roused his lust, in other words, stretched all the threads of the froenum of his now dreadfully throbbing cockey, to their utmost length.

Without making any noise, William slipped off his trousers, and suddenly flinging himself on his knees, between her open legs, he fondled her white thighs, parted the little curls around the great velvet lips, and rapidly engulfed his stiff standing prick, in the delicious quim all moist and ready to receive.

At this suddenly renewed attack, his mother attempted to rise, when again she felt the stiff, warm object entering. But he grasped the sofa on each side with his hands, and held her tight, while he worked away most vigorously. His mother, who had only aided him by her attempt to escape, entreated him to leave her, but he still persisted, and she concealed her confusion beneath her drapery.

After slightly rubbing her erect clitoris, glowing like a ruby in black wool, the bursting knob of his shaft fully entered her moist, hot and swollen sheath, every inch of its progress inward becoming more and more pleasant, and she soon became so much excited by the vigorous operations of his rampant rammer within her deep grotto, that her sensual passions mastered her completely.

First submitting patiently to his attack, this magnificent woman of a warm and erotic nature, ended by most actively seconding her son with the agile, wanton movements of her loins and bottom, each succeeding one giving her more and more pleasure. It culminated at last in a thrill so exquisite, that her frame seemed to melt. Nothing more was wanting, and she gave a sigh of deep gratification.

For a moment William lay still, and then he gave her half a dozen more furious thrusts. At each of which, her vagina was penetrated by a copious gush, which soothed and bathed its membranes, and she died away with her son in the delicious Crisis of erotic ecstasy. For a long time the lovers lay perfectly still, and the stiff rod, which had completely filled her sheath, diminished in size until it slipped entirely out.

After this, it was useless remonstrating with her son. She turned round when he arose, and at last relieved her of his weight by laying at her side, their legs being still entwined. She warmly embraced him, saying what a dreadful son he was, to commit incest with his own mother, and telling him that he must take care never to betray so dreadful a secret.

William promised, and also added that he would never divulge his knowledge of her intimacy with the baronet, even to him. He then added: "Oh Mamma! if you only knew how delicious it was to witness you together, how I longed to be a partaker in such charms, how beautifully you fuck, Mamma, as Sir Clifford calls it, and what a fine prick he has."

"How often have I envied him, when you were sucking his Jack, Mamma darling? will my pego ever be as big, just feel it Mamma dear, and do tell me." His mother took his virile member in her hand, and softly pressed it. It was only half stiff, but instantly became erect, as the blood rushed from his head and spine into his cock, filled it, and made it rise and swell out to an unknown size. His mother's eyes beamed with rapture, and as she was an exceedingly voluptuous woman, sensual passion quite transformed her. So William must now continue the story in his own words.

"I felt her hand grasp my lustful tool quite mechanically. I saw her cheeks flush with astonishment and delight. The old thrilling sensation in her breasts and large fanny became so intense, that she could scarcely resist the temptation to frig herself, so I slipped my own fingers over her prominent mount Venus and coral button, until two of them made an entrance, and were completely enclosed in the hot, moist tissues of her longing cunt, which instantly closed upon them and throbbed, making my prick respond and become as hard as iron.

"What a fine cock it is," she said, "I could not have thought, that a boy like you could have had one machine as large." "Oh, let me have another embrace, Mamma, with your consent and aid." I was frigging her cunt all the time, and could feel by its frequent throbbing, that her lubricity was gaining the day against prejudice.

"She stooped, kissed and then took the knob of my penis in her greedy mouth for a loving suck. My God, I thought I should have died, with the overwhelming sensation this produced on me. I felt as if every nerve was bursting, so intense was the enjoyment it afforded me. Providentially I did not however spend in her mouth, an action which would have exhausted me on this particular occasion.

"My mother left off her delightful occupation, and said: "As the wine is e'en drawn, we must e'en drink," it is a common county saying indicative of consent. She rose and bade me take off all my clothes, saying that as it must be, it had better be complete. This was rapidly effected. She then led me to the bed. She lay down on her back, extended her lovely legs wide apart, and told me to get between them.

"I did so, and she herself guided my rampant prick into her raging cunt, her legs closed over my back, she hugged me to her enchanting bosom, sought my mouth and covered it with kisses, thrusting her tongue within, and seeking out mine. After what I had already done with her, besides the frigging in the recess, I was not prepared to spend again without considerable action.

"This just suited the excited passion of my mother, for having now fully consented, the idea of incest with her own son acted as a special spur to her lust, and I am sure that she spent four times, before joining me in the joys of the final Crisis. It was most deliciously exquisite. I fainted at the last, and became perfectly insensible, but she had melted five times in my arms.

"My mother told me afterwards, that she had also been unconscious for some time in all the lovely after-sensations, greater as they were than ever she had experienced. She soon recovered by the aid of cold water and eau de Cologne, and when I returned to consciousness, she had thrown on a dressing gown, and a delightful languor stole over her frame. She fastened her mouth to mine in a passionate kiss, and I returned her a kiss as passionate as she gave.

"I begged her once more to lie down by my side, but she would not consent, saying, that she had extracted from me the most copious gushes, in the very ecstasy of filling her sheath with sperm, that I had exhausted myself too much already, and that I must rise and dress, it was too soon for me to melt with another thrill. I was obliged to comply and thus ended my first initiation into the divine mysteries of a mother's incestuous cunt."

CHAPTER X

SIR CLIFFORD

SIR Clifford's mistress was a young lady of such an ardent temperament and erotic constitution, that she had been unable to resist gently fondling the foreskin of William's lovely priapus, all the time he was relating to her his strangely exciting history, and the gallant page resumed it as follows, while his hand was eagerly slipping to her gaping slit.

"Of course, after my splendid initiation into the divine mysteries of an incestuous cunt, my adorable mother took every occasion to indulge me in the possession of her person. We always slept together on those days, when the baronet had spent a long afternoon in Mamma's arms. I was allowed to be a hidden spectator of their amorous transports, on condition that I did not impair my vigour by masturbation.

"On this occasion Mamma remained reposing on the bed, after Sir Clifford had left, and explained to me all the sexual mysteries which remained for me to know. She first used every artifice to keep me at bay, until my efforts should arouse her sensual passions, but they became so thoroughly aroused by this time, that she could scarcely help opening her white thighs, and letting me have free entrance.

"This allowed me to rush upon her foaming cunt and gamahuche it, in that state, namely wetted with their united abundant spendings, while I fingered the charming silky curls, which accumulated to quite a little wood, at the root of the thighs between which my head was buried, with my active tongue licking her coral button, or darted as far as possible into her vulva, sucking and rolling the inner lips and the sides of the outer ones, till with a shuddering spasm of lust, and a contraction of her vagina, she inundated my mouth with a flood of spunk, creamy and thick, shot out like a man's over the face and bosom of his mistress.

"My mother accustomed me to bottom-fucking. "You don't know how to sodomise properly," first said she, "there is no cleverness in buggering up to the hilt, remember that at the entrance there's a little muscle, a clinging ring." "Yes, the sphincter," said I. "That's where you must remain, if you wish to enjoy it, that's where you feel delicious contractions; never go right in! never bugger a woman completely."

"I obeyed my mother's orders, and stopped in the sphincter. She made me feel delicious contractions. It was the true kiss of the arsehole. So I used to slip my prick out of her cunt, and slippery as it was with her spending, sheath it in her wrinkly anus fully displayed, and finish my fuck in that soft and glowing sheath called rectum, till I felt a shudder pass through Mamma, as a warm flood of sperm gushed in her bowels. So I was soon completely initiated into the delicious science called Venery.

"My mother declared that another prick young and vigorous, just after exhaustion in another man's arms, imparted fresh life and passion to her wild lubricity, and I often fucked her twice without withdrawing, both of us being in the utmost state of excitement. But she never allowed me to spend above twice, as these meetings were always followed by a night of pleasure.

"Then I mounted her, and she would make me gain my way by the hardest pushing. Not only were her beautiful thighs locked, but she tightly contracted the muscles of her sheath at the lips. I would give a fierce but ineffective thrust, then I would squeeze and suck her breasts, until at last her wantonness became uncontrollable, and she gave way with a feeling that unnerved her, letting my rampant rammer plunge in to the hilt.

"My stalwart shaft would distend and penetrate her chapel, so much deeper than that cock of Sir Clifford. Her sheath with wanton greediness would devour every inch that entered it, and at my deepest thrust, my mother would melt with an incestuous rapture, never felt in the baronet's embrace. Again the wild incestuous thrill penetrated every part of her body. She fairly groaned with erotic ecstasy, and for a long time we lay in a voluptuous but motionless repose.

"Sir Clifford had a pass-key, and sometimes called at night, when he had been unable to do so during the day, but hitherto he had never done so, if he had enjoyed Mamma in the afternoon. It was reliance on this arrangement, that induced my mother to allow me to sleep with her all night, but this at last brought about the discovery of our liaison.

"The baronet had for time past been in the habit of calling me to him, and making me sit close to him on the sofa, passing his arms round my waist, and pressing me close to him, kissing me, and telling me he loved me as a son. I suspected his affection was more erotic than paternal, for I saw by the bulging out of his trousers, that this always excited him, and made his prick stand.

"The sight of his standing pego had the same effect on my priapus, and I saw that he always noticed this. One one occasion my mother had her dressmaker with her, and he had to wait before he could see her. He drew me to him as usual, and glided his tongue within my mouth, and begged me to suck it. I did so, and we were in a state of furious erection almost immediately.

"My dear boy," said he, "I see you are affected in the same manner as I am by these sweet embraces, and you seemed to be grown more, than I could have thought for your age," at the same time placing his hand on my throbbing Jack. "But nothing to your own, Sir," said I. "Would you like to see my machine." said he. "Above all things." "Well then, you may unbutton me, if you like, while I do the same for you."

"Out burst our two weapons, I took his priape that leaped and leaped as if it were an eel. Sir Clifford turned red and white with astonishment and delight. The old thrilling sensation in his cods and belly became so intense, that he could scarcely resist the temptation to frig himself. I was equally overwhelmed, when the baronet rose and locked the door, and begged me to lower my trousers, and stand up before him.

"He then rubbed my bottom, and gently handled my shaft with much enjoyment. The nobleman first frigged the staff of my glossy member, and then stooping took the rose-coloured knob in his mouth, tickling the point with his tongue, in the most delicious manner, at the same time contriving to frig the root of my now splendidly strutting instrument with one hand.

"Sir Clifford suddenly lifted his head, and inserting a finger in his mouth, moistened it well. He then renewed his sucking and frigging, and when he felt I was approaching the climax, he pushed his hand behind, and put his moistened finger up my bottom-hole, and pushed it in and out, in unison with his frigging and sucking, making me spend with more delight than I had ever experienced with Mamma.

"The baronet sucked me all out, and only stopped when not a drop remained. Raising his head, he asked me how I liked it. I told him the pleasure I had experienced, and begged he would allow me to suck him. For a few moments he allowed me to engulf the immense shaft of his cockney, with its glowing head thoroughly uncovered, and all the threads of its frœnum well stretched, but he would not spend, as my agile tongue would call forth the liquid of love, and pour it down my throat and drink it.

"He said he had other work to do, I must come to see him, but not tell Mamma on any account anything about it. I guessed what he wanted, for I had frequently seen him fuck Mamma in her arsehole, and she had in fact initiated me, and allowed me to do so to her also, and had also applied her finger to my bottom-hole, while we were mutually gamahuching, keeping the blissful in-and-out motion, till I felt dissolving and dying away, in the last throes of pleasure.

"When I visited Sir Clifford, he first locked the door, he begged me to strip naked, and followed my example himself. He then took me in his arms, and embraced me most lasciviously, then made me turn round, and handled and kissed every part of me, and then taking my prick in his mouth, began his delicious movement thereon, again exciting me by the insertion of an agile finger in my anus.

"When the baronet saw I was ready for anything, he desisted, knelt on the sofa, projecting his buttocks as far as possible, and told me to stand behind him, and let him take my cock in his hand. As I expected, he guided it between the cheeks of his bottom, and told me to push it in. I did so, and began to pass the ring of the sphincter and enter. He flinched a little, and told me to be quiet a moment, or I should spend too soon, and spoil the enjoyment.

"I obeyed Sir Clifford's orders, and stopped in the clinging ring, it made me feel delicious contractions. I could not resist the genuine kiss of his bottom-hole, and I buggered him up to the hilt, inserting my stalwart penis, at a single thrust, into the innermost recesses of his rectum. "Never bugger me up to the roots," ejaculated the baronet, and he told me how to sodomise properly as my mother did.

"Nevertheless he spent voluptuously, but I did not withdraw immediately, and the pressure he employed soon restiffened my tool. "Now," said Sir Clifford, "we will take it more leisurely, pass your hand under my belly, take my prick, frig it, stopping at intervals." I did so, and when we finally spent in unison, I thought it even better than my mother's bottom. It seemed hotter and tighter. I now withdrew, and after washing and partaking of refreshment, he requested me to stand up.

"I did so, then he knelt down behind me, and glued his lips to my pink bottom-hole, thrusting his tongue within, in a manner that fired my passions, and made me long to feel the sensation, that would be produced on me by the insertion of a prick. When the baronet saw by the state of my pego, the effect he was producing, he arose, saying that as his cock was so large, he would try to obviate the difficulty of penetration.

"Sir Clifford then passed his finger moistened up my arse, affording me great pleasure. Then bringing his magnificent prick to the spot, he soaped it, telling me to strain as if endeavouring to void something, and he, with little pain to me, succeeded in sheating the nut, and about an inch of the shaft within me, but when he attempted to advance, it hurt me and produced a sickening feeling.

"I should certainly have unseated him, but for the grip he maintained on my hips, which held me as though in a vice. His weapon was now so far in, that he speedily entered another inch and a half. He cried out to me to keep quiet, and the pain would soon cease.

"At this stage, I summoned up all my courage and did so, and shortly the throbbing of his rampant penis, within the narrow recess of my sphincter, began to affect my cock, which had shrunk to nothing during his first attempt. Upon the baronet's experience telling him, that my passions were now rising to fucking heat, he slipped a hand under my belly, and gently frigged me, till I spent.

"Sir Clifford then availed himself of the opportunity my wrigglings at this moment afforded him, and sheathed his immense shaft, beyond the clinging ring of my anus, up to the roots, without my being aware of it. When he had done this, he lay quiet, not having yet spent, and as soon as I had quite recovered, he told me to sink down on my left side.

"The baronet sank with me, without losing an inch of his penetration, his prick being still buried within me to the hairs. He now desired me to draw my knees well up, and stick out my bottom. He then took my cockey in his hand, and began to frig it again. This naturally excited him to fever heat, and the throbbing of my arse convinced him, he might proceed on the spot.

"Sir Clifford therefore began to move in and out, slowly and regularly, while he frigged me more rapidly. I soon begged him to be quicker in his movements behind. He did not immediately comply, but when he felt the electric increase in the size and heat of my pego, he worked rapidly within me. I became strangely wild in my feelings and when I spent, my very sobs of pleasure were checked by unutterable pain.

"The baronet had not even yet spent, preferring that I should be thoroughly broken in before he plunged in and out, with the violence and fury he enjoyed. Hence he lay quietly imbedded in me to the hilt, until I recovered my sensibility, and began to have my erotic sensations excited anew, and I once more commenced to wriggle under his caressing hand.

"Sir Clifford recommenced to plunge furiously in and out, and we at length came to the ecstatic Crisis, with an erotic fury on both sides rarely equalled. This thoroughly exhausted us both. The retention of his spunk by the baronet for so long a time caused a perfect body-killing discharge, and his prick immediately afterwards slipped out of my bottom-hole.

"We continued these delights for some weeks, till at last Sir Clifford spoke openly of the bliss of fucking my mother, and said how much he would like me to be buried in his arse, at the moment he was spending into my mother's palpitating body. I said I was sure she would never consent to that, I had only once come into her room when dressing, and had ventured to touch her bubbies, but she instantly turned me from the room.

"Nevertheless," said he, "you must fuck her yourself, she is very hot, I shall leave her some day only half fucked. I shall let you know when this happens, and as I leave, enter her room boldly, throw yourself into her arms, and if she does not consent willingly, force your way into her, her cunt will be all moist from my fucking, and your cock will easily slip in, and however angry she may be, she will be sure to forgive you, when you have made her spend."

"The baronet little thought I had long ago done so, but I promised to follow his directions. I told him afterwards that I made the attempt to no purpose. However he had some suspicions, that I had succeeded, I am sure, and a few nights afterwards, when we were in the Crisis of a delicious fuck, and I had given my mother the last convulsive thrust, just at that moment, I heard the front door softly open and shut: "Bravo," said a voice near us, and in a moment he threw off his clothes, and was on the bed.

"My mother screamed and struggled, pushing me away with a force that could draw my stiff shaft completely out of her quim, but as I thought I should take Sir Clifford's dreadful prick in me, while my young pego was buried in my mother, I held her fast, while he went to the foot of the bed, and inserting his face between our extended thighs, sucked my testicles, and rolled his tongue in the spendings, that were clinging to the roots of my rod.

"Then the baronet rushed up behind, and in a moment had penetrated me, and we were speedily in the agonies of mutual spending. After my mother's complaints had been silenced, she entered into the enjoyment of the thing, and henceforth we had the wildest orgies in company, till at length my mother was taken ill, and subsequently died to our great grief, and I have since travelled with Sir Clifford as his private page."

Thus ended this recital, in the course of which I had been unable to resist to spread my thighs wide open, and mount the gallant page, well astride, with my face towards him to give him a fair view of my most secret charms, my little tapering fingers playing with his limber shaft and wrinkled balls. As the story proceeded, I had toyed and fingered at the top of his prick the very pretty, smooth and glowing projection like the cup of an acorn.

While William was describing the bed-chamber scenes, I had contrived to enter this rosy knob into the crevice so directly above it, and kept undulating my loins as the story went on, till just as he finished, I was nearly ready to spend. My eyes were shut, but my mouth pouted for the kiss, which my lips longed for. I had been unable to refrain from emitting copiously several times during this exciting narrative, and the wanton situation had done its work upon me.

As soon as the page had finished his voluptuous story, his intrusive finger that had been in my vagina the whole time, perceived the throbbing of the lips between which it was inserted. His penis, that had been vivified as it was by the close retreat in which it was hidden, rose and rose until it became as rigid as bone. The glands clung to the base all ready for action. It was a beautiful specimen of a man's cock.

Furious with lust, as a wanton girl in quite an extraordinay state of rut, I wrapped my arms around the small of his back, and braced my whole strength for a thrust from his stiff and palpitating member. His crest was at once buried where his finger had lately explored. When William's knob went plunging in, and rammed my womb, my whole being seemed to center in my loins and gush out.

At the same moment I felt my sheath moistened with our spendings, and his prick drew out of my vagina, with a sucking noise which set me laughing. "Oh, God," I murmured, tossing my arms wildly upwards, and rolling my eyes towards heaven. Whether pain or pleasure was most exquisite, I did not know, but I sank prostrate and exhausted on William's shoulder, with my lubricity so much gratified that my head dropped, and the page caught it to his heart. I had fainted away.

When I again became conscious, I was lying on my back upon the sofa, in the arms of William, the lace of my bosom was parted, my heavy skirts were all turned up from my naked thighs, and the handsome page of Sir Clifford was in the very ecstasy of filling my sheath with sperm.

END

VICTORIAN EROTIC CLASSICS
AVAILABLE FROM CARROLL & GRAF

☐ Anonymous / Rosa Fielding: Victim of Lust		3.95
☐ Anonymous / Sharing Sisters		4.95
☐ Anonymous / Secret Lives		3.95
☐ Anonymous / Sensual Secrets		4.50
☐ Anonymous / Sweet Confessions		4.50
☐ Anonymous / Sweet Tales		4.50
☐ Anonymous / Tropic of Lust		4.50
☐ Anonymous / Venus Butterfly		3.95
☐ Anonymous / Venus Delights		3.95
☐ Anonymous / Venus Disposes		3.95
☐ Anonymous / Venus in India		3.95
☐ Anonymous / Victorian Fancies		4.50
☐ Anonymous / The Wantons		4.50
☐ Anonymous / White Thighs		4.50
☐ Anonymous / Youthful Indiscretions		4.50
☐ Cleland, John / Fanny Hill		4.95
☐ van Heller, Marcus / Adam and Eve		3.95
☐ van Heller, Marcus / Lusts of the Borgias		4.95
☐ van Heller, Marcus / Seduced		5.95
☐ van Heller, Marcus / Unbound		5.95
☐ van Heller, Marcus / Venus in Lace		3.95
☐ Villefranche, Anne-Marie / Passion d'Amour		5.95
☐ Villefranche, Anne-Marie / Scandale d'Amour		5.95
☐ Villefranche, Anne-Marie / Secrets d'Amour		4.50
☐ Villefranche, Anne-Marie / Souvenir d'Amour		4.50
☐ von Falkensee, Margarete / Blue Angel Confessions		6.95
☐ "Walter" / My Secret Life		7.95

Available from fine bookstores everywhere or use this coupon for ordering.

Carroll & Graf Publishers, Inc., 260 Fifth Avenue, N.Y., N.Y. 10001

Please send me the books I have checked above. I am enclosing $_____ (please add $1.75 per title to cover postage and handling.) Send check or money order—no cash or C.O.D.'s please. N.Y. residents please add 8¼% sales tax.

Mr/Mrs/Ms _____

Address _____

City_____ State/Zip_____

Please allow four to six weeks for delivery.